A LONG DECEMBER

Don Harstad is the author of *Eleven Days, The Known Dead, The Big Thaw* and *Code 61.* A ̶ d
̶ ̶ ̶ ̶ ̶ ̶ ̶ ̶ ̶ ̶ ̶ ̶ ̶ ̶ veteran of the Clayton County Sheriff's Department, he lives in Elkader, Iowa.

Also by Donald Harstad

Eleven Days
The Known Dead
The Big Thaw
Code 61

DONALD HARSTAD

A LONG DECEMBER

FOURTH ESTATE · *London* and *New York*

First published in Great Britain in 2003 by
Fourth Estate
A Division of HarperCollins*Publishers*
77–85 Fulham Palace Road
London W6 8JB
www.4thestate.com

Copyright © Donald Harstad 2003

1 3 5 7 9 8 6 4 2

A catalogue record for this book is
available from the British Library

ISBN 1-84115-547-0

Printed in Great Britain by Clays Ltd, St Ives plc

I WOULD LIKE TO DEDICATE THIS BOOK TO THE MEMORY OF

KEITH LEMKA.

HE WAS A FINE OFFICER AND A TRUE FRIEND.

15:26

SLUGS RIPPED THROUGH THE BARN'S OLD BOARDS, showering us with dust and debris. I got even lower than I had been before, pressing my cheek against the sooty limestone foundation. I could see George hunker down along the thick support beam he'd found, and I heard Hester, who was off to my right in the gloom, say "Shit." At first I thought she was just sort of venting, but then she kept going.

"Shit, oh shit, shit, shit."

Hester's no shrinking violet, but she's not one to curse for the hell of it, either. I rose and turned to her, and noticed that she'd rolled away from her vantage point near the rotted ground-level boards, and was half sitting with her back against the foundation wall.

"What? You okay?"

"My face," she said. She held the right side of her face with one hand while she struggled to reholster her sidearm with the other. I saw blood ooze between her fingers. "Shit, shit." she repeated.

George and I both got over to her as fast as we could crawl. "Let me see."

She reluctantly moved her hand from her face, and I saw blood and torn flesh. Not too much. It was hard to see in the shadows. I unsnapped my coat and daubed her face as gently as I could with the fleecy lining. It was all I had.

"Ahhh!" She pushed my hand away.

"Sorry, sorry, just a sec, just let me look."

"Don't press."

"Yeah, yeah," I said as I pulled off my gloves, fumbled under my sweater, and dipped into my shirt pocket for my reading glasses. I put 'em on and looked again. Sticking out of her right cheek was about a half-inch stub of an old, rusty square nail, flattened, but about half as big around as a pencil. It had embedded back toward the corner of her jaw. "I see it... it's an old square nail. Part of one. There's a chunk of nail stuck in your cheek."

"Don't touch it!"

"No, no."

"I can feel it," she said after a second, "with my tongue." As she spoke, a rivulet of blood dripped over her lower lip and onto her parka sleeve. "It's gonna hurt," she said, and then shivered violently. "It's inside my mouth. Oh shit."

"It doesn't seem to be bleeding very much," I said. "But spit, don't swallow it."

"I just had a first aid class," came Sally's voice from behind the rickety and rusty milking stanchions. "Somebody get over here, and let me come take a look."

George reached out and patted Hester on the arm. "It'll be all right," he said. "Okay," he said to Sally, "be right there. I'll get you my stuff."

Hester nodded, but said nothing as he crawled away.

"It's not a bullet," I said. She was shivering pretty hard, and breathing in deep, shuddering gasps, and I could see the clouds of frozen breath forming in the cold air. I didn't want her hyperventilating on us, and tried to reassure her. "It's just a piece of old nail, must have been hit by a slug. It's not life threatening, okay? It's not a bullet. Lots slower. There's no damage other than a little hole." It occurred to me that she might be worried about disfigurement. And it really wasn't a very big hole. "Real small," I said. "Try to slow your breathing, if you can."

She nodded. "It'll hurt," she said, with a quaver in her voice. "Hit my teeth. Numb now... but it'll hurt... oh boy." She didn't look at any of us, just stared at the concrete floor, concentrating, and beginning to try to breathe slowly and deeply.

If she was right about her teeth, it really was going to hurt like hell.

Sally scuttled over on all fours. "Hi, Hester. Let me see what I can do here, okay? You're gonna be all right ... "

"Sure," said Hester. Her words were less distinct. Swelling inside her mouth?

Sally briefly examined the wound. "We need some sort of compress," she said. "Just to protect it, if we can. Some water to irrigate it, maybe? Later, we better let the doc remove it, okay?"

As soon as I heard "irrigate," I reached into my parka pocket and pulled out one of my bottles of water and handed it to Sally. As far as I knew, all our real first aid equipment was still in our cars, and they were effectively out of reach. I thought for a second. "My T-shirt? It's clean today…"

"It'll have to do," said Sally. She too reached out and patted Hester on the shoulder. "You're gonna have the world's biggest compress."

Hester made a muffled sound, and I think she wanted to sound like she was laughing. I took off my coat and started pulling my sweater over my head.

"It starting to hurt yet?" asked Sally.

Hester shook her head gingerly. "Mumm." She tried again, making a real effort to be distinct. "Numb." It was swelling all right.

"Here, put your sweater back on," George called out to me, and I heard the distinctive sound of Velcro ripping open. "This stuff is part of my kit," he said, and tossed over a blue nylon bag with a red cross in a white square stitched on the front. "Take my muffler, too, it's warm and can hold the compress in place."

"All right!" Sally opened it up. There were several packets inside, each labeled for a different medical problem. "Fracture. Burns. Drowning"—Sally riffled through—"ah, Wounds and Bleeding"—then tore the pack open. There was a large compress, gauze, disinfectant ointment, and a scissors. "Shit, this is great…"

"I'll get an ambulance coming," I said. For all the good it would do. There was no way we cold get Hester to the paramedics until we got lots of backup. I keyed the mike on my walkie-talkie. "Comm, Three… ten-thirty-three."

Of course it was 10-33. This had been an emergency since the first shot was fired. But I had to say something to convey the extra urgency, and there's no code for "more urgent than before."

"Three, go ahead."

"Okay, we have an officer down now. Get me a ten-fifty-two down here at the old Dodd place. Fast…but tell 'em to hold until we clear 'em in."

"Ten-four, Three. Copy officer down?" She repeated it that way so everybody who was listening knew what we had, without her having to inform them separately.

"Ten-four, need as much ten-seventy-eight as you can get, and the ambulance. We are still pinned down. Repeating, still pinned down. How close is backup?"

"Ten-four the ten-fifty-two," she said, and I could imagine her hitting the page button for the Maitland ambulance service. "And…uh…backup is en route."

I was glad she acknowledged the ambulance request, but just telling me that the backup units were on the way, without giving me their current location, meant that it was going to take a while. I wasn't certain just why, but there was obviously a problem with backup. It was so damned typical of the complex kind of plan that we were working under. I was angry, but there was nothing Dispatch could do about it. I was just sorry she hadn't been able to give me an estimate. That was bad.

"Ten-four. Look, tell the responding units that we are still taking automatic weapons fire, from two or three locations. Repeat that, will you. Auto weapons fire from multiple locations."

"Ten-four, Three." She repeated the message, and as she did so she sounded about ready to cry. Being completely powerless in a tense situation will make you sound that way. "Can you be more specific regarding the location of the automatic weapons fire?"

"I'm giving you the best I've got," I said, as calmly as possible. "They were already here when we got here." The calm was mostly for Hester's benefit. The last thing she needed to hear was me getting all worried. "Just make sure you don't send the EMS people in until we clear them."

"Ten-four, Three. One says to keep them there until backup gets to you."

Well, that wasn't going to be too hard. It was them keeping us pinned down, not vice versa.

"I think we can do that, Comm," I said.

"The dumb one's coming back out," said George.

The "dumb one" was one of the group who was shooting at us off and on. This particular idiot wore a New York Yankees baseball cap and a gray sweatshirt. He'd step out of the old machine shed, half crouched, point his A K-47 either at our barn or the old chicken coop, and just blow out about thirty rounds in a couple of seconds. The first time he'd done it, George had said, "Look at that dumb son of a bitch!" It stuck.

So far, shooting from the hip the way he was, he'd not come very close to hitting the barn itself, let alone any of us inside. It wasn't for lack of trying, though. I thought it was pretty obvious he was trying to draw fire, and that was the other reason for "dumb one." There was something about the jumpy way he did it that told me it wasn't really his idea. The comfort was that it let us know they weren't sure exactly where we were.

"Back in a minute, Hester," I said. I crawled back toward my vantage point and pointed my AR-15 through a hole between the old foundation and the rotting boards of the barn wall. The elevated front sight just cleared the hole, but I had him dead to rights almost instantly. He was only about fifty yards away, and the upper two-thirds of him was in plain view. He'd be hard to miss. I squinted as I aimed at the white "NY" on his blue cap.

"Whadda ya think? Take him out?" I asked George. So far, we hadn't returned fire since the first exchange about ten minutes back. We hadn't because they had pretty much been shooting at the upper floor of the barn and into the loft, and we were down at the stone foundation. They were far enough off target; we'd been reluctant to reveal our actual position by shooting back. They had a lot more firepower than we did. But now Hester had been hurt. They were getting closer.

"Not yet, I think," said George. "Wait and see what he does."

The dumb one started waiving his assault rifle in the air and screaming something at us.

"Gotta be stoned," I said. "Gotta be."

"Any idea what he's saying?" asked George.

"No," I said. "Don't even know what language. But I don't think he's trying to surrender."

Suddenly, the dumb one lowered the assault rifle to hip level and pointed it right at us.

"Down!" yelled George.

CHAPTER 01

MY NAME IS CARL HOUSEMAN, and I'm a deputy sheriff in Nation County, Iowa. I'm also the department's senior investigator, which is a title that probably has as much to do with my being fifty-five as it does with my investigative abilities. It's also a title that can get me involved in some really neat stuff, even in a rural county with only twenty thousand residents. That's why I like it.

On that pleasant, twenty-degree December day, we were just beginning one of the mildest winters on record, the one that we'd later call "the winter that wasn't." I had some of my Christmas shopping done, was nearly caught up on my case files, and intended to take a few days off over Christmas for the first time in twenty-some years. On the down side, it was beginning to look as if it wouldn't be a White Christmas. Snow or not, I was already about halfway through my usual noon to eight shift, and it looked like I'd be able to coast through the rest of it. Hester Gorse, my favorite Iowa DCI agent, and I had just finished interviewing Clyde and Dirk Osterhaus—brothers, antiques burglars, and new jail inmates—regarding seventeen residential burglaries that had been committed in Nation County over the previous two months. The interviews had been conducted in the presence of their respective attorneys, who were both in their late twenties. The young brothers had thrown us a curve when they'd readily confessed to only fourteen of the break-ins. Why just those fourteen, when we all knew they'd done the whole seventeen? Some sort of strategy? A bargaining chip? It beat both Hester and me. Maybe it was just the principle of the thing.

Anyway, the attorneys had left and the brothers were back in the jail cells, arguing with the other prisoners over whether or not they were all going to watch *Antiques Roadshow* at 7:00 P.M. We only had one TV in the cell block. I was pretty sure the Osterhaus boys were going to win. Research comes first.

Hester and I were in Dispatch, having a leisurely cup of coffee. We were talking to the duty dispatcher, Sally Wells, about whether she should take her niece to see *Harry Potter* or *Lord of the Rings* when she got off duty. The phone rang, and our conversation stopped.

Sally answered with a simple "Nation County Sheriff's Department," which told me it wasn't a 911 call. They answer those with "Nine-one-one, what's your emergency?" I relaxed a bit, and had just brought my coffee cup to my lips when she reached over and snapped on the speakerphone.

"...Best get the Sheriff down here...there's this dead man in the road just down from our mailbox..." came crackling from the speaker.

"And your name and location, please?"

"I'm Jacob, Jacob Heinman," replied the brittle voice. "Me and my brother live down here in Frog Hollow...you know, just over from the Dodd place about a mile."

"I'll be paging the ambulance now," said Sally, very calmly, "but keep talking because I can hear you at the same time."

"We don't think he needs a ambulance, ma'am," said Jacob, also very calmly. "I saw 'em shoot him just about right smack in front of me. We went back up there. He's still laying there just like they left him. He's awful dead, we're pretty sure."

I suspect that even in departments where they have two or three hundred homicides a year, the adrenaline still flows with a call like that. In our case, with maybe one or two a year, the rush is remarkable. Hester and I headed out the door.

As we left, I said, "On the way. Backup, please."

Sally waved absently. She knew her job, and would have everything she could drum up out to help as soon as possible. But you like to remind even the best dispatchers, just in case something slips their mind.

The Heinman brothers were known throughout the area as the "Heinman boys." Confirmed bachelors, neither of the so-called "boys" were a day under eighty, and you couldn't excite either of them if you set his foot on fire. Or, apparently, if you shot somebody right in front of them. As I got into my unmarked patrol car, started the engine, and strapped on the seatbelt, I could hear Sally over the radio, telling a state trooper that she was looking the directions up in her plat book. Frog Hollow was an old name for a very remote stretch of road, about two miles long, that wound down through a deep, mile-long valley where there were just two farms. I don't think anybody except the rural mail carrier and the milk truck went there in the daytime, and only kids parking and drinking beer ended up there at night. Sally probably had a general idea where it was, but considering there were more than two thousand farms in Nation County, this would be no time to guess and end up giving the trooper bad directions. Hester, behind me in her own unmarked car, couldn't possibly know where we were going and was going to have to follow me to the scene. Her call sign was I 388, so I waited until the radio traffic between Sally and the trooper paused, and picked up my mike.

"Three and I 388 are ten-seventy-six," I said. That meant we were heading to the scene, and was meant as much for the case record as anything else. You always need times. "Which trooper you sending?"

"Two sixteen is south of you. I'm working on the directions..." There was no stress in Sally's voice, but I could tell she was really concentrating. "Be aware I've confirmed there are at least two suspects. Repeating, at least two suspects."

Two for sure. That always meant, to my mildly paranoid mind, that we were talking a *minimum* of two. Okay. Well, there was Hester, 216, and me. Fair odds, as 216 was new state trooper sergeant named Gary Beckman, who'd transferred into our area about six months ago. He was about forty and really knew his stuff.

"I'll direct him," I said, so she could forget the directions for him and concentrate on getting an ambulance and notifying our sheriff. "Two sixteen from Nation County Three, what's your ten-twenty?" I needed to know his location before I could give him directions. I also needed to find out where he was because we were both going to be in a hurry, and it would be extremely embarrassing if we were to find ourselves trying to occupy the same piece of roadway at the same time.

"I'm four south of Maitland on Highway Fourteen, Three." I could hear the roar of his engine over his siren noise. He was moving right along. Hester and I pulled out onto the main highway and headed south. The trooper was four miles closer than we were.

"Ten-four, two sixteen. We're just leaving Maitland now. Okay, uh, if you turn right at the big dairy farm with the three blue silos, take the next right, and, uh, continue on down a long, winding road into the valley. That's the right road, and the farm you're going to is the second one."

"Ten-four, Three." His siren was making a racket in the background. My siren was making a racket under my hood. Hester's siren was making a racket behind me. I reached down and turned the volume way up on my radio.

"Okay, and the, uh, subject is right in the roadway, so..." The last thing I wanted was for a car to run over the victim. "And Comm confirms two suspects."

"Understood."

I hoped so. After 216 and I shut up, I heard Sally talking to our sheriff, Lamar Ridgeway, whose call sign was Nation County One. From listening to their radio traffic, I could tell he was a good ten miles north of me. Since he drove the department's four-wheel-drive pickup, he wasn't going to be able to make more than eighty or so. Which begged a question.

I called Sally. "Comm, Three?"

"Three, go."

"Subject say whether or not the bad guys are still there?"

"Negative, not there. Repeating, the caller says the suspects have fled the immediate scene. He thinks they went southbound from near his residence, but he didn't get a vehicle description, just heard it leave, as it apparently was around the curve from his place, and out of his line of sight."

Great. "Give what you got to Battenberg PD." The small town of Battenberg was about five miles south of the Heinman boys' farm, and their officer could at least say who came into town from the north. Assuming that the suspects continued that way.

"He's already on the phone." She sounded a bit irritated. I wisely decided to stop interfering and let her do her job.

It had taken us about three minutes to cover the four miles to the cluster of three blue silos, and I braked hard to slow enough to make the right turn onto the gravel. I had anticipated the turn because I knew the road. Hester, who didn't, just about ended up in my trunk.

"Could we use our turn signals?" came crackling over the radio.

"Ten-four, I 388," I said to her. "Sorry 'bout that."

We were having a pretty mild winter so far, and there was no snow at all on the roadway. Just loose gravel. Almost as bad as ice and snow, if you oversped it. Without snow cover, though, there was much better traction. There was also a lot of dust from 216. Another reason I was unhappy he was ahead of me. Hester, behind both of us, had to back off quite a distance just to be able to see.

At that point, I heard "Two sixteen is ten-twenty-three" come calmly over the radio as the sergeant told Comm that he had arrived at the scene. After a beat, he said, "The scene is secure."

That meant that there was no suspect at the scene who was not in custody. Good to know, and it tended to affect how you got out of your car. Hester and I both shut down the sirens as soon as he said that.

I almost missed the next right due to the dust. It was just over the crest of a hill, and judging from the deep parallel furrows in the gravel, 216 had almost missed it, too. I was in an increasingly thick dust cloud for almost a minute, and when it tapered off I knew I was at the point where 216 had slowed. In a few seconds, I rounded a downhill curve and saw his car about fifty yards ahead, parked in the center of the roadway, top lights flashing. Excellent choice, as he was completely protecting the scene. Nobody could get by him on an eighteen-foot road with a bluff on one side and a deep ditch on the other. I stopped near the ditch and waited until I saw Hester in my rearview mirror.

"You go on up," I said on the radio. "I'll make sure nobody hits us." I carefully backed up around the curve until I was sure somebody cresting the hill could see the flashing lights in my rear window before they got into the curve. This was no time to get run over by an ambulance. Or the sheriff.

"Comm, Three, and I 388 are ten-twenty-three." I hung up the mike, grabbed my walkie-talkie, and opened my car door.

Sally's acknowledging "Ten-four, Three" just about blew me out of the car. I'd forgotten about cranking up the volume in order to hear over the sirens. I took a second to turn it way down, and then got out of the car, locked it up, and headed toward the scene. You always leave the engine running in the winter, so radio traffic doesn't run down your battery. It's also a good idea to have at least three sets of keys.

The Heinman farm sat well below road level, about fifty yards to my left. On my right, a steeply sloped, heavily wooded hill rose maybe a hundred feet above the roadbed. The farm lane came uphill toward the mailbox at a slant, with bare-limbed maple trees between it and the road. As an added measure, between the road and those trees was an old woven-wire fence covered with a thick tangle of brush and weeds. Put up, I was sure, to keep the larger debris from the roadway out of the Heinman property. There was an old, rusty Ford tractor from the fifties, quietly decomposing within ten feet of the galvanized mailbox that was perched on top of a wooden fencepost. That old tractor had been there the very first time I'd seen the farm, nearly twenty-five years ago. By now it and its rotting tires had become part of the landscape.

I saw 216 talking to the two elderly Heinman brothers. They were near the mailbox, looking toward the area ahead of the patrol car. As I approached, a body came slowly into my view in front of 216's car. It was lying kind of on its left side, parallel with the direction of the road, with its feet pointing away and downhill from me. I started making mental notes as I walked. Faded blue plaid flannel shirt, blue jeans, one black tennis shoe... and hands bound behind its back with yellow plastic binders. Damn. We call them Flex Cuffs, and use them when we run out of handcuffs. They're like the bindings for electrical wiring: once they're on, they have to be cut off. What we had here was an execution.

Two more steps, and I saw the head. More accurately, I saw the remains of the head. You often hear the phrase "blow their head off," but it's rare to actually see it.

Hester and 216 stepped over and joined me at the body.

"Hi Carl," said Trooper 216.

"Gary. Glad you could come."

"Notice the hands?"

"Right away. And the one shoe. And the head... or what used to be the head." From what I could see, from about the ears on up was gone. Although nearly all the cranium seemed gone, lots of skin was left and had sort of flapped around back into the cavity. One ear, perfectly recognizable and still attached to the neck by a flap of flesh, seemed to be pretty well intact. Seeing things like that always has a sense of unreality to it. Guess that's what keeps you sane.

"Uh, yeah," said Gary. "'Used to be' is right. I think I'm parked over top of some, uh, debris, from the head and stuff. I didn't even see it until I was just about stopped."

"Okay." His car was about fifteen feet from the top of the body's head, and still running. That was fine. We could have him move his car back when the crime lab got there.

Hester spoke to him. "Doesn't leak oil, does it?"

He looked offended. "No."

"Just checking." She smiled. "Wouldn't want oil all over the... debris. Just make sure your defroster or air conditioner's off. It's a lot easier if we don't get condensed moisture on the stuff."

"Right. Uh, you two better talk to the two old boys over there. Very interesting stuff."

"Just a few seconds more," I said. "Tell 'em we'll be right there."

Hester and I just stood and looked at the scene for a short time. You only get one chance to see a scene in a relatively undisturbed state, and I've learned to take in as much as I can when I have the chance. An ambience sort of thing, you might say. You just try to see, smell, and hear as much as you can. It helps when you try to return to it in your imagination, later in the case.

A sound was the first thing that distinguished this scene from the hundreds of others I'd been at before. The Heinman brothers had some galvanized steel hog feeders near the roadway. Looking like huge metal mushrooms, they had spring-loaded covers on them, and every time a hog wanted to eat, all it had to do was press its snout into the mechanism and open it. When it was done, out came the snout, and that spring-loaded lid slammed down with a loud clank. Usually two or three clanks, in fact. One, a beat, and then two very close together. All the time we were at the crime scene, those hog feeders made a constant racket in the background.

Now, bodies look smaller dead than they do when they're alive. I'm not sure why; they just do. This one was no exception, and it wasn't just the fact that he was a half a head shorter, so to speak. Even with the legs straightened out, he'd probably only be about five-three or five-four. It was sobering to see this wreck of a corpse, and think that he'd been alive and well only half an hour before. I just stood there looking for almost a minute, sort of taking it all in. Sometimes it helps, sometimes it doesn't. But if you don't do it, you always seem to regret it later in the case. I looked around for his other shoe, but didn't see it.

"Sure looks dead," I said.

"You must be a detective," said Hester.

"Kneeling, you think? When he was shot?"

She paused a moment. "If the debris is under Gary's car...I'd think it would have gone further if he'd been standing, maybe. But there's always the angles...but sure. I'll go with kneeling until we find out differently."

"Restrained and shot. Whether he was kneeling or not doesn't matter. Talk about malice aforethought." Binding the wrists surely eliminated sudden impulse. I took a deep breath. "Well, let's see what our witnesses have to say."

Hester and I crossed to the two old men standing by their mailbox. "I'm

Deputy Houseman," I said, not sure if they'd remember me, "and you've already met Agent Gorse?"

"Sure have. You was at the bus business, right?" asked the one I thought was Jacob.

He was referring to a car crash about fifteen years ago, when the two brothers in their old Dodge had been rear-ended by a school bus. They'd stopped in the middle of this very road to have a discussion, regrettably just into the hill and curve where I was now parked. The bus didn't see them until it was too late to completely stop. The brothers were just shaken up, but the bus driver was furious. I'd given them a ticket.

"Yeah, that was me."

"You put on a little weight," said Jacob.

"Yeah." I glanced at Hester, who was doing an admirable deadpan. "So, what happened here, Jacob?" I asked. "What did you see?"

"Well," he said, "I was comin' up to put a letter in the box, and Norris was in the barn feedin' the cows, and there was this commotion down the road there." He pointed downhill to where the road curved around to the right. "I said to myself, 'well, what's all that commotion?' and just then this young man here come a hell a kitin' round that curve, about as fast as he could go, and I thought there was something funny about him, and then I saw he had his hands behind his back, like he was ice skatin'." He shook his head. "Had to be hard to run that way."

"I'll bet," I said. I already had questions, but I let him go on with his story. Witnesses have a way of clamming up on you if you keep interrupting their train of thought.

"And he kinda came up short on one leg. I think that's 'cause he only had one shoe on. Anyways," he said, "these other two come runnin' behind him, and they was gaining pretty fast, and one of 'em had a shotgun." He paused. "I ducked down right quick. I was at Anzio, you know. Ever since, I see somebody runnin' my way with a gun, I duck." He smiled, almost shyly. "Instinct, they call it."

"Okay... me too, and I've never been to war." It still surprises me to see how much the WWII vets are aging.

"So I'm kinda behind the tractor, but I'm still lookin'. Then this one fella hollers something I didn't catch, and the one laying over there sorta turned his head to look, and he musta tripped, 'cause he just fell flat. Kerwhump." He shook his head. "Couldn't get up fast, 'cause of his hands, so they was on him just like that."

"Sure."

"They was saying something, but I didn't get it. Mostly another language, you know?"

"Like what?" I thought I could ask that without inhibiting him.

"Oh, golly. There was some different language...maybe Spanish? Sounds a lot like Italian to me, but I couldn't make out words I knew. Then English, too. That I could make out. That one word was 'motherfucker.'" He looked startled. "Oh, I'm so sorry, ma'am!"

"Think nothing of it," said Hester. "Did they say any proper names or anything?"

He shook his head. "Nope. They just seemed real upset, you know? Anyway, the one on the road over there, he was crying, I think, and they got him up on his knees, and the one with the shotgun, he just come up behind him, and put the gun to his head, and shot him. Bang. One time. A terrible thing. And that one there, he just flopped into the road so hard and fast the dust flew." He reflected a moment. "Musta been like getting hit with a truck, almost. That close and all."

"Musta been," I said.

"Then the others, they just looked around real fast, and I think they really saw the barn and the house for the first time, down there, you know? Like they saw it before, but it didn't register..." Jacob's hands had been in the pockets of his overalls throughout, and now he brought one of them into the conversation by pointing toward a cat in the barnyard. "It's like, you ever notice how a cat fixes on its prey? He's aware of everything, but just doesn't care about it bein' there. All he sees is the mouse, until the job's done. It was like that." Mission completed, his hand returned to his pocket. "Anyway, these two just turned around and ran back down the road and disappeared."

"Do you think they saw you?" asked Hester.

"Pretty sure they didn't. Their eyes just passed right over me."

I felt it would be best to lead him to the end before I backed up through the events. "Then what'd you do, Jacob?"

"Well, I didn't stand up right away, that's for sure." That shy smile again. "But when I did, I did it real careful, just in case they was comin' back for somethin', you know?" He paused. "But then I heard a car leaving down the way, and I supposed it was them. I don't take no chances, so I just took off for the barn lickety split, and got Norris, and we called from the telephone in the barn."

"That's what we did," interjected Norris. "Just that way."

"We thought it'd be best if we brought the shotgun, too," said Jacob, pointing toward a fencepost just behind the mailbox with a twelve-gauge leaning up against it. I'd missed it in the weeds and scrub.

"Figured we'd better," said Norris. "You never know." Given the afternoon's events, it was really hard to argue with that.

Jacob smiled again. "Norris, here, he was on Guadalcanal. Jarhead."

"Ah. Always good to have a Marine around. You two didn't happen to recognize any of the three, did you?" It hadn't sounded like it, but you can always hope.

"No, I didn't.... I think the dead one was a Mexican boy, but I'm not sure," said Jacob. "One of the other two might have been, too, but he looked... different than that, but like that? I don't know how to put it... "

I tried to help without planting anything in his head. "He was the one with the gun? The one who shot him?"

"Yes."

"What kind of complexion?"

"Well," said Jacob, "kind of dark, sort of dark... like a good tan would be."

"Okay. You happen to notice his hair color?"

"If I recollect, I'd have to say very dark, too. Black, maybe? Really dark for certain."

"What'd he have on?" I was taking notes now.

"Black pants, I think. Maybe navy blue. A dark sweater or something like it. Maybe a sweatshirt, with no sayings on it. Probably a sweater. I think maybe a real dark jacket, too. Maybe."

"Got it."

"And, oh... black tennis shoes." He considered that for a second. "Maybe just black shoes. Might not have been tennis shoes, now that I think about it."

"About how old? Best guess."

"I can't tell with them, the Mexicans. Not until they get really old, like me. Then it's the wrinkles, you know? But... old enough to know better. No kid."

"Okay." I wrote down ADULT. "So then, how about the other one, the white guy?"

"Well," said Jacob, "to tell the truth, I wasn't lookin' at him too hard, because I was givin' the one with the gun most of my attention."

"Understandable," said Hester.

"But if I had to guess, I'd say... about twenty-five or so."

"Why do you say that, Jacob?" I asked.

"Well, because he looked like that," said Jacob. "He wasn't a kid. I know that. But I'll tell you one thing. He looked as scared as I was."

A perfectly reasonable answer, especially if you were Jacob. I didn't think it was time to press him on just how you know when somebody's scared. If I needed anything, I needed a physical description. The fear indicators could wait for later. I'd get 'em, but eventually. Patience is very important in my line of work. "Can you describe him for me? What he looked like, just generally?"

"Oh, you know, pretty tall, a lot taller than the one with the gun. They were kinda like Mutt and Jeff. He had a pale complexion. Maybe blond hair, but it was tough to tell under the ball cap. Green jacket. That's about all."

"What did the ball cap look like?" asked Hester.

"A Forrest's Seed Corn hat. Ed Forrest down in Battenberg hands 'em out to anybody he thinks might buy seed. You know, yellow with the green lettering."

Hester didn't, but I did.

All could be local, then. "Can we go back to their ages?" asked Hester.

"Oh my," said Jacob, with a sigh. "Everybody seems to be so much younger these days. But I'd guess none of 'em was more 'n thirty. If that." He smiled at her. "I'm sorry, miss. I guess that's the best I can do."

"That's okay."

"This was a terrible thing," said Jacob. "To do that. Him bound up that way and all. Didn't have a chance. No chance at all."

There was a siren in the distance. Lamar, I was just about sure. I removed my walkie-talkie from my jeans pocket.

"You'll have to give me a minute here, Jacob," I said, moving two steps away from him. I keyed the mike. "One, Three... that you?"

"Ten-four, Three. Where you at?"

"Slow way down before the curve; we're blocking the road. Come in slow." Lamar was known for his fast driving on gravels.

"Ten-four."

I'd worked with Lamar for twenty-five years or so. He was going to hate this. Nothing appealed to him more than peace, quiet, and a placid surface to "his" county. "He's not going to be a happy man," I said as Hester stepped over.

"True." Hester knew Lamar pretty well, too.

She regarded the body for a moment. "You thinking what I'm thinking?"

I looked at her. "You mean dope?"

"Yes, I do."

"Could be. It sure looks like what the media calls 'execution-style.'"

I was rather startled when Gary, the trooper sergeant, said, "I'd say dope, too." He'd apparently come up behind me while I was on the walkie-talkie, and I'd missed it. "Sure looks like it to me." He said that with the complete assurance of an officer who wasn't working dope cases.

"It's sure as hell possible," I said. As the investigator who had the case, I didn't want to establish a mindset by labeling this "dope-related" unless and until I had hard evidence to back it up. I'd been racking my brain to try to come up with an instant suspect, and couldn't. We had meth labs in the county, and we had good-quality marijuana crops, but I wasn't currently aware of any really bad blood between local dealers. That didn't mean much, as a violent relationship in the dope business can spring up overnight. Nonetheless, at this point there was no evidence either way.

I shrugged and said, "All I know now is that he really musta pissed *somebody* off. Anyhow, you want to walk around the curve there and see if there are any tracks from the suspect vehicle?"

"Sure."

"Get photos and measurements, if there are any, and let me know, okay?"

Gary grinned. He had been a TI, one of the specially trained accident investigators for the state patrol, before he'd been promoted to sergeant. If anybody on earth knew how to interpret and photograph tire track evidence, it was Gary. "Want me to do plaster casts? I love doin' plaster casts."

"Better leave that to the lab team, but if you find something for them to cast, let me take a couple of photos right away, okay? Continuity in the courtroom," said Hester.

"Okay." I think Gary had been feeling kind of nonessential, and was anxious to get into his own area of expertise.

"And," said Hester, "I'd really like it if you could find a shotgun just laying around, you know? Or at least an empty shell."

Gary chuckled. "I'll see what I can do, Hester. You don't want much."

As soon as Lamar arrived at the scene, I briefed him on what I knew and then trudged back up the hill to my car while Lamar talked to Hester and the Heinman boys. I grabbed the big, padded nylon camera bag out of the backseat, and opened it to make sure everything was there. Other officers sometimes borrow equipment when you're on days off or vacation, and forget to put it back. They especially like to borrow 35mm film. A quick inventory revealed my 35mm SLR, my zoom lens, my digital camera, some ten rolls of 35mm film, and my short tripod. Mine in every sense, since the department didn't provide a camera or the supplies. The bag also contained a bag of Girl Scout cookies, a chocolate bar, and a box of latex gloves. Since we were beginning to draw a crowd, I grabbed the half roll of plastic crime scene tape I had left, and put it in my camera bag. I closed the trunk, reached into the backseat, and hauled out my jacket. It was going to get cold in a hurry when the sun went behind the hills. I was set. As I closed the car door, it occurred to me to try to call the department on my cell phone. We'd fought for years to get them, and had finally obtained grudging permission to carry them in the cars. We had to buy them ourselves, of course, even though we had to assure the county supervisors that we wouldn't be making personal calls. They didn't want us distracted. But it was a small victory, in spite of that. It had gotten smaller as we realized that they were pretty useless at our worst events. The really bad wrecks tended to be at the bottom of long hills on curvy roads, for instance, and we seemed to frequently find ourselves at crime scenes inside buildings with steel frames—both kinds of locations made it very difficult to reach a tower. I looked at the LCD display panel as I dialed. The little icon that indicated the strength of the nearest tower's signal was at the minimum. I tried anyway. Nope. I tried once more on the way back down the road. Nothing. Lamar glanced at me, and I knew he'd noticed I couldn't get a call through. I'd hear about that sooner or later. I made a mental note to tell him that there would be more towers in our area soon.

As I approached the body, Lamar excused himself and came over to me. "Hell of a thing," he said.

"Sure is."

"Any idea who did it?"

"Not yet. Not even close." I produced the black and yellow roll of crime scene tape. "We better get some of this around." Our tape says Sheriff's Line—Do Not Cross, and I knew that Lamar would want that up instead of Police. It's a sheriff thing.

"We better," he said.

We made a simple square of the stuff by tying one end to the Heinman boys' mailbox, stringing the tape across the road to a tree, then to a tree south of the body, to the Heinman boys' fence, and back to the mailbox.

That was a lot of tape, and I tried to placate the cost-conscious Lamar by saying, "That should look good in the photos." Then I held out my tape measure. "You want to do this, while I take the shots?" We always need a scale in each photo.

"Yep."

As I attached the flash to my 35mm SLR camera, Lamar knelt down about a yard from the body and extended the yellow steel tape from its chrome case.

"That's a new tape," I said, checking my batteries. "Don't let it snap back and cut you."

"You gonna use flash?" asked Lamar, ignoring my cautionary words about the tape. He never admitted to mistakes even after he made them, let alone beforehand.

"Yeah, the sun's going behind the hill here. Think I better." I looked through the lens and focused on an establishing shot.

"Don't get me in the damn pictures," said Lamar. He didn't want to have to go to court and testify about the photographs.

"Hell, Lamar, you know I won't even get your shadow."

I took eleven overall photos of the scene from different angles, with each camera, and then got to the close-ups of the body. Lamar, who was anticipating every shot, sort of duck-walked around the scene, standing and taking a giant step when he got to the area where the shooter had probably stood. It's hardly likely that you're going to get a good footprint on a gravel road, but you never know.

I used the digital camera in order to have photos on my computer as soon as I got back to the office. The 35mm was for the court, which didn't want to allow the digital stuff into evidence because it could be enhanced or manipulated too easily.

Finished with her notes from the Heinman boys, Hester came back over to the body. As we three got a closer look, we began to get an even better understanding of the extent of the damage. It was, as coroners say, massive.

It certainly appeared to have been a contact shotgun wound to the back of the head, just as Jacob Heinman had said. There really wasn't any entrance or exit wound. What there was was a U-shaped gap that had excised everything between the victim's ears. The entire top of the head was gone, and from what we could see without moving him, the missing area included most of his face.

"Christ," said Lamar.

"Yeah," I said, taking the last shot on the roll and stopping to reload. "Not much left."

"Where'd it all go?"

"Lots of it's under Gary's car," I said. "He couldn't get stopped before he realized he was just about on top of the stuff. We thought we'd leave it there until the lab gets here. I hope there's teeth and stuff under there, so we have some sort of chance of positive identification." I finished loading the camera and, lying down on the roadway, took three shots of the area under the patrol car. I could see chunks of tissue, and blood. I'd half been hoping to see the other shoe. No such luck.

"Well, we still got his fingerprints," said Lamar.

"Yeah. That's about all, unless we have tattoos or birthmarks." I got back to my feet and dusted myself off as well as possible. Frozen dust is still dust. "We sure can't tell eye color... unless we get lucky and find part of an eye."

"It had to be quick," said Lamar. "I mean, it wouldn't hurt at all, I think."

"Yeah. It looks like a lot of his head was just about vaporized." I thought I heard a siren in the distance. "Ambulance?"

"Should be," he said. "You two call for the DCI mobile lab yet?"

"I notified them," said Hester. "Haven't heard anything back yet."

"I'll check and see," he announced and headed back toward his car. "Radios still work better than those phones."

Ah, yes. But they weren't as private.

"You thinking dope on this one?" he asked.

"I'm leaning that way." I shrugged. "Way too early to say for sure, though."

Gary appeared around the curve and yelled out. "Hey, one of you?"

I looked up from my camera. "What's up, Gary?"

"You wanna come on down this way? I think I got some tracks here, where somebody spun as they left."

Hester and I headed down toward him. On our way, I checked in the right-hand ditch for a black tennis shoe. Nothing.

When I got around the curve to where the tire tracks were, they were pretty good indicators of a very fast turnaround and departure. There was a set of parallel furrows in the gravel and a partial track from one tire in the dust on the edge of the road.

I looked at them and snapped some quick shots. "So, what do you think?"

"Well, it's front-wheel-drive, from the relative positions of the furrows and the nonspinning tire tracks. Came from the south, and turned around and went back the same way." He sounded pleased with himself. I looked at the tracks and could see what he meant. I doubted if I'd have been able to decipher them, but once he explained it, it was obvious. "He couldn't get it turned on the roadway in one motion, so he went forward and to his left, backed around, then forward and cranked the wheel, and that's when he stepped on the gas and made the furrows."

I remembered that Lamar had my tape with him, so I laid my pen down alongside the partial track and took a photo of what seemed to be about half the tread-width, well impressed into the soft dust at the very edge of the roadway.

"You think they can get a plaster cast of this?" asked Hester.

"Maybe... if they just spray a mist of water to settle the dust first, it should go all right." Gary looked thoughtful. "I've got a box lid in my trunk, and that ought to preserve it until they get here."

The approaching siren was getting louder.

"We better stop the ambulance on the south side of these tire tracks," I said.

15:37

THE DUMB ONE LET LOOSE WITH A BUNCH OF ROUNDS. They hit the dirt about ten yards from the barn, and then he squeezed off some more that smacked through the barn boards just above the limestone foundation line, filling the air with wood fragments and an amazing amount of dust. George's admonition to get down had come a split second too late, but I managed to duck down an instant after the slugs started hitting the building. The rounds punched through the boards six feet to my left, but that was way too close for somebody as slow as I am. I stayed pressed up against the cold limestone for a few seconds after the firing stopped, my head down to protect my eyes from all the crud; then I very cautiously made my way to the holes to my left, took a deep breath, and looked through. The dumb one was gone, presumably back into the shed.

"Everybody all right?" asked George.

We all responded more or less affirmatively.

"Next time," I said, trying to slow my breathing, "we shoot first."

"You bet," said George.

I was getting a very bad feeling and stated the obvious, voicing what the rest of them probably already thought. "Hey. We lose sight of 'em every time." I put my face a bit closer to a hole to widen my field of view. Any closer, and I'd lose the cover of the interior shadow, and I sure didn't want that. "We just *think* they go to ground in the same place. They could be anywhere out there. And they could be getting closer." We needed a better view of the surrounding area. Unfortunately, it was not to be had from our location in the basement.

"I could go up into the loft," said Sally from behind George and me, where she was tending to Hester. "Great view from up there. I'm small. Harder to see me."

"Not with that red hair," said George. "I'll go up."

Being about six inches taller and seventy-five pounds heavier than George, I simply said, "I'll cover you from the steps." He was a lot faster than I was.

The open stairs from the basement came through the first floor about ten feet inside the open barn doors, on the side that faced our shooters. George was going to emerge from the basement, run across the main floor about thirty feet . to the right, and climb a vertical wooden ladder that went to the hayloft.

"How're you going to do that? Cover me, I mean." George tends to get right to the point. With the main barn doors standing open, he'd be in full view from the shed for the entire distance.

I looked up toward the main floor. "Why don't you let me get about halfway up the steps. Then you go by, and I go, too. Just stick my head out of the opening. I should be able to fire at floor level at the same time you get upstairs."

He looked skeptical. "Sure."

"Trust me," I said with a grin. "And rules or not, I'm gonna fire as soon as I get a shot at somebody. And screw it. If I don't see the shooter, I'll aim for where I think he is." We weren't allowed to fire unless we could see our target. A target that we could "demonstrate and elucidate" as a threat. An old machine shed that I just *thought* was occupied certainly wouldn't qualify. Well, not on a normal day.

"You got more than one magazine for that thing?" he asked, indicating my AR-15. He pointedly didn't say anything about my intention to lay down some fire. His department's rules were much stricter than mine.

"Three. Plus the one that's in it. That's about a hundred and eight rounds." I always carry twenty-seven or twenty-eight rounds in the thirty-round-capacity magazines. Easier on their springs.

"Save some for later," he advised. "Why does everybody always seem to leave those big barn doors open?" he asked. It was rhetorical. He took a deep breath, and as he exhaled I could see his breath against the sunlight upstairs. "Well, we might as well get started."

"You got a walkie?"

"Not one you can hear me on," he said. The feds use different frequencies than we do.

"Sally, you better give him yours," I said.

"Sure," she said, but I could tell she was reluctant. She was, after all, a dispatcher first and foremost.

"Okay, never mind, I'll give him mine," I said, unclipping it and handing it to him. "This way," I said to George, "you'll have Sally on the other end instead of me."

"And it's a good thing, too. Let me get to the wall," said Sally. "I'll look over left. Do I get to shoot, too?"

"Nope. Just me," I said. "No shots from the basement until they know we're really here."

She nodded and ducked over to the broken window. She patted Hester as she left her.

"Ready, Carl?" asked George.

"Yep," I said, and moved up the stairs. "Let me call it."

"Okay."

I eased into a position where I thought I could get through the opening in the floor above me without taking more than one full step, and could do it with my rifle just about leveled. I checked to make sure I'd left enough room for George to get by me. It looked about right.

"Okay, go," I said.

As my head emerged at main floor level, I felt George scramble by me and head for the ladder. I brought my rifle up, and aimed at the old machine shed. Out of the corner of my eye, I saw George trip on a bad board, then hit the old ladder about three rungs off the floor and nearly fly up and into the loft. It was over so fast, I found myself covering somebody who wasn't there anymore.

I ducked back down into the basement. There had been no movement anywhere in my field of view. Not a shot had been fired. Either they'd not seen him, or they hadn't had time to react. Excellent.

Sally and Hester were both looking at me. "He's up," I told them. "He's really fast."

Sally immediately put her walkie-talkie to her mouth. "George, you hear me?"

Silence.

"George?" she said, a bit louder. "George, you got a copy?"

Nothing.

She and I exchanged a glance, and I shook my head. "I know it was turned on," I said. "I just used it to talk to the S.O."

"Were you on Info or Ops?"

A good question. On the operations channel, or Ops, you could talk walkie to walkie, and walkie to car. On the information channel, or Info, you could only talk to the office, and no other walkie or car would hear you.

I looked at her. "I don't remember... damn, but I'll bet it was Info." Shit.

I headed back up the stairs. "Keep a sharp lookout," I said to Sally. "I can't see a lot from up here."

"Okay."

I crouched near the top of the steps, looking up toward the side of the loft where George had disappeared. It was a good fifteen feet above my head, and thoroughly covered with loose and baled hay. Insulation. He wasn't going to be able to hear me.

"George," I said in a loud voice. "George, you hear me?"

Silence.

Very cautiously, I stuck my head up past the floor level. I sure as hell didn't want to be yelling if there was somebody with a gun standing near the door. I glanced around. Clear, as far as I could tell.

I figured that I could spend half an hour trying to get his attention without yelling, or just let out one good shout and get it over with.

"HEY GEORGE!"

About two seconds later, his face appeared at the edge of the loft.

"You're on Info. The second button," I said, holding up two fingers. "Turn it to channel one!" I held up my index finger. "One! For Ops!"

He nodded.

I glanced back toward the big door, just in time to see somebody run by, going to my left. "Look left!" I yelled, and ducked back down below floor level. I'd had such a brief glance, and he'd been going so fast, I couldn't even tell what he was wearing.

Sally gave me a quizzical look.

"Tell him there's a guy just outside, and he's off to our left somewhere. Real close... maybe ten yards."

She spoke softly into the walkie-talkie as I moved left toward the south wall of the basement.

"He's over here somewhere," I said as I passed Sally. I wished I'd gotten a better look, because it would have been nice to give George some sort of color to key on.

"He can't see anybody," she said to me, meaning George couldn't make the guy from his position up in the loft. That figured. The guy was so close that George was probably going to have to lean out over the edge to see him.

"Okay…" I continued to the south wall. There were two small, quarter-framed windows at that end, probably only a foot or two above the outside ground level. There was very dirty glass in most of the frames, so it would be nearly impossible to see clearly into the gloomy basement from the outside. There were, however, two empty frames, both in the left-hand window. He'd have to go there if he was going to try to look in.

Either that, or go all the way to the back of the building, on the east side, where there was a walk-in door. The old door didn't fit well, and I could see daylight around all four edges of the rickety thing. Maybe there. Maybe. But if it was me, I'd kind of like to get a glimpse of what was inside before I came through the door. I put my rifle to my shoulder and pointed it in the general direction of the left-hand window, trying to keep the edges of the door in my peripheral vision in case I was guessing wrong.

"You keep looking toward the shed," I said to Sally. "I'll take this one."

"Okay."

There was a noise from Hester. It was like she was trying to talk with a mouthful of Novocain. I glanced at her, and she was pointing her handgun at the door.

"Got it," she managed to get out.

I just said, "Right." There wasn't time to tell her how impressed I was.

I slowly approached the window, half expecting to see a grenade or bomb or something come flying through. Instead, when I was about five feet away from it, the empty frames were suddenly filled by a New York Yankees baseball cap and a very wide-open mouth, which screamed something about "—die!!!!" Just like that, it was gone. I didn't even have a chance to squeeze the trigger.

He had to have been on all fours and to the right of the frame, just to get his head that low and at that angle. Almost instinctively, I fired four rounds through the old wallboards, at what I hoped was the right level to blow him to hell.

Mistake. The overpressure from the muzzle blast of that AR-15 in the confined area of the barn brought down a shower of dust and bits of stuff from the rafters and between the floorboards above my head. The concussion made my ears ring. The only plus was a series of high-pitched screams from outside the barn, which seemed to get weaker and weaker, and then stopped altogether.

I looked back at Sally, who was brushing the debris from her hair even as she was talking on the walkie-talkie, and giving me a dirty look. Over at Hester, who had put up her shoulder to hold the compress in place while she too tried to brush the dust from her hair and keep her handgun pointed at the old door.

I was sure I'd killed whoever it was. It was a funny, sad kind of feeling.

"George," said Sally, loudly, "says he can see him now."

I looked quizzically at her.

"He says the guy is running. Back to the shed. It looks like you might have hit him." She held the walkie-talkie closer to her ear. "In the hand, maybe… "

Damn. The funny, sad feeling left instantly, replaced by regret that I hadn't killed him. I thought that was really interesting. So much for the humanitarian deputy.

Sally continued to listen. She smiled. "He says it was the dumb one, and that you made him lose his hat out in the yard."

There was an upside yet. At least he'd left the immediate vicinity of the barn.

"Ask him," I said, "if he can see any others out there moving around."

"You don't have to shout," said Sally.

I hadn't realized that I was. The effect of the noise of the rifle, of course.

"Luuggg!" said Hester.

I stepped toward her, pointing my rifle at the door.

"Nunh," she said, and actually sounded happy. "Lugg." She was looking at me and holding out her hand. "I gawdd id!"

In her palm was the nail fragment that had been lodged in her cheek. She'd apparently managed to push it back out somehow, despite what had to be some considerable pain. She appeared exceptionally pleased with herself.

She held the piece of iron up to show Sally.

"Hey," said Sally into the walkie-talkie. "Hester got the fragment out of her cheek… yeah. Okay, ten-four, I'll tell 'em." She pointed a finger upward, toward the general area where George was in the loft. "He says, 'Good, now put gauze in your cheek,' and that he can't see anybody out there anywhere moving at all."

"Okay."

Sally looked me squarely in the eye. "I can't believe this is happening," she said. "I just can't believe it."

"Don't feel bad. Neither can I, and I know a lot more about this case than you do."

"So, we got a plan?"

I shrugged. "Wait for help. Best I can do."

Back to square one. Don't get me wrong. Sometimes that can be a very good thing.

CHAPTER 02

16:07

I WATCHED THE BLUE AND WHITE AMBULANCE COMING TOWARD US, lights flashing, the siren silent now that they had us in sight. I hoped they wouldn't be too irritated, seeing as how their patient was so obviously dead. It was just that we called them automatically, because we weren't about to take the chance that an amateur diagnosis was absolutely correct. There was nothing worse, from a lawsuit standpoint, than to take the word of a bystander that somebody was dead and decide not to dispatch an ambulance. I mean, we probably should call a mortician for those who we know to be dead, but if there's any doubt, we use the ambulances. The morticians are really nice people, but their save rate isn't too high.

The ambulance rolled to a stop, and the driver stuck his head out the side window. "What have you got for us, Carl?"

It was Red Schmitt, volunteer driver and emergency medical technician, who managed his uncle's clothing store in the real world. I'd known him for years.

"Hey, Red! What we got is one dead, and I mean *really* dead, dude lying in the roadway up around the curve. There's a bunch of tracks in the gravel right in front of you, so you gotta stop here."

"You bet," he said, setting his emergency brake and opening his door. He left the engine running. Years of experience with the rigs had taught him that. "What, a tractor roll over?"

"Nope. Not that easy. You guys just follow us on up, now." Hester and I started walking back up around the curve with the three members of the ambulance crew walking along behind. I felt like we were leading a little parade.

"Why are you way over there?" asked Hester.

"Lookin' for his other shoe in the ditch on this side. I was checking the other side on the way down."

I heard Red talking again, and turned around. "What you need, Red?"

"It's not one of the Heinman boys, is it?" He sounded really concerned.

"No. No, it's not." I turned back and we led them up to a good spot about ten yards short of the body, over on the left side of the roadway. "You can take a look at him, if you have to. Just close enough so you can see he's deceased."

One of the crew was Terri Biederman. She was in her thirties and had been an EMT with this crew several years ago. I hadn't seen her since about 1995, though, when she'd left for Milwaukee. I saw from the patches on her jump suit that she'd made paramedic. Cool.

"Mr. Houseman," she said. "Still here, huh?"

"Oh, yeah. How you been?"

"Pissy, mostly." As always, direct and to the point.

"Glad I asked." We'd always liked her.

The third member of the ambulance crew was Meg Hastings, about forty, and a clerk at the Coast-to-Coast store in her real life.

"I've been fine," she said, brightly. "No complaints at all."

Terri stuck out her tongue.

It wasn't advisable that we have the ambulance personnel actually examine the body, and they did not. If they'd left a footprint or observed something closely enough to form an opinion, they'd have to testify in court. They were volunteers, and it wasn't fair to have them waste time from their real jobs just sitting in court because some defense attorney wanted to try to trip one of them up. They did observe the body at a few feet, however, and all agreed that, whoever it was, he was most assuredly dead.

They decided to stick around for the medical examiner, who was on his way to the scene. He might want them to move the body fairly soon, and they were more than willing to help. Besides, EMTs always liked to watch the ME at work. In the meantime, they stood off to one side, watched us, and listened to the Heinman boys tell about what they'd seen. We could have stopped that, but the Heinman boys would be telling the same story in the coffee shop within hours anyway.

I motioned the ambulance crew over.

"Yeah, Carl?"

"You guys meet any cars on your way up here?"

"Sure," said Terri.

"Very many?"

"Well," said Red, trying to remember, "at least three or four, I think. Terri was in front, too, though. Maybe she remembers different."

"More like seven or eight." Terri was sharp. "You mean getaway-car kind of stuff?"

"Hopefully. We didn't meet any when we were coming in from the north." I shrugged. "There are at least four or five different gravel roads they could turn onto before they even got to the paving and into Battenberg," I said. The ambulance had come from Battenberg.

"At least," said Terri. "Anybody wake up the Battenberg cop to have him look?" She said it in a disparaging tone that let me know she had a very low opinion of the Battenberg police force.

"I believe he was up," I said, not knowing but not willing to concede the point. "There's no information that he's got anybody coming into town since we asked." But now I was wondering if he *was* awake. Crap. "You recognize any of the cars you met?" I asked, back on track and glad to change the subject.

"There was Hank Granger," she said. "Probably on his way home from his route. That's the only one I recognized."

Hank Granger was a rural mail carrier. With flashing yellow caution lights, and U.S. MAIL on the roof of his car, he tended to stand out. Good. He'd be very familiar with the cars he normally encountered on his route. A possible witness already. Things were looking up.

I went back to my car and contacted Sally on the radio.

"Three, go," came the reassuring voice.

"Yeah, Comm, uh, ten-twenty-one the Henry Granger residence in Battenberg, will you, and see if he's available for an officer to talk with him in an hour or so?"

"Ten-four, Three."

"Before you phone him, Comm, any traffic from Forty?" Forty was the Battenberg PD car's call sign.

"Negative, Three. I contacted the duty officer at his residence via ten-twenty-one, and he advised he'd contact us with any information."

So she'd phoned him at his house. Good enough. Battenberg was only six miles away from the Heinman farm. Easy reach with my car radio. "Ten-four, Comm. I'll go direct with him." He should be in the car, easily, by now.

I called six times, on two frequencies. No response. The Battenberg police department was a two-man operation, consisting of a chief and one officer. At least, they had been until the World Trade Center attack. It just happened that one of them was in the Air Force Reserve, and he'd been called to active service. That left Norm Vincent, the chief, to work most of the shifts. He'd scrounged up a part-timer who worked three evenings a week. Norm had been trying to do forty-eight hours on call, then twenty-four off. Not much opportunity presented itself for sleep, if he'd been at all busy.

"Comm, I get no signal from Forty." I tried not to sound testy, but Sally should have established radio contact a few minutes after the phone conversation when she'd originally notified him.

By the unabashedly testy "Ten-four, stand by," Sally agreed with me.

A few seconds later, Sally said, "He fell back asleep, Three. He'll be out right away." She sounded disgusted, probably as much with herself as with him.

"Okay, Comm," I said, intentionally dropping the 10 code. It's more informal, and friendlier. That's all I had to say for her to interpret something like, "Let's start looking a little sharper up there." "While we're at it, do you have an ETA for DCI mobile lab?"

"They're en route," said Sally. "My last contact was that they were going to be to you within forty-five minutes, and that was... nineteen minutes ago."

The "nineteen minutes" pleased me. It was her way of telling me that she was still pretty damned efficient, thank you very much. It also meant that they must have been at a scene fairly close to us.

"Ten-four, Comm. And the ME?" We wanted the medical examiner to be at the scene before it got really dark, because we didn't really have the good auxiliary lighting equipment we'd need to give him the best look at the scene. If night beat him, we'd have to call out a truck from the Battenberg volunteer fire department, with its auxiliary lighting equipment. That'd make for quite a crowd and only increase the chances that we'd obliterate some evidence.

"ME is Dr. Zimmer, and he's been en route from the clinic here in Maitland since seventeen-oh-one." She was sounding more at ease as the conversation progressed, but I knew that she was still kicking herself over the Battenberg PD call.

"Ten-four, Comm." I would have said something like "thanks" except we'd both have thought I was being condescending.

I walked back to the body in the road, and to the gathered ambulance crew. They had walkie-talkies, too, and I was sure they'd heard about the Battenberg officer sleeping. They had.

"Fell back asleep, huh?" asked Terri.

"Yep."

She just shook her head.

"So, then," I continued. "You didn't recognize any other cars on your way up?"

"Nope. So, who's this?" she asked, indicating Hester.

"Hester Gorse. I'm an agent with the DCI." Hester stuck out her hand.

"Oh," said Terri, extending her hand and shaking Hester's. "A state investigator. We've never met. I'm Terri Biederman. Recently of Milwaukee, but born here. Paramedic."

I walked over to Lamar. "You hear my radio traffic about Battenberg?"

"Yep. That dumb sonofabitch." He said it as one word. Calmly, though. "I told him he ought to loosen up on his damned budget and hire some of our reserves."

"I'll get with him as soon as I can," I said. "He still may be able to help."

"It ain't like he has before," said Lamar. "But go ahead. We gotta work with him."

I had a bit higher opinion of Norm Vincent than Lamar did, but I just let it ride. We *all* had to work together.

As it happened, both the DCI lab team and Dr. Henry Zimmer arrived at the same time. Both had been equally lost, as it turned out, and had actually met when the lab team flagged Henry down to ask directions. Henry got quite a kick out of that one.

Once there, though, it turned out to be like old home week. Henry and I were longtime friends. Hester and Henry had worked together off and on for years, and were glad to see each other. Like all our rural medical examiners, Henry was a general practitioner, and had a large private practice. Apparently he was the doctor for the Heinman boys, and they exchanged waves. He was also my doctor, and greeted me with "Still got the cookies in your camera bag?"

I got him some.

Hester introduced her lab crew to us, a youngish sort named Bob Ulrich and an older man named Dave Franks. Introductions over, she looked down the road toward the body of the still-unidentified victim.

"Well, let's get started."

We've found that, over the years, it's best if the investigators don't get too involved with the initial stuff the lab crew does. We want them to find things for themselves and not be distracted by us as we focus on some particular items of evidence. We proceeded together but separately, so to speak. That is, until it came time to move Gary's car back from the human debris field. At that point, we formed a little crowd.

Gary was told to back up very slowly and to stop when Bob signaled him. He did, and had backed up not more than fifteen feet when he was told to stop.

"Now, better call a wrecker, Sergeant," said Dave, the senior lab man. "We're going to have to have those tires."

"What?"

"We need your tires. They've been in our, uh, evidence. There may be small fragments and tissues adhering to them."

"You have to be shitting me." Gary was astonished.

"I assume you have to get permission," said Dave.

Dave was right. The tires had been in the blood and bone fragments, and some of that material was now transferred to them. The lab crew was going to take all four, as it turned out, and Gary was pretty disgusted. He'd have to get permission from high up, get the wrecker and four new tires ordered out to the scene. It was probably going to affect the maintenance budget for his entire post, and would reflect on his personal stats, as well. All just because he stopped a few feet closer to the body, in a well-intentioned effort to protect the scene.

"Don't let it bother you," said Lamar. "We'll get a receipt for the tires to you. And you ought to get 'em back in, oh, what you think, Carl? Three-four years?"

"Not any longer than that," I said.

I don't think it took any of the sting out.

"Look at that," said Lamar, pointing to the mobile crime lab truck. "I wonder when they got that?"

The lab crew had set up a portable generator with halogen lights attached to an extendable aluminum tripod, so we had truly exceptional lighting for our first real look at the extended debris field.

"Wow," I said. "Cool."

"Those halogens set somebody back," grumbled Lamar as he moved closer to take advantage of the brilliant lighting.

The debris field, if you could call it that, was roughly fan-shaped, with the small end closest to the body. There was blood, naturally, but a lot of it had been distributed in the form of a reddish haze by the blast, and we were confronted by mostly large droplets as opposed to pools of the stuff. It was a lot like spatter painting. There were two relatively large sections of skull, with the attached skin and hair. That would be a big help. The hair appeared to be either black or very dark brown. At that point, I appreciated any identifiers at all. There were a couple of chunks of bony tissue that would eventually be identified as parts of the maxilla. Most of the teeth were still attached, but some appeared to have been sheared off by the blast. They eventually salvaged four good upper teeth. "Good" in the sense that a dentist could use them to attempt to identify the former owner. There really wasn't an identifiable clump of brain tissue, except for one section about four inches by three that was near the far end of the debris field.

"This piece carried further, because it had more mass than the smaller fragments," said Bob, the younger lab member.

"Um hum," said Hester. She knew that, of course. It was just a matter of basic ballistics.

"That's the cerebellum, there," said Doc Zimmer. He got a quizzical look from Bob. "I'm no expert, but if it was a contact shotgun wound to the back of the head, we'd see the blast effect distributing the majority of the brain tissue." He peered more closely at the yellowish gray matter. "Whereas this bit was probably sucked out by the vacuum caused by the gases from the bore, and wasn't damaged all that much." He shrugged. "The brain divides pretty naturally into sections, with enough trauma."

"I've got some teeth and fragments of teeth scattered up here," said Dave, the older lab man. "Some still in pretty good shape, at least the tops."

"Maybe another fragment of jaw?" asked Bob, pointing to a light grayish item that was speckled with blood.

My turn. "Nope. That's the plastic wadding from the shotgun shell," I said. The plastic wadding holds the shot pellets and butterflies out as soon as it leaves the barrel. That was a good find, as it would enable us to nail down the exact caliber or gauge of the shotgun.

Our luck held, as we found about half an eyeball, mostly the retina.

"Looks like he had brown eyes," said Bob.

"Well, one, anyway," I said. It was an attempt at a bit of humor, to ease the stress.

We stepped back again and regarded the entirety of the scene.

"Mostly bits and pieces," I said. "That's only good if you like puzzles."

"It's not a lot," said Hester, "but we at least have someplace to start."

She was right about it not being a lot. Just some hair, partial dentition, and hopefully an eye color. The only concrete ID materials we had were his fingerprints, and we could only hope they turned up something concrete. In the meantime, we'd have to circulate a pretty basic description and see if anybody resembling it turned up missing. I was sort of praying that he was local. If not, we could be looking at the remains of somebody from just about anywhere.

Lamar and I pulled on some latex gloves and helped Henry turn the body over, so he could feel the abdomen and get a guess as to the core temperature of the deceased.

The absence of a face was a lot more pronounced when he was rolled over. What bothers me the most in the recently dead is usually the face. No problem here.

"Ugh," said Henry. "What a mess."

I noticed that there was a gold chain around the dead man's neck. Anything in the way of an identifier was good, although it looked like a perfectly ordinary chain from where I stood.

"Still some warmth in there," said Henry, mostly to himself. "Let me check his pockets to see if he has any ID."

"Watch for needles," warned Hester.

"Sure," said Henry. He went through the jeans pockets, and came up with a quarter and two dimes.

"That's it," he said. "No billfold, nothing else." He smiled at Hester. "And no needles."

Henry, as county medical examiner, authorized the remains to be taken to Maitland Hospital, where they'd be examined by one of the state forensic pathologists as soon as one was available.

"Are one of you," he asked Hester and me, "going to want to attend the autopsy?"

"Yes," said Hester. "If you could let us know when it's scheduled..."

"Sure," said Henry. "Shouldn't think it'd be too very hard to determine the mechanism of death in this one."

"God," said Hester, "I should hope." She motioned to Lamar. "Could you have an officer meet the body at the hospital and stay with it until the pathologist gets there?"

He could and would.

"Great. Either I'll be at the autopsy or Carl will," said Hester. "Bob, be sure to get case prints as soon as you can. That means you have to be at the hospital, because we leave the wrists bound until the pathologist cuts the cuffs. Okay?"

The senior lab technician agreed, a bit reluctantly. Case prints are "fingerprints" that encompass the entire hand, past the crease of the wrist. That way, even if the person being identified has just left a partial palm print on some surface, you can at least get a fair comparison. It was also for normal ID purposes, since our victim was without his face.

"And AFIS as soon as possible," she said. AFIS stands for Automated Fingerprint Identification System. Its computerized database is composed of links to FBI, state, local, and independent databases. If a set of prints has been recorded, AFIS can retrieve it, identify the owner, automatically link with the Computerized Criminal History system, and get any criminal record from CCH within seconds. It was a great system. They also make a portable print scanner, but Iowa hadn't chosen to provide one of those to its lab crews. Therefore, they had to do an old-fashioned ink and roll job, and then take the prints to a regional console. It was still a tremendous improvement over the old method where you had to have a suspect, and then the records were searched on that name. Those old manual searches made it impossible to obtain an ID from prints alone, simply because of the manpower required to search the millions of records.

"I wish this was happening about four years from now," said Bob. "The Iowa Laboratories facility ought to be up and running by then." He said it in a dreamy sort of voice.

The new facility was scheduled to have the DCI labs, the University of Iowa Hygienic Lab, the state medical examiner's lab, and the Department of Agriculture labs all under one roof, in Ankeny, Iowa. As opposed to today, where items that needed the attention of more than one lab could take hours just to transfer from one location to another. He was right; it would have been nice.

At this stage of the crime scene investigation, standard procedure was to allow the DCI lab team to do their thing with the collection and inventory of the evidence. It's the most effective way, and they do it much better if we don't interfere. So, since we were effectively done at the crime scene, Hester and I walked up to my car to discuss things. We didn't want to be overheard.

"If it's dope-related, or gang-related," she said, "we might get a tumble pretty quick. They do things like this to get a message out. We should hear pretty fast if that's what's going on."

"As long as they want to get the message out around here," I said. "If they're trying to send a message to this guy's cousin in Cincinnati, we're sort of out of the loop."

"Well, yes." She was making an entry in her Palm Pilot. Something else I was going to have to get.

"You like those?"

"Ummm… you bet," she said, closing the little cover. "Downloads right into my PC. Wonderful thing." She slipped it in the pocket of her slacks. "Just get a rechargeable one, not the AAA-battery kind. Much more convenient."

"You know of any DNE undercover stuff under way up here that I don't?"

"Nope. Just Harlan and Feinberg working the meth buys."

I thought for a second. "It sure looks dope-related, doesn't it?"

"Yes."

"I'm not quite convinced yet, though." I looked at her. "How about you?"

"Not yet," she said. "I'm at least open to suggestions."

We decided to head on in to Battenberg, and have a chat with Hank Granger, the rural mail carrier the ambulance crew had met on their way to the crime scene. He probably wasn't going to be a gold mine of information, but he seemed like a good place to start.

"Hey, you know, Hester," I said, "in all the time we've worked together, this is the first time you've actually been in our office when we got one of these calls."

"And it was truly exciting, Houseman." She grinned. "I just love driving in dust clouds."

"Oh, yeah. Sorry about that."

"I'll get even, sooner or later," she said.

At that point, Jacob Heinman came over to us. "Deputy?"

"Yeah, Jacob. You remember something else?" I always hope.

He gave us that shy smile of his, and said, "Nope. But me and Norris just wanted you to know… that ticket at the accident."

"Yes?"

"Well, we don't hold it against you. I mean we know you were just doing your job."

"Well, thanks, Jacob. I appreciate that."

"We still think," he added hastily, "that that bus was in the wrong. But it's okay with us, anyway. You did what you *thought* was right."

"I always try," I said. "Thanks." I thought his concession was sort of Nation County's legacy from the 9/11 attack. I was touched.

"What was that about?" asked Hester, when he'd moved back down the road toward Lamar.

I told her about the accident, and his statement.

"I think he's right," she said. "How on earth could you give a sweetheart like that a ticket?"

"Don't go there, Hester. I've had a long day."

"You old grump."

15:48

IT WAS TIME TO RETHINK OUR OPTIONS.

Now that the people who were shooting at us were fairly sure that we were in the barn, the main problem with our position was this: Both of our exits were covered from the area of the shed and chicken coop, where the bad guys were positioned, and the whole area from the barn to the road could be covered by somebody up in the old concrete silo. The barn's main door faced directly at the shed. Anybody trying to leave by that door stood a very good chance of being shot before they even got out of the damned barn. The second door, the old one with the daylight showing at all edges, would allow one or two of us to get out of the barn itself without being seen. Well, assuming that the people who were trying to kill us remained in the shed or the chicken coop. With that door option, it was subsequent movement that would get you killed. If you went right, you'd be visible from the shed in about five feet. If you went left, you could be clearly seen from the chicken coop after about forty feet. So, as long as you didn't want to go anywhere, you *could* get out.

And, of course, if they had got somebody to the old concrete silo, which in all likelihood they had, they could cover the second door from the get-go.

We couldn't get out. Tactical obstacle number one.

Seeing as how we couldn't leave, other problems just sort of popped up everywhere. Our field of view was absolutely rotten. Even from George's position in the loft, there were large areas of the farmyard we just couldn't see. Granted, we did have a good view of the shed. But, we only had a partial view of the chicken coop. And the concrete silo was out of our field of view completely. We weren't going to be able to tell if there was anybody up in the thing until one of us tried to get out the old door. Tactical obstacle number two.

We couldn't send somebody out to "draw their fire." Unlike the movies, you don't draw straws for that sort of thing. We were just going to have to stay put until one of two things happened. First, and most hopefully, backup would arrive and bail us out. Please, God. Failing that, those who were trying to kill us were going to either storm the barn, or do something downright shitty like set it on fire, and force us to make a break for it. Worst-case scenario, believe me. None of us had any idea just how many bad guys there were, but I was pretty sure there would be enough of them to cover both exits.

I figured we were pretty obviously outnumbered. Tactical obstacle number three.

Then there was the matter of firepower. So far, everybody we'd been able to see shooting at us had what appeared to be an AK-47, or something in that general category. Large caliber, and they had been shooting full auto. The 7.62mm rounds they were firing could easily penetrate our Kevlar tactical vests, even the ones with ceramic plates in the center of the chest. We, on the other hand, had my AR-15, Sally's shotgun, and four handguns. We were thoroughly outgunned, and except for my rifle, outranged as well. Tactical obstacle number four.

The only good thing was, so far, none of us was hurt in such a way that we couldn't run. If we had to make a run for it, maybe one or two of us could actually traverse the hundred-yard lane and get to the road. Not that that would do much good unless backup was there, since our cars were parked at the Heinman boys' farm about a mile up the road. So we had no place to go even if we did get out of the barn. Besides, I'd never been particularly fleet of foot, and at fifty-five years of age, six feet three inches, and 280 pounds, I was fairly certain that I'd not be able to make it up the lane at any great speed. I'd just be a large, slow-moving target. Tactical obstacle number five.

And I was sure I'd missed one or two others. No need to dwell on more than five.

It was pretty obvious that we were all running through those obstacles and concluding along the same lines. Morale was beginning to sink.

Sally spoke up. "Anybody want part of a Three Musketeers bar?"

Then it started to get dark. That meant that it was also only a matter of time before it got colder. I'd checked the forecast before we left, and they were expecting temperatures in the single digits. It was going to be a very long night.

Sally's walkie-talkie crackled. I couldn't quite make out what the message was, but she scooted over to me and held out the mike at the end of the pig-tailed cord.

"Forty is at the end of the lane," she said. "He says he can see the barn, and thinks he can make it up here."

Forty was Norm Vincent, the Battenberg chief.

"No way," I said, and took the mike. "Forty, Three."

"Yeah, go ahead, Three."

"Don't come up here. You won't make it past the old foundation."

"I can drive right up there. I don't see anybody."

"No, but they see you. Stay where you are, or go back a little further around the stop sign. They have AK-47s, I think."

There was a silence. Then, "Three, Forty?"

"Go."

"The, ah, ambulance is here now, too. We don't think it looks too bad."

"Stay there, Forty. Wait for more backup."

"Stand by, Three. Just a sec," said Norm. After a moment, he said, "We understand you have an injured officer?"

"Ten-four. Not life threatening," I said, glancing at Hester. She gave me a thumbs up. "Stay put until we advise for you to come up."

He acknowledged, but didn't sound too convinced.

I handed the mike back to Sally, and walked sort of half bent over to the road side of the barn. Looking out through the cracks, I could not only see most of Norm's blue patrol car, but I had a clear view of the top half of the Battenberg ambulance.

I gestured to Sally. "Tell 'em to back up, will you?" I went past her and back to the side of the barn where all the bullet holes were. We had to keep an eye on what our suspects were doing.

The light from the setting sun was streaming through the barn board cracks and was making it difficult to see when I looked to the left of the shed. The sunlight was also illuminating every dust mote in the place, and was beginning to make it equally difficult to see within the barn itself. If there was ever a worst time for us to have them make a move, it was about now.

"Sally..."

"Yeah?"

"See if you can contact George. Our visibility here is going to be crap until the sun goes behind that hill. Maybe he can see better."

The sunlight also meant that it was clear. Clear at night meant colder. Crap. This was probably the warmest part of the day in the barn, and I thought it was probably about twenty degrees. I could see my breath in the shafts of sunlight.

"Hang on," said Sally. "Lamar's here." Again, she handed me the mike.

"You there, Three?" It was good to hear his voice.

"Ten-four, One. Alive and kickin'."

"Is everybody all right?"

"Ah, negative. I 388 has been hit with a fragment."

"Is it ten-thirty-three? Do we have to get in to you now?"

"Ah, negative, One. Negative." I looked over at Hester. "How you feeling?"

I could just make out her answer. "No problem."

I thought for a second. "We need to get her out, but not urgently. I don't recommend anybody coming down the drive or across the yard. Not in daylight."

"Ten-four," said Lamar. "I got about a dozen state troopers ten-seventy-six. Should be here in less than ten minutes."

That was reassuring. "Glad to hear it. TAC team?" I was hoping. The TAC unit would be equipped with M-16s.

"Negative, not yet. They've been notified."

That was too bad. A standard issue state trooper would have a shotgun and a handgun. Shotguns, especially over several hundred yards of open ground, would be hopelessly outranged by the AK-47s our opponents seemed to have.

"Ah, ten-four. One, these guys have AKs. You ten-four on that?"

"Ten-four." He was. Lamar wasn't a ballistics expert, but he knew enough about 7.62mm rounds. He'd been hit just above the ankle with one fired by a barricaded suspect in 1996. He hadn't been able to walk well since, and hadn't had a single day without pain. He was lucky he still had a foot.

"Where you at, Three?"

Now there was the question. I felt the chances of the opposition listening in on our radio traffic were probably not too good. Nonetheless, I wasn't certain I wanted to reveal our exact position. I looked up at Sally, at the other end of the mike cord.

"What do you think? Should we just go ahead and tell?"

"I'd really like to get out of here."

That wasn't what I'd asked. But there was no rescue possible if they went to the wrong building.

"We're in the barn, One. The basement."

"Ten-four."

"Except George—he's in the loft. He's lookout."

"Ten-four," said Lamar, and as he spoke, I heard a siren over his mike. The troopers were beginning to arrive.

"We think most of the suspects are in the shed. The one on the other side of the barn from you."

"The one with the metal roof?"

"That's it. As far as I can tell. We haven't seen any movement in the last few minutes."

"Okay, Carl. I'll be back up on the radio in about five minutes."

"Ten-four, One. Glad to have you here."

Sally called George. He was fine, and hadn't seen any movement for several minutes. He thought he might be able to see fairly well to our front, as soon as he could finish up moving moldy hay bales away from the walls. He'd been unable to get even close to the front wall because they'd been stacked almost to the ceiling.

Sally and I both gave our full attention to peering out through the gaps in the boards and trying to see if there was anybody moving around the tin shed. Nothing.

"You 'spose they left?" she asked.

"Might have," I said. I didn't think so, though. "I think there's a better chance they're just gettin' reorganized."

We waited. About ten minutes after he'd said he'd be back in five, Lamar called.

"Go ahead," said Sally. She started to move closer to me, to hand over the mike again.

"You relay," I said. "I think I see something moving."

She just paused for a moment, and then said, "Go ahead for Three. He can hear you."

"We got people on the road on the other side of the valley, and in the bottom, and up on the hill past the farm," said Lamar. "More comin' all the time."

"Good," I said. That meant that the area was being surrounded, to cut off the escape of just whoever was shooting at us. But as I looked, I was certain something was moving, to our left, behind a screen formed by an old woven wire fence and a bunch of scrub that had grown up entangled through it.

"Three advises 'good,' One," said Sally.

"Tell him to stand by," I said, and brought my rifle up to my shoulder.

"Stand by," said Sally. I heard her move away to my right.

"Left," I said. "Behind the old wire fence. Really down low..."

As I spoke, a figure rose up, threw something, and disappeared back into the scrub.

There was a loud thump, as though a heavy rock had struck the barn above our heads.

"He throw a *rock*?" asked Sally.

Then the "rock" exploded.

CHAPTER 03

JUST AS SOON AS LAMAR WAS ABLE TO round up enough deputies and reserves to secure the crime scene, Hester and I headed for Battenberg. We took the scenic route, because we had to go back the way we'd come to avoid driving through the area where the lab crew was working. Or, as Lamar put it succinctly, "Don't go traipsin' through the scene."

The six miles to Battenberg, therefore, turned into fourteen. It gave me time to think, and I needed it. Our primary objective was an interview with our rural mail carrier, one Hank Granger. The tire track, which was being cast in plaster even as we drove, might allow us to ID the getaway car. The emphasis was on "might." Regardless, it was one thing to identify a car, and another thing altogether to identify the people in it. I was counting on Granger for at least a number of occupants. Assuming that the car had caught his eye, of course.

Great.

Then we were going to have to talk with Norm, the Battenberg chief. He had my sympathy, but it would have been really nice if he'd gotten out soon enough to give us at least an idea of some of the cars that might have come into town from the north.

He might, though, have some ideas regarding suspects.

Battenberg, in the late 1980s, had been a town of about fifteen hundred people—pretty much minding its own business, and trying to go gracefully through the decline that was hitting most of the rural areas. Then they got lucky. A meatpacking plant in town had changed hands and really started taking off. The plant was bought by a Jewish family, who started producing kosher meat products and shipping them to the East Coast. It was an excellent move on their part. Not having to build a plant from the ground up, they were able to produce for less, transport for less since they did their own shipping, and maintain complete quality control over the entire operation. Smart. And when asked why they'd chosen Iowa, one of the corporate officers had replied, "There wasn't a plant available over in Jersey."

After the plant got refurbished and up and running full tilt, things began to change in Battenberg, and mostly for the best. And due to the no-union, low-wage situation at the plant, it had suddenly become one of the most culturally diverse communities in the United States. Originally, Hispanics came in as inexpensive labor. That was a first in our area, and suddenly Spanish could be heard in stores all over town. With the large number of rabbis required for the kosher end of things, Yiddish could also be heard just about everywhere. In fact, it was rumored that, per capita, Battenberg had a higher ratio of rabbis than any other U.S. city.

Within fifteen years, the population had more than doubled. With the fall of the Soviet Union, Russian Jews began to arrive, along with Georgians, Ukrainians, and several other Eastern European ethnic groups. As the word got out, Guatemalans, Colombians, and several other South and Central American countries were also represented. There were a few Israelis, to boot. At last count, in fact, there were eighteen languages spoken within the Battenberg city limits.

Adjustments were not easy, and for a while things got sort of strained. They'd begun shaking themselves out, but they still had a way to go. The first drive-by shooting had caused quite a stir, for instance. That was when we were first truly aware that many of the Hispanics were illegal aliens. When we'd gone around trying to interview witnesses, there was nobody there. They'd fled or gone into hiding because they were afraid they'd be deported. Even the plant had to shut down for a couple of days, until it became evident that the Immigration and Naturalization Services wasn't going to be directly involved. Interviews went better as time passed, and the shooting turned out to be gang-related, involving some dope dispute. The perpetrator had been identified, arrested, tried, and sent to prison. All without ever saying why he'd done it.

We'd had a crash course in Spanish, but found that the Mexican Spanish we'd been exposed to (taught would be giving us too much credit) was unintelligible to the Hondurans and Guatemalans. Who'd a thunk, as we say. About all we could do was advise them of their rights in our brand of Spanish, and hand them a brochure. The Russians, the Central Europeans, and the Thai were on their own until we could arrange an interpreter. Yiddish wasn't a problem, as all the Jewish residents were fluent in English.

It really wasn't that we weren't willing to try to adapt. It was more to do with our budgets being very restricted. We were having a tough time replacing our tires, let alone budgeting for language courses. There was also a matter of instructing all three shifts. Our attempt at Spanish, for example, had the instructor trying to teach three classes of three or four officers each. One class at 07:00 for the night shift as they came off duty, one at 13:00 for the day crew, and one at 18:30 for the evening shift. It was pretty tough on the high school teacher who was doing it for some extra pay, it consumed our entire "continuing education" budget for the year, and at the end we were not much further ahead than before.

All of which made it a very interesting place to be a cop. Hell, it made it downright fascinating at times. More than once the chief, Norm, had made references to resigning and turning his job over to the U.N. We got a lot of mileage out of that, and even went so far as to get him a pale blue beret. But I could understand his frustration.

Which brings me right back to the current case. Jacob Heinman had said that one of the shooters had spoken Spanish. Wonderful. Or something that sounded to Jacob vaguely like Italian. Okay. The other had been "Norwegian"-looking. Ya. You betcha. Around here, that could be just about anybody.

Not a lot to go on.

The upshot was it was pretty damned hard to get informants, like I said. Hard, but not altogether impossible.

As we were getting out of our cars at Mail Carrier Granger's place, I stood outside for a minute, dialing the cell phone of one Hector Gonzalez, a twenty-two-year-old packing plant laborer whose acquaintance I'd made at a domestic call about a year ago.

"*Bueno?*"

"Hector, hey, this is Houseman."

"Oh, no."

"Oh, yes. Really, it is." I liked Hector. I made him nervous.

"Not now, man. I cannot talk now…"

When I'd gotten to that domestic call, I'd found a young Latino who turned out to be Hector defending his sister Selena from her boyfriend. The boyfriend was trying to beat Selena because she wouldn't give him her savings that she kept in a jar in the kitchen cupboard. It turned out to be all of sixty dollars. Hector was winning, but it had been a near thing. Both young men had black eyes and multiple abrasions. So did Selena. The Battenberg cop and I had hauled all three of them in, since they were all yelling at us and each other in Spanish, and we couldn't tell at the time just who had done what. Since none of them were speaking any English, even when addressed by us, we assumed they were illegal aliens. As we shook them down prior to putting them in the cars, I found a small bag of what we euphemistically call a "green, leafy substance" in Hector's pocket. After we'd sorted things out at the police station, and everybody had calmed down enough to communicate, we found that Hector and his sister spoke English very well, indeed. It turned out that both of them had been born and raised in Los Angeles. The boyfriend spoke no English at all, and Hector and Selena offered to translate for him. Right. I thought something a bit more unbiased might be needed, but I have to admit it would have been fun to hear what Selena would have come up with. While we waited for an interpreter, I'd taken Hector aside and told him that we were both going to stand in the rest room and watch the "green, leafy substance" go down the toilet. We did. I told him I appreciated what he'd done for his sister, that all three of them were likely to be charged with a minimum of disturbing the peace, and that I didn't think it was going to be in the interests of justice to hang an additional charge on him for the small bit of grass he had in his pocket. He'd asked why I was being so nice, and I told him that it wouldn't be worth my time to charge him with such a small amount. I did make it clear that I could still do it, however, if he preferred it that way. He thanked me, and in a weak moment said that if I ever needed a favor.... That's how informants are made.

"Now, I know you can listen, Hector. Just for a second."

"Okay," he sighed.

"There was a man just killed, out in the country, a couple of hours ago. Pretty close to Battenberg. Whoever did him blew his head off. He seems to be Hispanic. You with me so far?"

There was a silence, and then a faint, "Yeah, man?"

"We don't know who it is, Hector. There wasn't enough left of his face to even guess. Okay so far?"

"Holy chit, man. I doan know nothing about this." He tended to shift into an accent when he was getting stressed.

"That's gotta be a good thing. Look, Hector, all I want you to do is just give me a call if you hear who it was, okay?"

A pause, then, "Sure, man. I will do that."

"I appreciate it."

"No problem."

I caught up to Hester as she was knocking on Granger's door.

Most rural mail carriers know their districts like the back of their hands, and Granger was no exception. He hadn't noticed anything unusual on the road back to Battenberg, though. Nope. Not a thing.

It pays not to rush. He offered coffee, and I accepted. Hester looked a little anxious to get going, but I needed a cup.

As we sat around the living room, coffee in hand, Granger said something that made it all worthwhile.

"But, you know what? At the old Dodd place, just past the hollow? There was a cream-colored Subaru there earlier today. Parked by the barn. It was gone when I came back by, but I'd never seen that there before. If it helps…"

"About what time?" I asked. I knew the old Dodd place. The house had been abandoned, but whoever farmed the land still used the sheds and other outbuildings. The fire department had burned the house in a controlled burn for practice about five years back.

"Oh, it was after lunch…I always take my northern route after I grab a sandwich, so that would be about one-ten or so."

Punctuality is a trademark of the rural mail carriers. If he said 1:10, then he was within five minutes.

"Anybody around it?"

"Yes… couldn't see who, but three, four people. They looked like they were headed to one of the sheds or for the barn. I was by before they got there, if that was where they were going."

Cool. And there was still coffee left.

"You might want to check with Elmo Hazlett," he said. "The milk hauler. He drives route out that way."

"Thanks."

Granger chuckled. "He's got his head up his butt most of the time, though, so if he didn't run over 'em, he probably didn't notice."

When we got back in our cars, I checked in with the office on my radio. There was nothing new, the troops were still assisting the lab team at the crime scene, and Norm Vincent was waiting for us in his office.

Norm Vincent was really apologetic. The Battenberg chief was a decent guy, and like I said, was under quite a bit of strain with all the hours he'd been putting in. He'd seen and heard nothing of any use at all. The word was out in Battenberg that there had been some sort of murder just north of them. That wasn't unusual, since there were dozens of people in town with police scanners. But nothing had struck a chord, apparently, because none of his "informants" had contacted him. Well, he called them "informants." To put it nicely, Norm wasn't a really active sort of officer, and I don't think he had more than three or four "informants," total, and I suspected they were all high school kids who were lying to him about half the time. But he was trying, and I knew that he'd try even harder after having fallen back asleep on us that afternoon. Good enough. We gave him only one detail, and that was the nature of the wound. We wanted him to know the type of person he could be dealing with if he turned a suspect up.

"Christ," he said with some feeling.

"We'll have more for you, Chief," said Hester, "as soon as we get our evidence all sorted out."

"Thanks."

"Until then," I said, "just let us know if anything surfaces. Don't try to take somebody yourself. Get backup."

"Sure. You bet."

"I'm really serious. Don't take anybody alone, and I wouldn't try it with just a couple of cops, either. Whoever did this isn't gonna blink at the thought of killing somebody else."

"Okay, Carl. Okay. I get the point."

"Good. I'd hate to lose anybody over this one." I decided to trust him with another bit of evidence. "You think you can get hold of Elmo Hazlett for us?"

"He's probably asleep by now."

That was likely true, because Elmo would have to be up by about three

A.M. in order to get started on his milk route in time. I didn't think it would be worth waking him up and aggravating him. We didn't know that he'd even seen anything. There was just a chance that he might have. It was one of those decisions you have to make, and just hope it's the right one.

"You out till three or four?" I asked.

"Yeah."

"Well, if you see Elmo, tell him we'd like to chat with him for a few minutes. Whenever it's convenient for him, but sometime tomorrow."

The old Dodd place was kind of spooky, nestled between two large hills where the wind sort of hummed through the bare trees. Hester and I stopped at the mailbox and examined the powdery dust at the end of the lane, checking for tire tracks. Sure enough, there was one beauty about eighteen inches long, where somebody had come from the lane and turned north, toward the crime scene.

We did photos of it and called for the lab team to see if they could make a cast. Bob Ulrich hitched a ride down to our location with one of our reserves who we called Old Knockle. He was old, nearly seventy. He was also feisty, and knew the county very well.

We waited for them, pointed out the track, and then took my car up the lane to the buildings. One car was best, mainly because it would damage about half as much evidence as two.

There were four old wooden buildings, pretty dilapidated, on the left side of the gaping foundation that had been the Dodd residence. On the other side was an old concrete-block silo with rusty iron straps encircling it at about five-foot intervals. The rusted steel dome reminded me of an observatory. About fifty feet from it was an old platform for a windmill. It was really getting dark by now, especially down in the valley, and we had to use my headlights, spotlight, and flashlights to snoop about.

The paint was flaking from the weathered gray boards of the buildings, but you could still tell they'd been red, once upon a time. The floors were wood, as well—weathered pale and with the sunken grain that's peculiar to old wood. We'd go in the doorway of each one, stand there for a minute as we shone our flashlights around, and then enter carefully, making sure we didn't step on anything that was obviously evidence. With fortune typical of searchers, it was in the fourth and last building that we hit pay dirt.

"Hey, Houseman?"

"Yeah?"

"Look over here, in the corner." Hester pointed with her light.

"Well, no shit," I said. "Our missing shoe."

I went back to my car, got my cameras, took an establishing shot of the building, and then went inside and took six shots of the black tennis shoe, on its side, the laces still tied.

"I move we don't go any closer, and let the lab do the whole area," said Hester.

"Fine by me."

"When your flash went off," she said, "see over here.... Does that look like a bloodstain to you?"

Near the shoe, there was an old toolbox. At the base of the box, there was a large, fresh stain that did look like blood.

"You bet," I said, and started taking shots of that, as well.

"Try a couple of high-low angles, Carl. It looks from here like the dust has been wiped off the box and the floor near it. See if you can get that." Hester laid her flashlight on the floor, the low angle of the beam making the swipe marks in the dust pop out.

I took four shots using only the light cast by her flashlight. They'd be pretty stark, but they'd turn out fine.

"It looks," she said, "like somebody maybe was sitting on the box?"

"Yep." I squatted down to give myself a low-angle view. "And from down here, I think I get a couple of shoe prints over here, too, when the light's just right." I laid my flashlight on the floor like she had, and sure as hell, footprints just seemed to pop out in relief.

"Several," she said.

"Way cool."

"Lab team stuff for sure," said Hester, and I could hear the smile in her voice. "I think we've got ourselves a clue or two."

We sat in my car, waiting for Bob from the lab to finish his tire castings and come down the short lane to the outbuildings.

"So," I said, "why's the shoe here?"

"Beats me, Houseman. I just assist you guys." She laughed. "That means you get to guess first," she said.

"Okay... the easiest and least likely one first. How about they take him to the building to kill him, and he gets away?"

"Perfect. How far is it to the crime scene from here? Half a mile?"

"Pretty close, but a little more, I think."

"Long way to run, Houseman." She took out her Palm Pilot and started writing.

"Especially with one shoe on and your hands behind your back." I glanced at her two—by—two-inch screen. "You might want to make a note of that. I did say it was the least likely."

"Just a sec," she said, sounding distracted. "Okay, then. So he lost the shoe here, but he didn't run from here? I think that's right."

"Keep going."

"Right. So, they had a struggle here, though, don't you think?"

"Okay. Hell, if I thought they were going to kill me, I'd struggle."

She was really cooking. "But then, they put him in the car to take him somewhere else, and he got out..."

"Not with his hands behind his back," I objected. "Unless they had him in the backseat all by himself. And not if the car was moving. No abrasions on his clothes, for one thing."

"They took him up the road to kill him," she said. "He was in the back, they stopped, he made a break for it then. As they were getting him out of the car."

That sounded feasible.

She thought again and so did I. I got there first. Well, I think I did.

"Know what, Hester? If you're right, it would have been so damned much easier to kill him right here. They made an effort to take him someplace else to do it. So, they didn't want this place connected with him. You agree?"

"You bet. Now all we have to do is figure out why. And why, if they go to the trouble of taking him away from here, they go less than a mile. Why don't they take him way far away?"

That question had us both. Well, when you get to a place where you draw a blank, back up to the place just before it, and see what else you can pull from it.

"Well," I said, "let's go for what we know. First, let's assume they aren't completely familiar with the area. The rural mail carrier drove by and saw some people here after lunchtime. They may have seen him, too. Figured it was not a good idea to do what they were going to do after being seen?"

"Nope." She sounded pretty certain.

"Why?"

"Too much of a time lapse between then and the killing. But I think we're still on the right track. They want to get away from this place."

"So that means that the decision to kill him, regardless of when it was made, also took into consideration the fact that they didn't want a body discovered on this abandoned farmstead. We think we know that. So that means... what the hell else connects the suspect to this place, over and above the mail carrier?"

"Yep."

I sighed. "And you want to walk around the area, in the dark, looking for that particular 'something,' don't you?"

"I can wait until you finish a cookie," she said. "If you give me one, too."

I fished the Girl Scout cookies out of my camera bag. Fortified, we got out of the car and began to walk around each of the buildings in turn.

In a rural area, especially in a narrow valley, it gets very, very dark. The place did have a yard light, but it was one of the old ones that threw kind of a greenish cast over the area and created more shadows that anything else.

"Why keep the yard light hooked up," said Hester, "when nobody lives here?"

"Most do. Keep the vandals and kids out, as much as anything."

"It just makes it seem that much darker in the shadows," she said.

The scrub- and rock-strewn gully that ran near the back of the barn and shed kept us out of that area, but we did a fair job on the rest of the place. We didn't find anything of interest whatsoever.

Bob finished the tracks and came down the lane. We showed him the shoe. He said they'd do the area in the immediate vicinity of the shoe and then call it a day, returning early in the morning to finish up. We told him our theory about the suspects not wanting to connect the abandoned farm to the body for some reason.

"Why?"

It always went back to that.

"We don't know," said Hester. "Maybe you can come up with something when you get back here in the morning."

Bob grinned. "What's it worth?"

I didn't hesitate a second. "Lunch."

"For lunch," said Bob, pointing at the shed, "I can locate the remains of Jimmy Hoffa right over there..."

At that point, there really wasn't much for us to do until we had more information. We left instructions with the reserves that they were to protect the scene at all times, but especially while the lab crew got some sleep.

I figured that left the office and the preliminary report as all that stood in the way of a good night's sleep.

The media didn't agree.

CHAPTER 04

TUESDAY, DECEMBER 18, 2001 21:00

THE NATION COUNTY SHERIFF'S DEPARTMENT and County Jail sits on a hillside at the edge of the town of Maitland. I imagine the parking lot is about twenty or so feet higher than the approaching roadway. That being the case, the first hint I had of the presence of the media was as I glimpsed a four-wheel-drive with a conspicuous KNUG/TV on its side. Another hint, and one that boded no good for me, was the glimpse of Lamar's four-wheel-drive parked to the rear of the building. If he was there, and he was, then he was reluctant to come out of the building because he'd have to talk with the media. Lamar hated the media. So I knew who was going to be the spokesperson for the department. I just didn't know how he was going to order me to do it, since I had all that typing to do.

As we came up the steps to the main office entrance, I saw three reporters and their cameramen, and heard Lamar's voice saying, "Here's the man I was telling you to wait for. Just ask him anything, and if he can answer it, he will. He's been there, and he's seen it." This was followed by a big, hearty "Hello, Carl," as I reached the counter. "Glad you're back so soon."

I could tell by the look on his face that he had had just about as much media attention as he was going to allow for the rest of the year. I just smiled, turned to say something to Hester, and discovered that she'd disappeared. She'd probably ducked down the hall and into Dispatch. I was on my own.

"Hi, Boss."

"He's all yours, folks," said Lamar, and headed for his office in the back of the building. He didn't quite run.

I'd pretty much managed to avoid all media attention over the years, mainly because I was afraid that if they got me talking I'd say too much. Especially the TV reporters. Not that I'm all that chatty, but I tend to get very enthusiastic about my work.

"Detective Houseman?" asked a young, pretty TV reporter I saw on the tube just about every night. "I'm Judy Mercer, KNUG, and I'd like to ask a few questions..."

"Bill Nylant here, and I'm with KYYQ..."

"—Handy, with KKNN..."

I thought that maybe if we went outside in the cold, it would be shorter. "Come on out here, and I'll be glad to answer some questions if I can."

Once on the front steps, I remembered that I was on closed-circuit TV at the dispatch center from out there. With sound. As if the media weren't bad enough, our own people were now taping me, as well. Something for the Christmas party.

The cameramen had the tripods set up, cameras attached, and the lights came on, right in my eyes.

"Hey, do we need to do the cameras?"

Judy Mercer answered first. "Well, detective, I'm sure you've noticed that this isn't radio. We really like to have something to show." She paused and then said, "If you'd like to take us to the scene, we could shoot footage of that, and leave you as a voice-over."

No way in hell, and she knew it.

"Okay, just don't get reflections off the top of my head. And I'm not a 'detective,' I'm an investigator."

They asked standard questions before they rolled tape. Just so I wouldn't clutch on camera and cost them their footage.

"We need at least fifteen seconds of clear voice from you on camera," said Barbara Handy of KKNN. "We can do the parking lot and the jail for fill, and do our own narrative."

"Good. Okay, whenever you're ready, we might as well get it over with," I said.

"So, and we're rolling now," said Judy Mercer. "Deputy Houseman, can you just give us an idea what happened here today?"

I inhaled, held it for a second, and then said, "We received a call from the public that a body was on the roadway in the southern part of our county. The caller said that it appeared the victim was deceased, and that it appeared the victim had been shot."

"And what did you find when you responded?"

"The report was quite accurate. The victim was dead, and the initial evidence suggested a gunshot wound." Boy, I thought, did it ever.

"Have you identified the victim yet?"

"I won't be able to tell you who the victim is until after the relatives have been notified." I wasn't going to be able to notify relatives until I knew who in the hell the victim was, either, but I couldn't exactly say that.

"Do you have any suspects yet?"

"We're investigating now. I can't discuss that any further at this time."

"Has it been ruled a murder?"

"No," I said. "The autopsy results won't be in for at least twenty-four hours."

"Thank you."

That was it for Judy Mercer. Each of the other two, in turn, asked about the same questions. Then they were done. It occurred to me, during the first interview with Mercer, that they didn't care who or why so much as they needed the information to get to the stations. The tough questions could wait until later. That was all right with me.

The media types sort of milled about for a few minutes, taping themselves with the jail and cop cars in the background. I beat a hasty retreat and went directly to Dispatch. Just as I suspected, the duty dispatcher, Martha Behrens, along with Sally, Hester, and Lamar, were all sitting there, watching the external monitor.

"No popcorn?" I asked.

"Nice job," said Lamar. "I knew you could do it."

"The reflections off your bald top were pretty bad," said Sally.

"I'm surprised your nose isn't growing," came from Hester.

Martha, who hadn't been around us all that long, wisely said nothing. Her lack of tenure obviously didn't interfere with her enjoyment of the comments made at my expense, though.

"Being on TV doesn't seem to bother you," said Hester.

"Naw. Piece of cake," I said.

I made for the back room and my office, as if to take off my jacket and get started on my report. As soon as I got there, I picked up my phone and started to dial my home number to call my wife, Sue. I'd never been on TV before and sure didn't want her to miss this. As I did so, I happened to glance at my watch. Ten twenty-six.

The TV people were from either Cedar Rapids/Iowa City or Waterloo. Both were a good seventy miles from us. It was already too late to make the ten o'clock news.

Decorum forgotten, I hung up the phone, hustled back out the main door, and almost knocked Judy Mercer over.

"Hey!"

"Sorry, sorry, but could you tell me if my bit will be on tonight?"

She laughed. "No way. We haven't got a link. We have to go back to the studio and uplink from there. We'll send it in, but you won't see it until tomorrow morning at six."

"Oh. Well, thanks anyway."

I hustled back into my office and called Sue.

"Hello?"

"Hi! Hey, guess who's gonna be on TV?"

"You?"

"Absolutely!"

"What's happened?" She sounded as much concerned as anything else.

I told her we'd had a homicide, and that I'd be late, but that I was going to be on TV as spokesman for the department. I also included the information that it would be aired at six A.M. Since she was a teacher, and just getting up at that hour, she might get a chance to see it.

"Things are all right, though?" she asked.

"Sure. Just a murder case." I chuckled. "Nobody barricaded, or anything like that. Just have to use our heads and figure it out."

"Not one of my students, is it?" By that she meant any that she'd had for the last twenty years of teaching middle school English.

"To be completely honest, I couldn't tell, dear. Probably not, though."

She said she'd watch for me on the tube, and then told me there was some cold macaroni and cheese in the refrigerator. Being married over thirty years gives people a certain perspective.

"Got it."

"Good night. I'll miss you, but I'm really looking forward to seeing you on TV. If I knew anybody else up at that hour, I'd call them!"

"It ain't exactly prime time, but it's better than nothing."

"Oh, it sure is. Did you ask for a copy of the tape?"

I hadn't, but I made a note to do so as soon as I could next morning.

I went back through Dispatch on my way to the kitchen for some coffee, and was stopped by Martha, who was waving furiously at me from behind her console with one hand as she tried to write with the other and hold the phone to her ear with her shoulder.

"Yes sir, one moment," she said into the phone. She pressed the hold button, and said, "It's some dude for you, who says he knows who the body is. He won't give his name."

We had a fine phone installation in Dispatch, with a total of six instruments, two of which had full 911 capability and four where you could talk on any line you told the dispatcher to select for you. With twelve lines, we had lots of leeway unless things went to hell.

"Put me on this one," I said, picking up one of the phones at the end of the console.

She did.

"Houseman here."

"It was Rudy. Rudy Cueva," said the muffled voice. Muffled or not, it sounded so much like Hector I almost called him by name.

I wasn't able to connect any Rudy Cueva to anybody I knew. "Who is that?"

"He's a team supervisor at the plant, man. A really smart dude."

"What plant?" I knew, but if Hector wanted to play a game, he had a reason.

"The packing plant in Battenberg. That one."

"How do you know it's him?" This was going to be the telling point.

"I heard it just now, one of the workers in the kill room. He said that it was Rudy."

The kill room was just that, the location in the packing plant where they did the actual killing of the livestock. "How did he find out?"

"I cannot say, man. You know that."

There was absolutely no doubt that it was Hector, but if he wanted to remain officially anonymous, that was his choice. "Any idea why he was killed?"

There was a prolonged sigh on the other end of the line. "Because he knew something, and they dint want him to talk." He was getting exasperated.

"And what was that?"

"I got to go, man," and the line went dead.

"He hung up," I told Martha and Hester. "That didn't happen to be a 911 line, did it?"

Martha grinned. "It sure was. Cell phone, hit one of the two U.S. Cellular towers in Battenberg. Here." She handed me the printout.

```
PROGRAM: E9CONPRT PROCESS id: 2599 18-DEC-01 22:45:47
TRUNK SEIZURE: 22:45:16 ALI REQ: 22:45:19 FIRST RING: 22:45:19
MF RCVE READY:22:45:16 ALI RECV: 22:45:23 CALL ANSWERED: 22:45:20
PANI RECEIVED: 22:45:19 PILOT RTE: 22:45:19 CALL RELEASED: 22:47:02
PH: (563) 555-8290 CS: WRLS EXCH: 515-319-563 NO DESCRIPT. PILOT: 319-9132 NAME:
US CELLULAR (XYPOINT) LOC: 5633807343
ADDR: 1.16 MI SW BATTENBERG OMNI
CITY: 00054-0-198, NATION ID: 90-00789
ESN: 00069 MAITLAND---WIRELESS BATTENBERG PD VERIFY VERIFY VERIFY
DATE: 12/14/02 AAI:  SDN: 101
```

Nice. We were still in Phase One for cell phones, which meant that at some point in the future, several towers would triangulate the call and we'd get an actual physical location. That was what they called Phase Two. Right now, we got the tower that the cell phone had accessed and the number of the phone. Good enough for government work, as they say.

I looked in my billfold, just to make certain. The caller's number belonged to Hector Gonzalez, my buddy.

"Okay, Martha. Time to earn your keep. Run a OLN on a Rudy Cueva, no middle name available, so just first and last, if you can do something like that. Probably a Rudolph instead of Rudy, but do both. Probably within five years of thirty, but I'd be guessing. An address of Battenberg. See what you get."

Hester looked at me quizzically.

"The informant I talked to earlier. He thinks that this Rudy Cueva's our victim."

"Well, outstanding!"

The search for an Operator's License Number came back within two seconds. Nobody in Iowa by that name had a driver's license, nor an automobile registered in their name. In fact, the four Cuevas who were listed were all female. We couldn't try a Computerized Criminal History on a name without a date of birth.

"Try a dummy one," said Hester. "Give him a birth date sometime in 1971. It might work."

It had in the past, on occasion. This time, there was no such luck.

I looked in the phone book. Now, that's not as large a resource as you might think, because the entire Battenberg directory was only about fifty pages, and that included the government and business sections. No Rudy Cueva listed. No Cueva listed at all. The three of us checked the book for the entire county, using three books and taking sections. Took about five minutes. Nothing.

"Damn."

That had been the first real break in the case. Well, I'd thought so, anyway. It still could be, but we were at a dead end for the moment. I didn't dare call Hector back, because if he was at work, there were bound to be people around, and I was sure he'd preferred anonymity for a good reason. I figured he'd be the very best judge of whether or not it was safe for him to be chatting with a cop on his cell phone.

We checked with Battenberg PD. No Rudy Cueva listed in their city directory, but Norm Vincent thought the name sounded familiar. We had him go into the city manager's office and check the water bills. If you lived there, you had to be hooked up to city water, simple as that. Nothing.

"Well," I said, "our caller said he works for the packing plant. I sure as hell don't want to call their night shift and start asking questions, though. If he does work there, and if he's got family, the first thing that's gonna happen is that somebody calls his wife and tells her that we're checking."

"Couldn't you get there first?" asked Martha. Like I said, she was new.

"Not guaranteed, and we aren't sure it's him that's dead in the first place. Just a tip." I shrugged. "Let me call that anonymous caller back." It had to be done. Having made such a momentous decision, I was kind of disappointed when I got a recording telling me that the owner of that mobile phone had either turned it off, left the car, or left the dialing area.

"If it's who I think it is," I said, "he's turned it off. And he's at work in the plant, and I don't want to go there and..." Well, what the hell. "Give me the phone book," I said, holding out my hand. "Might as well call the owner."

He, naturally, was unlisted. I started with our Emergency Notification List, which was pretty much for fires and tornadoes, and started going down the chain of command for the packing plant. I finally got a very sleepy woman named Gloria Bennett. She was the head of accounting. She seemed to think I was INS or something. Finally, I got out of her that there might be somebody working there named Rudy Cueva, but she had no idea where he lived. I asked if her company records might indicate an address or a phone number. She said they might, but she wasn't about to go to the plant at this time of night to find out. She said she'd call us in the morning.

It's a free country.

Less than a minute later, Carson Hilgenberg called. He was the new county attorney. Really new, really young. About Carson's only experience with criminal cases was to accept plea bargains for fifth-degree theft. He wanted to know if there had actually been a murder.

"Oh, yeah," I said. "First-class one at that."

There was a slight pause, and then, "What do you mean, 'first-class'? Do you mean first-degree?"

I chuckled. "Let's call it 'first-degree-plus,'" I said. "Victim was found in the middle of a county road, wrists bound, and his head blown off."

This time the silence was a little longer. "No shit?"

"You betcha. Execution-style, as they say."

"Uh, well, has the state prosecutor been called?"

"Not yet, Carson. We won't do that until we have an arrest, or a really good suspect. No reason to. Nothing for him to do. Besides," I added, "you have to be the one to do that."

"What?"

"The AG's office only gets involved in county cases if the county attorney requests it."

"Right. Well then, do you have their number?"

I was having trouble keeping a straight face, and hoped it didn't affect the tone of my voice. "We'll get it to you. For now, though, we're going to be busy just developing a suspect."

"You don't have anybody in custody?" Carson sounded worried.

"Oh, hell, no. We don't have the faintest fuckin' notion who did it," I said. It was just too hard to resist.

There was another pause, and then, "Well, what are you going to do if you need help on a search warrant, or something, like an arrest warrant, or..."

"If we need help, Carson, we know where you live," I said. "We'll just call."

"Oh."

"We're pretty good with that sort of thing, really we are," I said. No sense in scaring the kid to death right off the bat. "But if you want, it's okay for us to take you along when we do the arrest. If you want."

"I'll let you know, Carl," he said, so seriously that it was almost touching.

"Okay," I relented a little bit. "It's not really necessary for you to be there; we'll try to videotape it. Anyway, as soon as the reports get done, we'll forward copies to your office. Interesting reading so far, and I get a feeling that it'll get better as we go."

"Thank you." He sounded absolutely grateful.

He wasn't such a bad kid, really. Just not much of an attorney. "Just remember, Carson, don't do any press stuff until you double-check with us to get the most up-to-date information. DCI will probably brief you tomorrow sometime. Okay?"

"Yes," he said. "I'm glad they're involved."

He meant that. It was almost a guarantee that the State Attorney General's Office would be available for the case, thereby relieving Carson of any practical responsibility other than making the obligatory phone call.

On that note, I went home, leaving instructions for Dispatch to call me if they got any more calls from anybody regarding our case. Anybody but the media, that is. I was very specific about that.

16:12

THE BARN WALL ABSORBED MOST OF THE FORCE OF THE EXPLOSION, but I could still feel the slap of the pressure wave. I wasn't aware of any fragments making it through the old wood siding, but the overpressure kicked loose a huge amount of dust and straw and hay debris. It was instant blindness.

"Holy shit!" said Sally.

"Stay down!" After a few seconds, I popped up and down at my peephole, trying to see if the figure was still behind the tangled fence without getting my head blown off in the process. That didn't work. Not really enough time to comprehend anything before I was down again. "Hester, you okay?"

There was a loud, mumbled "Yeah!" that would have been funny another time.

I took a chance and kept my head up for a longer look. Nothing... nothing. Then, so quickly that it made me jump, four or five figures rose in unison and began blazing away at the barn. It was quite a volume of fire, and we all hunkered down as wood chips and pieces of metal-jacketed rounds went whizzing through the boards. More fragments, more dust—almost enough to make me choke.

This time, though, I was back at my firing port as soon as the noise of the firing stopped. I was scared as hell, but I didn't want to give 'em a chance to advance toward us.

I saw them. I truly did, and for the first time I got a good look. There were four of them, all standing or kneeling and putting fresh magazines into their rifles. Now, as far as I was concerned, they were fair game.

I cranked off a full magazine as fast as I could pull the trigger. Probably just because I was firing, I heard Sally's shotgun blast twice, and I thought I heard other shots as well. My twenty-eight rounds went out, and at least two found their mark, because the two men in the middle twisted and tumbled and went down like sacks of meal. The other two disappeared, but not in the uncoordinated fashion of the middle two. I thought I'd missed both of those two for sure.

I replaced my magazine by feel, not looking down, not taking my eyes away from my field of view.

"Damn," said Sally. "You get anything?"

Her voice was strangely loud but faint at the same time. It took me a second, but then I realized the noise had screwed up my hearing.

"One or two, I'm pretty sure." As the dust and debris began to settle, I was sure I could see a booted foot tangled in the fence line. It wasn't moving. "One for certain. You?"

"I don't know," she said, with a tremor in her voice.

Then Sally's radio went nuts.

"*What the fuck's going on up there, Three?!*" Lamar's voice was easy to recognize on the radio.

"Tell him it was a…" and then I held my hand out for the mike. "One, Three?"

"Three, go ahead!"

I paused for a second or two, to make sure my voice was calm and pitched low. The last thing I wanted to do was to generate more excitement among our people down on the road. "Okay, One, that was a grenade, and then four or five guys with AKs, and then me. I think we got one of 'em."

"How about you people?"

I turned and saw that Hester had moved into the stanchions closer to the limestone wall. She looked at me and nodded.

"I think we're good. Hold your traffic, and I'll check with George."

Poor George, I believe he thought we'd forgotten about him. I reached him on the now-clear walkie-to-walkie frequency.

"You okay up there, George?"

It took a couple of seconds, and then he said, "Fine. Are you all right?

"We're doin' good. I think that was a grenade there. Did you see it?"

"I saw him throw it, but I didn't get a good look. Probably. We got two of 'em, Carl. I can see two bodies from up here. The others went back toward the shed."

"Excellent," I said. So the other shots had been George firing from the loft. "I thought I got one for sure."

Two dead. I hadn't been able to recognize either of them. And they had been reloading their rifles when I shot them, or at least as far as I could tell from my position. I took a deep breath. They weren't shooting at me at the moment I fired. Somewhere out there was an attorney licking his lips.

"I think there's somebody, maybe two or so, over by the silo," said George. "They were moving over that way when the explosion went off. That's why I couldn't warn you; I wasn't looking front all the time."

Interesting. Those two, plus the four or five at the fence line.... I was beginning to wonder where everybody had come from.

"That's fine. No problem. Hey, it's gettin' dark, George. Why don't you come down here when it gets dark enough to hide you?" I was also afraid that they'd zero in on him, now that he'd revealed his position by shooting, but I thought better of saying that over the radio.

"Okay. Good idea."

Chalk up a round for us.

CHAPTER 05

I'D GOTTEN TO BED WELL PAST MIDNIGHT, but rolled out of bed at 06:30, just missing myself on TV. Sue was apologetic, figuring that since I hadn't left her a note, I didn't want to be gotten up. She said it was "nice," but that I'd only been on the tube for about five seconds.

I saw her off to school at seven-thirty, which was pretty unusual since my normal shift started at noon, and I rarely awoke before ten. Being up, I'd figured on calling the office, seeing what was going on, and getting there by eight or so.

When I called, Lamar took the phone, said he was worried about my accumulating overtime, and ordered me not to be in before eleven. I said something about him never getting worried when I was tired, only when he thought I was getting rich. He thought that was funny.

I called Hester on her cell phone. She was already at the office, talking to the lab guys, who had finished late and stayed the night in Maitland to avoid a four-hour drive back to Des Moines with no sleep.

"Just a sec," said Hester. She spoke to someone up at the office, probably Sally. "You want to tell him, or can I? Cool." They must have said that she could. "Guess what they found in that ravine behind the outbuildings?"

"Four more bodies," I said. I couldn't imagine anything worse.

"No such luck," she said, altogether too brightly. "But the ditch is full of empty containers. Ether cans. Probably anhydrous ammonia was once in some of the buckets and plastic barrels. A whole bunch of busted open lithium batteries. Rags, other debris." She paused, and I could hear her grinning. "And empty shell casings, 7.62mm shell casings. Made in China, found just up the ditch from the ether cans. Many, many shell casings. How about that?"

A meth lab. Or, at least, the trash heap from one. And the shell casings were pretty typical, too. Lots of meth dealers liked to be armed, and Chinese SKS rifles, copies of Soviet ones, were easy to come by. "Meth. With guns, too, and target practice."

"You betcha."

"Son of a bitch." I chuckled. "Is there a functional lab there, or did we miss it?"

"No functional lab," said Hester, "but it was once. I've called DNE and they've called DEA, and we're going to need a professional cleanup. They'll be up as soon as possible."

DNE was the Iowa Department of Narcotics Enforcement, and DEA was its federal equivalent, the Drug Enforcement Administration. They had to be notified, and they'd take care of calling the Environmental Quality people. Lots of the stuff used to make methamphetamine was highly toxic, not only at the point of contact, but because of groundwater pollution as well.

"Think this is our motive?" I asked. "Drug-related?"

"It's very possible," she said. "Related, anyway. Want to hear my next news?"

"Go ahead... you're on a roll."

It turned out that the lab guys had done the case prints off the dead body late last night, and they'd been turned over to a state trooper at 07:00. He'd relayed them to the AFIS terminal at the Cedar Rapids police department.

"They're already being run, even as we speak," said Hester.

"Excellent."

"Next," she said, "the milk hauler... uh... Elmo Hazlett?"

"Yeah?"

"He was contacted, and should be back home around noon or so."

"Excellent."

"That makes three good things in a row, Houseman. Can you take a fourth one?"

There was no doubt in my mind. "Go for it."

"There's a young woman from Battenberg on her way up here to the office. Name is Linda Moynihan. She claims her live-in is missing, and she thinks he's our victim." Hester paused, and I could hear paper rustling in the background. "She's accompanied by... the EMT that was at the scene yesterday... nope, the paramedic... a Terri Biederman."

"Okay." That was curious.

"She said that she and this Terri were old high school friends."

"How soon they going to be there?"

"Pretty soon. They were leaving about fifteen minutes ago."

"Did she give his name? Her boyfriend?"

"Well, of course, Houseman." Hester sounded really pleased. "Jesus Ramon Cueva. Aka Rudy."

I was in the office in ten minutes. When Lamar saw me, he glanced at his watch and said, "Right on time." He does sarcasm really well.

"Hell, Lamar, I'm only an hour early. I'll just let my tires go another thousand miles before we change 'em." I think he liked that idea.

The black-haired, blue-eyed Linda Moynihan looked very small seated at the other side of my desk, and she seemed worried to the point of distraction. She was wearing blue jeans and a faded pink quilted jacket, and looked as if she'd been up all night.

According to her, the deceased was one Jesus Ramon Cueva, a thirty-one-year-old male, whom she'd last seen yesterday morning. Her description of the clothing he'd been wearing when he left the house matched the clothes on the body, with one exception. He'd been wearing a blue quilted nylon vest, with snaps up the front.

"Okay, Linda," I said, "I can understand your concern, but is there anything specific that makes you think the victim is Ramon? Any reason you have to fear for his safety?"

She shook her head. "Not really, I guess. No. No, but Terri and I were talking, and the more she told me, and the more we talked, and the more it got to look like..." She started to cry. "Him," she got out, after two tries. "Ramon."

"Okay," said Hester. "It's okay."

"We waited up all night, hoping that he'd come home," said Terri. "When he didn't, we called."

Terri was standing a few feet behind Linda's chair and was jerking her head toward the dispatch center.

"Hester," I said, "could you get something started here while I talk to Terri out at Dispatch?"

While Hester took a written statement, Terri and I went into the short hallway that connected the main office with the dispatch center. It was an area not covered by security cameras, and had very little foot traffic. It was about as private a place as we could muster without slipping the lock on Lamar's office door, and he really hated it when we did that.

"So," I said. "What ya got?"

"Hey, look, the more I think about it, the more I'm sure it's him. Really."

"Why?"

"Look, just a quick rundown here. Linda's always been head-over-heels in love with him, but Rudy was a prick. Okay? I mean, he was screwing around on her, he treated her like crap when there was company around, and he never told her anything about what he did."

"What did he do?" I almost hesitated, because Terri was so damned opinionated I hated to open the door.

"Well, he was working at the packing plant, when he'd decide to go in," she said. "That was his day job."

"Humm. How'd he get the nickname Rudy?"

She looked at me, surprised. "Who knows? Just what some of his little buds call him. Is it important?"

I shrugged. "Dunno. I just like to know as much as I can. So, like, what was he into that could get him killed?"

Turned out that Terri wasn't absolutely sure. I mean, she had thoughts, but no proof. She and Linda were pretty good friends, but they'd started to grow apart when Linda had started living with Rudy.

"He treated her like dirt when his shithead little friends were around. When they were alone, he was just fine. But he just had to turn her into his private little serving woman when they showed up. It made me sick."

"She didn't mind?"

Terri rolled her eyes. "Linda was in love. In the worst possible way. Her mom didn't want her seeing him, always gave her crap about a mixed marriage. Not because Ramon was Mexican, but because he was Catholic and Linda's Lutheran."

"Okay. So, who are these little friends?"

"I don't know names, I really don't. I just know he's into dope, Houseman. I just know it."

"I hate to use the term 'evidence,' there, kid, but you wouldn't happen to have any, would you?"

That produced a rare silence from Terri. Then she said, "No, but I know it's true."

I didn't want to argue with her, especially not now, for two reasons. First, it could very well be true. I had no information either way. Second, she was so damned bull-headed that if I were to push her just a bit, she'd do something foolish, like try to obtain the evidence on her own. No way was I about to allow that.

"All I can say at this point," I told her, "is that I need *evidence*." I held up my hand to forestall any objections. "And, no, I couldn't tell you if I did."

She sighed, mostly from frustration, and said, "Yeah."

"But don't try to find out on your own. I mean it. We'll know within a couple of days either way."

"Oh, sure."

"No," I said. "We'll know. I'm certain of that."

"Oh, right."

I didn't like the sound of that. "You concentrate on helping Linda deal with this. I'd like you to come with us when we have her view the body. She'll need that, and you've already seen him." I thought that was pure inspiration. If that didn't get her mind off suspected meth involvement for a day or two, I'd be very surprised.

"You're kidding? Aren't you?"

"Nope. She's going to really need a friend in there."

"Christ," she said. "Oh, I suppose. Shit."

"Have you described the wound to her?"

"No."

"Okay. Well, she'd better be a little prepared, don't you think?" I shrugged. "I suppose I can tell her..."

"No, let me." Terri had gotten sort of grayish in the last few seconds.

"You want to sit down for a minute first?"

"No, I'm fine."

"Just make sure," I said, "that there's no misunderstanding on her part. I know you can't prepare her for it, but give her a really good idea."

Having Linda identify her boyfriend's remains became more critical about fifteen minutes later, when the AFIS officer from Cedar Rapids PD called. The officer's name was Larry, and I'd known him for several years. He said there was absolutely no record of the fingerprints anywhere.

"Nowhere?"

"Well," said Larry, "the Pago Pago database is down, and we haven't got Mars on line yet..."

"Very funny."

"But really, no record nowhere, Carl. Absolutely nothing."

"What's that tell us?"

"Well," said Larry, "it probably just means he's never been fingerprinted. Lots of people have never been printed."

"Okay. Sure. Well, then..."

"Don't give up. They're recorded now. If somebody else picks him up, we'll put a flag on it for them to contact you."

"No good. He's, uh, dead."

There was a moment of silence, and then a chuckle. "You're having a *really* bad day, aren't you?"

"Aw, not really. Hey, I was on TV this morning."

"I saw that. Didn't realize you'd been promoted to sheriff."

"What?"

It turned out that one of the reporters had identified me as "Sheriff" Houseman. Great. Lamar was going to love that. I said as much to Larry.

"Tell ya what," said Larry. "We'll continue to run this set every week or two for a few months. Just in case there's a participating venue that's offline right now, or somebody who's new coming up online in the next while."

"Thanks." A glimmer of hope, regardless of just how faint, is still a glimmer.

"Think we'll have a white Christmas?"

"Not unless it would cover up a crucial piece of evidence," I said. "It's been that kind of week."

Since Linda's identification of the deceased was now critical, Hester, Linda, Terri, and I went to Maitland Hospital, where the remains had been placed in their morgue/autopsy room. It was a new installation, built with regional funds, because we were located in the center of a seven-county region. We didn't get lucky like that very often.

Dr. Steven Peters, our favorite forensic pathologist, had just arrived. I made the introductions and told him why so many of us were there. He unlocked the door to the morgue, and he and Hester went in so he could do a "preliminary examination" of the body. That had never happened before. I was curious. He reemerged about fifteen minutes later, and motioned Linda, Terri, and me in.

The room was about forty degrees, all tile and stainless steel, and very clean. Dr. Peters's large instrument and evidence case was open, and his camera was on a counter near the remains. The body was lying on a stainless steel table with an indented drain trough that ran around its perimeter and led into a large sink near the dead man's feet. I could tell from the silvery puddles of water that the body had just been hosed off. It was apparent, at least to me, that Dr. Peters had photographed the dead man, then washed the body so that Linda would have an easier time of it. That explained the "preliminary exam." The body had been covered with a simple white sheet. It looked really weird, because my eyes went automatically to where you'd expect to see the large lump made by the head, and there was no lump there. Just a sharpish rise, where some fragmented feature had remained attached to the body. Spooky.

"We won't be looking at the face," said Dr. Peters. "Just the chest and lower down. Before you look, can you think of any identifying feature you can name?"

Linda drew herself together and said, "He's got a mole on his stomach, just above his navel. And a tattoo that says 'Nortino' on his right arm."

"'Nortino'? North?" My Spanish is horrible.

"More like 'Northern,' I think." She was beginning to shake, almost imperceptibly.

"What's that for?" I asked. "The 'Nortino'?"

"I don't know," she said.

Dr. Peters moved the sheet aside. He'd placed a towel over the pubic area, and another was draped at the top of the shoulders. I saw the mole above the navel. Linda sort of squeaked, and just sat down on the floor and started to cry. Terri helped her up and sat her in a folding chair that faced away from the corpse. I looked across the body to where Dr. Peters stood. He pointed to the upper right arm. I could see —TINO tattooed on the flesh.

I looked back at Linda, who was shaking uncontrollably and making hiccuping sounds. That kind of gut-wrenching sobbing is almost impossible to fake. I hate to be cynical, but it pays to notice things like that. So. I thought the identity pretty much confirmed.

CHAPTER 06

I TOOK A MENTAL INVENTORY OF OUR EVIDENCE. Determining how somebody was killed is usually pretty easy. Most killers are in a heightened state and are frequently in a hurry. That often means the method is pretty obvious. It sure as hell was here. Check number one.

Determining just *where* somebody was killed is sometimes more difficult, but at least a general idea can be gotten very quickly. As in, "not where we found him." Here, again, that was absolutely no problem. Eyewitnesses coupled with debris are about as good as it gets. Check number two.

The identity of the victim is very important, because that can lead to just why he was killed. Check number three.

Knowing when the victim is killed is critical in being able to place the suspect at the scene. When was a piece of cake in this one, with an eyewitness, and an uninvolved one at that. Check number four.

We were ahead of the game already. At that point, I was willing to bet that we'd have our suspect nailed down within twenty-four hours, and an arrest warrant issued soon after. I was in a pretty good mood.

The next step was for the autopsy to be conducted. Hester stayed for that, and I went back to our office with Terri and the grieving Linda, to obtain some background information on the now positively identified Jesus Ramon Cueva. We just needed some confirmatory stuff, like date and place of birth, relatives, that sort of thing. And, incidentally, are you sure you don't know of any reason somebody would want to kill him?

At the office, Linda said Jesus Ramon Cueva, aka Rudy, was from Los Angeles. His family was there, and she knew of no relatives any closer than that, but had his mother's address at home. She said he'd been born on July 22, 1970. She wasn't certain where, but she assumed it was in the Los Angeles area somewhere.

"I've got his birth certificate at home, and some of his employment papers and stuff." She was retreating into that dull state that comes after a big shock. I was glad to see that, since I always suspect everybody until I can rule them out. Grief might be faked, but the dullness afterward seldom occurs to the actors. She was genuine, as far as I could tell.

"We'll need to see that," I said. "Also his Social Security number."

"Sure."

"And a photo, if you have one you can let us take for a while and get it photocopied." It was going to be a lot easier to ask possible witnesses if they'd seen the deceased if we had a photograph. I cleared my throat. "Fairly recent, if you can."

"Sure. Okay."

"Now, Linda, we have to talk about who killed him, and why."

"I don't know. I can't think of anybody. Really," she said, beseechingly. "I don't know…"

"Okay," I said. I hated to ask the next question. "You two have any kids?"

"No."

"I'm asking, because you may be in as much danger as he was." I leaned forward, toward her side of the desk. "I'm very serious. You, or people related to you, or friends of yours, may be at risk."

"Oh, come on, Houseman," said Terri.

"It's true," I said. "Until we know for sure why he was killed and who killed him, we have to assume relatives and associates might also be targets. It's the only safe way to go about this."

Terri didn't seem to buy it.

Linda looked up at Terri and said, "He wasn't into dope. I know you think he was, but he wasn't." That squelched Terri more effectively that I ever could. Then she turned to me. "You want to search our apartment? You can if you want to. I don't care."

"How about we just go back with you and get a copy of his birth certificate and the photograph? Maybe look around at some of his stuff, but that's not really too necessary." I hate to turn down an offer to search, but we really didn't have any grounds to even do a consent search of her premises.

"Fine."

"Now, we didn't find any ID of any sort on him. None. No billfold. Did he carry a billfold?"

"Yes. Always."

"Do you know if he had it with him yesterday?"

"I didn't see, you know? I mean, I didn't watch him put it in his pocket. It's not around the house, or I would have seen it." She looked at Terri. "We have to call the funeral people. I know there's lots of stuff to do."

"We have to call his mother first," said Terri. That was certainly true. The mother was the only true next of kin we had. One of the problems with living together. You may be the person in the world who is closest to them, but you have damned little legal standing.

Linda's attention was going to hell. I sure didn't blame her. "Just a couple more questions for now, Linda. Did he have any credit cards? A driver's license? Things like that?"

"Yes. He did." She was trying.

"We'll need the numbers from his credit cards," I said. "Since we can't rule out a robbery motive, we need to check if there's any activity on them in the next couple of weeks."

"Sure."

"Then..."

"You'll have to have her permission to do that," said Terri, interrupting.

"All you have to do, Linda," I said, "is look over your statements and make sure there aren't any charges you haven't put there yourself." I looked up at Terri. She seemed satisfied. I really didn't need her getting all overprotective on us. I looked back to Linda. "What state was his driver's license in? Do you know?"

"Iowa."

That caught me by surprise. "You sure?" I was assuming he still had a California license, since our record search indicated that all the Cuevas in Iowa who had a DL were female. "When did he get it?"

"After we moved in together. About five months ago."

"So, he had, like, a California one before that?"

"No," said Linda. "No, he never had one before, as far as I know."

Interesting. "Did he drive, though? Before he got his license?"

"Yes."

"Where did you two meet?" I needed to establish more background on Cueva, if possible.

"The plant. I used to work there."

"Okay, so, when was that? About how long ago?"

"About six months ago... early August, this year."

I'm always surprised at just how fast some people dive into a relationship. "So you've known him for a good six months, then?"

"Yeah," she said, and started to cry again.

Linda, who'd started in a bad state for an interview, was losing ground fast. I felt sorry for her, but... well, I really needed her in a frame of mind where she'd be able to focus, so I asked Terri to take her home to Battenberg and I'd be there after lunch.

"I'll take you to the clinic first," Terri told her. "You're going to need something..."

Linda just nodded.

I wasn't happy about the clinic, but Terri was right. Since Linda wasn't a suspect, we'd be able to talk again even though she may have had a mild sedative. Interviewing any witness who's in an induced state is a pretty slippery slope, but I really didn't see a problem with this one.

Hester and Dr. Steven Peters met me at the office for lunch. They had grabbed some burgers, but I was sticking to my new diet and had put rice and low-fat sausage patties in the microwave in the jail kitchen. To make the stuff palatable, I'd bought a bottle of Uncle Bob's Hickory Smoke Flavor, which I sprinkled liberally on the "food" in the plastic bowl before I nuked it. It hadn't tasted too bad the other times I'd had it, but the odor took a bit of getting used to.

"Is there something burning?" asked Hester.

"No, it's my lunch."

"You sure?" she asked.

"Yep."

"It does smell like smoke," said Dr. Peters. "Really."

I went to the cupboard and showed them the bottle. "Want some? It tastes better than it smells."

"Hard to believe," said Hester dryly. "No thanks. Besides, the smell's already affecting my taste."

"Suit yourself," I said. "So, I hope there was nothing unexpected about the cause of death?"

"The cause of death," said Dr. Peters, "was remarkably easy to determine, if that's what you mean. GSW, head. Massive trauma. More the effect of the gas pressure than the shot pellets," he said. He took a swig of pop from the can. "Toxicology will be back in a day or two, but I don't expect anything out of the ordinary." He grinned. "Anything toxic would have to work very, very quickly to beat the gunshot wound in this one."

"That's a lot to be thankful for," I said. "The simpler the better. You knew, didn't you, that we have a new county attorney?"

"No! Really? What happened?"

Hester laughed, but said nothing. Dr. Peters looked questioningly at her. "Better if he tells it," she said, nodding toward me.

"The old one developed a skin irritation, or an allergy or something. Really. They said it was the pollen, maybe herbicides, maybe mold spores. So he moved."

"Really?" Dr. Peters looked quizzically at Hester.

"That's not the funny part," she said.

"Nobody wanted the job," I said. That was quite true. The county considered it a part-time job, so they paid whoever it was about thirty thousand bucks a year. Nation County was lucky to get any lawyer at that rate, and what they ended up with was often an attorney who had to have a full-time regular practice on the side just to make ends meet. When they did that, they'd occasionally find themselves being asked to prosecute their own clients. Not good. Nobody who'd made it through law school wanted those hassles, with one general exception. Newbies.

"So you don't have one, currently?"

Hester laughed again. "I couldn't have put it better myself."

"We have one," I said. "Named Carson Hilgenberg. He passed the bar last July. This is his first job."

Hester couldn't let it drop. "Tell him the rest of it, Houseman."

I looked at Dr. Peters. Hell, he had to know, if for no other reason than to be able to anticipate what he might have to face with the courts. "He's the nephew of the chairman of the Board of Supervisors."

"Does that complicate things?" asked Dr. Peters. "It isn't really nepotism if he's elected."

"Carson didn't actually run for office. The Board appointed him. That's not the problem. Even his uncle can't stand him and was hoping he wouldn't pass the bar. The problem is, there were no other applicants. That and he literally couldn't find a job anywhere else." I cleared my throat. "He's kind of an idiot."

"Oh," said Dr. Peters. "What's he like in court?"

"Never seen him there," I said. "He even bargains traffic tickets. Far as I know, he's never tried a case even in magistrate's court."

"I guess we get really specific for him, then," said Dr. Peters.

"Pictures," said Hester. "I'd suggest lots and lots of pictures."

CHAPTER 07

13:27

HESTER AND I WENT TO BATTENBERG, stopped at Linda's apartment, above the local hardware store, and picked up a manila envelope taped to the door. It was addressed to me, and contained two photos of the late Jesus Ramon Cueva, along with what appeared to be copies of a birth certificate and a Social Security card in his name, and a home address for his mother Maria in L.A. Attached was a note saying that Terri and Linda were at the clinic and would be back later.

We took the stuff to the Battenberg City Clerk, to have copies made. The birth certificate said Cueva was born in Los Angeles County, California. Mother's name was given as Maria Helena Cueva, father as Jesus Ramon. The home address of Maria Cueva was 4024 Radford Avenue, Studio City, California, 91604. No phone number. I phoned the Social Security number in to Sally at the office.

"Hey, run this SSN for me in the criminal history files, will you? Nationwide, of course."

"You always want that," she said. "You sure you don't want international? That's fun."

"No, just the States and territories."

"Well, all right. So, then, what else? You always need more than that."

"Well, get a teletype off to LAPD, and see if a Maria Cueva still lives at forty-twenty-four Radford Avenue, Studio City, California, will you? She's our victim's mother, and they'll have to notify her that her son Ramon is deceased." We absolutely never notify the survivors over the phone.

"No problem. What else?"

"That ought to do it, actually."

"You kidding me?"

"Nope. That's all. Really," I continued, into the silence at the other end.

"You're no fun," she said.

While we were in Battenberg, I thought it was a good idea to connect with Hector in person. I wanted to introduce him to Hester and to check on what he knew about Rudy. I called his cell phone and asked if he could meet us at the Battenberg Public Library. Hector went there quite often to use their computers and check his Hotmail account. He said he was headed there anyway.

Martha Taylor was the librarian. She'd been in my class at Maitland High. Small, slender, and in her middle fifties, she waved as Hester and I walked in.

"Carl. Good to see you again." She said that while looking at Hester.

"Martha, this is an agent friend of mine," I said. "Hester Gorse." They shook hands. "You mind if we sit at that table over there? We're expecting my usual guest."

"No, that's fine. If you need anything, let me know." She pointed to the Christmas decorations festooning the children's section. "I'll be over there, putting tinsel on the tree."

"Thanks." Martha was just great about my meeting Hector at the library. Never asked. Never pried.

Hector was with us in five minutes. He seemed a bit taken aback when he saw Hester but was impressed with her credentials. His shyness lasted about two seconds.

"Rudy was in heavy with some very bad people," he told us. "Nobody knows why they did him, man, but they truly did it. His whole head was really gone?"

"Just about," I said. I pushed the photos over to him. "Those look much like him?"

He looked for a moment. "These are pretty good. This one, this is a very good likeness." He held up one that depicted a good-looking man with a mustache.

"Thanks," I said, and retrieved the photos. "We're going to notify his relatives in L.A. You wouldn't happen to know them, would you?" I always hope.

"Hell, man, he ain't got no relatives in L.A."

Hester and I exchanged glances. "You know that for sure?" I asked.

"For certain, man. *I* got relatives in L.A. Not Rudy."

"You know where I could find them? Mexico?"

Hector laughed in amazement. "Hell, man, Rudy wasn't no Mexican. He's a high and mighty dude from Colombia."

I don't know about anywhere else, but in the close confines of Battenberg, the Mexican and Colombian communities didn't get along very well. The Colombians tended to look down on the Mexicans for some reason, and the Mexicans reciprocated.

"How did you know him, Hector?" asked Hester.

"Oh, he started in the plant same day as me. We did the cleanup on the guts that spilled on the floor. Everybody's the same, that job," he said, with a broad grin. "Nobody better than anybody in that stink. Besides, he was illegal," said Hector.

"Illegal?" I asked. "How do you mean that?"

"He was an illegal alien," said Hector. "What you suppose? Hell, man, I thought you would know that already."

"We're just getting started," I said. Crap. Immigration and Naturalization should be notified, and that was very likely to add another layer or two of complication and delay.

"Okay. Anyway, Rudy, he needed somebody to help him out, and we talked about things on break. He wanted to know things about L.A., about if I was from a barrio, the names of places and streets, people and things." He smiled. "He was hard to make out, you know? He din' speak much English, and I cannot understand his Spanish hardly at all. All the Colombians speak funny."

You learn something every day. "Like the way we speak English here?" I asked.

"You got that right," he said, and laughed. "Ya, you betcha," he said, sounding just exactly like he'd been born in Minnesota. It was remarkable.

"Hey, that's good!" I said.

"Thank you, I think so too," he said. "My sister says I have a talent." He got very serious, very quickly. "Rudy's illegal. So are the ones who did this, but I don't know names or where they are right now."

"Do they work in the plant?"

"Rudy did, for sure. The others, though, I don't know. I doan think so. They're around, you know? The plant. But not regular, not like they gotta work there. They are there sometimes. But they ain't around any one special place. They sometimes hang around in the break room."

"Are they Colombians, too?" Hester asked.

"Not all of them, ma'am. Some are," and he leaned forward to whisper, "some are from other places. Some are Hispanics, some are dark-skinned from somewhere I doan know, some are whites."

Oh, great.

"One of those whites happen to be a tall, kind of blond dude?"

"I would say there is a very good chance of that," said Hector, with a smile. He did like to kid me. "But really, yes. I do not know his name, but I think they call him Cheeto, you know, like the corn chips in the bag."

"Any of 'em live here in Battenberg?" I hoped.

"I cannot say that, man. I never see them go home anywhere here."

"What do they drive?" asked Hester.

"More than one set of wheels," said Hector. "Sometimes in a Chevy pickup, sometimes a Jap car."

"What kind of Jap car?" I asked.

"Honda, maybe Subaru, or something like that."

"What color?" asked Hester.

"Kind of a calf-shit yellow," said Hector. He'd picked up local descriptors in a hurry, I noticed.

"Tan?" asked Hester. "Cream-colored?"

Hector looked about the room. "Like that," he said, pointing at a tropical poster on the far wall. "Like the sand in the picture."

It could have been described as cream-colored. Maybe. Under certain lighting conditions.

"Okay, got it," I said. I lowered my voice. "So, you're telling us that this is dope-related?"

"No way, man," said Hector. "Not with Ramon, anyway. I doan know what, but it's much bigger than dope."

"What is it?" asked Hester.

"I don' know." His accent was beginning to thicken. Hector was nervous.

"Got a guess?" I asked. I figured he knew.

"All I know," he said, "is that the word is 'you do not in any way fuck with these people.' And before you ask me, no, I don' know who they are. I have seen them, I think. I don' even know that for sure, man. I'm *tellin'* you, these are very, very bad men."

"Okay," I said. "If you think you've seen them—assuming it might have been them—what do they look like?"

He hesitated. "I don' want to say this," he whispered. He took a deep breath, and let it out. "Hokay. Look, there is one tall white guy, man, and two Latinos, one is very ugly in the face. Like an accident with a wall, man. And one dark-skinned man who dresses really well, you know? Expensive things. Very long nose. Very quiet. And one dark-skin dude with an Anglo nose. Maybe he comes from Argentina or Brazil or something. He's always got on a Yankees baseball cap. He's crazy, like wired, you know? But I doan think he's doin' much dope. He's natural crazy." He looked around. "I think maybe I should go."

"New York Yankees? You think he's from New York?" I always hate asking obvious questions.

"No way, man. Maybe he's a baseball fan," said Hector.

"The white guy... is he local?"

"I doan know." He looked around. "I never met this dude, man. That's the way I want to keep it."

White. Well, the local label sure fit. But Battenberg also had a substantial Russian, Ukrainian, and Georgian community, all first-generation and very recent. White would apply to them as well. I wasn't done with that line of questioning yet, but I thought we could keep up an informal but cooperative relationship if I didn't pressure him, at least not yet.

"At least some are connected to the meat plant, though?" I asked. We were going to have to start interviewing a broader set of witnesses. Well, just as soon as we developed something to ask them.

"There's a bunch that work at the plant who might know something, but good luck with that today."

"Why do you say that?"

"The plant is closed. They say it's in honor of Rudy, but the real reason is that most of the workers ain' there." Hector grinned. "Illegals. You know how it goes. They won't be back for a while... three, four days, most of them."

"You're kidding." The last time this had happened it cost us three days. There had been a murder in the Hispanic community, and they all thought they'd be deported if they talked to us.

"No, I am not. Some of them even went away last night." The grin got bigger. "Just like last time."

"Any idea where they went?" asked Hester.

Hector shrugged. "Probably most of them are here somewhere. Just not at work, where you can find them." He grinned again. "Not even to the Casey's for cigarettes, not today. Maybe not tomorrow, too." The grin faded. "The ones who know Rudy the best, they have probably gone a distance. They worry about the cops *and* the Immigration Service."

Well, damn. Now we'd have to go to the plant, get home addresses, and try not to scare any illegals into running before we could talk to them.

"Did he have any close friends you know of?"

"Maybe two. Maybe three. You already talk to Linda?"

I nodded.

"She better be careful, too. She don' know the way things are. She's from Iowa."

"You think she's in danger?" asked Hester.

Hector shrugged. "I don't know what she knows. Maybe *she* don't know what she knows, either. You know?"

I thought he'd summed it up pretty well. "Yeah, I know. Hell, Hector, there are some days I'm not even sure of what I know myself."

He thought that was funny. "I got to go, to look normal. But you be careful, Mr. Houseman. I would miss you."

"Stay in touch," I said. "Maybe it would be best it we just talk on the phone for a while."

He stood, and stuck out his hand to Hester. "Nice to meet you, ma'am."

Hester shook hands with him, and he walked over to the bank of half a dozen public access computers, picked one, and sat down, completely ignoring us. If someone had walked in ten seconds later, there would have been absolutely no indication we'd ever talked.

"Second one from the right," said Hester. "Remember that."

"Got it."

We headed out the door. "He works in the plant?"

"Yep. Well, that's his official job," I said, as soon as we were outside.

"Official?"

"Well, he's a dope dealer in real life," I said. "Ecstasy and meth, in small quantities. Makes a profit, though. That's what I hear, anyway. Can't prove it yet."

"You get interesting snitches, Houseman. For a Norwegian."

"He says he likes it here in Iowa," I said, as we got in the car. "Just like a lot of the Latino dope dealers do. They'll tell you that the cops here don't beat 'em up just because they're Mexicans. The other dope dealers don't shoot 'em here, and the local customers pay up front."

"What more could you ask for, right?" She shook her head. "Let's hear it for family values."

"Like Hector says, 'Ya, you betcha.'"

Hester and I headed back to Linda's apartment, to return the originals we'd been given. I called the office on the radio and let them know we were in the car.

"Ten-four, Three," said Sally. "Ten-twenty-one the office."

She wanted me to phone in. "Ten-four." I handed Hester my cell phone, and she dialed as I drove.

"Hey, Sally, it's Hester. Is this for us, or just for Houseman?" There was a pause. "No kidding? Really? Okay, I'll pass it along. Oh, he'll love this, all right. No, you tell him."

She handed the phone back to me. "It's Sally."

"I knew that," I said. I took the phone. "Well?"

"Well, looks like your case is going to shit, Houseman," said Sally. "The address in Los Angeles you gave me? The one where his mother lives?"

"Yeah?"

"It's a movie studio. A movie lot. Where they make pictures."

Sally sounded very much entertained. "The LAPD say it was a studio from year one. The old Republic lot, I think they called it. At least since the thirties. Never residential."

"Well, damn," I said. "That's great news. I just found out he was never in L.A. anyway."

"Sure, you did."

"No, really. But cross-check the Social Security book, and see where his SSN originated. That might not be California, either. And, hey, we still got those CDs with all the phone directories in the U.S. on 'em?" I suspected Hector was right, and that Rudy was indeed illegal. But it never hurts to check as thoroughly as possible. I decided not to share that information with Sally just yet. She'd be inclined to search harder, I thought, if she didn't know.

"Sure, but it's not *everybody,* you know. But I'll be glad to, before you even ask. Give Hester my best."

"One more thing," I interjected quickly, before she could hang up.

"What?"

"Call the packing plant and see if they're working a full shift today, will you?"

"Why, you hungry again already?"

"Just do it. Call me as soon as you get some hard data, okay?"

"You bet. Can I come out and do my Sheriff's Reserve thing on this one?"

I had to laugh at that. Sally was a reserve officer, and a good one. But it seemed to me that every time we had her put that particular hat on, things went to hell in a handbasket.

"Sure," I said. "But not until it gets worse than you can make it."

I parked in front of Linda's apartment.

"First thing," I said, "is to call LEIN, and see if there's been a one-oh-two submitted on anybody called Cheeto." LEIN is the acronym for the Iowa Law Enforcement Intelligence Network. A 102 is the standard form that an agency will submit when it has important data on a suspect. Narcotics involvement, burglary, things of that sort. The 102 includes a place to list nicknames.

"Let's do it," she said. She had the number programmed into her cell phone and was talking to the senior analyst in about five seconds. "Okay. Okay, yeah. Nation County Sheriff's Department. Okay, I'll tell him. Bye."

She put the phone back in her inside jacket pocket. "Norma says hi, and she didn't have anything in the standard fields. She's checking with the adjoining states. She'll get back to us."

"Good. Norma's cool." We got out of the warm car and into the sharp twenty-degree air. "So," I said to Hester, "what do you think? Do we tell her, or do we assume she's been lying to us?"

"I'd be inclined to trust her," said Hester. "I think Ramon was lying to Linda. Big time."

We headed up the stairs. "I hope," I said, "that she doesn't take this too hard. The kid's already had a bad day."

I needn't have worried. Terri answered the door and ushered us in. Linda was totally zonked in a recliner, wrapped up in a blanket with a pillow under her head. She was leaning her cheek against the head of a dark brown teddy bear that was cradled in her arm. She snored quietly.

"They gave her ten cc's of valium, IM," said Terry in a low voice, holding a finger to her lips to tell us to be quiet. "She's out."

"No shit." I whispered back.

"Yeah. She'll be that way for a few hours. Want a cup of coffee?" she asked, as I handed her the manila envelope.

"Sure." The three of us adjourned to the kitchen.

We talked in hushed voices, but we talked. Terri was in a talking mood.

"She's not sure of anything right now," she said. "And not just because she's out like a light."

"Sure."

"He had some strange friends, Houseman. I still don't have the names, but she's got some pictures of a wedding they went to in Minneapolis about three weeks ago. Rudy's friends. Strange people. Want to see 'em?"

As if I'd decline an offer like that. In a minute, they were spread out on the little kitchen table.

It looked like a big wedding, and an expensive one. Everybody happy, all dressed up and smiling for the camera. There was quite a mixed bag in attendance, about as culturally diverse as Battenberg. The theme was sort of Tex-Mex, judging from the attire of the band, but there were all sorts of people there. The composition of the head table caught my eye. The obvious bride and groom, of course. A nice looking Latino couple in their late twenties or early thirties. There was a thin-faced man at the table, maybe a bit older than the happy couple. Intense-looking, dark complected, and it almost looked like he was the center of attention instead of the bride and groom. Along with him were two blond young women; a reddish-blond young man; a studious-looking young man of about twenty with a good tan and black hair and glasses; and a small, very pale young woman with close-cropped black hair.

I handed the first photo to Hester. "Keep this one in mind."

She gave it a quick look and then glanced up at me. "Okay, but I must be missing something."

As we continued to go through the photos, I noticed that in seven of the thirty or so shots, the thin-faced man was depicted with various groups all around what I assumed was the church hall.

"You know who this one is?" I asked Terri, pushing a photo across the table to her and pointing at the thin-faced man.

She nodded. "Yeah, I do. I met him here, once. I was over here to see Linda, and this guy and Rudy came in. Nobody introduced us, so I stuck out my hand and introduced myself."

"Do you remember his name?" asked Hester.

"He never gave it. Just looked at me like I was some super ditzoid, and said,

'I greet you.' Or, really, more like 'I greed you.' That's an exact quote, by the way."

"Do you know if he works here in town?" I asked.

"I don't know another thing about him," said Terri. "Well, except that he's pretty highly regarded by Rudy. Was, I mean." She pushed the photo back over the table to me. "Check out the little Mexican dude in this one. With the ears and the hat. The one that looks lost."

The one she was pointing out looked to be in his late teens or early twenties. Chunky, almost. It looked like he was dressed in his very best shirt and string tie, with an absolutely outstanding tan Stetson in his hand. He also had an absolutely outstanding pair of ears. Literally. They stuck straight out from the sides of his head. He was standing stiffly, as if he was uncomfortable. He was smiling, but with his large dark eyes he did indeed appear lost. He looked very much like the poor relative you can see at just about any wedding or funeral you go to. "What about him?"

"That's the one they call Orejas. He's Rudy's little shadow, always hanging around. Works at the plant. He's harmless, but a real pest."

"How so?"

"Linda says he's over here all the time. Watching TV. Helping Rudy change the oil in the car. That sort of stuff. They even had him here last Christmas."

"Orejas his real name?" asked Hester.

"I don't know, but until she wakes up," said Terri, indicating Linda's zonked form, "Orejas will have to do. Do either of you speak Spanish?"

Neither of us, as a matter of fact. "Why?" I asked, knowing the answer.

"Well, I don't think Orejas speaks any English. He might not do you a lot of good. I mean, if you can't talk to him."

"Interpreters," said Hester, "should be just fine. Standard procedure."

"Orejas is the butt of lots of jokes about those ears," said Terri. "The best one is that he looks like he thinks Viagra's a suppository." She giggled. "I mean, I feel sorry for the poor guy, but that's really funny."

It struck me that way, I had to admit.

There was a loud snoring sound. We all glanced into the living room toward the sleeping Linda. Gone to the world.

"Is there anybody around for her?" asked Hester.

"Her mom and dad are on their way back from Arizona," said Terri. "We talked to them before she went to sleep. They'll be here early tomorrow."

"Good. I hate to say this," said Hester, "but just how sure are you that when she says there's no dope involvement here, she's right?"

Terri shrugged. "I always thought he was into dope. She always said he wasn't. She ought to know."

"Can you think of anything else it could be?" I asked.

Terri shook her head.

"Well, I said this back at the office, but she might want to go where there's some company. Just in case." I thought about what Hector had said about Rudy's associates. "Dope or no dope. At least until we know why this happened. Can we keep some of these photographs for a while?"

"Houseman, you want a lot. Ah, what the hell, why not?"

When we got to the car with the photos, I opened the envelope and took out the first one. I handed it to Hester. "This is the head table at the wedding reception. Want to know what I noticed?"

"Please."

"No parents. Nobody old enough to be the parent of a twenty-year-old, not by a long shot."

"And?"

"The parents sit at the head table. I can only think of two reasons they aren't there."

"Death," said Hester. "That would account for it."

"All four, for a couple in their twenties... what are the odds?"

Hester laughed outright. "Houseman, sometimes... look, at least as good as the odds that the young couple met at the orphanage."

"Okay. Okay, but *my* second reason is better."

"And that would be?"

"They're illegal aliens. They can't afford to bring their parents to the wedding and couldn't do it legally anyway. Hah, gotcha with that one, didn't I? Well, if you don't have available parents, you just might have the most important person in your circle of friends join you. Mr. Thin-face there. Look at all the pictures with him, and you'll see that everybody looks just pleased as shit to be in his presence."

"Well..." she said, after she'd looked the bunch over while I backed the car out and headed toward the packing plant, "that might be a stretch." She very carefully put them back in the envelope. "Oh, what the hell, for the sake of argument, let's say you're right. So, like, what?"

"I want to know who he is," I said. "I'm thinking Godfather-type of relationship in those photos." I paused while I turned a sharp corner.

"You're developing a suspicious imagination, there, Houseman," said Hester. "Let's make a bet... like for a milkshake. You go for"—and she made a two-fingered gesture with each hand, indicating quotation marks—"the Godfather." She chuckled. "I, frankly, will go for"—and again the quotation gesture—"the plant foreman."

I have to admit that plant foreman hadn't occurred to me. Damn. Just somebody's boss. Of course.

"Is there a Dairy Queen around here?" asked Hester. "I want chocolate."

"Let's just wait," I said. "Wait and see." I sounded lame even to myself.

We paused in the parking lot of the packing plant long enough for me to call Sally and see what she had found out. By the lack of cars in the parking lot, I was afraid I already knew the answer.

"They're closed, Houseman," she said. "No explanation, just that they aren't working today."

"If they're closed," I said, "who'd you talk to?"

"Well, the office staff is there. But the floor is closed down."

"Thanks. That's where we'll be until further notice. I'll leave this thing on in case you need us."

"You're all dedication. You have anything to tell Lamar yet?"

"Not really. When we get back."

The business office of the plant was smaller than you'd think, and was on the second floor of one of the large cement-block buildings. The receptionist in the sparsely furnished office handed us off to the assistant manager, a Mr. Chaim B. Hurwitz. I suspected the B stood for Benjamin, because the first time I'd met him he'd told me to call him Ben. Most people at the plant referred to him as "Mr. Hurwitz." I'd had dealings with him before, a couple of times, and I thought he was a pretty straight sort of guy. Ben had been the first Jew I'd met in Battenberg, and he had been an education for me. Like most of the residents of Nation County, my previous experience with things Jewish had consisted of the movies *The Diary of Anne Frank, Exodus, The Pawnbroker, Schindler's List,* and *Fiddler on the Roof.* Hardly a primer for knowing the twenty-first-century Jewish American.

Ben Hurwitz and I shook hands, and after Hester identified herself, he asked us to sit down. His office was small, crowded, and spartan. It reminded me of the interior of a mobile office you find on construction sites. Absolutely no nonsense, and extremely functional.

"What brings you to me?" he asked.

"Well, we originally wanted to talk to some of your workers, but"—I smiled—"they seem to have gone on strike again."

I was well aware that the packing plant was not a union shop. Not at all, and the plant would fight unionization to its last breath. And Ben knew that I knew that.

"No. No, the union is much stronger than that," he said, deadpan. "What we have here is a coffee break." Ben Hurwitz and I had been over the illegal alien issues before. His company asked for Social Security numbers, and the workers presented them. The plant had absolutely no way to verify the numbers. They started asking for birth certificates, and the workers began producing them. All indicated they were from either Los Angeles or San Diego or Houston. None of those county courthouses had the facilities to constantly search their records for confirmation of birth certificates, and the plant had no legal way of compelling them to do so. At one point, the plant started asking for driver's licenses as a way of confirming the other identity papers. Their attorney told them that they couldn't do that unless they were hiring a particular individual to drive for them. If they asked to see a green card, those they were shown were probably forgeries anyway. They also had no obligation or desire to spend the fees charged for the searches. If they had a question, they called INS. That agency had never responded by showing up. INS was grossly undermanned and Iowa was a long way from being the state with the largest immigration problem.

"Just so we're perfectly clear here," I told Ben, "as you know from before, I have no authority to ask for an individual's proof of citizenship. If I ask if somebody is a U.S. citizen, and they say yes, that's the end of it. I have no authority to demand. None." I shrugged. "Unconstitutional is unconstitutional, period. So, even if I do determine that somebody is illegally here, I can't arrest an illegal alien because, one, I'm not a federal officer, and two, I don't have a federally-approved facility where I could keep them." I nodded toward Hester. "Neither does she. So...I think we can afford to stipulate that none of us will go into that issue during this conversation. That sound okay to you?"

He nodded.

"We'd also like to get the word out on that, because we're gonna be needing witnesses, and it'd be nice if they came back into the world."

Ben chuckled. "I'll do what I can, but I've got to find them first."

"I hear that," I said. "So, I assume you've become aware that Rudy Cueva was murdered yesterday afternoon, about five or six miles from here?"

"Yes. My wife and I saw it on the news. They didn't say who it was, but we heard from the staff later." He gave me a wry look. "You know, on TV you looked pretty good. Even if the camera puts on some pounds."

"Thanks for blaming the camera," I said. "So, you knew Rudy, then?"

"Of course." Ben picked up the phone on his desk but didn't touch the numeric pad. "You want to see his employee file? It's no use to him."

"Sure."

He pressed two numbers and told whoever answered to bring in Rudy's file. "What else can I do for you?"

Hester opened the envelope Terri had given us and handed Ben the photo with Orejas in it. "Do you know the stocky short one there? With the hat. He's called Orejas, I think."

Ben didn't hesitate. "Surely. That's Jose Gonzales. You're right, they do call him Orejas." Ben chuckled. "Orejas is Spanish for 'big ears.' It's his nickname."

Ah. Big ears, indeed. "They only use one word for 'big ears'? I would have thought it would be two words."

"I don't want to embarrass anyone," said Ben, with a glance at Hester. "I have to say the way it was explained to me was that it means big ears in the same way that a woman nicknamed 'boobs' means a woman with large breasts. The words 'big' or 'large' in either case would be redundant."

"Like, 'mouth' would mean 'big mouth'?" asked Hester.

Ben was embarrassed. "I wish that example had come readily to mind," he said.

"You know where this Orejas lives?" I asked.

Ben picked up the phone again, dialed what looked like the same two digits. "Get me the address of Jose Gonzales. No. No. No, the one they call Orejas... with the ears... that Jose Gonzales." He looked up at us and smiled. "It's a common name... and I should warn you, they may have a family Social Security number, too." He spoke back into the phone, "Yes?" He wrote the information on a slip of paper and pushed it over to me.

Hester, anxious to score her milkshake, presented Ben with a second photo. The shot of the head table, with the thin-faced man so prominent. "Do you know the man with the thin face?" she asked.

"No. No, but I recognize the bride and groom. They work here, too." He picked up the phone and again rattled off two names. "Juan and Adriana Muñoz, their current address, please." Again, he wrote it down and passed it to me. "They were married about six months ago. Are there more?"

Never being one to let an opportunity go by, I just handed him a half dozen more of the photos. His next call resulted in five more names and addresses. "So, the person who gave you these didn't know who they were?" He sounded pretty skeptical.

"It's a long explanation," I said.

He just nodded. "Anything else I can do?"

"Any idea," asked Hester, "when this 'coffee break' will be over?"

"Unions. What can I say? Maybe tomorrow. Maybe two, three days? I think it will depend on the, ah, 'activity' around our plant."

There was a knock at the door, and a secretary entered with a stack of files. Ben picked out Rudy's and handed it to me after she left. "Look through it. You need copies, say so."

"Thanks. Any idea why Rudy was killed?" It was a long shot, but you never know until you ask. Frankly, I half expected Ben to pick up the phone and ask his secretary. Instead, he looked very thoughtful.

"Rudy was not our most ambitious employee. But he was liked. No, I don't know. So, do you know who killed him, or can't you say?"

"No comment," I said with a smile. "Union rules."

16:51

"YOU OKAY?" I ASKED HESTER.

She nodded, then spoke very deliberately. "How many grenades do you think they have left?" She shook her head, reached inside her coat, and pulled out a bottle of water. She took a swig, tilted her head toward the wounded side, and let the water do its work. She turned away, spit, and turned back to me. "God, that's irritating," she said.

"Now that you bring it up, I don't suppose you walk in someplace and buy just one."

"Right." She was looking out a wide crack that some past farmer had tried to fill with cement. It hadn't worked. "It's getting dark."

"Yeah. I was thinking about that."

"Me, too."

"George is comin' down as soon as it's dark enough." I looked around. "The yard light will cast a shadow on this corner, from about the big door over the whole left side of the place."

"They'll shoot it out," she said. "Damn thith thing."

"Be quiet and have some more water. No, they won't. If they leave it on, they can see anybody who comes our way up the lane."

It was the grenades that had me worried. "I've been thinking," I said. "Either they got modern frags, or concussion grenades." She looked at me questioningly. "Modern grenades have a fine wire wrapped around a central core. Notched. Tiny fragments, but a cloud of 'em. Lethal radius to ten or fifteen feet, not worth shit twenty-five feet away. Well, somethin' like that. Not like the old grenades in the movies, with the Hershey-bar squares."

She nodded in agreement.

"Concussion grenades don't have very effective fragments at all."

She nodded again.

"I don't think any fragments made it through the barn, so..." We left it at that. I had no idea if I was right or not. Just something to say.

"You want me to see if I can start George's heater for you?"

"No thanks. I'm just fine."

I patted her on the shoulder and moved back over to my position.

"Hester okay?" asked Sally.

"Yeah. You think dehydration could be a problem for her?"

"Well, she's thin, and she lost a bunch of blood...might as well not take a chance. How much water you got left?"

I patted the left side of my Canadian Army parka. "Three bottles."

"Better keep 'em on the inside," she said.

I only had two inside pockets that were available, so I gave her one of the bottles. Our body temperature would keep them from freezing.

"She has one bottle now."

"I'll make sure she drinks," said Sally. "What do you think's gonna happen when it gets dark?"

"No idea. Just stay alert. Everybody calling the shots is outside this barn, one way or the other."

"Yeah. You know what?"

"What, Sally?"

"I wish the people at the Academy could see me now."

"Really?"

"Yeah," she said. "All the guys gave us gals shit. About being smaller. About having to do only eighty-five percent as many push-ups and sit-ups and things. 'I suppose the bad guys will only try eighty-five percent as hard to kill you.' Shit like that."

"Sorry to hear that. I thought it might have changed since I was there."

"Oh, it has," she said. "They have electric lights now."

"You little shit," I said. "I'm not *that* old."

"Yeah, right. I'm about eighty-five percent as old as you."

She looked right at me as she said it, and the reflection of the setting sun bounced off the little gold and silver badge on her winter hat, and just about blinded me.

I told her what had happened. "You better unpin that hat badge and stick it in your pocket."

"Anyway," she continued, as she stuffed the badge inside her coat, "I think I can hold my own, huh?"

"With the best of 'em," I said.

"You're not just trying to cheer me up?"

"No, I'm trying to cheer myself up." I grinned. "Just getting back for the electric light comment," I said. "Can't think of anybody else I'd rather be pinned down with."

At that moment, Lamar's voice came crackling over the walkie-talkie and we both jumped.

"Go ahead, One," she said.

"Tell Three the TAC team's here."

That was good news. I told Sally to have Lamar give the TAC team leader my cell phone number, and I'd talk with him on the phone. I was still worried that the people trying to kill us might somehow be monitoring our radio traffic, or that the media would be monitoring us and broadcast something that the riflemen in the shed could somehow hear. I was also getting worried about the batteries in the walkie-talkie. Especially in cold weather, they will deplete really fast if you do much transmitting.

The Assistant TAC team leader was a trooper sergeant named Ed Henning. I'd met him once or twice.

"My boss ain't here yet. What you got up there?" asked Ed.

I told him, gave an approximate number of six suspects, told him where we thought they were, said they all seemed to have AK-47s, and that they seemed to have chucked at least one grenade at us.

"What you got cornered up there?" he asked. "Osama bin Laden?"

"Close enough," I said.

While I'd been on my cell phone, Sally had been busy on her walkie-talkie. "George says he's comin' down in about ten minutes," she told me.

Good. If we had any chance of making a break for it, I didn't want George stranded on the upper floor of the barn. Besides, I was really worried about these guys trying to set the place on fire. If we had to get out of a burning barn, anybody in the hayloft was as good as dead.

"Make sure he tells you when," I said.

"He will."

CHAPTER 08

WEDNESDAY, DECEMBER 19, 2001 15:12

OUR NEXT MOVE WAS TO GO LOOK UP ONE JOSE GONZALES, also known as Orejas. After Ben's comment about the common name, I was pretty sure even Jose Gonzales wasn't our man's real name, either. The address was 206 Jefferson, Battenberg. It was an old, two-story frame house, of the sort that the zoning board would call a single-family dwelling. We went up the porch steps and stood under the overhanging roof and knocked on the storm door. And knocked and knocked. No answer. I tried the knob. Locked. We could see through the cheap lacy curtains on the front windows, and there was no sign of life.

Hester tapped the printed list of about fifteen names neatly duct-taped to the mailbox. "At least one of these should be here."

I knocked again, and an elderly woman came around the corner of the house, clutching her hooded sweatshirt closed.

"They all left," she said.

"Pardon?" She'd taken me by surprise.

"They all left last night," she said, standing at the bottom of the porch steps and looking up at us. "I'm the part-time manager. I live right over there, and they all left. Just like that. There's nobody there now."

"And nobody's returned?" asked Hester.

"Nope. Nobody I've seen." She pointed to the single-lane driveway that led to a garage toward the rear of the house. "That's where they park their cars."

There were no cars there. A point for her. It sounded like she had the place under pretty close surveillance. "They ever done that before?" I asked.

"No."

"What's your name?" I asked her.

"Myra Gunderson. What's yours?"

"Carl Houseman. I'm a deputy here in Nation County. Could you tell me who owns this house?" I thought we could try the owner and see if he could do us any good.

"Helen Fritz," she replied. "But she's dead. Her son, Herman, lives in Cedar Rapids, I think. He owns this place now, but I think Mary Klein, the realtor, manages the rent and things for him, I guess. I just pick up the rent and call Mary when there's a problem with the plumbing."

"Thank you," I said. "Would you call us if you see anybody back over here? When they come back, or anything."

She sure would.

"When are the checks due?" I asked. I figured they'd have to be back by then.

"The first of the month. But no checks. They pay cash," she said.

I should have guessed. But a week and a half. Damn.

I tried to reach Mary Klein, one of the local real-estate agents, but got no reply. I picked up my aluminum logbook, opened it, took out my pen, and made a ceremonious check mark on my daily log sheet.

"What's the check mark for?" asked Hester.

"To remind me to tell Lamar how much time a cell phone saves me. He hates it when I do that."

Next, we tried Juan and Adriana Muñoz, the newlyweds. They lived in one of four apartments above the hardware store. The place had a long, very narrow stairwell with one dim light, a long, dark hall with old musty carpet, and a floor that creaked with every other step. The apartment doors were plywood, with a cheap dark stain on them and gold paper numbers stuck on them with tape. Dingy. Again, I knocked and knocked. No answer. It was apparent that Juan and Adriana Muñoz were gone, too. The only difference in this instance was that Myra Gunderson wasn't there to tell us.

Downstairs, the owner and proprietor of the hardware store said he hadn't heard footsteps all day.

"I don't know why they all left," he said. The defensiveness in his voice told me he damned well knew. "Maybe some beaner reunion or something. None of my business, though."

Beaner. That told me what I needed to know about his attitude toward Hispanics. I try not to be judgmental, but I'm always looking for a lever that I can use to move somebody.

It was an unhappy fact that a few landlords in Battenberg were gouging the illegal immigrants for rent and other services. We'd received few complaints, mainly because illegal aliens don't feel that they can go to the cops or the courts. And they're right, although it wasn't a trust sort of thing. We'd get the bad guy, but the illegal aliens themselves would be referred to INS. They'd be held in a facility a long way from Nation County, and maybe even deported before the bad guy went to trial. Either way, chances were that we'd have no complaining witness, and the bad guy would walk.

"You notice when they come back," I said, "give me a call."

"Sure." It was said with a noticeable lack of sincerity.

"State fire marshal's office is asking us if we know anything about people being warehoused in unsafe conditions. You heard anything about that?"

"Absolutely not."

"I just asked 'cause I noticed there wasn't a fire exit up there. Hate to have the fire marshal get the wrong impression." I nodded to him. "Thanks for the help."

Back outside, I said, "That might get a fire escape opened up, anyway."

"Pretty crude, Houseman."

"You gotta know your audience."

"I suppose. Now, speaking of knowing your audience," said Hester, "how many illegal aliens are we talking about?"

I thought for a moment. "In Battenberg, maybe three hundred. Give or take. Not necessarily counting their families....There's just no way to get an accurate count."

"That many? Good God, I didn't realize there were that many up here."

"That includes a bunch of ethnic groups. Not just Hispanic. And not all the new people are illegal, not by any means."

"Oh. But as many as three hundred gone for now, right?"

"Looks like."

Hester pulled out her Palm Pilot, slipped the stylus out, and did something. "Okay. So, answer this. Where did they all go?"

I didn't have to think about that at all. "Beats me."

We drove in silence for about a half mile, up the main drag of Battenberg.

"That's a lot of people to accommodate," said Hester absently. "We're at least a thousand miles from the Mexican border, and a good five hundred from Canada."

"Well, shit," I said softly.

"What?"

"The border. They can cross one. Anytime, and pretty damned quick."

Hester looked at me quizzically.

"The bridge at Freiberg, Hester. Sixteen miles from here, they can cross the Mississippi at Freiberg. I'll bet they've gone to Wisconsin."

It was 16:00 on the button when we got to the Battenberg police department. We needed to contact Harry Ullman, my investigative counterpart in Conception County, Wisconsin. The most secure way to do that was by land line. I didn't want any chance whatsoever of an intercept of what we were going to discuss.

The Battenberg chief, Norm Vincent, graciously let us into his private office. There were three phones there, sharing lines, and I wanted to talk to Harry with Hester on the line as well. What I didn't want was Norm overhearing the conversation. Unfortunately, he quite rightfully sat behind his desk and waited for us to begin.

"Norm?" I asked.

"Yeah?"

"Look, we're about to discuss a long shot with another agency. A real long shot. I wonder if we might ask you to step out for a few minutes?"

He looked hurt. Almost as if he thought I thought he couldn't keep a secret. Well, he was right.

"Oh, I'm sorry. You should have said something."

As he started to get up, I said, "Look, it's like this. If we're right, I'll tell you as soon as we know, okay? But if we're wrong, it's best this doesn't get out. At all."

That mollified him a bit, I think, but it also whetted his appetite.

"Sure, Carl. Just let me know when you're done."

Within a minute, we had Harry on the line.

"Hey, Houseman! How they hang—"

"Hello, Harry," said Hester.

"Oops," said Harry. "It's the fuzz."

We all went way back.

"Got a question for you, Harry," I said.

"Wouldn't have anything to do with a deader over there last evening, would it?" Harry loved homicides.

"Matter of fact," I said, "it does."

"Hot shit," he said. "Fire away."

"It's also kind of a missing persons case," I told him.

"Okay. Cool. Who you lookin' for?"

"Well, maybe as many as a couple of hundred people."

Good old Harry never missed a beat. "Got names and physical descriptions for me there, Carl? Let me get a pencil..."

He had me there. I did, however, give him the names of the people we had identified in the wedding photos. I placed particular emphasis on Jose Gonzales, aka Orejas.

"So. Okay on Big Ears," said Harry, before I'd had a chance to translate the nickname. "Now you wanna tell me why you need these guys?"

We explained to him what was going on. Or, more correctly, what we thought might be going on.

"Not all of 'em," I said. "But I'll bet a bunch just might be over there. They don't have the cash to go too far or to pay for much lodging."

"I'll let you know," said Harry. "And Hester, I just want you to know I'll only blame Carl for this one."

"Thanks, Harry," she said.

"Any of the ones I'm lookin' for suspects? Or we just talking witnesses?"

"I'd tell you if I knew," I said. "I don't think the names we gave you did the killing, but don't take chances. Just in case."

"Sure." Over the phone I could hear a tapping sound in the background. Harry had a tendency to drum on things when he was showing restraint.

"What is it?" I asked.

"Well, I hate to butt in, ya know, none of my business and all that shit, but... you think this might be dope-related?"

It always seemed to come back to that. "We don't know," I said. I explained about the meth lab, and the shoe linking the deceased to that location.

Harry chuckled. "Pretty fuckin' coincidental, ain't it? Oops...Sorry Hester." He cleared his throat. "An amazing coincidence, I'd say."

Hester laughed. "Either way. But remember, just 'related.' Not necessarily the main motive."

"You betcha," said Harry. "Three hundred missing persons...you want me to call you when I find the first one, or should I wait until I get the first fifty?"

"Just let us know how it's going," I said.

Since we were sort of at a dead end, we left Battenberg and headed back to the sheriff's department to get a running start on the paperwork. If you don't keep up with it, you can destroy a case that depends on a large number of precise details. Admittedly, the number of individual details now was small, but I expected it to grow rapidly. Well, I hoped it would. If it didn't, we were in deep trouble.

CHAPTER 09

WEDNESDAY, DECEMBER 19, 2001 **18:04**

I GOT A CALL TO RETURN TO BATTENBERG when we were only about five miles out of Maitland.

"Three, Comm." It was Sally at the office.

I picked up the mike. "Go ahead."

"Three, request you ten-twenty-five with Car Forty; not ten-thirty-three, but as soon as possible. He has a situation and requests your assistance."

Interesting. "Ten-four. What's the nature of the call, Comm?"

"I'll ten-twenty-one," she said, and a few seconds later my cell phone rang. "Yo!"

"Houseman, it's your lucky day."

"Uh-oh. What's he got?"

"Unattended death," Sally replied.

In Iowa, the sheriff's department is required to investigate all unattended deaths, to make sure they aren't crimes. An unattended death is one where a person dies without being under medical supervision for the thirty-six hours preceding their demise, unless they're prediagnosed as terminal. Then it's thirty days. We call it the 36/30 rule. If there's any doubt, call the sheriff. We have to go, even though ninety-nine percent of them are old-age-related. It's reasonable, really. Just time-consuming.

"Shit. Okay, where is it?" This was going to require a complete and thorough report, too. Just when I didn't need it.

"He gives an address of two-oh-six Jefferson, in Battenberg," she said. "It's a..."

"We were just there," I said, cutting her off. "There was nobody home."

"Well," said Sally, "in a way, that's probably true."

When we got back to 206 Jefferson, we met with Chief Norm Vincent, who was standing in the driveway. He was also beginning to look rather harried.

"What we got here, Norm?"

"It's a deader, Carl. Sounds natural to me. I told your dispatch that I'd take the call, but they said that you have to do it."

"Yep. Thanks for the offer." Norm knew the sheriff's department had to do it, so it had been an easy gesture on his part, but one that was well-meant. These little things count. "So, what happened?"

"You know why so many of the Mexicans left and all? Well, one of 'em was sick, I guess, and they called a social worker and told her about it, and she came to check up on him, and found him dead."

I looked at the porch and saw Myra Gunderson talking to a young, dark-haired woman I didn't know. "That the social worker with Mrs. Gunderson?"

"Yeah. Name's Sarah Deitzenbach. Oh, and I called the ambulance just before you got here. Figured we'd need it."

"You been in the house to see the body?" I asked.

"No. I wouldn't want to mess anything up." He wasn't being sarcastic. If he'd 'messed anything up,' it could cost him a long report, as well. It was typical of him to say it looked natural without having actually observed the body, too. Sloppy, but well intentioned. It was worth a lot of effort to keep him off the stand.

"Okay. So nobody has pronounced anybody dead yet, right?"

"Not as far as I know, Carl."

"Then I'm glad you called the ambulance and not a hearse." With that, I headed for the porch while Hester and Norm made some small talk. Hester, being a state officer, wasn't required at an unattended death. Lucky her.

As I approached Sarah, it occurred to me that she was my last hope of getting out of a lengthy report. If she knew that the deceased had been under any medical care, including an ER visit, I was off the hook.

"Hi, my name's Houseman. I'm a deputy sheriff here in Nation County. You're Sarah Deitzenbach?"

"Yes."

"You found the deceased?"

"I did." She sounded a little defiant.

"You okay?"

"Yes, of course. Fine."

"Could you lead me to the body?"

"Sure. You know," she said, once we were inside the house, "this is all so senseless. If they weren't so afraid they'd be deported, they'd go to the hospital or the clinic."

"I couldn't agree more," I said.

"Poor Orejas," she said. "I guess they thought it was the flu."

"Orejas? Sonofabitch." I only knew of one Orejas.

"Yes. Well, that's not his real name, really. It's just what his friends call him."

"Was his real name Jose Gonzales? By any chance?"

Sarah turned on the stair, and I almost ran over her. "Yes. It was. Do you know him?"

"Not yet," I said as I turned and headed back down the stairway.

Hester and I followed Sarah back up the stairs, down a dingy hallway, and into a very small room that had probably been occupied by an infant child in the heyday of the old house. Now it contained one cot, one card table, two folding chairs, an album cover poster of a beautiful woman that said "*Todos Mis Exitos*—Selena," and one body.

He was curled up in the bed the furthest from the door, next to the window. He was wearing blue jeans and a gray sweatshirt, socks, and a stocking cap pulled down to, but not over, his large, protruding ears. It probably got cold at night in the drafty place. He was half rolled up in an old army blanket. He looked pretty ugly, with his mouth hanging open, liquid on the pillow, and vomit on the floor and in a big dog-food bowl by the side of his bed. He'd tried not to make a mess, but had probably been too weak to get up.

I reached into my jacket pocket and got out a pair of latex gloves. The snap as they went on was the only sound in the room. Gingerly, I reached out and touched his neck. No carotid pulse presented itself. His lips were a bluish tint. His eyes were wide open, and as I shaded each of them in turn with my hand, the pupils didn't change at all. Fixed and dilated, as they say. It wasn't as if there was any question in my mind that he was dead, but you learn to check for the obvious signs in case you end up in court. I tried to move his left arm. It was stiff as a board. Rigor had set into the major muscles. At room temperature, that meant he'd been dead a minimum of twelve hours. I couldn't tell closer than that.

I lifted the blanket back and off the body and pulled up his sweatshirt. There was a purplish mottling on the right, or down side of the body. It was post-mortem lividity. It's produced when the blood seeks the lowest level after the heart stops. After about an hour or so of the blood clotting in the capillaries, it becomes irreversible, so it's a fairly good way to tell if a body has been moved after death. There was also a strong odor of feces. Either diarrhea or a post-mortem evacuation. I figured I'd leave that to the doc. There were no indications of foul play that I could see, meaning that there were no gunshot wounds or knives left in the victim. I noticed that there appeared to be a billfold in his right hip pocket. I reached in and removed it. Opened, it revealed a plant employee card in the name of Jose Gonzales. I was still willing to bet that wasn't his real name, but he did have documentation. He had a Social Security card, and I wrote the number down. It looked familiar. There was a photo of Jennifer Lopez that looked like it might have come with the billfold, and a small Roman Catholic prayer card in what looked to me like Latin or Spanish. Three dollars completed the inventory. I laid the billfold on his hip, because I'd noticed some liquid still escaping his mouth when I'd half-rolled him over to retrieve it from the rear. No point in creating more of a mess than necessary. The funeral director would hold it for next of kin.

I straightened up and looked at Hester. "Natural causes, so far. No idea what they might be, though. He sure looks like Orejas," I said.

Sarah, who had averted her gaze while I'd checked the body out, spoke up. "I thought you didn't know him?"

"I've seen his picture," I said. "So, how well did you know him?"

"I met him when his cousin applied for food stamps," she said. "He was a pretty good kid, I think."

I was doing a cursory visual search of the room, and I noticed three items that stood out. "That's what I heard about him," I said absently. The first item was a small bag of a green, leafy substance. "He seemed to be pretty benign." The second was a spray can with no label, and it only caught my eye because it was bright silver. Both were on top of an empty gym bag near the head of his bed. Probably hairspray. The paper labels frequently get removed, especially if the can is shoplifted. "He didn't have any record with us, anyway." The third item was a very nice Stetson, obviously the one in the wedding photos. It was hung carefully on a hook on the back of the door.

"How long had he been sick?" asked Hester.

"I don't really know," said Sarah. "His cousin stopped by yesterday afternoon and asked me to check on him around noontime today." She sighed, and her voice sounded flat. "I got stuck with a house call on a client in the country. I was late."

"I wouldn't worry," I told her. "He looks to have been dead for at least twelve hours." I snapped off my gloves and tossed them into a brown cardboard box that was obviously being used as a wastebasket. "I'm going to get my camera and take a few shots, just for the record."

I was almost out of the room when I turned and asked, "Can I have the name of his cousin? We need to know how long he'd been ill."

"Sure, it's Baldomero Gallegos."

"He live here?"

"Yes. Number six."

"Thanks," I said, heading down the stairs. Another witness to find and interview. Things were beginning to pile up.

Hester and Sarah followed me down the stairs.

Once in the car, I got the camera bag and did a check through my notes from the morning. Sure as hell.

I headed back into the house, got back to Hester, and motioned her aside. "Wanna hear somethin' neat?"

"Sure."

"The deceased Jose Gonzales up there has the same SSN as the late Rudy Cueva."

"Well, damn," said Hester. "Fascinating."

I grinned. "You think they're related?" It was an old cop joke.

She smiled back. "Just close enough to shop for documents together."

I did about a half dozen photos of the late "Jose Gonzales," or whatever his name actually was. I then did an "around the room" pan, snapping the photos as soon as the viewfinder stopped at the edge of the last shot.

I heard a noise under the cot. My first thought was rats. I took the little mini-Mag flashlight out of the camera bag and said, "You better not be gnawing on my body, here..." as I lit up the floor beneath the bed. "Damn," I said. It wasn't a rat. It was a little beagle, about a year old or less, lying very still and looking at me with those unique beagle eyes. "Who're you?" I knelt down and held out my hand. "Come on, it's okay, I'm not gonna hurt you..."

"Houseman, who are you talking to?" asked Hester from the hallway.

"Come on in, look what I found," I said, not taking my eyes off the dog. "That's a good boy, come on..."

He began to wag his tail, causing a soft thumping on the floor. Hester knelt beside me and was a goner from the first instant she laid eyes on him.

"He's adorable!"

He was also pretty frightened, and pretty reluctant to come out from under his late owner's cot. Well, for me, anyway. I was about to caution Hester about getting bitten when she reached her hand out and the little dog came right to her and started licking her hand and wagging his tail so hard that I thought he was going to torque himself right off his feet.

We took the dog downstairs with us and took him to Myra Gunderson, who was still standing on the front porch, trying to find out what she could about what was going on inside.

As soon as she saw the dog, she said, "Where did you get that?" She didn't sound too happy.

"Up in Jose Gonzales's room," I told her. "Do you know anybody who can take care of him until some of his friends get back?"

"We don't allow dogs. I don't want it. Have it put to sleep."

I wasn't about to do that. "You don't know anybody who will take his dog?"

"No."

"What about his cousin?" suggested Hester.

"Baldomero? He can't have it in that house, either."

My next thought was to give the little fellow to Sarah, but she informed us that she had four cats at home, and her husband wouldn't put up with a little dog to boot.

I ended up putting two garbage bags in the backseat of my car and explaining to the little dog that if he made a mess, we'd feed him to the prisoners. He seemed to accept the terms.

As I said to Hester, the upshot was, we were now deprived of a witness, maybe the best witness, who might have been able to enlighten us regarding Rudy Cueva.

"You're probably right."

I suspected Jose Gonzales had probably died of natural causes that had been left untreated because he was afraid that the local clinic would have to contact the Immigration and Naturalization Service, and he'd be deported. We'd tried to dispel that rumor by explaining that medical confidentiality would prevent the INS from being notified, but it just didn't seem to take. I said that to Hester, too.

"Right, again."

And, just to top things off, we'd inherited a dog. I said that, too. I looked over at Hester, who reached into the backseat and brought the puppy up to the front seat with her. "Aren't you so cute," she said.

"Thanks."

"Not you, Houseman. You're just grumpy."

"Hmmm."

"What should we name him?"

"Hold on, there, Hester. You name 'em, you own 'em forever."

She was holding the little beagle up in front of her face. "He's got such big, floppy ears. Don't you? Don't you? Yes. Hey, maybe we should call him Big Ears."

"You're doomed. That's now your dog."

It didn't seem to bother her a bit. Not even when she said, a few seconds later, "One little problem..."

"Oh?"

"I'd be glad to take him tonight, but they don't allow dogs at the motel."

Hester, like all DCI agents who stayed on a case in Nation County, had to grab a motel. The nearest agent actually lived in Waterloo, about seventy-five miles away, and after putting in a long day, nobody wanted to do what amounted to a minimum of a hundred-and-fifty-mile commute.

"I'm not taking him home," I told her. "Hell, we don't even know if he's housebroken."

"I was thinking the comm center at the jail," she said. "There's somebody awake there all night, and they could watch him for me."

"Lamar's gonna hate that."

"Oh, Lamar will be just fine. Trust me," she said.

As it turned out, Sally and a new dispatcher named Pam fell just as hard for Big Ears as Hester had. It was easy to see how. The damned dog charmed the socks off the whole bunch in seconds. They even prevailed upon me to go to the Pronto Market and get dog food for it.

"Treats," said Pam. "Don't forget treats."

"Treats?" I answered. "What you want?" I was thinking in terms of Mars bars and that sort of thing.

"Something like little bones flavored with bacon," she said. "Not the really big ones; he's too young for those. The smaller ones." She looked at me. "For the dog. Treats for *the dog*."

I was starting to get disgusted when one of our antiques burglars—I think it was Clyde Osterhaus—hollered out from the cell block and said, "What's going on out there?"

Big Ears curled his lip and growled at Osterhaus. Sort of a little rumbling sound. Treats on me.

CHAPTER 10

JUST AS I GOT BACK TO THE COMM CENTER FROM THE MARKET, Dr. Henry Zimmer was walking in from the parking lot to the door. I walked in with him.

"Hi, Henry."

"Carl, just the man I'm looking for."

"Why? Am I sick?" Sometimes I crack myself up.

"No, but that last ME case you sent to me this afternoon sure was. Really, really sick."

"Well, yeah," I said, buzzing the door and staring up at the security camera. "I mean, he *was* dead."

"Sicker than that," said Henry. He sounded much more serious than usual.

The dispatcher recognized us and triggered the unlocking mechanism. Henry opened the door for me, because I'd gotten a bit carried away and had a ten-pound bag of dog food and three boxes of assorted dog treats in my hands.

"Thanks." He and I walked back toward the comm center, where we caught sight of Hester with Big Ears on her lap.

"Was Hester at this unattended death, too?"

"Yeah. Turned out the dead guy was supposed to be a witness of sorts in the homicide."

"Really?"

"Yeah. Not been my day."

We entered the comm center, and pleasantries were exchanged between Henry and the gang while I divested myself of the dog rations.

"Can I talk to the two of you?" asked Henry, indicating Hester and myself.

"Sure," she said, and put Big Ears on the floor.

"Cute dog," said Henry, and leaned over and scratched Big Ears' head.

I closed my office door. "What's up?"

"This Jose Gonzales who you found this afternoon," said Henry. "Do you know where he's from, or where he's been the last few days?"

"Nope. Not yet."

"I think you better find out. We're going to need to know."

Hester and I looked at each other. "Sure," I said. "Why?"

"What killed this man," said Henry, "was extremely virulent. Much more than pneumonia. Much more. Acute hypoxic respiratory failure. Severe pulmonary edema. The man's lungs were absolutely full of liquid, and so was his upper GI tract. His nasal passages were completely shut, and even his eyes were infected. When I pressed on his abdomen to check for masses, he ejected about a quart of bloody liquid from his rectum." He shook his head. "I don't know what got him, but I've called the State Board, and he's being transferred to the University Medical Labs in Iowa City. Whatever it is, it might be transmittable from one person to another." He paused. "So, then, are you two feeling all right?"

"Jesus, Henry," I said. "You're kidding."

"Nope. I think I better see you both at the clinic yet tonight. Who else was present?"

I called Sally and had her get the contact information for the Battenberg ambulance crew, the social worker, and the Battenberg chief of police.

"I think I can guess," said Henry, "but where did he work?"

"The packing plant. Should I notify them?"

"Just let's find out when he last worked, and who the workers are in close proximity to him. Anybody who cohabits with him. I don't know if this is a poisoning, something toxic in their environment, or if it's a rare sort of disease, or what. Regardless, they'll have to be examined, too. Everybody in contact with him, or who works or lives in the same place."

I just stared at him for a second. "Uh, there might be a little problem with that...."

While Henry poked and prodded us at the clinic, I finally got to use my cell phone to its fullest extent. My first call was to Ben Hurwitz, the manager of the packing plant. I told him it was extremely urgent that we find out when Jose Gonzales, aka Orejas had last worked. He was reluctant, but I told him it was either that or warranted search of his company records.

"This is a joke, right?"

"No, Ben. Not at all. And I think I can promise we'll be there yet tonight, if we do the search warrant bit."

"I'll see what I can do. What's your number?"

I gave him the number at Dispatch, and then called Harry over in Conception County. I got him at home.

"This is gonna be good, isn't it?" he asked.

"'Fraid so, Harry." I told him that the search for the missing Hispanics was now just a whole lot more urgent than before, and then told him why.

"You gotta be shittin' me, Carl."

"Nope."

"Are you sayin' they're contagious? Like with a plague or like that?"

"Could be that, or it could be something toxic at the plant. Maybe the chemicals they use to cool the place, or to disinfect, or something like that. All I know is I'm standing here at our clinic, getting checked out pretty damned thoroughly. Here, how about I let you talk to Doc Z?" I handed Henry my phone. I noticed he wiped it off with a sterilization wipe before using it. He *was* serious.

A lab tech named Lois, who I knew all too well from my quarterly cholesterol tests, came in with the familiar tray of tubes. As she wrapped the ligature around my arm, I said, "Could we do my regular checkup now, too?" I expected a smile. Nothing. Deadly serious.

"What are we looking for, Henry?" I asked Dr. Z.

"His white count was astronomical," said Henry. "Whatever this is, it gets the attention of your immune system in a big way. That's what I'm looking for right now. Just to see if your white count is up." His eyes twinkled. I knew right then I was in deep trouble. "And, according to my little manual here. let's see, 'Useful testing includes a complete blood count (which may reveal leukocytosis), electrolytes, BUN, creatinine, glucose, prothrombin time, activated partial thromboplastin time, international normalized ratio, type and screen, fibrinogen, liver enzymes, amylase, and lipase. An arterial blood gas may reveal hypoxemia.' Well, what do you know about that."

"What?"

"I'll bet that, even if we leave out the blood gasses, we'll need at least...whatcha think, Lois? Five tubes?"

"At least," said Lois.

"Five tubes? Hell, Henry, you're gonna have to *feed* me for five tubes."

"Be brave," he said, clapping me on the shoulder. "This will hurt you more than it does me."

"Right," I muttered. "So, then, if it is, you treat me for the thing, right?"

"If I knew what it was, and if there turned out to be a treatment for it, you bet."

That didn't help much at all.

"Not even a guess?" I asked, watching tube after tube fill from the needle embedded in my arm.

"No. Remember when Alice and I went to Machu Picchu? How sick I got? Just some tropical kind of bug we'd picked up on the way. Still don't know what it was." He sort of cleared his throat. "Hell on wheels is what that bug was. But I still can't name it."

"Ah."

"It could be some strain of something I've never heard of. Or it could be a chemical that's toxic. Don't worry," he said. "With your cholesterol level, it might even be good for you."

Don't worry, my butt. I took a deep breath. "Okay. So, how soon will you know?"

"Shortly. If you don't have an elevated white count, it's a very good sign."

"I'm sure," I muttered. The needle came out, and Lois pressed folded gauze over the puncture and pushed my arm up so I'd hold it in place until she got some tape. "I got lots going on, Henry," I said. "I can still rule out foul play on this one, can't I?"

"There's no sign of it," he said. The way he said it left him a bit of room, though.

Lois pressed a Buzz Lightyear bandage over the gauze pad inside my elbow.

"Hey, thanks," I said. I looked back over at Henry. "So it's not likely?" I didn't want two homicide investigations going at the same time, and the ME was the only one who could classify Gonzales as a possible murder case at this stage.

"No. But if it's something like a transmittable disease or a toxic contamination of the workplace...we could lose a bunch of people."

My cell phone rang. Lamar.

"What in the hell is going on?"

"You mean about the dog?" I asked, trying to lighten it up a bit.

"Screw the dog. What's with all the commotion with the medical stuff?"

I told him. It's very important to manage information that might mean an impending plague with at least some discretion. Since the anthrax-in-the-mail thing after 9/11, it was even more important. In a small, rural jurisdiction, where just about everybody is known to or related to just about everybody else, it's absolutely vital.

"What does Doc Z think?"

Henry cleaned my cell phone off again before putting it to his ear. He told Lamar that the medical investigation was precautionary but absolutely necessary, and that the point of origin was probably not Jose Gonzales. "Gonzales is a victim, but I'd be surprised if he was the only one," was what he said. Doc Z was right, but in a way that never would have occurred to any of us at the time.

About fifteen minutes later I knew my white count was just fine, and so was Hester's. That was a real relief, I think, because we'd both seen what Jose Gonzales, aka Orejas, had looked like. It couldn't have been a pleasant way to go.

Henry was now leaning toward some toxic substance that Jose Gonzales had been exposed to somewhere, and fairly recently.

"How recent, Henry?" asked Hester.

"I don't even know that yet," he said. "Since we don't know what it is, we don't know how fast a lethal dosage will take to advance. But within the last week, I'd say. When I examined him, I half expected to find some chemical burns in his throat or windpipe, or in his nasal passages...Nothing. Inflammation, though. But chemical burns would have given me a toxic chemical to work with. Nothing." He was half talking to himself. "Chemicals would be faster acting, probably...."

Part of this was settled by my next cell phone call. It was the office, who told me that Ben had returned my call. They had strict orders not to give my cell phone number to anybody. I called Ben Hurwitz back, and he told me that Jose Gonzales had been at work Monday. He'd done his normal shift, which was from 3 P.M. to 10:30 P.M. A seven-and-a-half-hour shift wouldn't jeopardize his part-time status.

"Where does he work?" I asked. "In the plant."

"Well, he's logged in as doing his usual job. He carried meat into the refrigerated trucks."

"Semitrailer trucks? The kind where each trailer has its own refrigerant plant?"

"Yes."

"Would he be exposed to a refrigerant leak, or anything like that, maybe?" The checking had to start right now.

"There weren't any reported. We keep good records of that."

"We'll need the serials of the trailers he might have helped fill that shift, too," I told Ben.

"Yes."

"He'd be lugging swinging meat, right?"

"Yes."

"Couple hundred pounds, on his shoulder, like quarters that dangle from hooks?"

"Yes."

"So he'd have to feel at least okay, to do that, you think?" I was assuming that to do such heavy labor for a nearly eight-hour shift, he sure couldn't have any serious respiratory problems.

"I'd think so. Yes."

"Okay, Ben. I'll need to talk to some of the people he worked with. As soon as you can contact any of them..."

That was the problem. Everybody was still on that impromptu "coffee break."

"Can you tell me what this is about?" he asked.

I thought about it for a second. Why not? He'd likely find out very soon anyway, and I thought it was better for the relations between his plant and our department if he heard it from me first. "Well, Jose Gonzales is dead. It looked like natural causes at first, but now it looks like it might have been some toxic substance, not necessarily a disease, that did him. We don't know yet."

There was a profound silence on the other end. With either the toxic or the disease scenario, Ben knew he was now pretty likely to have the FDA pay a visit. Just to make sure that the product they shipped was not contaminated. OSHA would be equally fascinated, on the chance that the illness had been contracted at the plant by exposure to some substance or some unhealthy condition. Even though his plant routinely passed every inspection with flying colors, this would be a different sort of thing. An IRS audit would be mild in comparison. Also, any interviews with employees, assuming they could be found, could really complicate his life, and involve the INS paying a visit, as well.

The Immigration and Naturalization Service was in a perpetual overload state and had been for years. But if FDA and OSHA both hit them with a report, they might well actually respond this time. The odds were at least even, anyway. The Immigration violations and fines, bad publicity, and all that went with it could really hurt the plant. I was glad it was Ben's problem and not mine.

"I'll have our in-house inspection team on it as soon as possible," said Ben.

"That'd be great," I said. "Somebody from our office should be there, then, too."

"Was he worried about OSHA or the FDA?" asked Henry.

"I think so. Probably should be."

Henry chuckled. "Well, don't tell him yet, but this is also going to be reported to the Centers for Disease Control and Prevention in Atlanta. CDC has even more clout than the others."

"That's pretty heavy stuff," I said. It was also fascinating. I'd never worked a case with CDC being involved. This could be neat.

"The U of Iowa labs will refer it, if they haven't already. Since the 9/11 business," said Henry, "these things are moved along fast."

"Right." The anthrax mailings had been quite a lesson, not to mention the attendant media frenzy.

"I think our biggest concern will be the media—if they get this, and it gets blown out of proportion. I'd hope," said Henry, "that we could conclude this quickly enough to avoid that."

I just looked at him. "Good luck."

Henry gave us each a sheet of paper with a list of things he'd like us to find out about the late Jose Gonzales, and questions to ask of any of his close friends, relatives, and coworkers. He also told us to report to him at the clinic at 08:00.

"I don't know what it is," he said. "Therefore, I don't know how long it takes from exposure to onset of symptoms. We get to stick you again tomorrow morning." He grinned. "That's the fun part of my job."

The list of things Henry wanted answered ran as follows:

1. Did the victim(s) travel outside the U.S. in the last thirty days?
2. List common denominators of victims:
   a. Race
   b. Socioeconomic status
   c. Sociopolitical groups
   d. Associations
   e. Locations
   f. Events
   g. Travel
   h. Religion

3. What do the victims think made them ill?
4. Do the victims know of anyone else who has become ill?
5. Did they see any unusual activities or devices?
6. Have they noticed any unusual odors or tastes?
7. Have they noticed any sick or dead animals?

"We're gonna have a little problem with the items under question two here," I said. "The ACLU would be all over us like stink if we started asking those sorts of questions."

"At least he doesn't want questions asked regarding sexual preferences," she said. "Did you check out number seven?"

Actually, I'd been too busy talking. I looked at seven again, and we both had the same thoughts. First, our newly acquired mascot, Big Ears, had been found under the victim's bed and was still alive and well a short time ago. Second, these guys were meatpacking plant workers, and they'd likely seen lots and lots of dead animals recently. We went back into the clinic and told Henry.

"Where's the dog now, and where will he be? I want the vet to examine him as soon as possible."

"We'll keep him at the jail," I said.

"Okay...just don't let the other personnel be exposed to him until we get him checked out."

Talk about way too late. "How about if we just don't let the next shift be exposed," I asked. "Little dogs attract lots of attention."

"Sure. That's the little dog I petted, isn't it?"

"Yep, that was him. He belongs to Hester," I said, and got a dirty look.

CHAPTER 11

HESTER AND I MET AT THE CLINIC TO HAVE OUR BLOOD TESTED. I wasn't too worried, as I'd checked with Pam at Dispatch and discovered that Big Ears was still alive, well, and had peed on the floor. He'd been checked by the vet and pronounced healthy. Our personal canary, so to speak.

We were in the little waiting room outside the lab, just starting to get organized, when a nurse stuck her head around the corner, looked at us, and then disappeared. I heard her say, "They're right in there," and then Judy Mercer, intrepid reporter for KNUG, came hustling around the corner, followed by a cameraman.

I stood up and said, "No camera in here. Period."

"Sure, sure," she said. "No problem, we'll do an interview outside anyway. Better graphics. So, just what can you tell me about all this?"

"All what?" Not exactly a brilliant response, but she'd come right out of nowhere.

"The man who died from the toxic exposure. The sheriff said you were up here, and you'd talk to us about it."

"Just a sec," I said, and pulled out my cell phone. Before dialing, I checked. Damn. The signal strength indicator wasn't even visible. Well, of course not. I was probably five feet from the X-ray room. I closed the case and said, "Excuse me, but I need to move away from the lead shielding," and pointed to the X-ray sign. I indicated Hester. "You can ask her about the dog we have in custody," I said, indicating Hester, "while I call the office."

I hustled down the hall as I heard Judy Mercer said, "Dog? This can't be a dog-bite case."

I had to stand inside the rest room, near the little window, before the cell phone worked. Lamar was gone already, Pam told me. Didn't say where he was headed. But, yes, he'd told the media to talk to me. He really, really hates the media, but honest to God, he could have warned me.

"Look, did he give you any idea what he wants me to say?"

"Not really. He just said, 'My investigator is at the clinic; you better talk to him,' and left." Pam was new. Sally would never let him get away with that.

I sighed. "Okay. Hey, you should be off by now..."

"Midnight to eight," she said brightly. "Just finishing my logs."

"Lucky you. Well, give my best to Big Ears, and I'll see what I can do with the media crap."

"Okay," she said, sounding altogether too happy. "It's always great seeing you on the tube."

I looked at the rest room window. My only other way out, and I'd probably get stuck. The way Judy Mercer worked, I figured I'd still end up on the ten o'clock news, explaining how a man died from some toxic substance while I was protruding from a rest room window. Not quite the image I wanted to project. Reluctantly, I went back out into the hall and began to walk toward Hester and the TV pair. I heard the muted sound of at least two separate phones ringing. Just before I got to the waiting area, I heard Henry's muffled but hearty hello from behind the closed door of the lab. Maybe I could palm this one off on him, if I could just get him out in the hall.

Hester, as usual, had things firmly under control. "Why don't you," she said, as she saw me approaching, "tell Carl what you just told me. I'm sure he'd be interested."

There was no camera running, no recorder. The best way to talk to the media, as far as I'm concerned.

"Well," said Judy, "like I said, I got a phone call really early this morning. A friend who said that there was something really interesting over at the U of I med complex, and that I should check it out." She shrugged. "Just chatting, really, over coffee. I found out that there were people suddenly donning protective gear, that there was a seal down in one of the labs...that they'd encountered a dangerous substance." She looked at me in a kind of personal way, totally unlike the "reporter being sincere and caring" look we normally get. "My friend said it involved a cadaver that had been received from up here in Nation County. Yesterday. Is this your murder victim, the one found on the road?"

Okay. In my mind, the words "dangerous" and "protective gear" just screamed contagious. That was my first concern.

"Contagious?" I asked.

"I don't know. The personnel at the clinic have protocols they follow. Some of it is precautionary. But I'm assuming that it's contagious."

"But nobody said so," persisted Hester.

"No. Nobody."

"Maybe not," interjected her cameraman, "but you might tell 'em about the hazmat gear in the back of our rig."

"That's just in case," said Judy. "But don't stray on me, here. Is this the murder victim from the roadway? And if so, how could a gunshot make him contagious? Or was it suicide?"

Just then, Henry stuck his head out of the lab doors. "Oh, hello," he said to Judy and the cameraman. "I didn't know you were here. Carl, Hester, could you come in here a moment?"

We certainly could. "We'll get right back to you," I said to Judy. "Just a few minutes..." I thought it would be best to keep her in one place, instead of wandering all around the hospital and clinic, prying. I hoped it worked.

Once in the lab with the door firmly shut, Henry just said, "How do they do it?"

"Who?"

"The TV people. They are here about the Gonzales case?"

"Yep," I said. "I don't know. Tips, mostly, I guess."

"Amazing," said Henry. "Anyway, I just got a call from the U of I labs. The good news is that it's not contagious," he said. "Not from secondary aerosol exposure, which is what you seem to have had."

That was a genuine relief.

"The bad news is that they think it's a toxic agent, one that is frequently mentioned in the chemical and biological warfare handouts."

"What?" That was from Hester.

"I'm afraid so. They think it's ricin, or something very like it, aerosolized, and with the Gonzales exposure within the last forty-eight to sixty hours."

I'd never heard of ricin. Hester obviously had.

"That's made from castor beans," she said, "isn't it." A statement, not a question.

"Yes."

"Is it only dangerous in aerosol form?" Hester's background as a crime-lab technician was showing.

"Well, I've got the info right here," said Henry, and reached over and picked up a brochure. "It says that ricin's also potentially fatal if ingested. But that the preferred method of distribution is airborne."

It took a second for me to realize some of the implications. "Gonzales works with food. Worked. Is that a big factor?"

"Maybe," said Henry. "I know he worked at the plant. We don't know how he contracted the stuff. What kind of work did he do there?"

"He carried swinging meat into the refrigerated trucks," I said.

"Then I suspect there's a reason for concern," said Henry. "Direct physical contact." He picked up the phone. "There's going to be a lot of activity around the plant," he said. "A lot." He began pressing keys. "Thank God it's a mechanical vector," he said, half to himself.

"A what?" I knew what a vector was. I also knew what mechanical meant, but I wasn't connecting.

Henry looked at me and held up his hand, then began to talk on the phone. I looked at Hester. She'd started her career in the Iowa Crime Lab.

"Whatever caused the condition," she said, "won't grow. Won't change. Not like a mutating bacteria. More like a poisonous chemical."

"Good," I said. "We only have one thing to deal with, then."

"Right," she agreed. "But that should really be plenty."

Henry hung the phone up, and said, "U of I lab. Good news. They say that it has to be in a pretty heavy concentration for ingestion to kill somebody. The greatest risk is with the elderly or infants. Infants don't eat much beef."

Better and better.

"Now all we need to do," said Hester, "is find out how Gonzales was exposed to the agent. That's our key."

"Well," I said, ever hopeful, "where do they use that stuff?"

"Nobody uses it," said Henry. "It's toxic. No benefit whatsoever. It's a natural by-product of the castor bean. Ricin is a small percentage of what you have left over when you make castor oil."

"Waste," said Hester. "Or it should be. This stuff, if I remember, would only be used as a weapon, intentionally, and after some difficulty."

"That's true," said Henry.

"Wonderful," I said. "By who?"

"Whom," said Hester automatically. "Hard to tell. But if you thought that the 9/11 anthrax-in-a-letter stuff was a tough one, this is ten times worse to trace. Ricin doesn't even require a particularly sophisticated lab to produce."

"Where does this stuff grow? Castor beans, I mean."

Henry held up his brochure again. "This thing is a gold mine. It says that the plant originated in Africa, but it grows throughout the southwest United States. For example. Anybody manufactures castor oil, they probably have the waste that contains this protein."

"It's a protein?" High school biology and chemistry were a very, very vague memory. I knew that meant something, but for the life of me I couldn't remember what.

"That it is," said Henry. "It's just a whitish substance. But it's very toxic."

"So, I'm trying to remember *anything* about proteins..."

"It's synthesized by living things," he said, keeping it simple. "But it isn't alive itself. So it's biologically produced, but can't reproduce. That's good news, by the way. We're dealing with finite quantities here. Not a rapidly expanding and mutating organism."

"Okay." Sometimes a simple response is best for changing the subject, and at the same time concealing ignorance. "Do we know anybody who manufactures castor oil?"

"Well," said Henry, "nobody springs to mind. It can be used as a medicine, to treat constipation...and I think as a lubricant and as a replacement for other hydraulic fluids in machinery..."

"But the oil itself isn't harmful, is it?" said Hester.

"No."

"So, even if they used it as machine fluid at the plant, the ricin wouldn't be present..."

"True," said Henry.

"It's a kosher plant," I said. "Very high standard for cleanliness. And they're even careful about what lubricants are used in the machines."

"The whole plant?" asked Hester. "I mean, is there some sort of nonkosher processing, too?"

"Well, Ben told me that they only use about the front half of the beef in kosher stuff, and that's the half that gets the full treatment. The back half is used for nonkosher, but the plant's the same, really. The difference is that the nonkosher stuff doesn't get soaked and salted, that's all." I'd asked Ben about that stuff a while back.

Even while I told them all that I knew about kosher, I was beginning to get a very bad feeling about the case. I think it had something to do with the "front half/back half" part of my explanation. My mind works that way. But if somebody wanted Rudy Cueva dead, and did him...and the same somebody wanted Rudy's good buddy Jose Gonzales dead, and did him—very likely over a drug deal—and we had a Colombian connection, which we did...and castor beans were grown in southern climates...

"This ricin stuff's really hard to trace, isn't it?"

"That's pretty much what we've been saying," said Hester.

I ignored that. "So, let's say you wanted to poison somebody, and you were from a warmer area where castor beans can grow, and you had access to ricin..."

"You think our two cases here are connected?" Hester raised one eyebrow. "Well, sure. Sure, I think you might be right. Which takes us back to a dope connection..."

"Which," I said, with some relief, "takes the case away from the connection with the packing plant, and gets us out of that little problem."

"Not quite," said Henry. "Noninvolvement with the plant has to be confirmed. That's a very urgent requirement. Very urgent. If he was exposed at the plant, there could be lots of people at risk. We have to know for sure."

He was right. But I was now prepared to have most of the interviews done by the Iowa Department of Health. That would free us to interview those who could do double-duty as witnesses in the firming dope connection and the death of both men.

"Would this stuff be good for popping somebody, though? Real world, I mean. Not in theory." I just tossed it out, more than half expecting a vague answer.

"Oh, sure," said Henry. "That's how the Soviets got a KGB defector in London years back."

We both looked at him.

"Hey," he protested, "I watch the History Channel."

Judy was waiting right where we'd left her, cameraman in tow.

"So," she said, "what can you tell me?"

Hester gestured for me to go ahead. "Okay, look," I said, "in the first place, it's not the victim from the roadway. That was one Rudy Cueva. This guy, as far as we know, was accidentally exposed to a toxic substance. We don't know where, and that's what we're looking for. His name is, or was, Jose Gonzales. We're very interested in his whereabouts for the last several days, to see if there's a possibility that anybody else could have been exposed."

That was probably one of my most concise and very best statements to the press, and I caught her with the camera off. Just my luck.

"What poison are we talking about?" asked Judy, as the cameraman signaled he was up and running.

I noticed that it was "poison" and not "toxin." Ratings.

"You'll have to ask Dr. Zimmer here," I said. "I don't know much about toxic materials accidents." I was kind of pleased with myself, getting that on tape.

"I have to do rounds," said Henry, heading back up the hall toward the main hospital floor, trailing media behind him. "But I'll be glad..."

Hester and I went the opposite direction, towards the parking lot and away from the intrepid Judy. We had lots of people to talk to and soon, and sure didn't want to waste time.

Hester said she had to check on something at our office, so we went there first. The "something" turned out to be Big Ears. She did an admirable job of faking it, though. While she stood by Sally, ostensibly getting some information from Des Moines via teletype, she just sort of incidentally picked Big Ears up and held him in her arms, scratching him behind the ears.

"You are so hooked," said Sally.

I'd never worked a case with Department of Health involvement, so I wasn't even sure who was supposed to do what. As soon as Hester was off the phone, she explained it to me, with one caveat.

"I never have, either," she said. "My office says that the medical people do the medical stuff, the safety and health people to their thing, and we just assist with things like warrants if needed."

"Sounds easy," I said.

"They also said that we conduct whatever interviews are requested by the health people, but we don't *give* interviews with anybody."

"Damned good advice," I said.

"They also say that the AG's office will be involved directly, but they want the local county attorney to be involved, too."

"Uh-oh."

"That's what I said. But they insist. It's policy."

"They have to realize that the county attorney would be a loose cannon, don't they?" As an elected official, the county attorney was answerable only to the voters, not to the attorney general's office or anybody else. I mean, it was a fine idea and had a sound basis, and all that. But in this particular case...

"I expect," said Hester, trying to allay my fears, "that they'll snow him under with facts, scenarios, potential law suits, and"—she grinned—"tales of lynchings. He should be so nervous, he'll just go along with the flow."

"That assumes that he's bright enough to understand the implications."

She considered that for a moment. "You're right. Well, we'll just have to watch him."

I sighed. "Okay. So, where do we start with the health stuff?"

"We wait until they get here and we meet with them," she said. "Until then..."

"We can get on with our murder?"

"Don't see why not."

"Excellent!" I said. "Okay, look, let me bring Lamar up to date, and then we go to Battenberg."

I figured I'd better tell Lamar about the health and the safety people about to hit the county. That sort of attention was bound to stir up some political stuff, and Lamar had to be aware of what was coming. We talked for only a minute or two on the phone. He was pretty much okay with all of it. Except the bit about the county attorney being involved.

"He's gonna be a problem, Carl."

"Maybe not ours, though," I said.

"My ass."

Lamar sort of tends away from optimism.

CHAPTER 12

 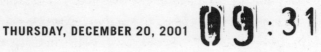

WE DECIDED THAT OUR NEXT MOVE WAS going to be to pay the late Rudy Cueva's girlfriend, Linda Moynihan, a return visit. Driving separate cars because we were probably going to have to be in different places throughout the day, we got to Linda's apartment in Battenberg at 09:30. No luck.

I called Terri on my cell pone.

"This is Houseman. You know where Linda's at?"

"She's at her place."

"That's where I am," I said. "No response on the phone, no answer at the door."

"Holy shit! She was sleeping when I left, but...look, over on the wall across from her door, there's a fire extinguisher. There's a key to her place wired to the bracket, behind the thing. I'll be right there...go ahead and go in. She might have ODed or something..."

"On what?" But I was talking to dead air.

Hester and I held a very brief discussion. This was fairly shaky ground, since Terri couldn't give us permission to enter Linda's apartment. She had, however, provided grounds for some concern as to Linda's well-being. That, and we had our own grounds for concern, as her boyfriend had just been murdered. Who knew?

About fifteen seconds after Terri hung up, we were in Linda's apartment.

We searched thoroughly and quickly, with Hester taking the bathroom and bedroom while I did the rest of the place. Nobody home.

"Her closet's got some big gaps in it," said Hester form the bedroom. "I think she might have packed."

I checked the kitchen and living room for notes of any sort, telling somebody she had gone. Nothing.

I heard somebody running up the steps and down the hall, and before I could get through the living room, Terri came flying through the open door. "Is she... is she..." she gasped.

"She's left," I said. "No OD or anything. Just gone."

Terri was in sweat pants and a hooded sweatshirt, no socks, and old tennis shoes. She'd hurried all right. She was panting and bending over to put her hands on her knees. "My damned"—she took a deep breath—"old car"—and another one—"wouldn't start." She took two more deep breaths and straightened up. "I hate that car," she said. She gasped again. "How cold is it?"

"About twenty, I think."

She nodded. "Original battery." Another deep breath. "So? What's up?"

Hester emerged from the bedroom. "Hi, Terri. Where do you think she went?"

"Boy, God, Hester, it beats me. You think"—and she took one last really big breath—"you think maybe they took her?"

"Who's they?"

"I don't know. Whoever killed Rudy." She began looking about the place. "I don't know."

"If they did," said Hester, "it looks like they let her pack. You have any idea where she might go?"

"Boy. Well, not right offhand. Maybe her mother's house? Shit, I don't know."

That sounded pretty good to me, except that Linda's mother lived right here in Battenberg. It didn't seem to me that she'd have to pack to go four blocks.

We let Terri make the call to Linda's mom. Zip. She had absolutely no idea where Linda might have gone. She was just getting ready to come over herself, to see how she could help, in fact.

Terri hung the phone up, having had the presence of mind not to mention us, and said, "So, then, her car's gone, too?"

"What's it look like?" I could also call Dispatch, and have them run all vehicles registered to her, but Terri would be much faster.

"Old wreck of a red Datsun pickup," said Terri. "It's always parked out back."

Hester said, "I looked out the back windows while I was in the bedroom," she said. "There's no vehicle at all parked back there."

Well, then.

A teddy bear caught my eye, sitting upright on the couch. "She left her teddy bear," I said. "I wonder..." and reached for it.

"Don't," snapped Terri, grabbing the bear. "She wouldn't have him with her." She paused. "It was a loaner. He's mine."

"Oh. Well, that's good, then." I looked around. No sign of any sort of disturbance, none at all. "It sure as hell looks voluntary," I said. "You gotta think, Terri, there's gotta be a place she'd go."

"I'm trying."

"Think about this first," said Hester. "*Why* did she go? Think if she's gone because she just can't handle it, or if she's gone because she's running from somebody."

"Hell," said Terri, "I don't know. I mean, you know I always thought Rudy was into dope pretty deep. I can't prove that, but the dude sure acted that way..."

"What way's that?" I asked.

"You know. They didn't have much money, but he always came up with what he needed to get things. The stereo. Clothes. He'd take off and come back a couple of days later, always had money for that." She gestured at the new TV. "That thing. Paid cash at my cousin's store for that. Didn't even have to go to Wal-Mart. Yet they couldn't afford a decent car. I heard him tell her that." Terri leaned against the kitchen counter. "He was always going to meet somebody, but wouldn't say who. For 'business.' That was all. I mean, I wasn't spying, but I saw him once, when he told Linda he had 'business,' and he was just driving around with some of his Mexican buds. You know."

"How long ago?" asked Hester.

"Four, maybe five, six weeks. At the Pronto Market. It was cold. I don't remember exactly when. It was after Halloween, though, because the candy was on sale." She shook her head. "Best guess is five weeks. Three, or for sure two, other guys in the car with him. Rudy was in the front, passenger side. I waved."

"He wave back?"

"No way. He pretended not to see me. That's how I knew whatever it was, it was no good. What he was doing."

Hardly an indictment. However, "You remember the car?"

"What car?" Terri was busy reading through the notes on the refrigerator.

"The one he was with his 'Mexican buds' in. When you saw him."

"Oh...yeah, sure. It was a kind of ugly tan, one of those Jap cars. Nissan, maybe? Honda? I can never tell."

Bingo. "You might describe it as maybe cream-colored?" I asked. "Or as we say around here, calf-shit yellow?"

She giggled. "I'd say calf-shit yellow fit it pretty well, tell you the truth."

That little exchange earned Terri fifteen minutes of our undivided attention.

Most of Terri's information was pretty vague. We went back over the photos we had, and she'd say "maybe" or "could have been" regarding everybody we thought might have been in the car with him. With one exception, and that was Jose Gonzales, aka Orejas. Great. The only two people in the car she could positively identify were dead. I said as much.

"Sorry."

"But the more you think about it, you're pretty sure there were four people in the car, total?"

"I think so, Carl. I know Orejas was in the backseat, and he was scoonched way over. There had to be at least one more back there, maybe even two."

"Why you suppose Gonzales was there? Is he a dealer, too? I mean, was—"

"Not much of one," interrupted Terri. "I think it was...well, Orejas wasn't Rudy's 'muscle' or anything like that...more like his portable witness, I think. I mean, like, you want to kill me, you're going to have to kill both—Oh, my God."

Couldn't have said it better myself. "It's a possibility," I said. "Nothing more. But we have to consider that."

"Linda figured it," said Terri. "She's running. Now I know that. Shit. She's afraid."

While Hester and Terri talked, I phoned in to the office to get an "all vehicles registered to" on Linda. There was just one, a red '74 Datsun pickup, Iowa license BHB 466. I told Sally to do an "attempt to locate," but just for our area, and not on the radio.

"You want an ATL, like, Teletype, surrounding counties?" she asked.

"Yeah. Use her DL information. Give the twenty-eight info, too." The 28 was the vehicle registration information. It was really 10-28, but we usually left the 10 off on the phone. "Tell our own people over the phone, or when they come in to the office. The teletype should say something about no radio traffic."

"So, what do you want me to give for a reason?"

"Say something like 'Wanted for questioning regarding a homicide investigation in Nation County.' That ought to do it."

"It sure as hell should," she said. "Stop and hold, or what?"

"If she's moving, do not stop, just advise location and direction of travel. We want to know where she's headed. Otherwise, like if she's at a motel or something, just have them notify us and keep her under surveillance until we contact them. We don't want her to get away, but I really don't want to scare her to death or piss her off by having her stopped."

"I'll try to rephrase that," said Sally. "What about out-of-state notification?"

"Just give it to Conception County by phone, attention Investigations. Harry'll take care of the rest."

Sally had already brought the correct form up on her screen and was filling in the blanks as we talked. "Armed, dangerous, suicide risk?"

"No, no, no."

"No clothing description, I suppose?"

"No."

"Warrant issued? Extradite?"

"Nope."

"Will we provide transportation?"

"Yes, we sure will."

"Good to go, sir!" she snapped out with enthusiasm. Sally had a cousin in the Marines.

I said, "You need anything else?"

"We're getting short on bacon dog treats. Forgot to tell you when you were here."

"I'll tell Hester," I said. "I'll call in later."

Hester and I left Terri with instructions to call us immediately if she heard from Linda. She said she would.

"And you might want to get out of here," I said. "If somebody is after Linda, you don't want to be mistaken for her."

We all left together, locking the apartment and replacing the key behind the fire extinguisher.

When we both got to the parking lot of Battenberg PD, Hester shut her car down and got into my car and we had a little chat.

Firstly, for somebody to kill two people over a dope deal, it had to be some pretty serious dope. Serious as to dollar value, not necessarily quality. Given either methamphetamine or ecstasy, we were talking a pretty large quantity.

"No way that much could be sold locally," I said. "Just not enough of a market."

"Could be a local thing, though," said Hester. "I mean, a message to lots of small dealers. Screwing with the franchise sort of thing."

"Yeah. We talked about that before."

"Yes."

It was quiet for a few seconds.

"Or, major amounts in transit," she said.

"Transit....Okay. If this is a major waypoint on the Mexican Pipeline, for example, they could have quite a bit of stuff. For that to happen—"

"—it would have to come in in quantity, for transshipment by another means," finished Hester.

"So we're both thinking the packing plant?"

"In via auto, out via meat truck," she said.

"Jose Gonzales humped meat into the trucks. What better way to ship crystal or X." That was certainly true. FDA rules mandated that a truck loaded with "swinging meat"—such as quarters or halves of beef—be sealed when it left the packing plant, and the seal not broken until the destination was reached. Any cop who wanted to search that truck, and consequently broke the seal, could be held personally responsible for the entire shipment. Several hundred thousand dollars worth of meat, all rejected at its destination because of a broken seal, and the cop would have to pay. Or, if he was lucky, his department would. Either way, it was just too expensive to risk unless you were absolutely certain the dope was there. Ergo, it was seldom done.

"Those trucks go all over the country?" asked Hester.

"I don't think so. I think they go to New York and Chicago, to major kosher delis there."

"All of it?"

"Ah...no. No, only the front half of the animal is kosher. The rest could go anywhere, I suppose."

"You think the management is involved?" asked Hester.

"I'd bet my life they were not," I said. "Not those guys. They're fanatics about cleanliness and reputation. No way."

"They'd cooperate with us, then?"

"I can't say for sure. They'd have to be convinced it was happening," I said.

"Ah."

We sat there in the car for a few moments, the only sound being the rush of air from the defroster.

Finally, I said, "I assume we're in agreement that we have two murders?"

"I think it would be safest to proceed that way."

"Best bet for a motive is dope?"

"So far."

I chuckled. "Okay, what's bothering you?"

"They'd have killed both of them the same time, same way," she said. "Poisoning just doesn't do it. It's not their style." She scooted around in the seat so she could come closer to facing me. "I've only had one toxic death in a dope murder, and that was years ago. They caught some dude ripping them, and they forced him to eat coke."

"Yeah?"

"Every other time, it was shooting, stabbing, or beating to death. Pain, humiliation, and in-your-face stuff. Something all the other little dirt-bags can identify with." She shook her head slowly. "Poisoning is too much like a Goddamned health issue, and too sneaky. Some petty-assed dope dealer is just too stupid to get a message from poisoning. Especially something like this ricin substance. No. No, it just doesn't fit."

"Okay," I said.

"Okay?"

"Yeah. Okay."

"Okay? *Okay?* All this great analysis and all I get is 'okay'?"

"You're eloquent. What can I say?" She was, of course, absolutely right.

"Well, anyway, I was going to talk with Ben about his. Maybe Hector instead?"

"Sounds like a winner," she said.

"But we *do* agree that they're related, right? The cases."

"Certainly. We just don't know how, and there's no physical or testimonial evidence indicating they are." She smiled. "Other than that little obstacle, sure, I think they're related."

"So, we just need the key, right? I mean, we've got lots of bits and pieces. I get the impression we're only missing one little bit of information, one little piece of evidence..."

Hester chuckled. "Well, you just keep thinking that, Houseman."

"I'm starting to hate this case. But I think we got it if we just get that one piece we're missing."

"It'll have to do," she said. "If it keeps you at it, that's what we need."

"Good enough for government work," I said, shutting off the car and opening my door. "Let's see if we can find Hector."

16:28

THERE WAS A CLATTERING, roaring sound outside that grew, then diminished.

"What's that?" Sally was peering through the cracks, straining to see.

"Sounds like a helicopter," I said. "Could be a police chopper from Cedar Rapids."

We heard it coming again. I hustled over to the door on the east side and cautiously peered out through the large, vertical crack. I just caught a glimpse of the helicopter as it went over, going from north to south. It was painted in the familiar red, white, and blue scheme I'd seen on TV so many times.

"It's the Goddamned KNUG 'Eye in the Sky' chopper. The news media."

If that thing flying over didn't stir the pot, nothing would.

My cell phone rang. It was the leader of the TAC team, who sounded assured, but not overconfident. That was good.

"We're getting in touch with that chopper, gonna get him out of here, but we want to check out his footage first. He's live, okay? He's givin' us a great view of the farm. He don't know it, but he is. As long as we're waitin' here," he said, "let's get back to who you got cornered up there." He was maintaining contact, probably to make sure we didn't do anything stupid before he could gain control of the situation. That was okay with me.

"I'm not sure who's got who cornered here," I answered. "We're more like a cork in a bottle, I think. You haven't been briefed by any feds, then?"

"I haven't talked to any here," he said. I heard him holler, away from the phone, "Anybody know of any feds around here? Check, will ya?" Then, more directly into the phone, and intended for me: "No. No brief by any feds, either."

Where to start and what to say. "Look," I said, "this is a federal sort of thing, and we have one FBI agent up here with us. He's on the second floor, kind of a lookout. He'll be down here soon as it gets dark. We've got three of us in the basement area. Limestone on three sides, hillside on the side facing west."

"Okay."

"Me and two female officers. One is a DCI agent, and she's been hit by a fragment."

"That wouldn't be Hester Gorse?"

"Yeah, it would."

"Sonofabitch," he said. "Tell her this is Marty, and we'll make sure we get her out."

"Okay, Marty. Mind if the rest of us come, too?"

"Sorry about that. You're all invited." He paused. "Feds still aren't here. What we got up there, anyway?"

"What you're gonna be dealing with is some people who have AK-47s. Some explosives, too. Okay?"

"Yeah?"

"They don't seem too...well...too capable. Don't get that wrong; they'll kill you if you screw up. But they don't seem all that aggressive to me. You know?"

"Okay..."

"Some of these guys, they got guts. Just not all that sharp. Be careful."

"Got it."

"We're getting a little concerned about it being dark real soon. I think they might try to get away. Watch the perimeter."

"We must have fifty cops out this way. Most of 'em are surrounding the area."

"Good."

"I gotta talk to my supervisor," he said. "Lieutenant Granger. He ought to be here shortly. But what I'd like to do is get you guys out of there, and put my people in your place as the cork."

"Sounds good to me." Boy, did it.

"Okay, I'll get back to you real quick, soon as the lieutenant gets here and I have a chance to talk to him. But be careful yourself," he said. "Instead of making a break for it, they might go for you in the dark."

This had occurred to me. "Right. Sounds like you got a good plan going there," I said. "Go for it."

"We just have to be real heads-up until they get up to us," I said to Hester and Sally. "We don't want a fuck-up at this stage."

"Oh, yeah," said Sally.

"The TAC team leader's a guy named Marty," I said to Hester. "He says hello and that he'll get us out."

"Marty's all right," she said. She sounded encouraged.

About two minutes later, my cell phone rang again. I answered, surprised that Lieutenant Granger had gotten to the perimeter so quickly.

"Hello!"

"Deputy Houseman? Is that you?"

It took me a second. "Hector? Is this Hector?"

"Yeah, you betcha," he said, brightly, in his best Norske accent.

"Hector, I'm kinda busy right now..."

"I know, man. I just heard about the cops trapped in the barn out there. It's all over TV. I thought I might have some information for you to tell them..."

"To tell the cops in the barn, Hector?"

"That's right. About some people. The ones I think might be up there with them."

"I'm one of the cops in the barn," I said. "I'm really busy."

"Holy shit," he said. "You are in the barn?"

"Yeah."

"Right now?"

"Hector..."

"Look, you gotta be *really* busy," he said, speaking very fast, "so I'll make this really quick. There are four people I have never seen before, they been asking questions around town today, about Linda, man, and Cheeto, and all of them. They wanted 'specially to know where the farm was, man. They ask lots of people. They ask me while I am in the Pronto getting cigarettes."

"They cops?" I asked.

He laughed. "No fuckin' way, man. They ain't exactly TV personalities, either."

"You don't know who they are?"

"No, but they look to me like they were in a hurry. You know? No hanging out. Right to the questions."

"Hey...what kind of car, you know?"

"Sure. I am your best informant. You know I know. It is a green Dodge van, pretty new, with Nebraska license plates. I don't have the numbers; I gotta admit I missed the numbers."

"Plenty good enough," I said. I thought Hector was on to something. If so, we now had the identity of the people who were shooting at us. Just to firm that up, I asked him what time he'd seen them.

"One o'clock or so," he said.

That pretty well fit in with what had happened. I figured they must have gotten to the farm just before we did. I thought I had what they call a "high probability" of being right on this one. "Excellent," I said. "Very good. Tell you what: give it about three minutes, okay? Then call nine-one-one and give the information to the dispatcher, okay? I can't get the information to everybody from here. Okay?"

"Sure, man. Three minutes. *Tener cuidado*, Mr. Houseman. You be careful. I see the barn on the TV, and it looks pretty fuckin' lonesome up there where you are."

"We'll be careful," I said. "Just make that call." I broke the connection. "That was Hector," I said to Hester and Sally. "Just a sec..." and I called the office private line and gave the information that Hector was going to call 911.

Then I called One on the walkie-talkie and asked him to check the chopper broadcast for a green van parked somewhere on the farm, outside my view.

"I don't know for sure," I said, "but it looks like it might be the vehicle that brought these guys."

"Ten-four, Three."

"Call the office on a phone, One, and they can give you the background." I was still not convinced the men in the shed didn't have a scanner.

"Will do." I heard his breathing change. "I'm goin' over to the TV truck right now. They got everything on tape."

"Ten-four. How we comin' with the TAC team?"

"The lieutenant is here...just got here."

"Ten-four."

About five minutes later, Marty, the TAC team leader, called me on my cell phone. He was pissed off.

First, there was a question about watching the tapes. The technician in the TV truck said that, as far as he knew, anything that went out over the air could be shared with the "authorities." He just wasn't sure how much of the chopper footage had actually been broadcast by the station.

"You gotta be kidding."

"Negative. We got a call in to the station manager. He's gonna call."

"Right. Okay. Well, that's great."

"That's not so bad. I was watchin' most of it as it came in, before it got 'official,' and I didn't see a van. But," Marty asked, "you ready for this?"

"What?"

"Things are kinda stalled on this end."

The lieutenant, apparently, had decided that, since this was a federal matter, his TAC team would act in support, but not take any overt action until the federal agents in charge were at the scene and could assess things for themselves.

"Policy," said Marty. "I can't change it."

"Right." Crap. I really didn't need this.

"What I can do, though, is deploy my people on both sides of the lane. We can give you supporting fire toward the silo and in the main yard right up to the edge of the barn."

"Right." I didn't say anything more for about two breaths. "I guess that's what we get, then."

"We can give you covering fire if you can make a break for it," he said.

"We'll keep that in mind."

"Does that yard light up there work, do you know?"

"It did the last time we were here in the dark," I said. "Two, three days back."

"Then we'll take it out. We've got night-vision goggles. No problem."

"Don't do that! Jesus, we're gonna have little enough light here anyway. You take that out, we'll be blind."

"But then they can see my people as soon as they break cover."

It was hard not to tell him how little that bothered me. "Just don't do it, okay? If that light has to go, it's on our request only, understand?"

This time, he was the one who paused. "Okay. You bet. Look, man, this wasn't my idea. If I had my way, we'd be up there right now. But they tell me it ain't an *active shooter* situation."

"Yeah. Yeah, I know. They sure as hell were pretty active a little while ago." I thought I'd try to lighten it up a bit. "Do we have anybody on scene that can promote you to captain?"

"Let me ask around," he said, after a pause. "I like that."

"Okay. Gotta go. Call as soon as you have a change of orders, okay?"

"You bet. Be careful up there."

"Hey!"

"Yeah?" I caught him just before he terminated the call.

"I don't know if anybody told you or not, but there's only one uniform here in the barn. Female sheriff's officer. The rest of us are in street clothes. Just like the bad guys."

"No, nobody told me that. Thanks."

"My pleasure," I said.

"Okay. You be careful up there, now."

I was getting a little tired of people telling me to be careful.

Not five seconds after I broke the connection, there was a really weird sound that came floating down from the area of the shed. It was a human voice, no doubt about that, and it sounded kind of like...well, a rebel yell with lyrics covers it pretty well. I certainly didn't understand the words, if that's what they were, but it sounded as if it were meant to be intimidating.

At that moment, for some strange reason, it occurred to me that I'd very likely killed two men. I thought about that. I didn't feel any remorse. None at all. I didn't feel different. I didn't feel happy, either. It was weird. I'd never killed anybody before, and I'd always thought it would affect me strongly. Whatever the effect it was having, I was pretty sure it wouldn't stop me from shooting the next guy who lobbed a grenade at me.

There was a loud thud against the barn, and then another. Having learned my lesson with the first grenade, I hunkered down and yelled "Get down!" just as the two explosions went off, not more than a second apart.

I caught a lot more dust this time as the blast wave whipped through the gaps in the boards and cleaned off the top of the foundation stones.

Like I say, I'd learned my lesson. I got my head up as high as I had to in order see out my little peephole, stuck my rifle through the boards, and looked for a target. Nothing. Nothing in sight, no movement, nothing. And it was getting really dark there in the shadow of the hillside.

I fired three shots in the general direction of the shed, just to discourage whoever was thinking about throwing some more at us. Sally, who apparently thought, "If Houseman has a reason to fire, so do I," blasted one twelve-gauge round from her position a split second after I stopped. Silence.

"How damned many of those things you think they got?" asked Sally.

"I dunno," I said. "A bunch, I guess. You okay?"

"Yeah."

I turned to Hester. "How about you?"

She nodded and gave a wave of her hand.

I looked up through the stair opening and toward the hayloft. "Why don't you give George a try," I said to Sally. As she began to talk, I squinted out my peephole again.

The light had gone, and if I were going to be able to see anybody, they'd have to be wearing white.

"George is on his way down," said Sally. "Look sharp!"

I looked as hard as I could, for all the good it did me. About ten seconds after she spoke, there was a loud thump on the floor above us, and then George came clattering down the steps.

Not a shot was fired. In the gloom, that didn't surprise me.

"Boy, it's dark down here." George took a deep breath. "How's Hester?"

"I'm fine," she said, from her post near the rear wall.

"Oh, there you are....Boy, I don't have a clue where those last two bombs came from. I couldn't see shit up there."

"It's no better down here," I said, "but at least we can act as a unit again."

"Right. Is there a TAC team up yet?"

"Well, yes and no," I said. I thought I heard a radio squawk. "Anybody hear that?"

CHAPTER 13

WHILE I TRIED FOR HECTOR AND BEN, Hester was on the phone to her headquarters in Des Moines, checking for assistance. There was just too much to do for us to be able to get it done in a timely fashion.

Hector wasn't answering his phone. He virtually slept with the thing next to his ear. There was only one place where he'd turn it off. While Hester was still contacting her boss, I said, "I'll be over at the library."

I walked the two blocks. Normally I would have driven, for the sole purpose of having the cop car immediately available if I needed it. You learn to appreciate wasted time when somebody calls for help. This time, though, I thought it might be better if I were to keep it out of sight. My car was unmarked, but in a rural area, an unmarked cop car becomes very well known very quickly, and I was pretty sure just about anybody who I didn't want to recognize it would do so immediately. Hector, being the nervous sort, might appreciate that.

The big electronic thermometer outside the savings and loan read twenty-two degrees. It would get worse in the next thirty days, so I tried to enjoy the twenty-two degrees as I walked toward the new library. I met two rabbis walking toward me. Both were dressed in black hats and ankle-length black coats. Quite a contrast to the blue jeans and brightly colored down vests I was accustomed to encountering.

"Hi," I said as we passed.

I got looks of complete incomprehension. They were probably New York born and raised, and strangers just didn't say hi out of the blue. I chuckled to myself as I walked. Sooner or later, they'd be greeting me back. Well, if they stayed long enough. Like Ben had told me, "You can take the rabbi out of New York, but it's very hard to take the New York out of the rabbi."

I walked another fifty feet toward the library, toward the building the rabbis had left. Meier's Deli. It hit me as soon as I saw the sign. I stood outside, and called the sheriff's department on my cell phone.

"Nation County Sheriff," said Sally.

"Hi. It's Houseman. Can you do me a favor?"

"What a unique request," she said.

"Just a fast one. We have any more reports of sick or dead people? Anybody been in the ER, or the clinic, or anything?"

"Beats me," she said.

"That's the favor. Call Henry. The unlisted cell phone number he gave us. Ask him. It's really important."

"On TV once," she said, and I could hear the keyboard clicking in the background as she called up Henry's listing in the Dispatch database, "they had something called the 'blue men' or something, and they were trying to get a common location, or... let me put you on hold..."

That was what made her such a good dispatcher. She could think. Sometimes faster than the rest of us.

A few seconds later, I was back on the line. "Houseman, you still there?"

"Yep. Whatcha got?"

"No cases. Zip. Nothing at all."

"Excellent. Thanks, kid."

"It was a story I read in high school," she said. "'The Eleven Blue Men.'"

"Okay."

I went into the deli and spoke to Abe Meier, the owner.

"Abe, where do you get your meat?"

"Our meat? You want to know where we get our meat?"

"The beef is what I need to know about," I said. "Where does that come from?"

"The plant."

"The plant here in town?"

"Of course here in town. There is a problem?"

"I dunno, Abe. How often do you buy beef from them?"

He thought for a few seconds. "We go through one, one and a half quarters each week. If we're having a good week. Not so good, maybe one. We sell fresh; we don't freeze."

"You buy any since last Monday, maybe?"

"We buy each Wednesday. You're asking me this for a reason?"

"Give me one more answer, and then I'll tell you," I said. "What kind of truck do they use to deliver it? One of the eighteen-wheelers, or one of the smaller trucks?"

"We get it ourselves. In my wife's truck," he said.

"Your wife's truck?" I'd seen his wife driving around on occasion. "I thought she drove a four-wheel-drive Subaru?"

"For the taxes," he said, "it's a truck."

As I entered the library, I almost turned and left. There was a class of about thirty fourth-graders and a teacher sort of invading the place. They were all over, and Martha Taylor, my former classmate and current librarian, was helping round them up. She saw me, glanced over toward the computers, looked back, and gave a little wave. That triggered the memory that she'd been one of our high school cheerleaders, and that we'd called her "Boom Boom." Boom Boom the librarian. I couldn't suppress a grin.

I recognized the back of Hector's head at the second computer, and that's just about all that could have persuaded me to stay.

I waded over to the computers through the noisy herd of runny noses and tennis shoes, and tapped Hector on the shoulder.

"Hi there," I said.

He just about jumped out of his skin. "Holy shit, man, doan do that!" he said, startled. "I coulda had a heart attack, man."

"Sorry. It's probably all the noise in here. Got a minute?"

"Ah, not right now I don't..."

"Sure you do. Let's go to our table."

I let him lead. I couldn't see anybody else in the place who might be making him so nervous, but I only looked as we traversed the place toward the table. There could have been somebody else in there I didn't see.

"Have a seat," I said.

He pulled out a chair and turned it about forty-five degrees from the table before he sat in it. Easer to bolt that way, and easier to make it look like he didn't want to talk to me if somebody was to observe us. I really liked Hector.

As I sat, I said, "Okay. Now I know much more than I did when we talked the last time, and so do you. Let's compare notes."

"I don't know much more," he said.

"Sure you do. You know Orejas is dead. Or Jose Gonzales, or whoever he wanted people to think he was."

"Sure. That's common knowledge, man. Orejas, he got sick."

"He sure as hell did," I said. "But I think he got sick and died because somebody made him sick."

Silence.

"I think you know who did that, and why."

"I doan know why you would think that," he said, but a smile was trying to break out on his face. "I just work here."

That was one of my old lines. "I don't buy that any more than you did," I said. "Let's talk about where Rudy got his money."

"The plant." The grin was trying harder.

"Yeah, right. For three bucks an hour. Thirty-nine hours a week. That's a hundred and...seventeen bucks a week. Tell me more."

"Okay," he said. "I'm cooked." The grin came out, and he looked around. "Okay, this is gonna be fast."

"Right."

"You think because he's Colombian, he's connected, he sells dope, and he gets rich, doan you?"

"It *had* occurred to me," I said.

"He used to be, man. Dope-connected, okay? But no more." His smile disappeared. "He still is connected. He is still Colombian, see? But not dope, okay? Not dope. No more dope."

"Okay?" That didn't leave much.

"If I say more they will kill me, too."

"Well, neither of us wants that," I said, kind of surprised at the sudden intensity.

"I doan want it much more than you," he said.

"Sure. So, Orejas was killed by the same people as Rudy, then?" I was just fishing, but sometimes that produces pretty good results.

"You know he was."

Well, I pretty much did now. "Why?"

Hector was about to crap, I swear, but he hung in there. "They used him, and Rudy did not like it. They lied and they used him."

"Who?"

"Hey, you got to earn that big money sometime," he said, and the smile tried to come back. It didn't make it.

"The calf-shit yellow car, the thin-faced man, and two or three others." I said it flat, matter-of-fact, because I wanted him to think I was really confident that they were the ones. Well, hell, they were the only ones I had.

"You should eat well this week," he said.

"Why? Why did they do him?"

"Rudy?" He glanced around again. "He got pissed. About Orejas. It surprised him."

"Wait a second. Orejas died *after* Rudy was killed," I said.

"He was not pissed because Orejas was *dead*," said Hector, sounding like a very patient teacher. "Because Orejas, he was still alive at that time. It was something else. Somethin' they did to him. But it was before Orejas was dead, I can tell you that, because I heard about it last Saturday. That's all I know, man," he said. "I gotta go. Too many people could come in here."

Looking back, I know he wasn't just making an excuse, but at the time it struck me as kind of lame.

He simply stood, zipped his jacket, said, "I will listen for you," and walked out the door. With a room full of fourth-graders, there wasn't a damned thing I could do about it. I sure as hell didn't want to go running out the door after him. Way too much attention.

But I had more than I'd started with. Not too bad for ten minutes' work. I stood more slowly than Rudy had, pushed our chairs back under the table, and waved at Boom Boom.

Now, if I could just find Linda...

I was just getting back to the PD when Hester came out, looked around, saw me, and waved for me to hurry. I got all hopeful that she'd gotten some key bit of information. No such luck.

"We've got to get back to the office; the Public Health people are here and we need to go to the briefing."

"How soon?"

"Noon. Let's go."

I looked at my watch. Eleven thirty-four. Damn. "Any word on Linda?"

"It's only been an hour or so, Houseman. Patience. You find Hector?"

"Yeah," I said, and told her what I'd learned.

"This just gets stranger and stranger," she said. "*Before* he died, huh?"

"That's what he said, and that he heard about it last Saturday already."

"Couldn't you get him to say more?" She had her car door open. "He's got to know more."

"I was surrounded by munchkins," I said across the top of my car as I opened my own door. "Tell you about that later."

We hit the office at about five to noon. The parking lot was jammed with vehicles, including all our officers, on duty or off. Three unmarked cop-type cars, four smaller cars with the white decals of the State of Iowa on the side, the County Health nurses' Bronco, Doc Zimmer's car, and three or four I didn't recognize.

Hester and I had to drive around the back and park in the prisoner-unloading area.

"Jesus," I said as we got out of our cars. "It looks like a football game or something."

"It's getting worse," she said, pointing to the street below the jail hill. "Look who's here."

Judy Mercer, her cameraman, and their white and blue KNUG four-wheel-drive were backing down from the main jail parking lot.

"Well, this time she's not our problem," I said. But we hustled into the jail anyway, just to be sure we weren't caught on camera again.

Once inside, we were crammed into the kitchen with all the drivers of those cars we'd seen, plus the county attorney, two people from the state attorney general's office, and three DCI agents. I recognized the oldest of them: Art Meyerman, an ex–Nation County deputy, and a royal pain in the butt. I waved at him across the room. He barely acknowledged me. Crap. Art was an obstructionist martinet by temperament and choice. What the hell was he doing here?

"I see they sent Art," said Hester.

"Yeah. Whoopee." I glanced around the kitchen. "Why him?"

"Beats me," she said. "Last I knew he'd been transferred out of Intel. Don't know where he went, but I thought he'd been pretty much moved out of useful."

I could buy that.

Lamar gave a general introduction that lasted about fifteen seconds. More or less, a "listen up and take notes" word to the wise. He then turned it over to an assistant attorney general, whose name eluded me when the compressor for the kitchen refrigerator kicked in. He apparently concentrated on health and safety issues. He was brief, and only told us how important it was for everybody to cooperate.

Next, we got Iowa's Deputy Director of Emergency Preparedness, who outlined the pecking order for conducting the investigation. She also gave us a good five minutes on keeping our mouths shut, and measures in place for preventing panic. Good stuff. She had handouts, which I also like.

Next, the Iowa Department of Health people briefed everybody on ricin, its effects, and its methods of transmission. I had one moment during that part of the briefing, when the speaker asked if anybody knew what a mechanical vector was. Hester and I were the only two cops who raised our hands. That scored points for us, even if I'd only known for five or six hours.

From that point on, it was emphasized about every five minutes that what we were dealing with was not "catching." One of the Health folks, a Dr. McWhirter from Iowa City, also briefed us on prophylactic measures.

"Basically," he said, "all you have to do is wear a decent filter mask, like this one." He held up something that looked like a simple dust mask for working in a shop. "This is a very fine filter system; you can't pick them up in a hardware store, but you can buy them at your local pharmacy. And," he said, "remember to wash your hands. That's it. That's all it takes." He paused. "Oh, also," he added, "if you come across some contaminated food, just don't eat it."

It sounded like an afterthought, but I thought that was a pretty key point. So, apparently, did Lamar.

"You hear that, Carl? No lunch!"

There were a couple of laughs. There would have been more, but lots of the people in the room had no idea who I was.

After that little tension-breaker, I felt a bit silly, but I raised my hand, getting a dark look from Art. He was the sort who thought any question was a matter of showboating. That went a long way toward explaining why he never seemed to get completely with a program.

"Yes?"

"Would cooking decontaminate food?"

"Protein is pretty tough stuff," McWhirter said. "Might. I wouldn't want to rely on that, though. Iffy at best."

"So we get this stuff," asked Lamar. "Then what? You haven't said anything about an antidote."

"That's right," said Dr. McWhirter. "There is no antidote."

That sank in for a second.

"The treatment is supportive. That means we do what we can for the symptoms and let things take their course." Dr. McWhirter looked out on the unhappy faces. "I wouldn't be too concerned; the LD50 levels are really high for this substance."

"What's LD50?" asked Lamar.

"LD50 is shorthand for what would constitute a lethal dosage for fifty percent of the exposed population."

"Oh."

"Any more questions? Okay then, let's get on here..."

The Health briefing continued, with them handing out the same sheet of questions we'd gotten from Henry that morning. They then went over each question, explaining why it was being asked, why it was important, and how that answer would be used to further the investigation. It seemed to take forever.

When that segment was over, the assistant attorney general got back up and outlined the approach to the groups of people to be questioned.

"Since we are starting off with the supposition that Gonzales was exposed at his place of work," he said, "we'll begin with his coworkers."

My hand shot up.

"Yes?" He seemed irritated.

"Most of them are unavailable at this time," I said.

"Pardon?"

"Most of them are Hispanics who worked with Gonzales at the plant. Most of them are here illegally. There was a murder Tuesday up here, and it involved a member of the Hispanic community. The illegals all went missing. They're afraid we're going to find them and deport them." I paused. "We're looking for them right now, but so far, no luck."

"Just how many people are we talking here?"

"As many as a couple hundred," I said. "They had to close the plant on Wednesday, and it's not back up in operation yet."

I had to give him a lot of credit. He didn't miss a beat. "So, we talk to the plant management first. I assume they're not illegal aliens, too?"

"Absolutely not," I said.

"Excellent. We'll assign a team to interview them, along with health and safety inspectors to go over the plant, and you can let us know when you find the missing people."

"Okay," I said.

Just when I thought we were done, our own county attorney got to put his two cents' worth in. His "Hi, I'm Carson Hilgenberg, and I guess I'm supposed to say something here" was vintage Carson. What followed didn't exactly enhance his position.

"I think this is, uh, a really worthwhile endeavor. I want you to know my office is open for you, and I'll be there to help you understand these heavy legal complications as they come up."

Honest. He even made little quote mark gestures with his fingers when he said "legal complications."

He paused, and then said, "I'll be happy to answer any questions regarding this case, if you have any."

I was about to raise my hand and ask him for a definition of protein, but Hester beat me to it with a real question.

"What authority do we have to act here?"

"Pardon?"

"If somebody asks us under what authority we are questioning workers and inspecting premises, what do we tell them?" she asked, just as though she didn't know.

Carson Hilgenberg simply looked toward the assistant attorney general and said, "Maybe you'd like to take this one?" He had assumed the role of emcee without blinking an eye.

The deputy AG never missed a beat. He pulled the appropriate citation from his open briefcase and read it to us. "According to Chapter 135.35 of the Code of Iowa, 'All peace officers of the state when called upon by the department shall enforce its rules and execute the lawful orders of the department within their respective jurisdictions.' You have officially been 'called upon.' Any other questions?"

I love those "toss it to the nearest cop" sections of the Code. They were put there by legislators who didn't want to fund any enforcement arm for Health, but who just couldn't leave them with no muscle at all. So they assigned cops to them upon request. The problem is, having virtually no prior training or experience, if we were requested, we had to spend time in long meetings just to get up to speed.

"What do we charge somebody with for noncompliance?" Lamar. Good boy.

"Ah, just a sec...the next one...here. Cite them under 135.36. Interference with authorized agents of the Department of Health." The AGA looked at his audience. "That's you."

"Talk about potential!" said Deputy Mike Connors, one of our longtime guys. "Spread your cheeks and freeze!"

"Knock it off. How much penalty does that section have?" Lamar, again.

"Simple misdemeanor. A hundred and fifty-five dollars, with court costs," said the assistant AG. He spread his hands at the groans. "I know. But let's just make a procedure now. You bring 'em here; you don't cite into court. Haul 'em in. Fill out a complaint and affidavit. No automatic ten percent bond. You call a magistrate. That way, it gets 'em out of the hair of the other members of the investigative team. For a while. How's that? If you can't beat 'em, annoy 'em," he said.

That went over well. I leaned over to Hester. "I like this guy," I said. "Who is he?"

"Morton Bligh. Really. And *everybody* calls him Captain already, so don't start."

"Which of you are the ones who first saw the body of Mr. Gonzales?" asked Bligh.

Hester and I held up our hands.

"I'll need to talk to you two in a few minutes, so stick around, okay?"

Hell, why not. We'd shot most of the day by now already.

CHAPTER 14

BY THE TIME EVERYBODY GOT SORTED OUT AND SQUARED AWAY, we ended up sitting down with Bligh in my office at 3:30 in the afternoon. He brought Dr. McWhirter along with him.

"So, you two were the lucky ones," Bligh said.

"Yep. You have our preliminary reports yet?"

"Attached to the main case file already. Good reports. What else can you tell us about this Gonzales?"

I figured what the hell. "Gonzales was the best friend of a man who was murdered, execution-style, the day before we found him, Gonzales, in his room. Dead guy's name was Rudy Cueva. Both claimed to be either U.S. or Mexican citizens, but as far as we know, Cueva, the guy who was shot, was from Colombia, and we think Gonzales was, too. Both seem to be illegals."

Bligh and McWhirter just stared.

"Both were employed at the meat-processing plant. Both are suspected of some sort of narcotics involvement, past or present, but we can't confirm that. We have reason to think both of these men were murdered, but we're having one hell of a time getting any hard evidence for Gonzales."

Bligh cleared his throat. "You're saying that ricin was deliberately...applied... to Gonzales?"

"It begins to look that way," said Hester. "The only problem is, that's not the way drug-related killings go down. Not poison, at least not delayed action. They're usually really violent: knives or guns, like this Cueva murder. Instant gratification."

Bligh leaned forward in his chair. "Let me get this: Cueva was killed on... ?"

"Tuesday," I said.

"And your investigation led you to Gonzales."

"Only as a witness, and one before the fact. Gonzales wasn't an eyewitness, as far as we know. He was Cueva's best friend."

"Right. And who sent you to Gonzales? Who thought it was a murder?"

"Nobody," said Hester. "The county needed a response to an unattended death. Carl and I were together working Cueva's murder. We were all that was available," she said. "The Battenberg officer called us for assistance in a simple unattended death, and that's what we thought it was at first."

There was a scratching sound at the door. I thought it was somebody playing a joke, and said, "Not now. We're busy."

It persisted. I got up and opened the door. Big Ears, who had been standing on his hind legs to scratch, tumbled through the door, spotted Hester, and galloped over to her outstretched hand.

"That's Big Ears," I said, smiling. "Named after Gonzales. It was his dog, and now there's nobody but Hester who wants him."

I got a questioning look from Bligh.

"Uh, okay, Gonzales was called Orejas, that means 'big ears,' or so we're told. The dog was under his bed."

Dr. McWhirter spoke up. "The dog was in the room with the dead man?"

"Yep. Been checked by the vet. He's just fine."

"So," said Bligh, getting us all back on track. "You think Cueva *and* Gonzales were murdered."

"Yeah," I sighed. "I'm afraid it sure looks like it."

"Because of some drug involvement?"

"It's the only thing that even begins to fit," said Hester, lifting Big Ears up to her lap. "It fits the pattern, except for method in the case of Gonzales."

"You aren't absolutely certain as to motive, then?"

"Nope," I said. "Not yet, anyway. Cueva's live-in girlfriend might be a big help with that, but she split on us early today. We've got an ATL out on her, but apparently nobody's seen her yet."

"She's illegal, too?" asked Bligh.

"No," said Hester. "She's local, born and bred."

Bligh shook his head. "You two really stepped into one, didn't you?"

"Houseman's cases are always like this," said Hester. "He never has a simple one."

"I try," I said, "to make it interesting for everybody. So far, I've succeeded beyond my wildest dreams."

Bligh got out a notepad. "So, you two have any information as to how the ricin was, uh, applied, to Mr. Gonzales?"

I looked at Dr. McWhirter. "I was thinking the Doc here might know that."

Dr. McWhirter cleared his throat. "I helped with the autopsy, and the subsequent testing," he said. "We had a wide variety of symptoms, from gastrointestinal chaos to virtual drowning from pulmonary edema. That perplexed us. It appeared to us that we had a case involving both aspiration and ingestion."

"Really?" said Hester. "Both?"

"Yes. And in highly concentrated doses in both methods. Highly. In my opinion, he was as good as dead after the exposure. No amount of care would have come close to saving him." He paused again. "We were wondering just where he could have been to acquire that heavy dosage."

"His last day of work was Monday," said Hester. "We know that. He worked the late shift. We found him on Wednesday, about 18:00 or so. He'd been dead, what, Carl? You thought about twelve hours?"

"From the rigor, yeah. About that."

"Makes the time of death about six A.M. Wednesday," said Hester. "Infection at thirty-six hours puts it at six P.M. on Monday. End of his shift at the plant, or thereabouts."

"So, it happened at the plant, then? Could it be an accidental exposure? An informant claims it was 'something they did to him.' But the informant wasn't a witness," I said. "Could we be talking accidental here, after all?"

"I'd expect a broader contamination, if that were the case," said Dr. McWhirter. "We only have one victim here. That's a pretty narrow exposure."

We decided that Hester would accompany Dr. McWhirter to the Gonzales apartment, along with two techs, to recover any dirty laundry he might have had and to test the shower and washbasins. Everything would be tested for contaminants.

Bligh and I were to go to the packing plant and get the ball rolling. Two health and safety inspectors came along.

Bligh suggested that the county attorney, Carson Hilgenberg, go with Hester and her team so we had a legal presence at both locations. Hester rolled her eyes, but accepted it.

Bligh and Hilgenberg did a fast application for a search warrant, and I went with them to a local magistrate's office, where I signed as affiant. At that point, even though we'd lost most of a day, we were finally getting back on track.

Bligh and I got to the plant at 16:21, according to my watch. I'd called ahead for Ben, and he'd agreed to wait for us. I hadn't told him much, but I'd made it clear that this was very, very important.

We were ushered immediately to Ben's office. When the door opened, I saw a very familiar face with Ben.

"Hey, George!"

"Carl." He didn't look at all happy.

"Who's that?" asked Bligh.

"That's Special Agent George Pollard, FBI," I said to Bligh. "We know each other from way back. How ya doin?" I said, sticking my hand out to George.

"Wonderful," said George, flatly. "Just wonderful."

"This is Mr. Bligh," I said, unable to remember his first name. "Iowa AG's office."

"Call me Mort," said Bligh.

"Glad to meet you," said George.

"And this," I said to Bligh, "is Mr. Chaim B. Hurwitz."

"Call me Ben." When he spoke, I looked at him more closely. Ben looked terrible. My first thought was that he was sick.

"So, what brings the FBI to Nation County?" asked Bligh.

Now, that was a truly good question. FBI anywhere in Iowa these days was a rare event all by itself. It was another example of the effect of 9/11 on everybody. On September 10, 2001, there were tweny-six FBI agents working in Iowa. By September 15, about twenty-four of them had been assigned to terrorism investigations. You didn't even expect to see one at a bank robbery anymore. To spend one on a meatpacking plant was most unusual. What was more unusual was that I knew for a fact that George had been assigned to counterterrorism.

"I'm afraid it's an aspect of what brings you two here," said George, reaching behind us and closing the door. He stepped back toward Ben's desk and picked up a file. "I assume you're here about the ricin?"

"We are," I said. "You, too, huh?"

"Yes."

"What's up?" I found it kind of difficult to believe that the Bureau was concerned with the death of one illegal immigrant.

"We were notified by CDC in Atlanta that there had been a case of ricin ingestion in Nation County," said George. "Maybe you two should sit down," he said to Bligh and me.

We two did.

"Like I just finished telling Ben here, CDC found themselves working two separate but contemporaneous cases involving ricin poisoning," said George. "Yours, and an outbreak in New York City."

"New York?" I was surprised, to say the least.

"This is terrible," said Ben. "Terrible."

"We have four dead people in New York," said George. "All from ricin. We have fifty-seven who are ill, with at least one more who is not expected to survive." He checked his file. "The lab people say that they think many of the ill are psychosomatic reactions, because several are good friends of deceased, but didn't eat the same things. Not all of them, though. It takes time for this stuff to finish its job. They started getting sick enough to need medical attention on the fifteenth. Three cases. Eight more on the sixteenth, twenty-two on the seventeenth, twenty-nine on the eighteenth. One of the first three died on the seventeenth. He was a deli employee, by the way. Three of the cases from the sixteenth were also fatal. They're all older people, so far."

"Holy shit."

"It gets worse," said George. "All the victims except two are Jews. We have a vector of three specific delis in the city. Everybody who was infected either worked at those delis or ate meat purchased there. Everybody."

"Oh, crap," I said. I saw what was coming.

"During Hanukkah," said Ben softly. "They got sick eating our meat during Hanukkah."

George nodded. "Right. As luck would have it, those three delis get most of their beef products from this plant." He looked at Bligh and me. "What we have here is very possibly a hate crime. Regardless of the motive, we suspect an act of terrorism. Domestic or otherwise."

George shut his file. "Carl, could we meet at the local PD, or your office, when you're done here?"

"You bet." I looked at Bligh. "Why don't you get your information from Ben here, and George and I'll go over to the PD. Call over there when you're done; I'll come get you." I was really anxious to hear more from George, and I was sure he didn't want to talk in front of Bligh and Ben.

George and I were in the Battenberg PD within five minutes. The chief wasn't there, but the city clerk let us in just as she closed up.

"Jesus, George. What's up?"

"We're considering this a terrorism case, Carl."

"Okay. Sure. Domestic, though, I assume?"

"Not necessarily."

"You're kidding?"

He wasn't. As it turned out, several known terrorist groups, including Osama bin Laden's Al Qaeda network, were known to have recruited the services of non-Muslim terrorists to do some of their dirty work. The "recruits" were readily available through the terrorists' established drug connections, and came equipped with at least some expertise in the required areas.

"Most important," said George, "these individuals aren't tagged as extremist Muslim terrorists. Some Thais, some Laotians, some Colombians, Mexicans, and...you know, Carl. Anywhere there's a foreign importer of illegal drugs, they have a connection. France, Afghanistan. they use those connections to recruit. Lots easier to conceal their activities that way. And," he added, "they're always overseen by the faithful. Well, 'the fanatical' would be more accurate. The radical, fundamentalist Muslims are always in control."

"Recruiting unemployed muscle from the cartels..."

"Yep. That's one source."

"And that's what we have here?"

"With your Mr. Jose Gonzales, I think it's possible, if not downright likely," said George. "What makes you think he's from Colombia?"

I told him what we'd discovered and included the fact that the main information had come from a confidential informant. I did not name Hector.

"We did establish, based on the tip, that the address for Cueva in L.A. was false," I said. I went on to explain the duplicate Social Security numbers. "It sure would explain some stuff...they're recruited, but for money, I suppose?"

"Mostly," he said. "At least they would be, if I'm right about the connection."

"So, like, 'hired' might be a better term, though? Not to split hairs or anything..."

"Hired," said George, "is a good term. We prefer 'recruited,' though, because if we collar some of them, we don't want to piss around with the defense demanding a paper trail for their 'hired' services." He produced the first honest smile I'd seen from him that day. "I'd hate to have to produce a W-2 for one of 'em. It's a practical thing."

"Gotcha."

"I called my office a couple of hours ago," he said, "right after Ben told me about this Gonzales man. Our experts assure us that there's virtually no chance that the ricin was contacted accidentally. That say there's no chance it's used in meat processing. No way, not even if they used castor oil to lube the machinery. Ricin's a by-product, and nobody anywhere near here refines castor beans." He gave me a worried look. "Ricin was one of the major weapons of mass destruction that Saddam Hussein was trying to produce in quantity. Lots of the research was done there, and we destroyed a bunch of the stuff right after the Gulf War. That's another reason we think it's not a home-grown problem."

"You're kidding."

"No. Iraq produced a lot of it. But, hell, they weren't the only ones. Anyway, last I heard, CDC was sending two people up anyway, and they may send more now. Look, I better set you up for our briefing."

"You gotta be kidding," I said. "You're gonna have a briefing? Christ, George, we just got out of a state briefing." George was a friend. Maybe. "Could you get me out of this one? I'm losing valuable time on my homicide case here."

"Not out of this one," he said. "You'll be doing part of it." He looked at his watch. "The plane carrying the CDC people has already landed. Cedar Rapids. They should be driving up now. The FBI joint intelligence team has members on their way from D.C., and they should be getting to Cedar Rapids within a few hours now. Can you be ready to give them a summary of what you have in, say, four hours or so?"

Shit. "Ah...let me call Hester. She'll have to be there, too."

"Hester is DCI's agent on the homicide? Excellent!" George and Hester had worked together before, too.

"Yeah. It's just been old home week around here." I stood. "Look, I've got an informant I'm looking for, and a missing female who was the live-in with Cueva, who split on us."

"Are these already set to be interviewed, or are you just planning to talk to them at some time?"

I thought that was a strange sort of question. "Oh, planning, I guess. Actually, we have an ATL out on the woman, probably APIA. No response yet, as far as I know."

"Why don't we go to your office? Just a suggestion, but don't you think you should expand the APIA?"

APIA stood for All Points, Iowa. That meant that every police teletype in Iowa got the relevant Attempt To Locate data.

"Upper Midwest?"

"Let's go national," he said. "From you, though, not from us. Just for now. It's a security thing. How long has she been gone?"

"Not more than twelve hours."

George and I rounded up Bligh from the plant and went to the Gonzales apartment, where we linked up with Hester, Carson Hilgenberg, and Dr. McWhirter. When George walked in, it was one of the very rare times I've ever seen Hester floored.

"George? What on earth...?"

Carson Hilgenberg stepped forward. He didn't know George, but he'd apparently decided he was important. He introduced himself.

"Glad to meet you," said George. "I'm Special Agent Pollard, FBI."

"Really?" asked Hilgenberg.

"Really," said George.

While George filled in Hester, Hilgenberg, and Dr. McWhirter about why he was there, I called the office on a land line and had a chat with Sally.

"Hi. Hey, we gotta go national on the ATL for Linda Moynihan."

"Uh, sure...okay...but I'll need more information. That's a formal request, so we need a wanted/missing person's report...just a sec..." and I heard her mutter to herself, "page 939..." She was looking at the NCIC manual. "Uh, can I do her as a missing person? For that she has to be mentally disabled, or abducted, or..."

"No, no. Just wanted."

"Has a warrant been issued for her? I really need a warrant for that."

NCIC, the National Crime Information Center, is the overseeing authority for all police teletype messages, and they have pretty stringent rules. "Not yet. Can we just say one will be, ah, obtained in the future?"

"Yeah..." Sally sounded reluctant. "WWBI, Warrant Will Be Issued. But I better have a warrant number within twenty-four hours, or I'm in trouble. With a bond attached. And it better include a 'Will Extradite' or you ain't gonna get much of an effort out of anybody. But you gotta get a warrant..."

"Okay. Do that. WWBI. Call her a material witness in a homicide case."

"Right. That was the easy part."

"Hey, is the media around up there or anything?"

"Around? Well" and I could hear her voice fade slightly as she stood and walked to the window "out here in the parking lot I count three TV Broncos. Is that enough?"

Even the press, apparently, had a problem with keeping secrets. I'd thought that only Judy Mercer from KNUG would be there.

"Thanks," I said. "We'll be back in a while. Get ready for some company."

"What?"

"Better break out the thirty-cup coffeepot. You're going to have guests. That's all I can say." I looked over at George, who was listening to my end of the conversation. "Sally," I said, indicating the phone.

George came over and said, "Let me talk to her." I handed him the phone.

"Hi, Sally! It's George of the Bureau." He knew his nickname, apparently. "Yes! Pretty soon, you bet. Hey, this really has got to be kept pretty quiet for right now, okay? You have any trouble with getting any of the messages you want out, or accepted, or anything, call this number..." and he pulled out a business card and read a series of numbers to her. "Tell her it's on my authority, S.A. Pollard, and give the word 'buoyant.' Yes... b-u-o-y-a-n-t. Got that? Okay, and I'll be looking forward to seeing you!"

That done, Hester drew our attention to the unmarked spray can that I remembered seeing the first time we were in the apartment.

"We think there's a good chance that this could be the delivery system for the ricin," she said. "We haven't touched it yet...but we have to wrap it securely and forward it to the FBI labs in D.C. It looks just like an ordinary spray can. But if you look at it really closely," she said, pointing with her pen, "you'll see that it's not a can that's had the label torn off. No glue marks, no residual paper patches, nothing. But, it *does* have a commercial serial number on the bottom."

"So, where'd it come from?" I thought that was a good question.

"Not sure," she said. "I do know, though, that major paint stores will make up spray cans to special order. You buy the paint; they put it in the can and pressurize it for you. That's a possibility."

"I didn't know they did that," I said. "Cool."

"There's also a box of synthetic vinyl exam gloves inside a shoe box in the closet over there," said Hester. "It's opened, but I don't know if any are gone."

The things you miss if you only think it's an unattended death. "No smoking guns?" I couldn't resist.

"Well, not exactly," she said. "However, there's also a pair of dust masks, labeled N-95 Particulate Respirators, in the same shoe box. They're just for dust, though. Tell them what you said, Doc," she said to Dr. McWhirter.

"I don't think that kind of mask would be particularly effective against the ricin spray," he said. "I'd wear something with much finer filtration if I was going to be around that. And it isn't really adjustable enough to make a good seal."

"It's labeled in English," said Hester. "We've had absolutely no indication that Gonzales, or whoever he really is, had any English at all." She shrugged. "Or that he'd understand the finer points of filtration, anyway. A mask is a mask."

"Right."

"I figure the can isn't leaking," said Hester, noticing that I was edging back toward the door, "because Big Ears didn't get sick."

"Sure," I said, backing up and leaning up against the doorframe. "Good point."

"So," said Hester, "lacking any other information, I'd say that our man here used this spray can to spray the meat that went to New York. Most likely when he carried it into the trucks. I'd say that he used the mask and gloves to protect himself, and somehow either failed to do it right, or soon enough, and the mask was inadequate anyway. Maybe contaminated himself when he took the gloves off. He used a mask that provided some protection, but not enough. Maybe it slipped. Maybe it wasn't tight."

"Inept," I said. "Nontrained, then. Just told to use it but not how?"

"You just earned a place on the speaker's stand," said George to Hester.

"What?"

He told her about the next meeting.

"Swell," said Hester. "Just swell. Not that I'm not glad to do it," she said, "but we really need to get moving on the homicide."

"I know, and I'm sorry," said George. "We'll free you up as soon as possible. Really."

"Just one of those little adjustments," I said.

"But we do have an hour or so, I suspect," said George. "Why don't we make some appointments to talk to the fellow workers...you know, the ones who worked with Gonzales and this...?"

"Cueva," I said. Hester and I exchanged looks. "You wanna tell him?"

"No, go ahead," she said. "You do it."

"Tell me what?" asked George, falling neatly into the setup.

"Well," I said, "we've got a bit of a problem interviewing the coworkers. The majority of them are not here...well... legally."

That really got his attention.

"It appears that they all left the area the night after Cueva was shot," I said. "A couple hundred of 'em, at least. They had to shut down the plant, so many were gone."

"Well, damn," said George.

"That's what we said," said Hester.

"We're looking." I explained about Wisconsin, and Harry's search over there. "No luck yet."

"They could have run to a major metro area," said George. "Gone forever, in a practical sense, if they did that."

"We're hoping," said Hester, "that they drift back when the heat's off. Next day or two."

"I hope you're right," said George. "We're all going to need to talk with those people."

"We have a couple of names," I said helpfully. "Maybe you guys could help us find them? They could lead to all sorts of good things..."

During this exchange, both Attorney Bligh and Dr. McWhirter started to get a little fidgety.

"Ah, we're sort of out of our purview here," said Bligh. "Our concern is the toxic substance and its effects. Ah, if you think this is a criminal matter..."

"You're in this for the duration," said George. "We might be wrong. Unlikely though that is. But we need your work to establish a basis in fact for our case, sort of the antithesis, so to speak. Or the thesis, and we do the antithesis. Whatever. We need you to prove that an accident either did or did not occur. This is going to be a really multijurisdictional effort, in all respects."

Neither Bligh nor McWhirter looked particularly pleased at that.

When we all got back to the sheriff's department, Hester and I ducked in the back door to avoid the media people who were sitting in the main parking lot with their engines running. I really thought that somebody should have at least had the courtesy to ask them in to the booking room, where there were a couple of seats and it was warmer, but I didn't say anything. I didn't say anything because the first person I met was Lamar, who greeted me with, "Where'd all those damned reporters come from?"

"Beats me," I said. "George Pollard is right behind us, and he wants to talk to you. When he does, you'll know why Hester and I have to get our reports up to date in the next couple of hours. We gotta get busy," I said, passing him and heading down the hall.

"You got us in trouble again?" he called after us.

"You betcha!" I called over my shoulder.

About an hour later, when Hester and I were about done typing and sorting things out, Lamar came into my office. He even knocked before he opened the door. That was rare.

"You think this is really this big?"

"You spoke to George, right?" I asked, looking up from my stack of case photos.

"I sure did. What do you think about this? Is he right?"

"I think so," I said. "It sure takes care of some very loose ends."

"How about you, Hester?" he asked.

"There's a good chance they're on to something," she said. "The connection to the delis in New York just about clinches it."

"Damn," said Lamar, and sat down in on my desk. He picked up a few photos, but wasn't really looking at them. "As soon as the media got wind of the CDC people showing up here," he said, "they started pissin' and moanin' about 'access.' God, I hate it when they do that."

"Wait until after the briefing," said Hester. "I think the feds will have a spokesperson assigned. They'll handle that."

"I hope so," said Lamar. "I'm always afraid I'm gonna say somethin' and accidentally give somethin' away. It's worse 'n court."

"This is so far out of our hands," I said, "I think we can just concentrate on making sure we know who killed Cueva."

"Easy for you to say," he said. "I been on the phone with Abe Goldstein." He glanced at Hester. "He's the guy who owns the plant. The media have been calling him at his office, and at home, all day. He claims he's the victim of anti-Semitism. Hell, he's right. But I don't know what to tell the poor bastard. He says he's about to be ruined, that he and his family have spent their whole lives making good on his father's reputation for top products. Now he says the 'authorities' say his food kills his friends and relatives in New York. What the hell can I do?"

"It's not his fault," said Hester. "Not that that'll mean a damned thing."

"He wants to know if we can help him make sure it won't happen again."

"We'll do our very best," she said. "You *could* tell him that the plant being shut down right now is the best thing that could have happened to him. With the health people going over everything, we can make sure he's off to a clean start when production starts again."

"Maybe," said Lamar. "Oh, and while I'm at it, I had to send an officer back to court with another application for a search warrant."

"What?"

"Yeah. Mr. County Attorney Hilgenberg walked off the premises after the first search and left his file folder in the apartment. He didn't discover it was missing until after he got back here."

One of the things about search warrants is, you have the right to be there as long as it takes you to do the search. But you can't go back ten minutes later, not without another, separate search warrant.

"That man," said Hester, "is going to drive me crazy. I hope nobody got into the apartment and read his file."

"He doesn't think so," said Lamar. "But, like I say, the media gets things that way."

Hester and I got on with what we were doing. One thing you have to be constantly aware of when writing a good police report is that you need to differentiate between what you know and what you suspect. Cueva's origin was a good example.

"We know he's not from L.A., and that he used forged a Social Security number and birth certificate," said Hester. "We have anything confirmed that he is actually from Colombia?"

I leafed through my notes. "Nope. Well, Hector said Cueva was Colombian. Nothing confirmed, though."

"Okay..."

We both assumed Hector was probably right, and I felt that he'd given us good information. But we hadn't been able to confirm it.

Another thing you have to be able to do is be absolutely certain you don't leave anything out. Bad leads, for example, have to stay in the report, and you handle them until you're satisfied that they're bad. You *always* say what criteria you used to discount information. Otherwise, the defense gets hold of it and tries to make it sound as if you ignored the *real* evidence just to focus on their client. This can lead to some pretty interesting conversations between investigators.

"Okay, we believe anything she's told us?" I asked, meaning Linda Moynihan.

"Sure," said Hester. "Just the indirect, though. Emotional state." I knew she was referring to Linda's reaction at the autopsy, and later.

"So...really grief stricken...maybe even surprised?" I was referring to Rudy Cueva's death in general. Hester picked that up right away.

We both thought about that for a moment. "Not surprised," said Hester. "Not necessarily. Maybe just really unhappy."

"So the reaction could have been...well, probably was more like 'Holy shit! They said they were gonna do it, and they did.' You think?"

"That's fair," said Hester, going through her own notes and looking for something else. "Might even be a case of 'I told you so, Rudy.' Maybe that..."

"Gotta find her," I said, and went back to the keyboard. "Really quick."

"That goes in your part of the report," she said. "I'm still on the scene."

"Okay. Be sure to tell me when you figure out who the white guy is standing there when Cueva gets shot." I was only half kidding, because we really needed to figure out who in the hell that man was.

"Sure. When you tell me who Rudy really was."

"And then the ricin..."

"Oh, no. The ricin's yours. All yours. I'll go the connections route, summary, thing." She was already typing on her laptop again.

"Good enough."

George stuck his head in once, bringing us coffee that Sally had made. "She says this is her best stuff," he said.

I was impressed. Sally had a small bag of specially ground coffee she'd picked up in Dubuque. Nobody had gotten to do anything but smell it brewing, except Sally herself.

"I, uh, made a couple of calls, based on what you told me. ATF's going to helicopter an agent up from Des Moines."

"ATF?" said Hester.

"The shell casings," said George. "We think there may be another connection.

We're having all of them dusted, by the way. Thumbprints..."

When you load a magazine with shells, you tend to press down pretty firmly on the shell casings as they go in, especially the last few. It was a possibility.

"The DCI lab hadn't gotten to that?" I was kind of surprised.

"Probably not," said Hester. "The legislature had us get rid of overtime for the lab personnel for this year. I'd think the technicians would be concentrating on the homicide evidence from the scene itself."

"We picked the casings up from your lab. They're being flown back to our labs in Washington." said George. Then he added defensively, "Well, we had a plane going that way anyway."

"Some got resources, some don't," I said, trying to lighten things up a tad. "We could have offered our facilities, but the high school chemistry lab closes at three forty-five."

"Speaking of labs, George," said Hester, "you wouldn't happen to have a couple of large hazardous material containment packages, would you? I need two tubes, concentric, the smaller one being able to hold this can, plus a couple of hazmat or biohazard stickers."

"In my car," he said, "I've got evidence tubes. No biohazard stickers, though."

"I've got some of those," I said absently. There was a silence. I looked up. "What?"

"What on earth are you doing with those?" asked Hester.

"Oh, Sally snagged a bunch of 'em from the hospital. She stuck the things all over my lunch containers and my sauce bottles. She had a couple of rolls left... they're in that drawer over there."

"Figures," said Hester. "I don't suppose you'd have any address labels for the FBI labs?"

"Check with Dispatch," I said with a straight face.

George let us get back to our reports.

16:56

IT WAS LAMAR ON THE RADIO AGAIN. Apparently he'd been calling, but in all the commotion we hadn't heard him.

Sally cranked up the walkie-talkie volume and reassured him that we were still alive and as well as could be expected. However, as she so succinctly put it, "We could sure use some company up here, One."

"We're working on it," said Lamar, and I could really hear the strain in his voice, even ten feet from the walkie-talkie.

"What do we think?" asked George. "We haven't seen any movement for a while."

"But we've sure seen grenades," I said. "I think they're still there, if that's what you're asking."

"I was thinking about that," he said. "Could those have been a blind, to distract us while they slipped over the bluff?"

"Possible," I said. "Lamar says there are about fifty cops watching the perimeter, though. Maybe more by now."

I heard Hester's voice, but I couldn't make out the words. "What?"

She stood, took a big swig from her water bottle, and then did sort of a gargle thing that ended in, "Ahh!"

The water had hit one of her broken teeth. She shuddered for a few moments, shaking it off, and then said, "No. They won't be leaving."

"How so?"

"They're protecting something," she said. "By stayin' here, distracting us some way." She made as if to take another swig, thought better of it, and said, very deliberately, "Deception."

"Okay," I said. "You want to sit back down?"

She shook her head.

"You're above the wall," I said, indicating the limestone foundation. She crouched.

"So, you think they will stay at us, not trying exceptionally hard to take us out, but to keep us here?" George didn't sound fully convinced.

Hester made an exasperated sound in the back of her throat and said, "Not just us!" She made a sweeping gesture. "Us!"

I got it. "They think we were headed up there. They aren't trying to *get* out. They're trying to keep *us* out."

"Yes!" she said.

Sally, as usual, put her finger right on it. "Why?"

Damned good question.

We didn't have any sort of a good answer. We all moved back to positions where we thought we could cover the approaches to the barn fairly well, and made that our priority. The whys could wait.

"Hey, George?"

"Yes?"

"Can I have my walkie-talkie back?"

He tossed it to me. "Sorry about that."

"No problem." I checked the frequency setting and keyed the mike.

"One, Three?"

There was a momentary wait, and then, "Three, go ahead!"

"Yeah, One, get Marty on the TAC team to call me on my phone, and you try to listen in, okay?"

My phone rang about two minutes later.

"Houseman," I said.

"Anything new we should know about?"

"Marty, we been thinking up here, and we tend to believe that they're keeping us out, rather than us keeping them in."

After about a two-second pause, Marty said, "No shit?"

"Yeah."

"Hang on for one."

If we were right, it meant that the allocation of personnel out there could drastically change. Rather than concentrate on preventing the remaining shooters from leaving, they could concentrate on advancing and go at them more aggressively. I hoped.

"Okay, Carl. Could be. We'll check it out. Okay. Look, about the van...we got the station manager to let us look at all the footage, and we can't see any van parked up there." He paused, and then said, "But that really don't mean shit, because we think it could be parked in one of the sheds."

"Oh. Sure."

"We see two, ah, objects, about fifty feet west of you, along a fence. They might be people, we aren't sure, but they didn't move."

"I believe they're dead," I said.

"Say again?"

"If those are the two I shot," I said, "they're dead."

"Way to go!" Marty sounded genuinely pleased.

"That's the location where they toss grenades," I told him. "You might want to keep an eye on that area."

"You bet! Okay. We got two choppers headed up: one from CRPD, and the other is a National Guard bird, an OH-58. Both have FLIR, so we can check the heat from the shed and see if we can maybe find that van."

"Great."

"And once they get here, we're gonna be able to see the whole area like it was daylight, so we can keep you advised of movements. And the feds just got here. A whole bunch, and a chunk of the FBI Hostage Rescue Team is already in Cedar Rapids."

Things were looking up, and I said as much.

"You got that right," said Marty. "Okay, now, about them bein' there to keep you out? Is that right?"

"That's what we think, yeah."

"Any idea why?"

"Nope. None. But you might ask the feds."

Ten minutes later, I was concentrating even harder on trying to see in the dark. My eyes were getting used to the shadow, pretty much, and I thought I could discern individual things like rocks and scrub. But try as I might, I couldn't see that fence where the two dead men were.

I thought about calling Sue. She wasn't the sort to watch the news all that much, but I thought it might be a good idea to let her know I was okay. Just in case somebody called her and told her there was something up. On the other hand, if she didn't know anything was going on, and I called, then she'd start watching for TV spots, and God only knew what kind of speculation she'd be hearing then. Well, now was the best opportunity I'd had to do it, and I thought I shouldn't waste it.

I dialed home.

"Hello?"

"Hi, there."

"Carl, oh my God, what's going on? Oh, I'm so glad you called. Are you all right? We're watching the news...are the officers in the barn all right?"

It all came out in a rush.

"Well, yeah, I'm fine. Really good, in fact. Who's the 'we' watching TV?"

"Phyllis came over about ten minutes ago, and told me that Nation County was on CNN."

"Oh, okay." Phyllis is our next-door neighbor.

"You're sure you're all right?"

"Oh, yeah. I'm fine. Really." Maybe, I thought, she won't ask about the barn again.

"Who's in the barn? Lamar?"

"Well, no, actually. Ah, it's George, and Hester, and Sally, and, well, me."

"You!!!!"

"Yeah, but I'm fine. Really."

"My God!"

"Now look, I didn't call to worry you. I'm really sorry about that. We're going to be fine." Now would be about the worst time for one of those damned grenades, I thought. All I needed was a loud bang in the background.

"Can't you get out?" A reasonable question.

How to put it. "Well, we probably could. But Hester's been hurt a little, and we think we're much safer in here. Mostly we're going to wait for an ambulance..."

"Hester? Oh, Lord."

"Hey, don't tell anybody anything about that. Nobody knows that except us folks, okay?"

"Yes."

"Look, I called to tell you that everything is going to be just fine. Really."

"Okay."

"I'm gonna have to go in a sec, but I just wanted you to know."

"Oh, I'm so glad you called," she said.

"Me, too. Look, don't worry. If I thought I was in really serious shit, I wouldn't call. You know that."

She didn't. But she said she did. "Yes."

"Okay, well..."

"I love you."

"And I love you, too. I'll be home as soon as I can." That, for sure, was absolutely true.

Now, however, I had an additional problem. Prior to talking with Sue, it honestly hadn't occurred to me that I might not be going home after this one. I pushed that thought to the back of my mind, but the new awareness was now there. Damn.

Sally was back at her lookout. "Can you see anything, Carl?"

"Nope."

"Me, either," said George.

After a second of unnatural silence, I glanced back at Hester. She was just taking a good swig from a water bottle. When she finished, she said, "No!"

Well, that had been enlightening. Either there was truly nothing moving, or it was just too damned murky out there to see anything.

"Where's the Mr. Heater?"

George turned. "I'll get it, Hester. You're right, it's getting cold in here." He went to his heap of luggage, turned on a pocket light, and hustled the portable heater over to Hester. "I'll have it lit in just a second," he said. "How are you getting along?"

As the two of them talked, I kept peering into the gloom. Ah. Over by the left edge of the shed, just where the fence started, and where the two dead men were, I thought I caught movement.

"Left of the shed!" I said.

George was back at the wall in a second. There was a moment, then, "I don't have it."

"Where the fence starts. Nothing moving there, but there's a really dark spot right next to the shed..."

"Yeah...." From the tone of his voice, I could tell George still hadn't located the object.

"Just wait. If it's really something, it'll move again."

We waited. When you stare at an area in the dark, if there are variations in the shadow, you're eventually going to see something move. Whether it does or not. I was just beginning to get the feeling that my eyes had been playing tricks, when a figure suddenly stood, right where I'd seen the movement, and a very loud voice called out.

"Fuck you! Fuck every one of you!"

Then he was gone. Just like that.

We in the barn looked at each other. "What the hell," said Sally, "did he do that for?"

"They're trying to provoke us," said George.

I laughed. "Too fuckin' late."

CHAPTER 1 5

THURSDAY, DECEMBER 20, 2001 **19:30**

SEVEN-THIRTY IN THE EVENING isn't a really good time to start a meeting. Nonetheless, there we were, once again crammed into the kitchen of the Nation County Jail. The attendees of this second meeting of the day were considerably more upscale than the first. There were people representing the FBI, DOJ, CDC, FDA, DEA, ATF, OSHA, and the NSA. Iowa had sent command level people from the DCI and DNE, as well as the EMD. I felt like I was watching CNN.

It all hardly seemed real, the unreality enhanced by the faint strains of Christmas music coming from the adjacent dispatch center.

FBI was represented not only by George Pollard, but also by our old acquaintance Special Agent in Charge Volont. We'd had some, well, difficult times with him in the past, but nothing horrible. Volont was a good agent, just a bit Bureau-centric, as they say. This time, he seemed genuinely happy to see us. With him were two others: Special Agent Gwen Thurgood, a counterterrorism specialist, and one super special sort named Special Agent Milton Hawse. Hawse was younger than Volont, but obviously someone of great importance in the Bureau. All the other federal employees deferred to him. It wasn't a respect sort of thing, so much as just really lots of rank. Well, that's the way it looked to me.

The Department of Justice had sent a deputy U.S. attorney from Cedar Rapids, named Harriet Glee. She'd been working out of the Cedar Rapids office long enough to be known to most of us as "Dirty Harriet." It was a compliment, and a heartfelt one at that. She was hell on wheels, and one of the best prosecutors in the business.

The Centers for Disease Control had sent a team of three; the Food and Drug Administration, one.

The Drug Enforcement Agency had hustled two of our old friends up from Cedar Rapids, one of whom was Katie Martinez. I was particularly glad to see Katie, as she had worked both L.A. and San Diego for DEA, and we were going to be in dire need of a Spanish-speaker we could trust absolutely.

The Bureau of Alcohol, Tobacco and Firearms had also sent somebody I knew and respected, Agent Brian Chase. I didn't know the two Occupational Safety and Health Administration people, but they both looked pretty intense. I like to see that in somebody who's been sent to help on a case.

The National Security Agency was just so far from my experience, I wasn't even really sure what they did. They'd sent two people, though, both of whom were about as un-spy-looking as anybody I'd ever seen. All the feds treated them with great deference, though. Unlike the FBI's Hawse, these two were treated that way from pure respect. One of the NSA men was introduced to me as Edward Peasley, an expert in biological warfare. Cool. The other was Herb, no last name, who simply said he did "some code work."

Present from Iowa's Division of Criminal Investigation was Hester's boss's boss, Special Agent Barney England. Iowa's Division of Narcotics Enforcement had sent Bob Dahl, who'd worked closely with us when one of his fellow agents had been killed on a dope stakeout back in 1996. Sitting next to him was a guy from Iowa's Emergency Management Division. He was going to be a critical player, as all requests and demands for emergency management were going to have to go through him. I thought that, with the rather bizarre health hazard that was being revealed, he was going to be one busy man.

Present from Nation County was County Attorney Carson Hilgenberg, along with Deputy Mike Connors and Dispatcher Sally Wells. Sally was key, as most of the communications were going to have to be coordinated by her.

I tried to count heads, and got at least twenty-one people in a room that should have held ten. With only sixteen chairs, including the ones from Dispatch, all the Nation County personnel were seated on the kitchen counter. We were the hosts, after all. George gave Hester his chair, and joined us.

Lamar and Volont threaded their way over to the refrigerator, where they called the meeting to order and made brief statements about cooperation and common goals. Volont explained that those present were part of a newly constituted team that had been assembled at very short notice by Special Agent

Hawse, under the new multiagency mandate that had occurred after 9/11. Volont told the assemblage that Hester, Lamar, Sally, and I had worked with him before, on a fairly well-known case against an extremist called "Gabriel." He said that we were to be trusted. Thank you, Agent Volont. Then he tossed me a real curve.

"I've checked, and the ricin didn't come from our U.S.-based right-wing extremists."

The "What?" just sort of came out of my mouth unbidden. "I never knew that they were into that."

"Oh, yeah," said Volont. "It was my assigned area when we worked our last case together. The extreme right had a strong interest in ricin at that time." He shrugged. "You just didn't have a need to know."

That sort of pissed me off, since the case he referred to had been a major terrorism investigation we'd worked. Together, supposedly. "I sure could have come up with one, if you'd asked me," I said. I shrugged. Volont was a bit of a jerk sometimes.

Hester and I briefly outlined our cases to date, Hester doing Cueva, and then me with Gonzales. Sally'd made copies of the case file, and passed them out to everybody present. We'd managed to wangle the use of the super-copier at the *Nation County Bulletin*, and were therefore able to pass out good copies of the photos from Linda and Rudy's album. As I got to those, we got two instant hits.

Katie Martinez's hand shot up. "Katie?"

"Hell, this is Rudolpho Orejuela," she said, holding up her copy of Rudy Cueva's photo. "We associated him with the Cali cartel in Colombia, a couple years ago. He was busted by the Colombian authorities. He escaped from the Cathedral a while back, along with a whole group. I know this man."

"Past tense, Katie. And what's the 'Cathedral' thing?"

"Oh, right," she said, and laughed. "Knew. Sorry. The Cathedral is a Colombian prison. Orejuela broke out the same time as some of the Medellin cartel people, you remember Pablo Escobar? Rudolpho Orejuela, he got his start with Escobar, and then got hired by the Cali people. After that, he was identified as a FARC associate. We IDed him in a surveillance in San Diego last year."

"FARC?" I asked.

"Big-time bad," said Katie. "That's the Fuerzas Armadas Revolucionarios de Colombia. A guerrilla organization, terrorists, based in Colombia. Hates the U.S. Strong drug ties."

"Oh," I said, thinking, Jesus Christ! "So, what did he do? Sales?" I asked. Hopefully.

"Oh, no. Not smart enough. Orejuela was muscle. He killed people for hire, or burned down their houses, or friendly little things like that. He was only fair at it, though." Katie tapped the photo with a forefinger. "I heard they tossed him out, but I can't say for sure."

"So, he would have been...what? Working for the cartels?"

"Oh, no," she said. "He screwed up enough to get caught for offing somebody, they didn't want to use him much after that. He was known to the cops. They busted him out along with the rest, to send him back into the hills where he could just work inside cartel territory. That's where we think he hooked up with FARC."

"Would he have prints on file?" I asked. "We have case prints."

"Oh, sure. I'll run them through our people in Colombia. He was *booked* into prison," she said. "Even though he just pretty much walked out when he wanted to."

"Thanks, Katie." It was the best news I'd had all day.

Because of the way we'd divided the briefing up, I got to tell about Hester discovering and seizing the spray can, the gloves, and the mask. Serious excitement. We then asked if there were any questions.

"Where did you say most of these 'witnesses' had gone?" asked Barney England, Hester's superior's superior. He knew. He just wanted to emphasize the point.

"Well, that's the problem," I said. "We aren't too sure. Possibly into Wisconsin or Illinois, across the Mississippi bridges. One at Dubuque, one at Freiberg, and one at Lansing. Or straight north into Minnesota."

"About this Moynihan woman? Everybody's been notified?"

"Oh, yeah." I directed him to the last page of the report, where we'd attached Sally's entries. "Nothing yet, though."

Special Agent Milton Hawse raised his hand. "I'm not sure that I'm completely clear as to why this number of illegal immigrants have been allowed to work here without a word being said. Could you clarify that for me?"

Well, I certainly could have, but Lamar spoke up in a loud, clear voice from his perch on the counter.

"Let me tell you somethin'," he said. "We called. We called INS every damned time we found some more of 'em comin' in on a bus. We called every time we found 'em living in crappy conditions. We called every time one of 'em got into trouble. And every time, we were told that INS was busy, and that it was a federal matter, and that we better keep our noses out of it because we didn't have any damned jurisdiction to arrest 'em or to hold 'em on federal charges." He was steamed just remembering. "They wouldn't come up for less 'n thirty, if we had twenty-five. They wouldn't come up for less 'n fifty if we had forty. They were 'snowed under.' I know they were snowed under. There ain't enough INS agents. I know that. I believe 'em. But it ain't a local problem, it ain't a county problem, and it ain't a state problem. So maybe you should do what we have to do: ask your representative." He shook his head. "It don't do a shit pile of good, but it's all we got."

I was just a little embarrassed, but also glad he'd said what he had. I watched George, who was trying very hard to make it look as if he'd been so absorbed in our reports that he hadn't heard anything. Volont was grinning from ear to ear.

Hawse seemed somewhat taken aback, but not at all flustered. "Good, clear answer," he said.

"Lamar's right," I said. "But I want to make something very clear here. We don't need INS moving in at this point, okay?" I looked at the kitchen full of heavy-hitters. "Not yet. We don't want INS up until after we talk to these witnesses. Just hold off on notification. The illegals will be back. I'm certain of it, and pretty soon, too. They need the work."

Silence.

"And Hester and I can't afford to drive to a federal detention facility, or worse, to Mexico, every time we want to talk to a witness. Okay?"

Hawse nodded. He didn't say a word. It was the best I could get.

"Any other questions?" I asked.

Hardly.

I looked around the kitchen. I don't think I've ever felt so out of place in my life. I just wanted to get two things done: I wanted to get the killer of Rudy Cueva, or whoever the hell our dead man really was. And I wanted to get whoever put Gonzales up to spraying toxic shit all over some beef. That was all.

"Well," I said, "that's about all I have here. I can't see that I'll be much help with the rest of this, the way it's going, but if you need anything from our department, just ask. My main interest is the Cueva murder and the actual placement of the ricin in the food." I was simply telling the truth. I was also getting a feeling that, regardless of the information we were able to gather on Rudy Cueva's murder, other concerns were going to have to come first. National concerns. I could just see us having to hold off on an arrest of Cueva's killer to further a broader and more important investigation. Not that I wouldn't be willing or able to see the reasoning behind that. It was just that I was willing to bet that this was the last time most of the people in the room were going to listen to a word I said.

Harriet Glee, Deputy U.S. Attorney, replaced Hester and me in front of the refrigerator.

"Let me summarize to this point," she said. "One: we have a terrorist act. Foreign or domestic, it's a terrorist act. If it's domestic, it's also a hate crime. Two: we don't know who's behind it. Three: I think Nation County and the State of Iowa should be complimented on their investigation to date. They've done a fine job."

It wasn't like there was any applause or anything, but I gave her my most cavalier bow from the kitchen counter.

"Their reports," said Harriet, "will be appended to the reports of Agents Pollard and Volont." It was an order, and both Volont and George nodded. "I'll need those before I leave tonight. I'll present this information to the Federal Grand Jury tomorrow, probably before noon. If we need subpoenas for any data, let's ask for them then." She looked directly at Lamar. "I'm going to suggest that we not flood the area with agents at this point. Just the absolute minimum of federal people to inspect the plant in a timely fashion, and to assist Nation County with legwork. Especially in finding those illegals. Let me take care of any waiver necessary, so interviews can be done without compelling custody."

It was a pleasure watching her work.

"Given the possibilities here," she said, "I suggest that Mr. Hawse assemble an action group, within a reasonable response distance, and arrange for liaison between them and the officers and agents working this area." She looked directly at Hawse, and I saw him nod again.

I made a mental note to ask George what constituted an "action group." A surveillance team and an interview team we could call on would be nice.

"CDC will do the public information and news release on the ricin. The FDA will handle the recall of all the meat shipped by the plant since December ninth, to be on the safe side. I believe that's already begun?"

Fred Nichimura of the FDA held up his cell phone and said, "Even as we speak. We contacted the customer delis in Chicago early today, so both the New York and Chicago delis have been notified. They're checking their subsequent shipments. That's only coverage for the kosher meats. The nonkosher is the subject of a nationwide recall, as well. That will begin in a few hours. Without making any presumptions," he said, almost as an aside, "it seems that the most easily traced meats, the kosher shipments, were the only ones affected."

"Excellent, Mr. Nichimura. Thank you. So, then, I will maintain very close contact with Mr. Bligh and Mr. Hilgenberg," said Harriet. "Cooperation is key here."

That was the last thing of import said, really. It was 20:44 on the nose.

We mostly stood around in little clumps after that. I talked mostly to the state people, as just about all of them were heading home. No budget for overnight stays. They'd be driving back and forth to Nation County for the next few days. It was gong to be more expensive, but their funds were in the mileage budget. We were a one-to-two-hour commute for most of them, one way, so it also cut into the time they were able to spend on-site. Hester, being the lead DCI agent on a homicide case, was the exception. Most of the feds, on the other hand, were staying over.

We all went over possibilities, made many suggestions to each other, and just generally tried to get a grip on what was happening. The public needed to be reassured that there was no risk of contagion from contact with an infected individual, and CDC could emphasize that.

Hester and Hawse were talking about the ricin developments, and she happened to mention the funny little episode with my biohazard labels. I overheard that, and drifted over to them.

"Don't worry about getting that evidence to our lab," said Hawse. "They'll be here soon. I've got our Evidence Response Team from the St. Louis field office on the way. They can handle that when they do the apartment and the packing plant."

Volont, standing over by the sink with Lamar, was sort of listening in with half an ear.

"I didn't know you'd alerted them." His voice was light enough, but he didn't look too happy about it.

"Always on top of it," said Hawse. "That's why you let me come along." He, too, was lighthearted, but there were undercurrents. Boy, were there undercurrents. I made a mental note, all in caps, to stay the hell out of the way of that little pissing contest.

Hawse said they felt the deliberate aspects of the crime should be deemphasized for the present, until we had more information we could act on. The specter of another anthrax scare loomed over everything. Fred Hohenstein from Iowa's Emergency Management Division said, "This is much more manageable. It's got a solid mechanical vector, and the incidence rate is falling off. We know where it came from, and where it went. Very localized. It's not like an indiscriminate mailing."

I, for one, felt better.

For a moment. Carson Hilgenberg sidled up to me and asked if I thought there should be a separate "County Attorney's" news conference.

"Absolutely not," I said. I thought that was pretty restrained, since I didn't add "you idiot."

He looked hurt. "Well, I'll go with what you guys want. But I just was thinking we should, ah, emphasize that the local officials are, ah, in control."

"I think," I said, as nicely as I could manage, "they'll be really happy that the state and feds are on the case. Relieved, even."

It was nearly 11 P.M. when I got home. Sue was waiting up, but very nearly asleep.

"Why are you so late?"

It was a good question, but since I'd just been required to sign an agreement that I wouldn't talk about anything with anybody at any time, it was going to be tough to explain.

"I can't tell you, dear," I said, as I leaned over and kissed her hello. "National security concerns." I thought she'd think I was joking.

"I understand," she said.

"What?"

"I understand. It must be really busy for you right now. Did you see the KNUG news at ten?"

Uh-oh. "No, I really was busy."

"I know. I thought you might miss it, so I taped it for you." She picked up the VCR remote and turned the tape on.

I was appalled. Judy Mercer and her cameraman had managed to get almost everybody who had attended the meeting on camera as they came through the parking lot. The only ones she'd apparently missed were George, Hester, Bligh, McWhirter, and me. I was never so glad I'd used a back door in my life.

She did get Volont, Thurgood, and Hawse, though. That camera had quite a zoom, apparently. The worst part was, she identified Volont correctly, and although she didn't name Thurgood, she did say that she was a counterterrorism agent who had "testified in the Cedar Rapids Federal Court for the Northern District of Iowa." Hawse she didn't ID, and that was at least a blessing.

Judy Mercer's voice-over was, when not identifying attendees, busy outlining the "mysterious death" of "an unidentified worker" at the plant in Battenberg. "After a mysterious death in Battenberg, is there any reason for Eastern Iowa to be concerned about an infectious disease?" She then cut to about fifteen seconds of an interview with Fred Hohenstein, from Iowa Emergency Management. Good old Fred simply stated flat-out: "There is no involvement of an infectious agent. There was some contamination with a toxic substance, and we're here to make sure there is no further exposure." Judy Mercer didn't repeat what he had said. That worried me. I knew she was pretty damned good, so I was now wondering just what she'd heard about the New York connection. I was pretty sure that wasn't going to take the major networks too long to piece together.

When it was over, Sue asked me if there was any reason to be concerned about the unspecified disease.

"Do we need shots or something?" was what she said.

"Nope. Noncommunicable. Absolutely no problem."

"Okay..." But she sounded just a teeny bit uncertain.

I showered and shaved just before I went to bed. You learn to do it that way, so you're at least half presentable if you get called out early the next morning.

CHAPTER 16

ONE OF THE THINGS I HATE about working a major case is that I always seem to be getting wake-up calls about an hour too early for me to be really rested. Today was no exception.

I turned over on my right side, pushed the covers down far enough for me to reach an arm out, and picked up the phone. As I did, Sue murmured, "What?"

"Just the phone." I picked it up. "Yeah?"

"Hate to bother you," said George's familiar voice, "but we have a development you should know about."

"Good or bad?"

"Both, maybe."

"Okay, go for it," I said, sitting up and throwing the covers aside. That created a breeze, disturbing Sue, and earning me an angry mutter.

"Linda Moynihan," said George. "She's surfaced."

"Alive or dead?" I had a bad feeling he was just being polite about a drowning victim.

"Oh, very much alive, according to her attorney."

That woke me up. "What?"

"Yep. We were contacted by Ms. Moynihan's attorney about an hour ago. His client will turn herself in, if we promise her immunity and protection."

"What?" The protection didn't bother me a bit. But a request for immunity came at me from left field.

"That's what he says. He won't say where she's at, but since he practices in Madison, Wisconsin, I'd guess she's not all that far away."

"That lying little shit," I said. "Does Hester know?"

"Volont just called her. She's in the room next to us here in the motel. Want to meet us for breakfast?"

"Give me ten," I said. "Maybe fifteen. Where you want to eat?"

"How about your jail kitchen?" he said. Local restaurants, especially during a major investigation, were a bad idea. Way too many ears.

"How about here instead," I offered. "The media won't be outside."

I heard him ask Volont something. "Sure. Okay if we bring Gwen?"

"Sure. Absolutely. And Hawse, too, if he wants."

George chuckled. "He left last night, went back to Cedar Rapids. He didn't like the accommodations."

"That's too bad... it's a long drive, especially late at night."

"Not for him," said George. "He took a helicopter."

As I replaced the phone on its cradle, Sue said, "Did I just hear you invite some people over here in ten or fifteen minutes!?"

"More like twenty, I think," I said. "I'll just run to the bakery and get some rolls, and put on some coffee..."

She'd have none of that. While I dressed, walked one block, and spent ten minutes investing in pastry, Sue managed to dress, put on some makeup, start scrambling eggs, and make two quarts of orange juice. When I got back home, she was all set.

Two minutes later, Hester and three hungry FBI agents came through the back door.

Volont sat back in his chair and put his hands on the dining room table. "Sue," he said, "that was a truly great breakfast."

Sue smiled. "Anytime." Well, I knew better, but the feds sure didn't.

Hester, George, and I helped clear the table, and then Sue discreetly went back upstairs, ostensibly to give us some privacy. I figured she'd be collapsed on the bed and out like a light in five.

I called the office and told Sally we were all at my place. Then, over coffee, we tried to sort things out.

"The immunity request tells me she's got some complicity in what's going on here," said Hester. "Either that or her attorney is just being very cautious."

"And she *thinks*," said Volont, "or at least wants us to, that she's got something of value to trade for it." He sipped his coffee. "That's what I got from the request for protection, at least. Or, maybe just dramatic games. But if she really thinks she's got something we want, we gotta figure out just what that might be. Then we see if it's worth it."

"Think she knows who's behind the thing?" I asked.

"We should be so lucky. In my experience," said Volont, "they always want to 'trade up,' so to speak. You got to be real careful."

"How long has she known Rudy Cueva, or whoever he really is?" asked Gwen.

"About six months," said Hester. She glanced at me. "Isn't that what she said?"

"Yeah. The way she put it, they started living together pretty close to the day they met," I said.

"Ah," said Volont, "love at first sight."

"Sounds like," said Hester.

"She said he wasn't into dope," I said. "I guess she should have said 'not anymore.' But she was really firm about that, the no-dope stuff. She offered to let us search her apartment. She had to know it was pretty clean to take that chance."

"Not to worry," said Volont. "We don't trade *zip* for dope information on this case. We need warm bodies, we need the source of the ricin, we need to know who wasted her boyfriend, or the deal's off."

"If we can pop her as a material witness before a deal is cut, can we..." I said, thinking aloud.

"Well, now," said Volont, "let's think about that. Because she's *implied* she's more than a material witness. She implies that she could be an accessory. That's a long way from probable cause, even with the totality of the circumstances. I talked with Harriet this morning about this. We can still hold her under your 'material witness' ATL, assuming we can find her, but as soon as serious negotiations start between the attorneys, we shouldn't question her. Even with a Miranda warning. Her attorney will have to be involved all the way at that point, as soon as an agreement on the immunity is tentatively reached. Glad you said something."

I was glad I had, too. I went into the kitchen and called the office, and asked Sally if there had been any response to the ATL. Nothing.

"Is that all?" She sounded a little harried.

"Busy?"

"Like a cat burying poo-poo," she said. "We've got the media clogging up the parking lot, Lamar is really pissed, and we have two prisoners who have to go to court this morning. Go away, Houseman."

As I got back into the dining room, Hester was saying, "Just who is this attorney, anyway?"

"Not sure yet," said Gwen, stirring her coffee. "We're checking."

The way she said that was just so cool. It just reeked of staff scurrying about while she stirred that coffee.

"I wasn't expecting an attorney from Madison," said Hester. "Our only connection so far was the wedding in the Twin Cities."

"Speaking of which," said Gwen, "I scanned in those photos last night, e-mailed them to some people. They're working on those, too, now. Multiagency. Recognition software gets better every day."

"You know," said Volont, "we sort of owe that Gonzales, the one they call Orejas. We'd be a few days behind the curve if he hadn't gotten sick and croaked."

"That's true," said Gwen. "Hawse said as much last night."

"Speaking of," Volont asked her, "Did God's other son say if he'd be back today?"

She grinned. "He said he would. After he talked with some people."

"We're talking about Agent Hawse, I presume?" asked Hester.

"My favorite super agent," said Volont. "Yeah. That's who."

"Is he going to be a problem for anybody?" asked Hester. "We should know that now, before it gets important."

Volont shook his head. "Nope. He won't be here that long. He'll just drop in long enough to encourage us, and then he'll hightail it back to D.C., to report in person to the really important people. The boy is just hell-bent to be an assistant director. Like they say in Texas, 'He's all hat and no cattle.' Just one of life's little irritants."

"Okay," I said. "Just as long as he frees up the resources."

"Oh, he'll do that," promised Volont. "Really. He's very good about that." He stood. "Time to go to work."

When we got to the sheriff's department, the first thing I did was call Ben at the plant. He was up to his armpits in health inspections, but he took the call.

"We need to know who loaded trucks with Gonzales over the last few days he worked," I said.

He sighed. "Okay. You coming down here today?"

"I hope to, but I'll probably need the information sooner than that."

"The information you can have in five minutes," he said. "But my boss Mr. Goldstein wants to talk with you. If you aren't too busy."

"Tell him I'll be there if I possibly can," I said. "He must be having fits."

"Yes," said Ben.

There was something about the tone of his voice that prompted me to say, "Hey, don't let him start digging on his own, now. We don't need that."

"You're psychic?"

"Not by a long shot. But Mr. Goldstein isn't exactly the kind to sit on his hands," I said. "But he's gotta rely on us."

Ben had been right. We were just getting everybody settled at desks in the main reception area when Sally buzzed us. She had the information on the loading crew. It had been just about five minutes. There were eight male subjects, not counting the late Gonzales. We started running the names and Social Security numbers the secretary gave us, and came up with two bona fide people and six complete unknowns. Not the normal sort of unknown we normally got, which just meant that they had no police records. These six were just not anywhere to be found in any records, except at the plant. Two of them had the same Social Security number, but all were different from the Cueva and Gonzales matched set. That may not have meant much, as Gwen Thurgood was of the opinion that average forgers tended to print them in a recognizable sequence.

"To do more than one of each number is very sloppy. Lots of them are sloppy, though. But we might have a connection."

Swell.

Just to make my morning complete, Iowa DCI Special Agent Art Meyerman came striding through the open door. He sat down on the edge of the first desk, normally used by our secretary, and announced, "Well, this is real bullshit."

"What is?" I asked.

"All this media stuff. They follow you guys around like flies," he said.

"It's because we're sweet, Art," said George. "Didn't get to talk to you last night. How've you been?"

"Fine," snapped Art. "If you ask me, this whole thing is a wild-goose chase, just like that anthrax thing in the mail."

"About a half dozen people died there," said George. "And we'll be lucky if we don't have a dozen dead here before we're done."

"Oh, sure. I know. But, look out there. There must be five or six stations out there now, and look at that big rig coming up the hill...."

We all looked. I'd never seen one of the big microwave trucks the major networks used for direct broadcasts. Well, not up close. As it reached the intersection at the bottom of the department driveway, it turned left, and we could read the printing on the side.

"CNN," said Hester. "We better not screw up now." She was only half kidding.

"I never start to worry," said Gwen, "until the crew from *Monday Night Football* shows up."

We all moved back from the window and back to our desks.

"You got time to type up a report for me?" Art asked Gwen.

"Pardon me?"

Art spoke more slowly. "I said, 'you got time to type up a report for me.' I have to make some phone calls."

"Depends," she said. "You got time to make me a cup of coffee?"

"What?"

I figured I'd better intervene before Art got himself shot. "You two must not have been introduced last night," I said. "Special Agent Art Meyerman, Iowa DCI, meet Special Agent Gwen Thurgood, FBI counterintelligence/counterterrorism unit."

"Nice to meet you," said Art. He turned back to me. "Well, you got another office I can use? One with a *real* secretary?"

"Sure," I said. "How about your old one? We'll see if we can get a typist for you." He and I walked down the narrow hall to the cramped office we'd shared years ago, when we were both on the night shift for the county.

"Boy," he said. "She's pissy, isn't she?"

When I got back to the main office, Gwen was on the phone, and holding up one hand to get everybody's attention.

"Thanks, Manny," she said, and hung up the phone. "Well."

We all looked at her. Well, indeed.

"That was Manny Ortega," she said. "Best intelligence analyst in the business. He's done the photo images I sent last night. This man, the thin-faced one in the wedding photos? The one you say looks like the boss?"

"Yeah?" I said.

"Manny thinks this is a man named Odeh. He's not a hundred percent certain, but he believes it is. Do you have prints on him, too?"

"No. Not as far as I know, we don't." I had to ask. "How's that spelled? I mean, it sounds Irish..."

"It's Mustafa Abdullah Odeh. Oscar, delta, echo, hotel," said Gwen. "That's okay about not having the prints. That's what I thought, but I had to be sure. Anyway, Manny didn't know Odeh was in the country, but he's just about positive it's him. Manny Ortega is really, really conservative on this sort of thing. This is the first photo he's seen of Odeh without facial hair, but even so, I'd say we have a 'for certain' here. Just exactly where and when were these photos taken, do you know?"

Always keep your handwritten notes. I checked. "Minneapolis, or the Twin Cities, anyway...about three weeks ago. No closer data than that, at least not yet." I made a note to attach to the first one. "It was probably in conjunction with a Catholic wedding, bride and groom were Juan and Adriana Muñoz...we'll just check with the Catholic churches in the Cities, and see if there was a wedding party by that name." I added a big *S*, to remind me to stick Sally with this.

"Right." She made a note, too. "Why don't you let us do that? We can do that for you, and really fast."

I crossed off the *S*, and thereby added a few months to my life. "Excellent."

" So, then," continued Gwen, "without going into too much detail, Mustafa Abdullah Odeh has a U.S. education, mostly at City College in New York. He's got connections throughout the Middle East, with all sorts of terrorist cells and organizations. He gets things started, mainly. Plans. He's kind of like a staff officer would be in the army. Manny says that Mustafa Abdullah Odeh pledged *bayat* to Osama bin Laden. That's an oath of fealty. He's also been associated with Hammas, Hezbollah, and the PLO. Over a period of fifteen years or more. The Hezbollah connection is the most important, by the way. They're the most capable of 'em all. Anyway, this is a dangerous man. Not necessarily directly. If he's involved, directly or indirectly, it means that there is a serous foreign terrorist involvement somewhere in the area."

Great. Just great. "Everybody but the Popular Front for the Liberation of Dubuque," I said. I don't know if it eased the tension much, but it helped me.

"I'll double-check that," said Gwen. "Anyway, members of the cell, the cell he works with, would probably call him something like the 'Wise Man' or the

'Wise One.' He carries plans that are forwarded to him from higher up. He also controls their finances. They need money, they come to him."

"Okay." We were getting way out of my league.

"But he normally won't be directly involved. He's too valuable to have him get himself killed, and way, way too valuable to have him get himself interrogated." Gwen looked around. "I feel certain it *is* Odeh," she said, quietly. "We all should be very, very careful from now on."

There was a momentary silence.

"Well, all right!" said Volont. "This is more like it." He was serious. The man thrived on this sort of thing, but I couldn't help thinking about last time Volont was in his element. We'd gotten one of our officers killed on that one, along with several others, and all those terrorists had been homegrown. "I wouldn't worry too much," said Volont. "This group is probably dangerous if provoked, but just from the people we know who are involved, they aren't a top-of-the-line terrorist cell. The only one who's probably spent any profitable time in a training camp would be Odeh."

The intercom buzzed.

"Yeah," I said.

"Hey," said Sally, "Special Agent Hawse is out at the airport. His helicopter just left, and he'd like a ride in to the office."

"Get one of the marked cars, would you?" I said, without even checking with the FBI agents in the room. "He'll look a lot less inconspicuous in one of those, and they can get him past the CNN people out there. We really should make sure he's up to speed before the media grabs him."

"CNN? Holy shit," exclaimed Sally, but not to anyone in our room, "turn on the tube, CNN's outside..." and the connection went dead.

That broke the tension a bit.

Once he'd arrived, having successfully ducked the news teams outside, Hawse seemed very pleased with himself. "The art of distraction works every time. When I was a kid," he said, taking off his coat, "my brother and I used to do a magic show. I never realized how useful it was going to be."

Volont looked at the ceiling.

"So, boys and girls," said Hawse, "what have we got this morning?"

"You might want to sit down," said Volont.

"Go for it," said Hawse, who remained standing.

"The skinny-faced dude in those wedding photos, with the Hispanics? The ones we saw last night? Well, we've got him IDed as one Mustafa Abdullah Odeh, a bin Laden associate. Money and plans man."

"Who did the ID?" asked Hawse.

"Manny Ortega," said Gwen. "He gives it a ninety-nine percent probability."

"I suspected something like this," said Hawse, not missing a beat. "I was going over scenarios in my room last night. It fits."

That was something to see. He'd not only fielded the news with remarkable aplomb, he'd managed to make it appear just slightly out-of-date because he'd already considered it. I'd only seen that kind of thing once before, in Art Meyerman when he was just a new deputy. No matter who was turned as a suspect in any case, Art always said, "Oh, yeah, I figured it was him." I knew he was fudging most of the time, but Lamar didn't pick up on it. But that was how Art had gotten promoted to chief deputy, by making Lamar think he was always on top of everything. I was willing to bet my next month's check on Hawse making assistant director before too long.

Within ten minutes, Sally buzzed from the dispatch desk. "You guys might want to come out here, we're on *Headline News,* and we're being tied in to a terrorist act in New York..."

By the time we got to the dispatch center, our segment was done, and we stood around for almost fifteen minutes, waiting for it to be rebroadcast. But, then, there it was. They showed footage of a deli in New York, and a hospital, and a bit of an interview. But all the time, the voice-over was giving out remarkably accurate information. They had the three delis the FBI had identified, the total number of casualties, the correct number of deaths, the current status of the hospitalized victims, and the date of the first admission to the hospital.

What they didn't have was the substance. Not yet. I said as much.

"Don't be too sure about that," said Volont. "They're probably doing their verifications right now."

Then, when we thought we were going to dodge the bullet, they showed the Nation County Sheriff's Department, complete with a lot full of media vehicles and our unmarked patrol cars. Then, they named the plant in Battenberg and identified it as the source of the suspected contaminated meat.

"Damn," I said. "They're good."

"Yeah," said Gwen. "They are. Uh-oh..."

They had just announced that there would be a special report on CNN in thirty minutes.

Sally looked at Gwen. "Bad news?"

"It means they have enough to do a long version," Gwen said grimly. "That means they have more information, and probably interviews."

"Time for a good statement," declared Hawse. "We better get a press conference organized." He turned to me. "Is there some sort of auditorium available around here?"s

"Well," I said, "there's the Opera House. Seats about four hundred. Stage. Balcony. Even has footlights, if you want 'em."

We assigned Lamar to get the Opera House opened and available for the media. I say "we" in the broadest sense. I suggested his name, and Hawse did the actual assigning. Sometimes, you just have to get even.

CHAPTER 17

12:21

THE FEDERAL SEARCH WARRANT for Jose Gonzales's apartment arrived in our office at 11:55. We were divided into two teams, search and security. As the original case officer, I was listed on the search team. Hester got security. Everybody else was a federal agent. We were just on our way out the back door of the sheriff's department, when I got called on my walkie-talkie.

"Comm, Three?"

I fished it out of my coat pocket. "Comm?"

"Three, return to the office immediately, authority officer One."

That meant that Lamar had ordered it. There was no questioning. I caught up to Volont and George, who were with Hester. "I gotta get back to the office. Lamar needs something. I'll catch up."

As soon as I got inside, Lamar was waiting for me.

"What's up?" I was as polite as possible under the circumstances, but I really wanted to go on that search.

"Quick," he said, turning and leading me down the hall to his office. "I wanted you to get this first, before anybody else finds out."

That was unlike him. "What?"

"Just pick up the phone," he said as he shut his office door very firmly behind us. He sounded happy as hell.

I lifted the phone off the desk. It was obviously an active line, and Lamar hadn't even put whoever it was on hold.

"This is Houseman."

"Hey! Boy, have I got some good shit for you. You owe me dinner at Mabel's for this one!"

It was Harry, from Conception County, Wisconsin.

"Harry, my man. What's up?"

"You want one each Linda Moynihan and one each Yevgenny Skripkin?"

Hot damn. "We sure as hell want her, but who the hell is this, this Yevgenny whatshisname?"

"Ho ho, my boy. Da plot thickens. Your girl Linda is sitting in our jail, bawling her eyes out and screamin' about some attorney she needs. You know anything about that?"

"Sure. She's got some attorney in Madison who's trying to arrange an immunity and protection deal for her."

"Okay," said Harry. "That's about what she said to us. Shit, she's about as safe as possible, she's the only sad broad in the whole women's cell block. I don't know nothing about no immunity," he added, laughing. "I can assume you still want her?"

"Oh, yeah!"

"She was shacked up with this Skripkin dude over in Blue Mound, where we found 'em. The Whispering Pines Motel."

"Maybe they're just friends," I said.

"They were in the sack together, naked," said Harry, with some relish. "We used to call that shacked up, when I was a kid."

"Yeah, we did, too. Okay, but who the hell is he? I don't know anybody by that name."

"You shittin' me?" asked Harry. "You really don't know who he is? Hell, Houseman, I thought you were one shit-hot investigator!"

"Get to the fuckin' point, Harry," I said. He found that uproarious.

"Okay, Carl. Okay. This Skripkin, a white male Ukrainian, twenty-six years of age, was with the guy who blew away this Rudy Cueva boyfriend of Moynihan's the other day."

"What?" Glib in the face of surprise, as always.

"You betcha, Norske. This Skripkin was right there when one Juan Miguel Alvarez, also known to his friends as Hassan Ahmed Hassan, stuck the shotgun in the back of your boy's head and pulled the fuckin' trigger. Makes no bones about it. Seems to think he's part of the immunity deal or something. That's why I thought you knew him."

The white boy. Harry'd found the white boy.

"You still there, Carl?"

"Yeah, yeah, Harry. Just thinkin'. I don't know this Skripkin. Whatever else, though, we got enough for an accessory to murder charge. I'll get the paperwork started on that right away. I don't suppose they're gonna waive extradition?"

"I didn't ask," he said, "but I'd be willing to bet your ass that they won't."

"Me, too. How soon can I talk to 'em?"

"You got a free pass to this facility anytime you want," he said. "Should I put the coffee on?"

"You better put on about sixty cups," I told him. "You're gonna have a crowd. And Harry?"

"Yeah?"

"Get a photo of this Skripkin over to me as fast as possible, okay?"

"Your e-mail up and runnin'?"

"You bet."

"You'll have it in less than a minute."

I did, too. Printing it took about four, and then grabbing a half dozen photos of other white males out of our Jail files took another five. Sally did the picking, while I called Hester on her cell phone and told her what we had.

"Oh my God. You're kidding!" She was as delighted as I'd ever heard her.

I left, and made a flying trip to the Heinman brothers' farm, where I showed the photos to Jacob. He picked Skripkin out immediately.

"This one. This is the white boy. No doubt in my mind. Is he from around here?"

"Well, Jacob, kind of. In a way. I can't tell you more right now."

"That's fine. Good job."

Well, it would have taken too long to explain about Harry, and Linda, and...

"Thanks, Jacob. We appreciate it."

The trip to the Heinman farm and back, plus the identification process with the photo lineup, took twenty-eight minutes.

We got the ball rolling with the county attorney, who we told to file a complaint and affidavit with the district court and get an arrest warrant out for Skripkin. Carson needed some help, so we told him to come on up. We then called a judicial magistrate, who was just wrapping up his morning traffic court tour, and he came up to the sheriff's department with his sack lunch and dined at a desk while watching us with a look of bemused detachment. With me dictating, Sally typing, and Carson Hilgenberg signing it, it only took about thirty minutes.

I grabbed a second with Volont. "Do you know Harry over in Conception County?"

"No."

"Okay, look... Harry uses some pretty rough language. He doesn't mean anything by it, and he's one of the best cops I've ever known. All you have to do is give it a few minutes, and you don't even notice it anymore."

"That sort of thing," said Volont, "doesn't bother me at all."

"I know," I said. "But I think you might want to, well, alert some of the other federal officers. You know. Like Hawse."

Volont looked like a kid about to pull the wings off a fly. "Oh, sure. Thanks for the warning."

That look told me that he wasn't about to mention anything to his superior. I made a mental note to try to be out of the room if Hawse ever met Harry.

Fifteen minutes after that, arrest warrant in hand, the four of us left for the Conception County Jail, George and Volont in one car, Hester and me in another. We arrived there at 14:14 on the dot.

"For Christ's sake," said Harry. "It took ya long enough!"

Harry had run all the data on our Mr. Skripkin, and gave us a brief run-down.

"Three or four minor entries on his CCH," he said. He was referring to the Computerized Criminal History check that is run on every prisoner upon being booked into jail. "One simple po; two traffic, both speed; and one public intox."

"Okay," I said. A first offender, then, in the felony world. "The simple po and the intox come on the same date?" I suspected that possession of a small amount of marijuana and being stoned could easily arise from the same incident.

"Damn," said Harry, glancing at the dates. "You still got it."

"Thanks. It's not much of a rap sheet, is it?" I noticed that, while it would have been normal to just hand me the thing, Harry was keeping the sheet to himself. Knowing Harry, that was an indicator that there was something else lurking on that piece of paper. Like he said, I still got it.

"Well, maybe it's more than you'd think," he said. The familiar grin spread over his face. "The charges were all filed by the San Diego PD. Less than a year ago."

Ah. "No kidding?"

"Yep. And when we inventoried his shit when we booked him, we found DLs from California, Oregon, Pennsylvania, Iowa, and Kentucky." He handed me the sheet, finally. "All with his name, but all with different dates of birth. All bright and shiny, and all 'issued' on 02/18/2000." He looked very pleased with himself. "We ran 'em all, just to see, but there's no record of any of these except the California one. Like the others don't exist, which they don't."

"Fascinating," I said, looking at the sheet. "Just checking...the OLN on Iowa licenses is the same as the SSN. Just wanted to see if he was using a familiar number...but he isn't." I was just a bit disappointed.

"Any chauffeur's licenses?" asked Hester.

"Oh, yeah," said Harry. "All but California, as a matter of fact. Hester, you are one sharp lady."

"Did any of them have hazardous material certification on them?"

That stopped him. "Shit. Shit, I'll be right back," he said, and headed out to the booking area to check the DLs.

George looked at Hester. "Nice one."

It had become something of an indicator, the hazmat certificate on the fake chauffeur's license. It looked like somebody high in terrorist networks figured that, in case they wanted to ship dangerous materials by road, if they had somebody with that type of license drive the vehicle, they could just breeze through any encounter with the cops. What they apparently didn't quite grasp was that, with the additional testing for hazardous materials transport, nobody got those certifications just for the hell of it. Only those who did that for a living would have them, and they were able to answer any question a cop had about the proper procedures right off the top of their heads. Arcane questions like which letters on the diamond-shaped warning were required for particular materials.

Harry returned. "All the chauffeurs have hazmat certification. Every fuckin' one of 'em."

Volont had been on his cell phone to Harriet Glee at the U.S. Attorney's Office in Cedar Rapids during most of the conversation with Harry. Dirty Harriet had told him that there had been no agreement reached regarding the immunity or protection, but that she'd be talking to Linda's attorney within an hour. In the meantime, she'd emphatically told him that the name Skripkin had never been mentioned, nor had any other individual. Period.

"So," said Volont, "it looks like Skripkin's fair game. That was a nice bit," he said to Hester, "about the hazmat certification. Good job." The way he looked at George when he said it meant that he thought that George should have caught that first. "You advised him of his rights?" he asked Harry.

"Fuckin' ay."

"And he's fluent in English?"

"Sure sounds like it," said Harry. "He tells a mean story."

"Okay." Volont, who was sitting in a tipped-back chair with his feet on Harry's desk, made a tent shape with his hands and tapped his chin with the tips of his fingers. I'd seen him do that before, and it told me that he was really being careful.

"Tell you what," he said. "Why don't we do it this way? Carl, you've got this Skripkin cold as an accessory to murder, based on an admission against interest after being advised of his rights pursuant to Miranda." He glanced at Harry. "He did *waive* those rights, didn't he?"

"Of course, my man," said Harry. "Here." He handed Volont a rights waiver form, signed by Skripkin. "Black and white."

"Excellent. Carl, here, owes you supper." A satisfied smile appeared on Volont's face. Things were coming together. "So, then, Carl, you and Hester interview him regarding the Cueva murder. Now, your witness is sure that this Skripkin was not the trigger man?"

"Absolutely certain."

"Good. Okay, so let's see what he says to you. Don't let him know we're anywhere around. Find out all you can about motive, and just why this Juan Miguel Alvarez is also called Hassan Ahmed Hassan. And remember, you aren't allowed to even *mention* the possibility of an immunity agreement with Linda. It could look like an intimidation tactic, by making him believe he was being hung out to dry by his friends. It could contaminate the whole interview." He looked over at Harry. "Do you have a room where we can view and hear the interrogation without being observed by the suspect?"

"Shit, yes," said Harry. "Where do you think you are, Iowa?"

I wanted to come back with something snappy in defense of my state, but Harry's jail was three years old, and ours was over a hundred. The only way we could have done what Volont wanted would have been to hide somebody in a closet.

"Go get 'em," said Volont to Hester and me.

"Just a sec," I said. "If this guy asks if he's covered under some sort of immunity deal..."

"We tell him he's not," said Hester. "But only if he brings it up. He has to introduce it himself. You gotta be truthful. He asks, you tell him. Then, if he chooses not to talk, at least we give him something to think about while he waits for his court-appointed attorney."

"Good enough," I said. "Okay with you?" I asked Volont and George.

It was.

Hester and I stashed our handguns in individual lockers and gave a jailer the keys. She gave us each a number to be used to repossess our weapons when we were leaving.

As Harry led us back to the interview room, he said to Hester, "This Skripkin is one worried dude."

"I would be, too," said Hester.

I noticed how busy and noisy it was in the halls. Lots of staff. In our jail, you could clap your hands and get an echo.

We entered a room without windows, about fifteen by twenty-five feet, a mirror on the wall, and a long table with four chairs, arranged two to a side.

I knew the mirror was one-way, but it still could have fooled me. "Holy shit, Harry," I said. "This looks like a movie set."

He chuckled. "Strange you should mention that...the video camera is up in that corner there," he said, pointing, "and the real video equipment is behind the glass. Great sound, so don't say anything to each other in a whisper if you don't want Skripkin's attorney to hear you. That mike system picks up everything. It's all digital."

"You have popcorn on the other side of the glass?" I asked.

"I ain't tellin'," he said.

There was a knock on the door, and a uniformed jailer ushered Skripkin in. "I'll be leaving you now," said Harry, and meaningfully picked up the fourth chair and took it with him. Now, in order to obtain a weapon, Skripkin was either going to have to ask Hester or me for our chairs, or stand up and use his own. Not too bad an idea.

My first impression of Skripkin was that of a tall, very thin young man, with large blue eyes, blond hair, a large and narrow nose, and a very pale complexion.

He was about two inches taller than I was, making him close to six feet six. He had very long fingers, with the nearly round nails you sometimes see in an ectomorph. He appeared pretty calm to me. Like they say, always take your cue from the suspect.

"Hi," I said. "My name's Carl Houseman, and this is Hester Gorse. I'm a deputy sheriff over in Nation County, Iowa, and she's a special agent of the Iowa Division of Criminal Investigation. We'd like to talk to you about the murder of Rudy Cueva."

"Sure, no problem. What do you want to know?" Although he spoke pretty slowly and did have a Russian accent, his English was pretty damned good.

"Have a seat," I said. "We need to explain a few things to you before we go any further."

"Sure, whatever you need." He sat, and so did we. I was rather surprised at his seemingly relaxed demeanor. I'd expected more tension, especially since Harry had told us he was worried.

"Okay, your first name is..." I said, wanting him to say it so I had a pronunciation guide.

"Yevgenny Ilyavitch Skripkin," he said. "I am U.S. citizen since July 23 of this very year."

"Excellent," I said, and meant it. It was nice to be on familiar territory. "Congratulations."

"Thank you."

"First, let me advise you that you have the right to remain silent, and that anything you say can and will be used against you in a court or courts of law. You have the right to an attorney, and to have him present during questioning. If you cannot afford an attorney, one will be appointed to represent you at no cost to you." I said it slowly, and with as little expression as possible. "Do you understand those rights?"

"Yes, I do."

"With those rights in mind, do you still wish to talk with us without the presence of an attorney?"

"Sure, why not?"

I hate it when suspects append things like that. An attorney can have a field day, asking why you didn't explain to him why he shouldn't really talk to you. All over what is essentially a figure of speech.

"Okay. You know that you have been charged as an accessory to the murder of Rudy Cueva, is that correct?"

"Please explain this 'accessory' to me. Please."

"In this case, it means that you were there when Rudy Cueva was killed, and you either helped to kill him or did nothing to prevent him being killed."

He considered that for a moment. "I did not think Hassan was going to kill him, okay?"

"By Hassan, do you mean a man who calls himself Hassan Ahmed Hassan?" asked Hester.

"Yes I do. I mean, too, a man who calls himself Juan Alvarez. This person is the same."

"That would be 'Juan Miguel Alvarez,' as far as you know?" asked Hester.

"As far as I know."

He looked at us for a second, digesting Hester's use of Alvarez's middle name. He was smart enough to have picked up on it, but did he realize the implications? It had definitely dawned on him that we already knew something about Alvarez. I wondered if he realized Hester had done it deliberately.

"Can I ask here a question?"

There might be a time when you say something about being the one doing the questioning, but we wanted Yevgenny relaxed and as comfortable as possible.

"Go ahead," I said.

"Do you think truly that I wanted Rudy to be dead?"

"I don't know yet," I said. "I don't have enough information."

He thought again. "Okay. I understand. I did not want to die, this Rudy, at all. I will explain to you why I mean that."

"Fine. What happened that day?" I asked. "What were you doing there in the first place?"

According to Skripkin, he had come to the Midwest with his friend Hassan Ahmed Hassan, also known as Juan Miguel Alvarez, back in August. They lived in Harmony, Minnesota, for about a month, and then moved to Iowa City, Iowa. They were unemployed but Hassan always had cash. Skripkin claimed that he had no idea where the money came from. That seemed to be the first lie.

He then claimed they would drive around sometimes, and on one of those little drives, they came up north to Battenberg, and that was where he and Hassan met with Rudy Cueva for the first time.

"You came up specifically to meet Rudy Cueva?" I asked.

"I don't know."

"You don't think that a hundred-mile drive without knowing who you were going to see was a little...strange?"

"How would I know that? I think...no, I am guessing that Hassan he knew Rudy already. Is that right, guess?"

"Could be. Why do you say that?"

"That was my guessing when we got there, because he...just a second, I reach for word...*recognized* him. That is it, recognized." He looked genuinely pleased.

"How do you know that?" I asked. "That he recognized him."

"Because we were driving around looking for address of Rudy and Linda, and we went by the Casey's store, and there was a man filling gas into his car, and Hassan turned in the driving place and said, 'That's him there.' That is why."

"Does it for me," I said. "So, you two came up to see Rudy and Linda, then?"

"No, just Rudy. I did not know both of them, and I think Hassan, he also met Linda that night for first time when we went to the apartment."

"So," asked Hester, "why did you come up to see them?"

Skripkin leaned a bit forward. "It was business, lady agent." And he winked.

Lady agent. I suspected that the troops on the other side of the glass were going to have a good time with that one.

"Narcotics?" asked Hester, not missing a beat. "Drugs, dope?"

"No. No drugs. No."

"What for, then?" She was pretty insistent.

"This makes me frightened," he said. "I do not know what to say."

"Why's that?" I asked.

He thought. "I tell you, because you have my fingerprints. You will know soon, if you do not know already." His whole demeanor had changed, just like a switch had been tripped. He became much more confident, and more assertive.

"My real name is truly Yevgenny Skripkin. I am wanted in Ukraine for murder, which I did kill that man, because I am hired to do that. I do that for a job. I was brought to this country in 1996, arrangement from my old boss with the boss of Hassan. I come to this country from Canada, then to Chicago. I had job, and pretty good visa and not so good green card. I was cook at restaurant there." As I started to speak, he held up his hand for silence. "No, I do not know boss of Hassan. I do not know that Hassan knows boss of Hassan." His prominent jaw muscles clenched. "It is good for me not to know those things. I know this." He appeared to relax a bit. "So, I am wanted to become hard to find in Ukraine, and this is good deal for bosses. I am to help the boss of Hassan whenever he asks. Otherwise, I am to be a U.S. citizen as soon as I can, so I keep my nose pretty damn clean."

I thought I heard a muted thump from behind the one-way glass, and imagined that Volont had just sent George scrambling to run Skripkin's prints through AFIS.

"What's the name of your old boss?" asked Hester.

"Vladimir Nadsyev." He said it very freely, which surprised me.

"And you don't know the name of Hassan's boss?"

"Of course not."

"But you would tell us if you knew it?" she asked.

"Of course not," he said, with a big smile. "I am not stupid."

"Then," she asked, "why did you tell us the name of your old boss?"

"He is husband of my sister," said Skripkin. "Everybody knows I work for him for years."

"Then are you really a U.S. citizen?" I asked. I thought I could get away with the question because I was asking it for verification purposes for a prior statement.

He sighed. "No, I am not U.S. citizen."

"Okay." Lies were piling up. Now we had to determine if we were actually getting closer to the truth of the matter, or if we were just getting more lies. Filtering can be a real pain in the butt. I looked at my notes. "So, back to this Hassan and his boss..."

"This is first time boss of Hassan asks for favor. I am to come with Hassan and be his guard, and be his strong right arm if there is to be trouble."

"And this is the first time you met Hassan?"

"To be truthful, yes. I never met Hassan before then."

It's amazing how many times the people we interview say things like 'to tell the truth' or 'to be truthful.' It's a dead giveaway that they've been lying to you. That's the easy part. The hard part is determining just where and why.

"Just what was it that this Hassan was supposed to be doing?" asked Hester.

"He did not tell me, so much as I figure it out." That's how Skripkin began, but I thought he'd figured it out very well, indeed.

First, he said that Hassan was supposed to do some "contamination" in the meat plant. Skripkin had thought, originally, it was to "make the meat bad," and to force a recall.

"Why did he want to do that?"

"To hurt the Jews who run the plant," he said. "This is what I think. This is the...impression I get. From him. He tells he hates Jews. I figure it out."

He said then that as time passed, and things happened, he began to think that something more was being planned.

"You know, of course, that Linda, she and I are lovers." It was a statement, not a question.

"When did that start?" asked Hester.

"From the moment she sees my eyes," he said, with a completely straight face. "We start to be with the other that same time, only one day after we meet."

That surprised me, but considering where Harry said he'd found them, it did fit.

"You started bagging her the day after you met her, then?" I asked.

"Yes."

"Well, okay," I said. "So you're sleeping with Linda almost right away, then?"

"We never sleep together until last night." He smiled in a friendly way. "That is how we find ourself caught. Never sleep together, just screw together. Hard to catch you."

I imagined Harry was rolling on the floor by now. I tossed one in for the audience when I said, "I'll make a note of that."

"So, then what happened?" Hester brought us back into line.

As it happened, Linda, at some point, had told Skripkin that Rudy was getting worried about just what was up, and that Hassan and company were asking him to do something he objected to.

"Why didn't he just walk away?" asked Hester.

"Agent lady," said Skripkin, "Rudy had been bought like me. They had...hired him, out of Colombia, to do a job for them, and he had agreed to do it. This man who was boss of Hassan? He was, too, boss of Rudy, but Hassan was boss of Rudy too. Same man. Do you understand? Very important man."

"Okay," I said. "So you have this boss, and under him you have Hassan, and under him you have Rudy, right?"

"Absolutely correct," he said.

"So...?"

"Rudy got very mad because Hassan and me, we also...ah, recruit...the Orejas man who is friend of Rudy. Rudy cannot get to the right place in the processing line, okay, to put the stuff on the meats. Rudy said he would not take a—what do I want to say—lesser job to do that. You know many Colombians? No? They are that way. I do not know. But Rudy was higher than the meat carrier, and he also said that there would be suspicion if he asks for a lesser duty. So, then, we do not ask Rudy, we ask Orejas. Orejas carries meat into trucks, and is very often having privacy for a several seconds as he is in the truck. He is in right place to do this deed."

Ah-ha. "Just what deed?"

"He was to use this substance, this white stuff, and...what is this word...place it on, like butter you place on bread. Only this it was on the meat. Spread! That is it, spread. At first." ·

"At first?"

"Yes. We do experiment for spread, we see it cannot be done...well...with a plastic bag and a rubber spreading tool. Hassan telephones his boss, and a few days later, the ups," he said, pretty clearly meaning United Parcel Service, "they deliver a very nice package, and in the package we have cans that spray."

"No shit?" I said.

"No shit, yes. And we give cans to Orejas, and Rudy gets very mad."

"Why was he so mad?" asked Hester. "Orejas worked for him, didn't he?"

"Rudy says that when this Orejas was very small, he gets very bad injured in his head. Orejas is made to be very easy to persuade. Rudy takes care to see Orejas stays out of trouble from that day. Rudy says that Orejas, he is 'too fucking dumb to know if he wants to do it or not,' and Hassan should leave Orejas alone." Skripkin shrugged. "I know for a fact that Orejas, he is not smart. He does it because Hassan tells him that it will help Rudy. I was there."

"Okay..."

"Then Rudy finds out that Orejas is supposed to use a mask and gloves, and he gets a lot worried. He says that Orejas cannot do things like that the right way."

"Just a second," I said. "Orejas just wasn't quick enough to follow the procedures?"

"That is correct. Rudy is very mad, and Rudy is making talk like he is going to tell Orejas to stop. So we take Rudy to the old farm, and we have talk with him."

"Who's we?" I asked.

"That would be me, and Hassan, and the one they call Chato, and Rudy."

"Chato?" Another unknown.

"Yes. Chato, he was the driver. He works at the plant, he knows Rudy and Orejas, and everybody there."

Hester and I exchanged glances.

"You know his real name?" asked Hester.

"I do not, lady agent. I swear." And he gave her another wink.

"So, what happened? First, why did you pick the old Dodd place?" I asked.

"What is this 'old Dodd place'? I do not know it."

"Sorry. The old farm where you took Rudy."

"Ah. Dodd? That is funny name, Dodd. We take Rudy there because we know where it is. We go there sometimes, to do private meeting and talk about plan. Hassan, he is very worried that FBI listens in at walls of apartment."

"How did you ever find that place?" I asked.

"I do not know this. This Rudy would know."

"Okay. But you'd been there before?"

"Oh yes," said Skripkin. "Four, five times."

"Okay. So, when you got to the farm, what happened?"

"I am sorry to say that Rudy knows by then about Linda and me. He is very angry at that. Hassan is very angry. He is angry at Rudy, and he is angry at me. We start to beat up Rudy a bit, you know. To make him to listen. But my heart is not in my work, because I feel bad about Linda. Hassan gets mad at me again, too. I tie Rudy's wrists, and Hassan hits him many times. Rudy falls down and starts to kick Hassan. It was very bad."

"Why was Hassan so mad?" asked Hester. "Did Rudy talk to Orejas and tell him to stop?"

"No. Rudy came to us first, I think. Me and Hassan. He never had a chance to talk to Orejas about it after that."

"So why was he so mad at Rudy?"

"Because, Rudy, if he go to Orejas and tell him to stop, the experiment cannot be done, and the boss of Hassan will get very angry at Hassan."

"So Hassan pisses off his boss...so what?"

"Boss of Hassan is very bad man. Very bad. Very important in many places. Hassan would be killed in a slow way and the way will be full of meaning to others."

"So," I asked, "just how did Rudy find out that Orejas was involved in the first place? Do you know?" It wasn't adding up.

Skripkin lowered his eyes. "I am afraid that I tell Linda after we are making love. She likes Orejas, he is like a little pet to her. So she tells Rudy. But she tells him *everything*, you know? About me, about screwing, about all these things." He looked up again. "Women I do not understand very well. I think very hard that if Rudy did not have so much on his mind, he might not have done what he did."

"Good bet," I said. "Okay, now, back to you four at the farm. Rudy was kicking Hassan. What happens next?"

"Yes. Sure. So, after Hassan is kicked by Rudy, Hassan gets very, very angry. He says, 'Okay you motherfucker, we will see how you talk to the boss.' He says it just that way. You understand, they are speaking Spanish to each other most of the time, okay? I don't understand Spanish. So I don't know all that is said. But when he wants me to know, he speaks English. You understand he is not Arab person. He is Mexican kind of person. He calls himself Hassan because he says he has come to that religion. You see?"

"I think so," I said.

"Good. Do not forget this, that Hassan is not Arab. So he tells me and Chato in English to put Rudy in the car, in the back, and he has me in the back, too, because I am so big to Rudy. Hassan and Chato, they are in front. Chato is our driver. Hassan gets the shotgun that is in the...back. No, trunk, in trunk, and has it in now with him. He tells Chato to go to Iowa City."

"Iowa City?"

"That is where we can meet the boss."

"And that would be...?" asked Hester.

"Pardon, lady agent?"

"What's the name of the person you refer to as 'the boss'?"

"I tell you before. This is something I do not know." He gave her an intense look. "You must believe me, lady agent."

"I'll try," said Hester, dryly.

"Okay," I said. "Then what?"

"I am feeling badly about things, and not looking at anything but Rudy, but Hassan is starting to really talk loudly at Chato about going the wrong way. So Chato, he stops in a hurry, and starts to back up, and when he does this, Rudy opens the car door and he just falls backwards out of the car, and he gets away."

We questioned him more closely, and established that he was on the left side in the rear of the car, and that Rudy was on the right side. As Chato started to try to turn the car around on the narrow, sixteen-foot gravel road, he pulled toward the left and stopped very close to the ditch on that side. Most of that was explained with hand motions, and I was very glad we were on video. When they were stopped for a second while Chato shifted into reverse, Rudy got out the back door on the right. Skripkin figured that Rudy's hands, being bound behind his back, had been near the door latch, and that he had grabbed it when Chato braked hard. At that point, Skripkin was trying to get out on the left side and go after Rudy, but Chato apparently didn't realize that Rudy had gone out of the car, and started to back up. That also slowed Hassan's exiting down, and actually knocked him over when his open car door pushed him to the ground. It also made him even madder. Skripkin said that they both were delayed for a second or two, and that Rudy disappeared around the curve. He also said that for a moment, he thought Hassan might shoot Chato for being so stupid.

It had a ring of truth. It seemed to have been the sort of total screw-up that was typical in most crimes.

"So, then what happened?" I asked.

"We were running up this road after him," said Skripkin, "and Hassan was in front of me, and then Rudy falls to the ground. And Hassan catches him and so do I, and Hassan is very, very angry. He yells at Rudy, and Rudy, he begins to cry. I do not know what was said, but I think it occurs to Rudy that life is over. And Hassan, he calls him a motherfucker again, and then he just shoots him in the back of the head, while he is kneeling on the ground. Bang. Just like that. Very quick."

"Just the three of you, and then just the two of you, right?" I asked. I wanted to know if they'd seen old Jacob there.

He grinned. "Good way to say it. Yes. Three, then bang, then two."

He never mentioned seeing anyone else, so I guess Jacob Heinman had been right with his theory about the cat and the mouse.

"I was not expecting the shooting," said Skripkin. "I was taken by surprise. I said, 'What do we do now?' because we had a body to get rid of. And Hassan says, 'We leave now,' and I did not think it wise to argue as I did not have a gun."

"So you just took off, and left the body on the road?" asked Hester.

"Sure."

"And you thought you should, what, take it with you?"

"If we take it back to the farm, nobody would ever see it again," he said. "Nobody would know Rudy was dead. Leaving it on the road is stupid mistake. I search for word...ah, no money for work...Olympics say this."

"Amateur?" I asked. It sure fit what I was thinking.

"Yes! Amateur is a good word for it."

"That sounds right," I said. "But I think you're pretty damned lucky."

"Why is that?"

"If Hassan hadn't left the body in the road, you and Chato would have been the only other persons who would have known where it was. I got a feeling that you're both pretty damned lucky you didn't help him hide it, because I think he would have shot you, too."

He thought about that. "Probably."

"Maybe not so amateur all the time," I said. "Okay, now, why..."

"I have question," said Skripkin. "Can I ask?"

"Sure. Ask away."

"This immunity that Linda is doing. Am I included? She said I was to be included."

It was time to set that straight. "No. As far as we know, your name has never been mentioned."

"I see." He shook his head sadly. "Women. They tell you anything to get you to love them." He tapped his fingers on the tabletop. "So, I can be taken to trial?"

"Yes. You can be charged, and I intend to do that."

"So, good as it gets," he said.

"Pardon me?"

"I got to be in jail. Somewhere. I know this. I am in jail here or I am in jail in Russia. I will take here. Much better places in U.S.A."

I thought that might depend on which definition of "better" was being used, but didn't say anything.

The more I thought about it, the more something wasn't quite right about Skripkin's information regarding the boss, but I couldn't put my finger on it. I made a quick note, just a question mark and the word "boss." I'd go back there later.

"Okay, now," I said. "Just why was all this stuff being done? The substance on the meat, I mean. What was it intended to do?"

"It was intended to kill Jews," he said. "Of course."

17:03

AFTER THE SHADOWY FIGURE YELLED AT US, it got very quiet for what seemed a very long time.

When we looked back, later, and tried to piece together the moment when everything went to shit, we decided it was about now, when George's, Hester's, and my cell phones all rang at the same time.

There was a moment's confusion, because nobody was really sure just whose phone was ringing.

Sally helped Hester with hers, while George and I tried to talk, understand the messages, and keep lookout at the same time.

"Yeah," I said, after fishing mine out of my pocket.

"Carl," said Lamar, "call the office. They just got a 911 call from somebody they think is up there at the shed area west of you. Caller says he has something to negotiate."

"What?" I was totally surprised.

"Yeah. They've got a call-back number, and we got a federal agent who's a negotiator, and he's callin' that number right now."

"Okay..."

"And the CRPD chopper is gonna be makin' a pass over you real shortly with the FLIR. So make the call to the office. Then contact the chopper on AID."

The Forward-Looking Infra-Red viewer in the helicopter would enable them to see just about anything that would be visible in the daytime, and some things that wouldn't be. It measured the heat differential to about a tenth of a degree, and that made for some very high-definition viewing, indeed.

"Sheriff's Department," said the harried but familiar voice of Patty Neuman. She wasn't yet up to the standard we'd come to expect from Sally, but she'd do the job.

"Hi. It's Houseman. Lamar said to call—"

"Jesus, are you guys all right? Is Sally okay?"

"So far. What you got?"

"Just a sec." I heard her rummaging around on her desk. "God, Houseman, I got pictures of where you are on the TV in front of me. Okay, here you go....Okay, so the call came in at 18:22:09, from the Battenberg OMNI, and the caller said that his name wasn't important, but that he wanted to arrange a truce so they could get a male subject treated for a wound." She was reading the E911 printout.

"No shit?"

"Yeah, no shit is right. You want the number?"

"Can't write it down just now. What is it, though?" I really wanted to know who the hell it was that had called.

"Okay...that's area code 781, 555, 8811."

"Where's area code 781?"

"Minneapolis. For mobile phones."

"Well."

"I think the FBI is talking to that line now."

"That's what Lamar said. Okay, I gotta go, unless you have more on that..."

"That's it. Oh, boy, you all be careful down there, now."

"Oh, we will," I said. "We will."

After I terminated my call, Sally came over. "That was Hester's boss. It looks like we might have a deal where we get an ambulance up here for one of the wounded assholes, and they're going to try to get Hester out at the same time."

Ah. "Not in the same ambulance," I said. "We need two ambulances. And we load Hester first."

George came over. "That was Volont. They've got a negotiator talking to one of them now, I guess. They want to get an ambulance up for one of their wounded."

"That's what I hear. DCI wants to get Hester out then, too."

"That would be good," said George. "She's got to be wearing down."

"I want to call Lamar. I don't want her going out in the same ambulance with some terrorist. Too risky."

"I agree," he said. "Oh, and Volont says they didn't get anybody in Michigan or Nebraska. He thinks something might have gone wrong... that the informant might have had the wrong date, or something. At any rate, it doesn't look like the other operation is going until later."

"Their informant a liar?"

"Possible," he said. "But Volont and Hawse and Gwen are here. The HRT is in a helicopter right now, and on the way. We wait for them, then we go."

The FBI Hostage Rescue Team was rightly considered to be the best tactical team ever invented. I was as happy to know they were on the way as I would have been to have the Marines. Well, close. HRT doesn't come with artillery, tanks, and integral air support.

My phone rang. It was Lamar.

"Carl, it looks like we're gonna have to get an ambulance up there in the next five or ten minutes. They insist, and the negotiator says it's bad for us to play with the times for a wounded subject. The press is all over us. We gotta be prompt, I guess."

"Okay. Make it two ambulances, though. We don't want Hester in with them."

Apparently nobody else in the whole damned world had thought of that. "Oh. Oh, yeah. We'll do that."

"Let us know when to move," I said.

George's phone rang next. It was Volont. The FBI negotiator had tried to delay the pickup of the wounded terrorist until the HRT arrived. No such luck. Whoever was on the other end of that negotiation was aware that there were two or three ambulances stacked up on the gravel road south of the farm. Volont suspected it meant that the bad guys had a vantage point that was pretty high up.

After George told me, we both looked in the direction of the silo. Even money said there was somebody up there, although we couldn't see anyone.

"I told Volont that we thought the terrorists were trying to block us, not the other way around," said George, never taking his eyes off the area around the silo.

"What'd he say to that?" I asked.

"He thinks it's possible," said George. "But he said that they might just be so fanatical that they just want to sucker more of us up there to be killed, before they die for the cause."

"You think they're that fanatical? I haven't seen any of that."

"Not particularly, no," said George. "But Volont would tend to think they were. That sort of thing appeals to him, I think."

As we were talking, my walkie-talkie announced, "Nation County Three, 918."

Just from the background noise, I could tell it was a helicopter. I twisted the knob on the top of my walkie-talkie to channel 4, the AID channel, and cut off the scan function. I didn't want any interruptions at this point.

"Nation County Three, go ahead 918," I said.

"Stand by for one, Three. TAC Six from 918?" TAC 6 answered, and I recognized Marty's voice. "Yeah, Three and TAC Six, we're just about overhead, now. We can see two people moving behind the shed closest to the barn. Two people near the base of the silo, on the ground and stationary, and one on the ladder on the west side. He's stable at about three-fourths of the way to the top. All those are stationary, repeat, stationary. We have a strong IR signature in the other shed, the one more northerly, and it looks like they've got a car running in there, possibly to keep the injured subject warm. Three, maybe four subjects in that immediate area. We've got a strong glow in your barn itself, and four individuals. Do you guys have a heat source in there?"

"Ten-four," I answered. "We do."

"Right. We got the TAC team members spotted, and one, no, two deer in the wooded area to the northeast about a hundred yards."

"Ten-four. Can you tell if that's a car in the shed, or is it a van?"

"Nope, not a van. That's definite. It's a warm enough target to give us an outline of the vehicle. Wrong shape all the way. It's a confirmed passenger car, mid-sized, maybe."

"Ten-four."

"We'll be working the area, but we're gonna avoid being overhead. Advise when you want close watch. Understand you have a 10-52 that's going to be coming up that lane toward the barn?"

"Ten-four," said Marty. "Last I heard, two of 'em. Go up on Orange for a minute."

That was a signal to change to a scrambled, restricted access frequency, so that TAC 6 and the helicopter could discuss something that wasn't for just everybody. They were being careful, and I liked that.

Sally was holding up her fingers. "Shit. That's at least eight of 'em," she said. "Eight."

"Yeah. With the two, that would have been ten."

We all looked at one another in the faint orange glow of the heater.

"That's just too many," I said, "for one fuckin' car. Where the hell's Hector's van with the Nebraska plates, then?" A van made more sense, although it would have been pretty crowded with ten people in one. The van plus the car, on the other hand, would just about fit.

Sally held up her walkie-talkie, "It's Lamar for you on Ops."

I switched my frequency to channel 1, and said, "Three."

"Okay, now everybody listen up." Lamar must have called a radio conference. "Here's the deal. Two ten-fifty-twos go up. They take their crews and one officer each. They stop in the yard, right in the middle. Nobody, I repeat, nobody goes outside the circle of the yard light." There was a brief transmission break as he organized his thoughts. "Okay, everybody listenin'? They will bring their wounded man into the light, and the EMTs from the first ambulance will go to them with a stretcher. Both officers in the ambulances go to the stretcher with them. Nobody else. Repeat, nobody else."

Another transmission break, followed by, "While they do that, I-388 will come out to the other ambulance. I-388 can walk on her own. She will get into that ambulance. Both ambulances leave at the same time. Nobody else moves into the area. It goes smooth and quick. If you're ten-four on that, sound off in order, starting with Three."

"Three's ten-four," I said. That was followed by acknowledgments from eight or nine team-leading officers, and both ambulances; Battenberg 51 and Maitland 52.

"Okay," said Lamar. "We go in ten minutes."

It sounded like a plan, all right.

As Lamar finished, my cell phone went off again. This time it was Marty.

"Carl, look. The HRT is going to be here really soon. The plan is, as soon as the ambulances clear the area on their way out, the HRT goes in, and then we go in. Get ready to move, because when HRT reach the barn in good shape, you guys will leave with us. We take you out, down to the road, and then move back up. The HRT will advance on the suspects. They want you out of there as soon as you can get out."

"What about the people at the silo?"

"They'll neutralize them."

I wondered just how to neutralize somebody two-thirds of the way up a silo. I hoped he was right when he said they could do that. "Okay. Sounds like a plan."

"We call you one more time, just before we come to get you."

"Got it."

"Should be within fifteen minutes or so. If the HRT gets here while the ambulances are still up at the barn area, we wait until they clear."

"Right."

"The word is, if anybody tries anything with the ambulance, we take 'em out."

"Good."

"Okay. See you soon."

CHAPTER 18

"SKRIPKIN'S BULLSHITTING," SAID VOLONT.

"No shit," I said. "Which part?" We were sitting in the taping room, getting ready to replay the Skripkin interview for the second time. We'd been joined by FBI agents Gwen Thurgood and Milton Hawse, who had broken off from the searches in Battenberg after Volont had called them from the Conception County Jail.

"Let's start with when he says 'to kill Jews.' That's bullshit. If somebody wants to kill the Jews who get meat from some delis, all you have to do is break into a deli and put the stuff on the food right on-site. Hell, it'd be a whole lot easier just to toss a bomb in the front door. Nope. Won't fly. He's lying."

"Okay, I'll buy that. So now tell me why," said Hester. "Why lie about what they've already done?"

Volont had a satisfied look. "Okay, *lady agent*," he said. "To keep us from figuring out what they're going to do."

It was quiet. Volont leaned forward just slightly. "What we have here is the warm-up. The game hasn't started yet. Now, assume you want to poison a food supply. On a big, big scale. Kill thousands, maybe hundreds of thousands of people."

"We don't really have any evidence for that," said Hawse.

"Now, just hang on here," said Volont. "Like I said, *assume* that and just listen for a minute. But, no, we don't. No direct evidence, anyway. However, we do have an involvement with Al Qaeda through our Mr. Odeh. That's not theoretical. We do know that much. Keep with me for a minute," he said, forestalling another comment from Hawse. "You can't just try a method and then try it again and again until you get it right. Won't work. The first big attempt, the one where you tip your hand, really has to work right from the start. Otherwise, you set off alarms all over the country, and you don't get a second shot. Not these days." Volont glanced around the room. We were all listening.

"Right..." said Hawse.

"Okay, then. You start small. You do a little test. An experiment. Very small scale. Where? You go to a sparsely populated area with virtually no cops." He made a sweeping gesture around the room. "Well, shit, here we are. Like they say, the heartland will never be a police state, because there just about aren't any police."

He was right about that, at least.

"Then, you pick the most closely supervised, cleanest, most sanitary operation you can find. A kosher meat plant fills that bill. For one thing, this one just so happens to be located in the middle of a rural area, okay? For another, it hires nonresident labor. This whole area is just about made in heaven for these bastards to waltz in and do their thing without anybody picking up on their being here."

"An experiment?" asked George.

"Sure. If you get it to work in a kosher plant, you can get it to work anywhere. Even the FDA guys say that the kosher plants are the best in the business. Sanitary. Clean. Safe. Closely supervised. It's a family business, for Christ sake, not a big corporation. The guys who own and run that place get involved in the whole business."

"Your point?" asked Hawse.

"It's coming. But there's one more thing," added Volont. "With this one, you get the added benefit that your experiment, if successful, also kills Jews. That works two ways."

"How?" asked Gwen.

"Like this. First, we have Mustafa Abdullah Odeh. An involvement by him is almost a guarantee that I'm on the right track here, all by itself. We've got the ricin in the meat that sure as hell didn't get there by accident. We've got a Colombian connection, Rudy, who hired out to work with Mustafa and whichever particular group he's fronting for right now. So what we've got is a carefully planned, controlled experiment. Look, the Jews are a secondary target here. Frosting. It's really sensitive because the victims are Jewish, but don't let that distract you from understanding the real intent, here. Don't forget these people are connected to the 9/11 bunch. Their primary objective is to kill Americans. They want to destroy American icons, like the World Trade Center. And they want to terrify as many Americans as possible. Hell," he said, "I'd bet even money that if Juan Miguel Alvarez , aka Hassan Ahmed Hassan, *does* have a hatred of the Jews. It's an acquired taste. It's like Osama bin Laden, you remember? He hardly said diddly shit about Jews until we started goin' after his ass in Afghanistan. Then, all of a sudden, he's a crusader against Jews in general, and Israel in particular. Smoke screen, just like the one Skripkin's trying to blow up our ass."

"Well…" said Hawse, drawing the word out, "I'm not so sure. We'll need more than this before we submit it to the NIPC."

He was referring to the FBI's National Infrastructure Protection Center, which was responsible for disseminating warnings to law enforcement agencies regarding terrorism.

"Stick with me for a minute yet," said Volont. "Then decide that. Just exactly what stage of the experiment are we in? Right now? An experiment requires an act that has measurable results. With this one, all you have to do is run your experiment, and then you just turn on the news and see how effective it was. The media hand you your measurable results. All the numbers, sick, dead, critical condition. Just like the Air Force's Bomb Damage Assessment does. The terrorists have access to all the data, on every major network, and in every paper you can name. You, as the experimenter, know how much meat you screwed with, and you know how much 'product' you used on it. You know when you did it. Turn on your TV, and you now know how many you killed and wounded with it. All your post-strike analysis is done for you. Data in, data out, and an independent analysis of the damage when it's done." He looked right at Hawse. "BDA by CNN, as they say. You want to finish for me?"

Volont was baiting him.

"You go ahead," said Hawse. He gave no indication that he'd noticed.

"Now we get theoretical. But, do this. Think a big, fat, juicy target. Think fast food," said Volont. "Just a theoretical, but that stuff's the greatest symbol of the U.S.A. since Coca-Cola and the Hershey bar. Even more than some statue or monument, because fast-food places pop up all over the whole world. 'In your face,' in every sense of the word. I'd be willing to bet that what, maybe a dozen packing plants, and you'll cover at least some of the beef source for a lot of the major fast-food chains. And it doesn't have to be beef. Remember that. Fish, chicken, vegetables... Also keep in mind that lots of packing plants use nonresident labor, as they put it. Easy to get the foreign terrorists in, easy to have them keep a low profile until you need 'em."

"Sleepers," said Hawse.

Volont gave him a fast glance, said "Yeah. Sleepers" dryly, and then went on. "But let's go with the fast-food scenario. Doesn't have to be, so pick any other food target you want. But let's say it is. Either way, all you have to do is fill a bunch of those spray cans with ricin. Ship the cans to the people you already have in place, set a date, wait for the damage assessment on the news, and then send out the order to hit 'em all at once. Bingo. Maybe a whole bunch of dead Americans. Maybe just a few. It really wouldn't matter, to produce the desired effect. I mean, we're talkin' about making a statement here. So, either way, you get to destroy some 'capitalist icons,' and scare the shit out of half the country at the same time. And you don't need a single employee at the target restaurants, so anybody trying to protect them won't ever know what hit 'em."

"Christ," said Gwen. "It works for me."

"Sure it does. And what's more," said Volont, "it already *has* worked. Their experiment at Battenberg was a complete success." He leaned back in his chair. "Hell, they probably already have the cans shipped out to the other plants."

"It's a pretty long shot," said Hawse, half to himself. "It's a stretch..."

He was right, it *was* a long shot. But Volont was right, too, I thought.

"You just gotta balance the consequences," said Volont, softly. "What happens if we run with it and we're wrong? We get a kick in the ass. What happens if we don't run with it and we're right?" He looked at each of us in turn. "Who knows how many dead Americans, lots of economic damage, and God only knows what else."

"Well, now that we've thought of it," said George, "I'd say we're pretty much committed." He looked pointedly at Hawse. "I'd say we don't really have much choice. I think it's enough for NIPC."

The look he got from Hawse said that what George thought was of little consequence. But Hawse did say, "NIPC can decide, but I think I can recommend on this one."

I wondered if I was the only one who noticed he didn't say which way he'd recommend. That guy was slick.

"NIPC will buy it," said Volont. Hawse scowled, but didn't reply.

I was fascinated. While Hawse pronounced the NIPC acronym "nigh pick," and George had enunciated each of the four letters, Volont pronounced it an irreverent "nipsy."

"They tried the World Trade Center twice, so we know they'll persist. The second time, look what happened. They've got to have learned from their success. The difference is, this time they used a surrogate target for the controlled experiment. Just a few delis in New York City, and just one kosher packing plant way far away in the Midwest. The mega-shot comes next. They'll know we'll assume Jews are the target, because they're the victims of the test shot. They fake us right out of our shoes. We're wrong, but they not only do a deceptive move, after it's all said and done, they get to take credit for being anti-Israeli, or anti-Jewish with their friends. It's a slick deception, and we already started to bite. Time to change focus. They're aiming at a much bigger target than that. And they already have all the data they need to make it work."

"If that's the case," said Gwen, "we better hurry."

At that moment, Harry, Hester, and I were, as Hawse would have put it, "out of the loop vis-à-vis the big picture." Or something like that. Regardless of how it was stated, our part in this large investigation was just about back where we'd had it before the feds had shown up.

Half an hour later, we three "noninvolved" were just setting things up to talk with Linda Moynihan, when we were informed that her attorney had advised her to say absolutely nothing to us. Well, swell.

Volont, Hawse, Gwen, and George were in another office by that time, all busy on the telephones. I knocked on their door, and, after identifying me, George stepped out to talk to me in the busy hallway. Things had, indeed, changed.

"I'm really sorry, Carl, but we're doing 'need-to-know' on everything," said George, almost closing the door behind him.

"No problem," I said, and meant it. "We just need to know," and I smiled, "no pun intended, if it's okay if we do another interview on Skripkin."

This was a deceptively sensitive matter. We figured, based on the first interview, that Skripkin was now a key federal witness. We didn't want to mess up the feds' case, and had to know just where we stood. If they wanted guidelines for us to abide by during our questioning of him, we'd be happy to go along with that. Unfortunately, there was a strong possibility that a comprehensive set of guidelines would reveal way too much about their current operation. It had to be their call.

"Beats me, Carl," said George, raising his voice a bit to be heard over the noise being made by the copier in the little alcove next to us. A Conception County deputy and a secretary were running copies of something and having an animated conversation while doing so. "How soon you need to have an answer?"

"Just as soon as possible," I answered. "He's pretty cooperative right now. You know as well as I do that that can change in five seconds. Besides, Linda Moynihan's attorney has told her not to talk to us. We really need to put it to Skripkin."

"Oh, boy," said George. "Let me see what I can do." Due to the noise level in the narrow hall, he didn't notice the door opening behind him. "This is one for Hawse. By the way, did you see how he made himself look like he was as smart as Volont back there?"

"Is there a problem?" asked Hawse, from the now fully open door behind George.

"Uh, oh, yes," said George. "Uh, Carl here wants to know if he can do another Skripkin interview."

I didn't know if Hawse had overheard everything George said or not, but he sure as hell had to have heard that last part about him being as smart as Volont.

"Ah. Step in for a moment, Carl," said Hawse. "We'll kick some things around a bit." I got the impression he was including Special Agent George Pollard on that list of things that were going to be kicked around.

I stood leaning on a four-drawer filing cabinet while the four agents had a brief conversation about the status and value of Skripkin. They didn't ask why we wanted to talk to him again.

Hawse glanced at his watch and said, "The plane will be here in fifteen minutes, and this gentleman needs an answer before we go." He glanced at me. "You've been a great help, and I don't want to appear rude, or high-handed. You are aware of the need-to-know requirements, I'm sure."

"Oh yeah. No problem with that."

He sighed. "Sometimes these rules of engagement can be a pain in the ass," he said. I really think he was trying to make me feel better. "In this instance, I think I have the perfect solution."

This was going to be good.

"Rather than burden you with the need to keep us posted, why don't we just assign an agent to you as liaison? If you'll allow him to monitor the interview, and to keep pace with your investigation in case you turn up more valuable information..."

"That'd be fine." I said that an instant before I caught George's stricken look.

"Excellent." He looked around the crowded little office as if he were making a choice. So he *had* overheard George in the hallway.

"I think we can spare Agent Pollard, here. He's up to speed on lots of things. He'll remain attached to you for the duration." He smiled, very pleased with himself. "I'm sure he won't be in your way."

"We'll consider ourselves lucky to have him," I said, and I meant that.

George looked crestfallen. I didn't know where the plane they referred to had come from, or where it was going, but I was sure that George had originally been intended as one of the passengers. This could really hurt his career.

Volont looked perplexed, but since he hadn't heard what George had said, he had no idea about the main reason for Hawse assigning an agent to us. "You okay with that, George?"

George had absolutely no choice. "Fine with me," he said, and managed to make it sound convincing.

"Well," said Volont, "as long as you're okay with it, why don't you also take on the press relations over in Nation County? The media won't be able to find us for quite a while, and we want them to think the locus of the investigation is still over there. If that'd be all right?"

"Excellent idea," said Hawse.

"Oh, sure," said George. "Fine. Absolutely."

"Good," said Volont. "Now, don't lie to 'em or anything like that. Don't even mislead 'em. Just don't acknowledge what else is going on until we give you the word."

"Look what the FBI gave me," I said as we joined Hester and Harry. George half waved, sheepishly. "Hi, gang."

"Shit," said Harry. "Who'd you piss off?" He was kidding.

"Hawse," said George, who wasn't. "Big time."

"The rest of the federal group is flying out in about ten minutes," I said. "We have permission to do Skripkin again if we need to, but George has to monitor. And George is to handle media for the feds over in Nation County. Volont wants the media to think that we're still the focus of the investigation."

"Sound," said Hester.

"Where they gettin' a plane?" asked Harry. Conception County Airport had just extended its paved runway, but so far there were no business flights actually based there.

"Hawse had one on standby in Milwaukee," said George. "Corporate jet kind of thing. Contracted to the Bureau."

"Hot shit," said Harry. "Must be nice."

At that point, the door opened, and Volont, Hawse, and Gwen Thurgood squeezed in.

"We have to be leaving," Hawse told us. "But we wanted you to know that we really appreciate all the good work you've done on this case. Really. It's excellent. If there's anything you need," he said, "let us know. We're going to be concentrating in other areas, as I'm sure you've guessed, but we're as close as your phone, as they say."

"What he means," translated Volont, "is that if you turn up any more good stuff, be sure to contact us."

Hawse smiled. "That, too. But if you do need something, I'll do everything in my power to see that you get it."

The "Flying Feds," as Harry now called them, hadn't been gone for more than ten minutes when one of the Conception County secretaries stuck her head into the room.

"Is one of you Deputy Houseman?"

"Me," I said.

"I have a teletype message for you that says that the 'missing plant workers' are starting to drift back into Battenberg."

It was about time. "Thanks," I said.

"Is there still a federal agent here?"

"Yeah," said George. "That's me."

"Then this is for you," she said, handing George a manila file folder. "That other FBI guy, the old one, requested this about an hour ago."

George thanked her, looked at the teletype information in the folder, and smiled. "Thanks." The secretary left, and George skimmed the papers in the folder. "Well, at least his name really is Skripkin," he said. "Based on fingerprint records. Nothing in the States. Nothing in Russia, or any of the former states of the Soviet Union. But he really *is* wanted...in the U.K., by the London Metropolitan Police."

"What for?" asked Hester.

"Apparently passing counterfeit securities and counterfeit bonds, and something they refer to as 'other suspected offenses of a subversive nature.' We better call on this one."

"Call who?" asked Harry.

"The Metropolitan Police, for starters," said George.

"I hope you brought your fuckin' phone card," said Harry.

"Don't worry, Harry," said George. "Uncle Sam's picking up the tab on this one."

The Metropolitan Police were quite cooperative. George, just to share the fun, put them on the speakerphone while they talked.

"Oh, yes," said Inspector Blythe, with a very British accent. "Lived in a tatty flat in Lambeth with a half dozen others. They styled themselves the 'People's Freedom and Reform Movement.' That was two years ago, when we had contact with our Mr. Skripkin."

"I hate to jump the gun," said George, "but was that some sort of...well...terrorist cell, by any chance?"

"Hardly. But I know how you feel since September. We used to feel the same way about the IRA. But, no. We weren't able to make any connection to a truly functional terrorist organization. The People's Freedom and Reform Movement's counterfeiting activities were directed toward some lunatic scheme to destroy our economy by printing up false securities and bonds, in fact. There were many, well, holes in their approach to that."

"Okay," said George.

"Their source of income, at the time we had them, was by making their services available as protestors. They were for let to anyone, actually, but they seemed to have a decided preference for any demonstrations against capitalists in general and the European Economic Union in particular."

"So, that's the part about 'other suspected offenses of a subversive nature,' then?" asked George.

"No, that part's a direct reference to a stack of Kalashnikovs we found in their flat. We were unable to discover just what it was they actually intended to *do* with the things. There was no ammunition present. Our Mr. Skripkin denied any association with that part of the scheming. They all did, at first. We filed charges on four of them for the weapons. Mr. Skripkin's fingerprints were found on several of the weapons. He was on bond, awaiting trial, when he fled the U.K. He would have been deported eventually, at any rate. We didn't feel a loss. Interestingly enough, we came up with a dead trace on the Kalashnikovs. Chinese manufacture, originally. Turned up next in Libya, in fact. Then, if I remember, Spain. No routing available after that. So you might have a connection to bona fide terrorists through the weapons, but it would be tenuous at best. And, truthfully, I wouldn't have the vaguest notion which direction you'd even start, over there."

"And cold, to boot," said George.

"By the way, would you mind telling me your interest in him? You obviously have his latents at hand."

"We have him in custody here, on a state charge of conspiracy to commit a murder."

"Really? He actually went through with it, then?"

"He sure did," said George. "He was five feet from a man who was murdered execution-style. Near contact shotgun wound to the head. He'd helped bind and restrain him."

There was a chuckle from Blythe at the other end. "Yes, I'd say that was a conspiracy, indeed. Well, it's nice to hear that Mr. Skripkin has come up in the world. I'm glad you have got him."

"We also have a fair link to a more authentic terrorist group. We can keep you posted on that."

"Excellent."

"Did he say anything to you about being wanted in Russia?" asked George.

"He did, but we weren't able to confirm the information. That," he hurried to say, "shouldn't be taken conclusively either way, you understand. Even today, they have some things they don't tell us on inquiry. The Russian mafia, as an example, isn't always freely acknowledged in communiqués." There was humor in his voice.

"Did you know Skripkin personally? Have you met him?"

"Oh, yes. Indeed I did know him. I conducted the interviews with him, and with some of his friends."

"Was he such a compulsive liar then, too?" asked George.

"Oh, my, yes. Yes, indeed. Quite the ladies' man, too, according to others."

"Still is," said George, grinning at Hester. "Look, we'll let you go now. Thank you very much for the information."

"I'm sorry there's not more. If you do turn up anything you need, though, be sure to let us know."

"Just a sec...could you forward a list of his group in London?" asked George. "The names, and if you have any idea where they are now?"

"I'll send a complete list just as soon as we can pull the files."

Hester held up a note.

"And...and, can you tell us anything about a Vladimir Nadsyev, in connection with Skripkin?"

"Just a moment...now, there's a name I haven't heard since...but yes, Vladimir Nadsyev was living in the same flat with Skripkin, now that you mention it."

"Skripkin refers to this Vladimir Nadsyev as his boss. Can we believe him on that?"

"I don't believe I can verify that either way," replied the Metropolitan Police detective. "I can check for you."

"Please," said George. "We'd really appreciate being able to verify some of what he tells us."

That produced a chuckle in London. "Would you be so good as to send a photo of him telling the truth? We'd very much like to see that one."

"It looks like everybody agrees Skripkin's a liar, then," said Hester, when George hung up the phone. "So, just what do we believe?"

That was the real problem. We had a major step about to be taken by several federal agencies, because Volont believed he had seen through the lies. Thus far, we had confirmed that he *was* a liar. We had no specific information as to just where the lies actually crept in. We really needed to talk to Linda Moynihan.

CHAPTER 19

SINCE WE COULDN'T TALK TO LINDA, we did the next best thing. We talked to Skripkin again. This time, things were a little different.

As soon as he saw Hester, he smiled and said, "Hello, lady agent. I dream about you."

"It's the jail food," said Hester. "Trust me."

"Deputy," he said, acknowledging me. "And who is...?"

George said, "Special Agent Pollard, FBI Counterintelligence."

Just a tiny flicker of surprise showed on Skripkin's face. "How do you do." He was definitely more alert.

"Just fine," said George. "You know you have the right to an attorney..."

After the second Miranda, George just leaned back in his chair and said, "You're a very interesting fellow."

"Thank you."

"As soon as I heard that you were wanted in Russia, I thought I'd like to talk with you sometime."

"I am glad."

"Then, when I found out you were really wanted in the U.K., I thought I'd better talk to you right away."

"What is this U.K.?" The tension was back.

"You lie too much to be of any real use to us," said George. "Maybe the English will want you back. I've talked to someone who knew you when you lived in 'a tatty little flat in Lambeth.' With your friends the Kalashnikovs."

"I do not think I want to talk any more with you," said Skripkin.

George began rummaging through his file folder. That was my prearranged signal to ask a wild-card question.

"When did they start to call you 'Cheeto'? Way back then? Or is it more recent?" We'd decided that was to be tossed into the line of questioning because I remembered that Hector had referred to one of Rudy's acquaintances by that nickname. It was a question that could serve two purposes. First, if Cheeto wasn't Skripkin, it might be just enough to distract him and cause a little worry about what false information we had about him that *he* hadn't supplied. A liar always wants to be in control of the lies. Second, if he was Cheeto, then he could worry about what truth we knew about him, and just where we obtained it. For us, there wasn't a downside.

"Who told you that?" It was an indefinite response.

I put on my reading glasses, took a paper out of my folder, which happened to contain a bunch of throwaway teletypes regarding God knew what that I'd pulled off the dispatch desk, and pretended to read. Keeping my head slightly down, I looked up at him over the top of my glasses. "Three days ago, when you came up during an interview," I said.

I had a feeling that he was a lot less accustomed to getting evasive answers than he was to giving them.

"Three days ago?" asked Skripkin.

"The day Rudy was shot," I said. "That was three days ago, wasn't it?"

He didn't answer.

I gave as genuine a chuckle as I was able, all things considered. "I'll bet that all along, you thought it was *Linda* we were looking for, didn't you?" I mean, it was Linda, of course. I never said it wasn't. But he sure as hell didn't know that.

Like they say, silence is golden.

I figured I was on the right track. "Well, you're sure right about one thing. You really don't know much about women. I'll bet you also thought Rudy was the only one she told about the two of you."

"You are such a smart person...who else did she tell, then?" I had to give him credit, he didn't give in easily.

We'd talked about this beforehand and had decided that the second, and last, wild card we had to hit him with was the name of Mustafa Abdullah Odeh. We'd agreed to make it an indirect reference, to be used by any of the three of us, at our discretion.

"I can't give you the name of the other person she told," I said. Dangle the worm.

He leaned back, beginning to smile.

"But I can tell you that the other person subsequently told one...one"—and I looked at my bogus folder again—"told one Mustafa Abdullah Odeh." I looked up and was able to watch the blood drain from his face. When you're on a roll, you might as well go as far as you can. "And I guess he's pissed," I said. "From what I'm told. You happen to know him?"

The question produced a first, as far as my history of interviews went. Skripkin got a funny look on his face and just said, "I must use rest room. Hurry, please."

He was serious. Hester hit the buzzer on the desk, and a jailer stuck his head in the room.

"He's gotta go," she said. "Rest room."

Skripkin was on his feet and halfway to the door before she finished speaking.

As our suspect disappeared down the short jail hallway, Hester said dryly, "Think he might know him?"

"Nice job, Carl," said George. "Volont's going to be sorry he missed this."

It was fifteen minutes later that Skripkin finally reentered the interview room. He didn't look too good. We went at him gently at first, with Hester taking the lead. He told her that Mustafa Abdullah Odeh was a very bad man. As if we didn't know that. He also told her that Mustafa Abdullah Odeh was the boss. Just that simple. As far as Skripkin knew, Odeh was the source of the plan to spray the meat at the Battenberg plant. He was also the source of anything that Juan Miguel Alvarez, aka Hassan Ahmed Hassan, had needed or had thought necessary to complete the mission.

"Like what?" asked Hester. "Money?"

"Money. Yes. The spray cans, too. Weapons. For security of the operations."

"Is that where the shotgun came from?" she asked. "The one that was used to kill Rudy?"

"No. That one was purchased by Hassan at a store. For hunting, he said."

"Okay. Do you know which store?"

"The tools and things store in Battenberg."

"You mean the hardware store?" she asked.

"Yes. That is the one."

Hester made a note. "Hassan didn't happen to get the spray cans filled there, too, did he?"

"No, no. Those came UPS to sweet little liar Linda. She brought them to us. That way," Skripkin said, "they go to U.S.A. citizen. No questions."

This was turning out to be a really productive day.

About that time, Skripkin began having second thoughts. I suspect the picture of himself locked up in either a state or federal prison and being stalked therein by one of Odeh's associates was beginning to loom large. Or maybe he was just tired of urgent bowel movements. Either way, he suddenly decided he needed to talk with an attorney. From that point on, we could not question him without his attorney present.

Finding him an attorney presented a problem. As soon as the local attorneys found out there were going to be Iowa felonies, federal felonies, and the possibility of extradition to the U.K., they all refused to represent him. They said it was "outside their expertise." We had to go to a judge, and she had to *order* one to talk with him. It was a lot of fuss for nothing, as the appointed attorney just told Skripkin to shut up until he was able to talk to a good Federal Practice attorney, and then submitted his bill. But it had to be done.

We were happy, though. We had a good start at getting Linda Moynihan charged with a federal felony for aiding and abetting foreign terrorists. That was a good. All we had to do was check with UPS, see when the package was delivered to her address, see where it had come from, and tell her the bad news as we handed her a federal warrant. No wonder she'd wanted guarantees of both immunity and protection.

Harry put it rather succinctly when he said, "Your girl Linda probably don't know enough to save her ass, just enough to get herself killed."

"I wonder," said George, "if she knew what was in the package?"

"I'll bet she had an idea," said Hester. "Maybe not exactly, but close enough to count. The picture I'm getting of her, she tends to find those things out."

CHAPTER 20

IT HAD BEEN A LONG DAY. HESTER, GEORGE, and I got back to Iowa at about 9:15 P.M., and had been at the Nation County Sheriff's Department, mostly wrapping up the reporting for the day.

George had held a briefing for the swarming media, along with Iowa and federal health officials who provided the technical details of what was becoming known on the networks as the "Kosher Killings" case.

Hester, Sally, and I had watched George's briefing live from the safety of the dispatch center. We all groaned when the "Kosher Killings" headline was flashed on the screen. George, on camera, had no idea about the label until we told him afterward. We played the tape back for him. He'd been speechless.

We were still talking about that when Judy Mercer, KNUG's bureau chief from Iowa City, buzzed the outside door and asked for admittance to the sheriff's department. We could see her on the exterior camera. She was alone. That in itself was unusual. I couldn't remember ever seeing her without a camera operator in tow.

When the duty dispatcher asked her the purpose of her visit, over the mike at the door, Judy replied, "I'd like to speak with the officers who're working the meat poisoning case." I think the fact that she hadn't referred to "Kosher Killings" was the deciding factor in letting her in.

George, Hester, and I ushered her into the jail kitchen. I put on a pot of coffee, and we listened to what she had to say. To her offer, actually.

"I really want to be up front with all of you," she said. "Let me start with the fact that this case could be the break I need to go to the network. Just so you know why I'm here."

"Sure," said George. "We understand that."

"Good. Look, I'd like to be on air with something just a half hour ahead of the big boys out there. Something good that they'd die to get. All right?"

"We know what you want *from* us," said Hester. "What do you have *for* us in exchange?"

"Okay, look. I don't know just what this means, but I think it could be important."

We waited.

"Okay, so you know where Coralville is?"

We all did. It was a town that shared a border with Iowa City.

"I've got a girlfriend who lives in an apartment in Coralville. She says that there's been an Arabic student in the apartment next to hers, who comes and goes at odd hours and who has Hispanic and Caucasian men visit him on a regular basis."

"Okay, and...?" said George. "I mean, in Iowa City, there must be thousands of foreign exchange students."

"I know. But my friend called me about an hour ago and said that an Hispanic man had pounded on her door and asked to speak to a Mr. O'Day. She spoke to him through the closed door, but he was very insistent. She said that she was just about to call the cops when the door next to hers opened, and the Arabic man stuck his head out, and the Hispanic said, 'Mr. O'Day!' and they both went into his apartment. She thinks it's strange that an Arab is using an Irish name."

"Go on," said George.

"Well, what she said was the really weird part is that the Hispanic man was the same man she saw on one of the interviews I did down at the plant today. She swears it." Judy Mercer looked at each of us in turn. "I mean," she said, "she tapes every segment I'm on. So she replayed tonight's and double-checked. She says she's certain. Now, I don't pretend to know just what's happening here, but it seems to me that that's the sort of thing you might want to know."

"Could be," said George.

"Okay, she also says that, in the daytime, she can look out her bedroom window down to the parking lot, and this Arab's car, when she can see it, has lots of maps in the seat. Regular ones, like you can get in gas stations."

The three of us didn't say a word.

"Well? I think you should check that out."

"You might be right," said George. "Who is this friend of yours, and where does she live?"

"Now," said Judy Mercer, "we negotiate." She had a dazzling smile. "Don't you think?"

Within an hour, Coralville PD had gone to the apartment, interviewed Mercer's friend, and staked out the apartment unit next door. The suspect was not at home. His vehicle, which they said was a red Dodge van with Michigan plates, was also gone. We talked to Barry Goodman, the Coralville chief and longtime LEIN member. He assured us that he would keep the place under very tight surveillance until we advised it was no longer necessary. He'd also see what he could find out about Mr. Odeh from other sources.

In exchange, we promised Judy Mercer that she would be the first told of an impending arrest. She bargained us up to include an exclusive interview with the first suspect we took into custody. Just in case, as she said, the impending arrest turned out to be made in Florida or California.

We got the best of that deal.

I finally got home at 01:30. I let myself in as quietly as I could and found a note on the refrigerator. *"Lasagna in white container. Tastes good! Watched TV and now I'm really worried. Wake me when you come up to bed, so I don't worry. On the bright side, the weather report says we might get a white Christmas yet. Love, Sue."*

The lasagna was really good. I sat in the living room, eating it and watching our segment every fifteen minutes on *Headline News*. They changed the background footage twice, so I stayed up for another thirty minutes waiting to see if they'd change it again. They didn't. Between times, I surfed through other news channels and got to hear some fascinating commentary about what was happening in New York City and Nation County, Iowa. Nobody seemed to have either the delivery method or the targeting anywhere near right. I learned a lot about ricin, and even got a five-minute segment regarding the "legitimate uses of castor oil." This case was getting to be a real education.

So far, nobody had managed to link the poisoning to any specific terrorist network. Speculation was rife, though. Some poor bastard from the Israeli Embassy had been cornered, and was badgered about who he thought had done it, and if he thought it was an anti-Semitic hate crime, if he thought it would lead to a U.S. strike in the Middle East, and if he thought Israeli citizens felt safe in Tel Aviv. He did a very credible job of avoiding saying anything, and spent most of his time trying to reassure the reporter that "the U.S. authorities, I am sure, are handling this case with great expertise." I thought that was nice of him. I also think he deserved a little credit for not calling the reporter an idiot.

I woke Sue and told her I was home. It must have been reassuring, because she was asleep again in two minutes. I think she only beat me by a minute or two.

CHAPTER 21

SUE AND I WERE AWAKENED BY the telephone at the head of the bed. I remember wondering for the umpteenth time why I'd ever thought I needed to buy an alarm clock, and then I picked it up.

"Houseman."

"Did I get you up?" It was Volont.

"Uh, yeah. Yeah, you did."

"Well, rise and shine. We got one!"

I sat upright. "What?"

"We got some of Odeh's people, that's who. One sad bastard was driving the vehicle that Odeh was using in Coralville. It was observed at about three this morning in Michigan. The troopers notified us, and we all just followed the idiot to an apartment building. We just walked in with him and watched where he went. We hit the place as they opened the door. It was great! Odeh wasn't anywhere around, and we're sure nobody got out of the apartment unless they were with us. One of 'em started talking. He says that there are two plants—one in Michigan, one in Nebraska—which they've targeted. He says something's supposed to happen tonight, about four A.M. He's given us some names of some of the workers."

"No shit!"

"No shit, old buddy. Hawse says to tell you guys down there that you've done a terrific job. I couldn't agree more. Just keep the lid on for another day or two, and we should have these people in the bag."

"No problem. Hell, just the report-writing ought to keep us out of trouble for a month."

"You got that right!"

I didn't say it, but I also thought it would be nice to get back to finishing the work on the Rudy Cueva murder case.

After I hung up, Sue said, "What?"

"Oh, good news. About the big case. Can't tell you what, but I'm going to be spending the next few days behind a keyboard, writing endless reports."

"Oh, that's great!"

It was, in a way.

"This means that you'll be home for Christmas," she said.

"You bet." It was just about certain, in fact.

Today was Saturday, and Christmas was Tuesday. I thought I just might coast right into the holidays. We had Skripkin, we had a warrant for Hassan also known as Alvarez, we had a strong potential witness in Linda, and we had a motive. We needed to find this Chato, get an ID, and charge him with conspiracy to commit murder. That wouldn't take long. The warrant for him at least. I suspected he was wherever Hassan/Alvarez had gotten himself to, and if he was, I figured he could well be dead by now. No great loss, and it would lay a second murder charge on Hassan/Alvarez. Him we needed. It would take time, but somebody, somewhere would snag him.

I rolled up to the parking lot at 09:35, past the media's three huge microwave rigs, and allowed myself to think just how empty the place would be without them. As it was, the residents near the jail were getting a little upset since the trucks were set up in the only available space near the jail, the main highway leading out of town. As a consequence, the normal eighteen-wheeler traffic was being routed through the residential streets and bothering just about everybody. It was a good thing there was no snow, or we'd have been completely screwed.

Hester and George were both in the kitchen as I got there. The late shift had bought rolls at the local bakery, and Sally had put on some fresh coffee. In the jail kitchen, Big Ears was curled up at Hester's feet, and George was reading the *Des Moines Register.*

"Good God," I said as I walked in, "how domestic can we get?"

It was strange. I don't think we'd realized just how much we had been running on adrenaline the last few days. Now that we were out of the main effort in the ricin case, everybody just got tired all at once.

"You know," said George, "I really don't feel like working today."

"Not until Hawse and Volont want your report," said Hester.

"Well..."

"It's gonna take me the better part of the day just to get stuff sorted out," I said. "I've almost lost track of where we are with Rudy..."

Five hours later, after going over all the notes, all the statements, all the prior reports, and combining them in my report on the death of Rudy Cueva, I declared myself ready for lunch.

"Me, too," said Hester. "George?"

"Yeah?"

"When's your next news briefing?"

"No later than 4:30 this afternoon. Closer to four if I can manage it."

"Anything new to tell?" I asked.

"Not until I hear from Hawse and company. Just the same old 'the investigation is progressing' statement. Then refuse to answer questions about anything but the weather." He was totally relaxed. I though he was beginning to enjoy being the PR man on the scene.

The three of us ambled out to the kitchen to scrounge up something to eat. It was amazing. None of us had even had a phone call since about 9:00. It was almost like a vacation.

We cooked up tomato soup and toasted cheese sandwiches, with Sally's help. I was assigned to stir the soup, since everybody seemed to think I overcook everything I put in a frying pan.

"Toasted cheese sandwiches are *supposed* to be black."

It was a fine meal. Just as we finished, a phone call came in for George.

"It had to end sometime," he said cheerfully.

It was Volont. George talked to him for a few seconds, then said to me, "He'd like to talk to you."

"Really?" I took the phone, trying to think of what could possibly be left.

"We're doing the hits on the two plants later today. All the action is on the plant's late shift, so the fun should start about eleven tonight," said Volont. "Just wanted to keep you posted."

"Excellent!"

"So, they want us to make this one 'airtight.' That's the word Hawse is using now. 'Airtight.' He said to check with you to see if you had any additional information develop in the last couple of hours."

At that point, I could have just said no, and let it go at that. Maybe I should have. What I did instead was say, "You think maybe we should stake out the farm where Rudy Cueva was taken before he was killed? And Rudy and Linda's apartment? Just in case somebody rabbits on the arrest teams, and might come here."

There was a long pause at the other end of the conversation. "Well, sure. Yes. I mean, that's a pretty good idea." He sounded surprised. Not at the suggestion itself, but at the fact that I'd been the one to make it.

"You might also want to touch base with the Johnson County folks" I said. "Hell, if they don't reassemble here, I'd suspect Odeh's apartment in Coralville."

"That's been arranged," said Volont testily. "Would you notify Conception County for us?" he asked. "Special watch on Linda's and Skripkin's cells, and the jail in general. Just in case."

"Well, sure," I said. "How late you think we ought to maintain surveillance?"

"Until eleven tomorrow morning," said Volont, taking charge again. "Either that, or you can call it off if we contact you before that. Sorry." I could hear the grin in his voice.

"Got it," I said. I couldn't resist. "Anything else I can do for you?"

"Just let me talk to George," he said. I relinquished the phone and told Hester the gist of what he'd said.

"You're kidding," said Hester. "Driving time from Nebraska is what? Eight hours, maybe? The Task Force goes in at eleven or a little later tonight. That's seven A.M. any suspect can be here, at the earliest. On the off damned chance that they would ever in a million years come back this way." She smiled and sighed. "Way to go, Houseman."

"Well," I said, "they might...oh, charter a plane..."

She laughed. "Around here, that would take longer. Did they happen to say just when they want us to begin?" she asked.

"As soon as possible, so we can be in place and completely hidden before four this afternoon."

Me and my big mouth.

I had to tell Lamar, of course. He was pretty enthusiastic and thought we should have four or five people at each location.

"That's gonna be a little difficult," I said. "Isn't it?" Lamar had something up his sleeve.

"Tell you what, why don't you and Hester and George do the farm. Hell, Sally's a certified reserve. Take her, too."

"Okay. So, then, who does the apartment?"

"Me," he said. "I can't do outside stuff with my Goddamned leg, but I can stay in an apartment or in a car someplace. Just so I don't get too cold. I'll take Mike and a reserve and Martha with me." Martha was a fairly experienced dispatcher, in her early sixties. Lamar was going to be in with the second team.

"Why don't we split it a different way?" I asked. "Maybe Hester and Sally with you, and..."

"Nope. If these bastards come back, they ain't gonna go to the apartment. Too many witnesses. I want the most experience out there on that farm."

That was that.

I knew we wouldn't be able to have our cars at the old Dodd place. We'd either have to be dropped off or park a long way away and walk in. With the manpower allocations going the way they were, I suspected we'd park somewhere and hump our stuff in. Either way, that meant no heat.

"How cold's it supposed to get tonight?"

"Oh, I dunno," said Lamar. "Probably in the twenties, like last night. Hell, you been in colder places than that. Just dress warm."

This was Lamar's idea of a good time.

George and Hester weren't too excited about the idea, but I thought it was because we'd be spending a night in the cold, not the actual assignment. Sally, on the other hand, thought it would be great fun.

"If we set up in the barn," I said to Hester, "we'll be out of the wind. Maybe a couple of us in one of the sheds? How about me and George in the biggest shed, and you and Sally in the barn, then."

"What kinds of night-vision equipment do you have here?" asked George.

"About a dozen flashlights," I answered. "That's all that works, anyway."

We'd mail-ordered a surplus Soviet night scope several years back. It was a first-generation outfit we thought was called a TBC-4, but we weren't sure of the Cyrillic characters. The department joke maintained that the letters stood for "To Be Charged." At any rate, it came with one rechargeable battery that had been left in the charger for so many years it had drained to a five-minute "memory," rendering it useless outside the office. Nobody in the States manufactured a battery that would fit the thing. It had been a bargain, though.

"We can use the time," said Hester, "to chat about the cases. Sit in the dark and tell scary stories about supervisors, paperwork, and court. How about we all meet back here in half an hour. If I'm going to this slumber party, I want to get my warmest stuff."

That was an excellent idea.

We left singly, spaced a few minutes apart, so we wouldn't tip off the media.

I hit the house like a herd of buffalo. I kissed Sue as I passed her on the way up the stairs.

"What's going on? I thought the case was over."

"It is," I said from the top of the stairs "This is a wrap-up stakeout. We gotta be out all night, but all the action is way far away."

I heard Sue coming up the steps as I fished out my thermal underwear and thermal socks.

"You must be going to be outside," she said.

"Well, part of the time. And if somebody tries to get away, it'll be a good idea to be wearing warm clothes." I sat down on the bed to put my socks on over the thermal long johns.

"I thought nothing was supposed to happen," she said, pulling my Gore-Tex boots out of the closet.

"You always gotta be ready," I said as she handed me the boots. "Thanks."

"Sure. You need anything else?"

"Well, if I can remember where I put that big thermos, I'd like to fill it with hot soup. Just a couple of cans of minestrone will do. Could you put," I said, lacing the boots, "maybe a couple of cans in the mike? Make sure they boil, and I'll look for the thermos when I get downstairs..."

As she left, I slipped my thermal knit undershirt on over my head, then a short-sleeved sweatshirt, and my green woolly-pully sweater. Perfect. I clipped my gun and holster to my right hip and put two extra magazines in my back pocket. Handcuffs in the other back pocket. Badge case and ID in the left front. Always on that side, since if you stuck your gun in somebody's face, you really didn't want to have to put the thing down to get your badge out of the right-hand pocket. My Canadian Army parka was in the trunk of my car, equipped with Gore-Tex gloves, a woolen muffler, and a stocking cap. My rifle, an AR-15, was there, too, along with three extra magazines. Now for the important stuff...I headed downstairs to the kitchen.

I thought I remembered where I put the big thermos. I bent down to open the lower cupboard door.

"What are you looking for?" said Sue, over the hum of the microwave.

"The thermos..."

"I've got it right here," she said. She was washing it out at the sink.

"Oh. Okay. Good. We got any crackers?"

We did. A whole box. A new pack of string cheese, a small bag of pretzels, and six half-liter bottles of water, and I was ready to go.

I gave Sue a kiss. "See you tomorrow."

"Okay." She took a step back and looked me up and down. "Carl goes to camp," she said.

"Well, yeah. Sort of."

She handed me the thermos of soup. "Stay warm," she said, and kissed me again.

I opened the overhead garage door, to have enough room to stash my stuff in the trunk, and almost stepped on KNUG's very own Judy Mercer.

"Going somewhere?"

"Well, yes, actually." Damn. We'd promised to tell her when things started to go, and here she was.

"Mind if we," she said, indicating her cameraman, who was stepping around the back of their four-wheel-drive with his camera at his shoulder, "tag along?"

"Actually, yes," I said. "Kill the camera."

He did.

"Just like you were afraid of," I said, leaning in my trunk and packing my food carefully around the spare tire. "The focus has moved elsewhere. We're a backwater again. We're gonna be staking out a place where, if anybody gets through the FBI, then they might show up."

"Shit."

"Tell me," I said. "Anyway, the best I can do for you is going to depend on whether you can get away without the rest of the media seeing you."

"No problem," she said. "Shoot."

"Okay. Here's the deal..." and I told her to go to Battenberg and sit someplace where she could watch the north end of the town. I told her that she'd probably hear any commotion starting up on the scanner and be able to get into position to do her story long before the other media were alerted.

"Just where do I go? When it starts to hit the fan?"

"If," I said. "If. Not when. But I don't know, so I can't tell you. You'll get aware in a hurry, though, on the off-chance it does heat up. Lots of cop traffic will either come in from the north, or go out from the south. And we ought to light up your scanner." I thought that was vague enough.

"You gotta do better than that!"

"You already got an exclusive on the dude in Coralville," I reminded her. "Talk to that lady in the apartment as soon as you can."

Her eyes lit up. "Really!?"

"Yep. You ought to have your groundwork pretty well done before any other reporter even gets started on that end of it. It was a good break."

I shut the trunk. "Now, listen really close to this...if I catch you following me, you'll have four flat tires, a free trip to the Linn County Jail, and a federal felony in your pocket. No question about it."

"Yeah, right."

"No. For real. I'm absolutely serious."

"You can't arrest us for a federal offense," said her cameraman. "I know that much."

"Too true," I said. "But the federal agent with me sure as hell can, and will."

Just to make sure, I took a back road out of Maitland, turned on a Class B, minimum-maintenance road, and came back to town from the opposite direction. I pulled up in the driveway of Sally's place and beeped the horn.

She came out looking like two winter boots underneath a laundry pile. She was carrying a large red cooler stacked high with blankets, a parka, a large box of crackers and a Girl Scout backpack.

I opened my door and got out. "Need a hand?" I called to her across the roof of my car.

"No, I got it!"

"You sure?" It didn't look like it to me.

"This is the twenty-first century, Houseman," she said.

Consequently, I was still on the driver's side when she walked right into the side of the car, and I heard a faint, "Jesus Christ, Houseman, give me a hand!"

I did. Her stuff took up the whole backseat.

"Got enough?" I asked, wondering if the back door would shut.

"It could get really cold. I've got hot coffee, and water, and sandwiches, and pop, and string cheese, and pretzels, and trail mix, and tea..."

"There aren't any rest rooms out there," I said.

"You and George will be in the shed anyway," she said primly, while sliding into the front seat and closing the door.

There was to be no radio traffic unless absolutely necessary, in order to prevent the media scanners from picking us up and giving a hint that there was something afoot. Sally and I met George and Hester at the motel. They were already seated in Hester's car as I drove into the parking lot. George gave a thumbs up, and I just kept on driving right back out and headed south. They followed us.

"Where we gonna park these cars?" said Sally, still trying to get her seatbelt fastened. It was completely out of sight under the left edge of her heavy winter coat.

"I thought we'd park in the yard at the Heinman boys' place," I said, reaching down and lifting the edge of her coat so she could find the buckle.

"Oh, cool. The crime scene in daylight." She clicked the belt in place. "Thanks."

"Yep."

"Wait a minute," she said. "How far is that from the barn we're going to be stuck in?"

"About three-quarters of a mile," I said.

We drove in silence for a moment.

"You're just gonna have to help me carry some stuff, that's all."

I laughed. "Oh, I will. Especially since you'll be taking the shotgun." We carried our shotguns in a case that ran along the lower front edge of the seat.

"What the hell do I need that for?"

"If I knew," I said, "I'd tell. Always take as much firepower as you can reasonably carry," I said. "You know that."

"How about I take as much as *you* can reasonably carry?"

"I don't think so..."

"Sooner or later, you're gonna want a sandwich," she said. "Think about it."

We got to the Heinman boys' farm about fifteen minutes later. We pulled both cars into the lane, and all got out as Jacob came to the door.

"Jacob! How's it goin'?"

"Fair. You need somethin'?"

"Yep," I said. "We need to park these two cars here, if it's all right with you."

He scrutinized us very closely. "Looks like you're goin' squirrel huntin'."

I just explained that we were going to be watching the old Dodd place, and we needed to keep our cars out of sight of anyone who might be going there. Jacob directed us around the back of the barn. He seemed glad to be of assistance.

"Think you'll catch the people who did it?" he asked.

In the spirit of cooperation, I said, "We already got one of 'em, Jacob. I think we'll have everybody pretty soon."

"Mind if I tell Norris?" he asked me.

"No, not a bit. Just keep it under your hats for a day or two, though."

The bemused Heinman brothers watched us loading up all our gear.

Sally gave George and Hester a run-down on all the great stuff in her cooler while I loaded up as much gear that had straps as I could. That meant my AR-15, the shotgun, my ammo bag, my camera bag, and Sally's Girl Scout backpack over one arm.

"We better start moving," I said, "or I'm gonna poop out just standing here."

"Right," said George. He slipped a full-fledged super pack with frame over his shoulders, and carefully adjusted a tube that emerged from the bottom of the pack and ran up over his left shoulder.

"What's that?" I asked, beating Sally by an instant.

"What? Oh, this tube? This is what they call a 'hydration pack.' Carries lots of stuff, and has a water bag attached at the bottom."

"Okay," said Hester. "So what's with the pickax there?"

There really was a strange looking tool dangling from a loop on the side of the pack.

"That's an ice ax," said George.

"There's no ice," I said. "There's not even snow."

"That's okay," said Hester. "He can use it to break up the ice in the pack when his hydration system freezes up."

"Ah, but look," said George. "*Voilà!*" He reached into the backseat of Hester's car and produced a black box, about a foot square and about half that thick. "Meet Mr. Heater," he said, grinning. Sure enough, that's what the label said. Mr. Heater.

"Runs on a one-pound bottle, puts out 9,000 BTUs for six hours on one. I've even got a spare bottle in my pack."

"What the hell," said Sally. "I'm sticking with George tonight."

"Me, too," said Hester. "Carl, you can stay in the shed if you want."

"Where," I asked George, "do you *get* that stuff?"

"I shop around," he said. "This was only a hundred bucks. Want to see what all I've got in my pack?"

"There's gonna be plenty of time after we get there," I said. "We've got a way to go."

Hester produced her own duffel bag. "I don't have a shotgun. Department's a little short right now, and we keep 'em in the office and draw one out when we think we're going to need one."

"I don't, either," said George.

"I'm disappointed, George," I said. "I was sorta hoping you'd have a small cannon with wheels."

We set off down the road, with George and me carrying most of the packs and blankets, and Hester and Sally toting the rest along with the cooler between them. When we got back up onto the roadway, Sally said, "Is that dark spot...?"

"Yep. That was where the body was," I said.

"Boy," said George. "This is sure a lonely spot to die."

"Well," I said, "Rudy really didn't have much time to think about that."

"Do you and Hester think you've got the right man?"

"If you mean Skripkin," I said, "yeah, I think so. But I really want that Hassan or that Alvarez, or whoever he is. That sonofabitch is the trigger man." I adjusted my load, nearly dropping the shotgun off my shoulder. "Skripkin's only a co-conspirator. That, and a lying sonofabitch, to boot. We'd really like some solid physical evidence."

The law says that you cannot convict an individual based solely on the testimony of a co-conspirator. It's a very good rule, when you think about it. But it also means that you have to have something else linking the suspect to the act. Like a large amount of physical evidence, for example. I didn't think other testimonial evidence, such as that available from Jacob Heinman, would be enough in a strongly contested case.

Along with that, Skripkin's lying continued to haunt me. I knew he was telling mostly the truth about the murder, but there were little holes in his account that a decent defense attorney would be able to drive a truck through.

"Like what kind of evidence?" George asked, more to make conversation than out of real interest.

"I'd be happy with the murder weapon," I said. "It's a twelve-gauge shotgun, and we have that plastic wadding. It will have some marks, so I think we can maybe do a match. His fingerprints all over the gun would help, too."

We rounded the curve, and Sally said, "Shit, Houseman, how much further?"

"Way down around the next curve," I said. "It's all downhill."

"Way down there?"

"Yep." I turned around and walked backwards for a few steps. "Gettin' tired?"

She stuck out her tongue.

Another hundred yards down the road, and Sally spoke up again. "You mind tellin' me why you didn't just drop us off down here, and then go park the car?"

"Too many tracks. People make lots of tracks, especially when they stand around waiting for somebody. It's best this way."

"Be sure to tell me that on the way back up," she said.

"Wait till you see the farmyard," said Hester. "It gets worse."

When we turned into the farm lane of the old Dodd place, Sally let out a groan. It was quite a distance to the abandoned barn, all uphill and over rutted, frozen tracks. A gust of ice-cold air whipped down the little valley, right into our faces. It was going to be chilly tonight.

CHAPTER 22

SATURDAY, DECEMBER 22, 2001 15:23

WE PAUSED AT THE END OF THE LANE and set most of the stuff down to give ourselves a break.

"Anybody know anybody else who's crazy enough to go on a winter picnic?" asked Sally.

"It won't be so bad," said George, "once we're out of the wind."

Sally shivered. "Yeah. But it's a long way to that barn. I just hate it when it blows right in your face. Makes it ten times colder."

George turned his back to her. "The zipper pocket on the upper right," he said. "There's a muffler in there. Go ahead and use it."

Sally pulled out a maroon and gold muffler, complete with fringed ends. "Wow, thanks," she said, wrapping it around her face.

Hester lifted one end of the cloth. "Hogwarts?"

"USC," said George. "Same thing."

Rested and wrapped, we loaded up again and started up the lane.

"Where's the house?" asked George.

I pointed to the top edge of the stone foundation ahead on our right. "Used to be over there. When the original owner leaves, if another farmer who lives fairly close buys the place, they don't have much use for the residence. They only spend the money and the time to maintain the useful buildings."

George chuckled. "I've got to tell my little sister that I've found the fixer-upper she wants."

We piled everything in the barn. It was built on a slope, with the big doors on the main floor facing the uphill side, away from the driveway. There was a door on the second story that faced the driveway, designed for loading the hayloft, but it didn't permit much observation unless it was wide open. The basement, which grew out of the slope at main floor level, had windows and a walk-in door, as well as a large Dutch door for animals. The basement walls that extended out from the slope were limestone, which meant that the wind wasn't going to be blowing through the basement. Better yet, the basement door faced the driveway.

"Well, we might as well do the lower barn level," I said.

"Looks good to me," said George.

"Fine," said Sally. "I'm not about lug all this stuff up into the hayloft."

That pretty much decided it.

After we got our gear comfortably set in the barn, we decided take a look around outside to get a good idea of the whole layout of the place. We'd already been inside long enough to notice how much colder it was when we went back outside.

As the four of us stood in the middle of the barnyard, Hester and I pointed out the features we were familiar with. Facing upslope, the barn was on our immediate left. About fifty yards upslope from us, and a little more to the right, was an old shed. Another shed was across the yard, and also about fifty yards upslope. A large, concrete-block silo was on the right, about twenty-five yards from the barn, and had a small shed adjacent to its base. Between the barn and the silo was the wooden telephone pole that mounted the yard light. There was some old wooden fencing that ran on three sides of the silo and butted into the rising hillside on the right.

The foundation of the old house was behind us and to our right.

"How far up this little valley does this lane go?" asked George. From our vantage point, it made a bend to the left and went out of sight around the hillside.

"About a hundred yards," said Hester. "It ends at the gate to a field up there."

"And that one?" asked Sally, pointing over toward the right, behind the silo.

"That goes up along the little creek bed," I said. "I didn't see anything up there, and it kind of stops being a lane and starts being a cow path."

There were faint markings on that lane, two parallel lines, that looked like they could be tire tracks.

"Were those tracks there when we were here?" I asked Hester.

"I don't remember," she said, "but it was pretty dark."

The problem with tracks in the winter, especially when there's no snow on the ground, is that any grasses or other small vegetation don't spring back up after a while. You can't tell if it's recent or not. I did look, but there weren't any tire impressions at all, just the two parallel lines of depressed vegetation.

"Farm wagon?" asked George.

"Probably. Either that," I said, "or the lab van backed in there, maybe to turn around?"

"Sure," said Hester.

That was it.

"Well," I said, "if somebody comes here to hide out, they'll come up the drive. Maybe check it out as they go, so they might come up pretty slow. I'd think they'd want to park behind the barn, here. Wouldn't be seen from the road."

"So, what's the plan if they do that?" asked Sally. "I mean, do we just step out and say hi or what?"

"I'd say," said Hester, "that two of us go up the stairs to the main floor, and one of us goes on each side of the barn. At the word 'go,' we all confront them at once. No place to hide. No place to run."

"Excellent," said George.

"It'll probably be after dark, so just remember not to concentrate on the headlights. Really screw up your night vision." I looked back down toward the roadway. "As long as we can hear 'em driving, we really don't need to look out much at all. And headlights will light up faces through the slats," I said.

"Yes, Mother," said Hester.

"Yeah, yeah. The important thing," I said, "is that, once they're in, they don't get out. No matter where they stop, we have to have somebody between them and the roadway just as fast as we can."

"Well, then," said Sally, "let's get inside where it's warmer."

As we all started walking to our right, back to the barn, with our backs to the sheds, there was a yell, then another. I think we all turned at the same instant to see what was going on.

Three dark shapes emerged from behind the right-hand shed, near the path that wound up along the creek bed. All three were bobbing and weaving like crazy, and it took me about a second too long to figure out what they were doing. They were trying to confuse anybody who was shooting at them. Only nobody was. Then they opened fire.

I swear to God, there must have been fifty slugs smacking into the dirt, the barn, fence posts, and the limestone foundation all at the same time.

Hester, I think, reacted first. None of us did the proper move, which would have been to fall to the ground and crawl for cover. All four of us just took off for the barn as fast as we could go. And I mean fast. George, who was in front of me, spun around with his handgun drawn, and popped off three or four rounds as I passed him. I noticed him turning back toward the barn as I went by. That made me third through the door, as Sally and Hester were much faster than I was. George came thundering in right behind me.

"Fuck!" That was me. I didn't have enough breath to say anything more.

"Who in the hell is that?" came from Hester.

"Jesus Christ!" said Sally. "They're shooting at us!"

George said, "Three subjects. They all got down when I shot, but I don't think I hit anybody."

Hester was breathing hard. "Where in hell," she gasped, "did they *come* from?"

I shook my head. "Those are automatic," I said, referring to the rifles.

I grabbed my own rifle off Sally's pile of blankets and headed to the right side of the barn. As I got there, I saw movement in the middle distance, going to my left.

"They're going toward the biggest shed," I said. "Heads up!"

We took up positions against the long limestone foundation on the upslope side of the barn. That foundation was the only bulletproof feature in the whole barn.

We were all able to find cracks or holes in the vertical boards of the siding, about four feet off the floor. We all looked out onto the long, brown grass of the slope that led to the big shed. We couldn't see anything moving.

After about ten seconds, when the shock began to wear off a bit, Hester said, "Maybe we should watch all four sides?"

Hester went to the right, George to the left, and Sally took the side facing the roadway.

"Call the office," I said to Sally. "Get backup coming."

Sally picked up her walkie-talkie mike, and said "Comm, Three!" She used my number because she didn't have one.

No answer.

She tried again, and again. Nothing. Before I could stop her, she was crouching near the top of the stair, holding the walkie-talkie up above the floor line with one hand, and talking into the mike at the end of the stretched pigtail cord.

"Comm, Three, ten-thirty-three. I repeat, ten-thirty-three."

She got an answer. "Three, I'm ten-six. Hold your traffic unless ten-thirty-three." Somebody wasn't paying attention.

"Comm, Three needs ten-seventy-eight, this is very ten-thirty-three, multiple ten-thirty-two, shots fired. Repeating..." Ten-seventy-eight meant that we needed assistance, the 10-33 indicated an emergency, and multiple 10-32 meant more than one armed suspect. With all the rest, 10-33 might sound redundant, but it was an official declaration of an emergency and enabled certain authority to accrue to the dispatcher automatically.

I heard the voice on the radio say, "Nation County has ten-thirty-three traffic." That meant that everybody else had to shut up and only speak when spoken to.

"Where's backup at?" asked Sally, speaking to me from her perch on the stairs.

"Lamar's in Battenberg," I said. There really wasn't anybody else within fifty miles, at least not on duty.

"He might want to stay there for a few minutes. If we've got some here," said Hester, meaning the terrorists, "there might be some where he is, too."

All well and good, but we were dealing with very limited resources. "There won't be more than two troopers within thirty miles of us," I said. "Get our next-out duty officer, and local cops from Maitland and Battenberg. Call out the rest of the department after that."

"Where's the cell phone tower from here?" asked Hester, as Sally began talking to Dispatch again.

I pointed back toward the road. "That way."

"Good," she said, and pulled her phone from her jacket pocket. "I'll get the state TAC team headed up this way."

That was an excellent idea, and I said so. I looked back up the stairs, just in time to see Sally stick her head up past floor level to get a quick look through the big barn doors. I just started to tell her to get down, when a burst of fire ripped through the slats above her, and she ducked so fast she fell most of the way down the stairs. I thought she'd been hit.

I was over to her in four steps. "You okay?!"

"Yeah," she said, uncertainly. "Shit. Yeah. Yeah, I think so."

"Jesus, keep your head down."

She stood. "Yeah, just my knee hurts…skinned it, I think. Holy shit, did you see that!?"

"I saw it all right," I said. "That's a good way to get killed."

"I saw one of 'em," she said, her voice wavering slightly. "Looked right at him. He was in the big shed, looked right at me. No shit. Just like a neighbor. Somebody else shot. He didn't. He just looked."

"Okay. Just don't stick you head up like that again, okay?"

"No shit." She brushed off her uniform pants. "I don't know why you let me do things like that."

"And if you do it again, lose the scarf. You really stand out with that."

George and Hester were both on their cell phones, talking in muted tones and trying to get a view of whoever had been shooting at us. I did the same, but couldn't see anybody along the whole upslope side of the barnyard. Belatedly, I remembered to pull the cocking handle of my rifle sharply to the rear. I never carried a round in the chamber and had nearly forgotten to load one in. That could have been embarrassing, to say the least. I searched my mind to see if there was anything else I should have done, or should be doing. Little mental lapses like that mean that you aren't getting up to speed as quickly as you should, and are lagging behind events. Not permissible, if you want to survive a bad one.

Hester was off her cell phone. "Anything?"

"Nope," I said.

"Not from back here," said Sally. It occurred to me that she was in the position that guarded the only fast entrance to the barn, the two doors that faced out to the lane.

"Hester? Could you take this side for a sec?" I said. As she moved toward my position, I hustled over to Sally.

"You got a round in the chamber?" I asked her, touching the barrel of her shotgun.

"Oops. No." She jacked a round in. "God, I feel dumb."

"Don't. I asked because I forgot to do the same," I said. "We got to get up to speed here." Our training emphasized that long weapons such as shotguns and rifles should not have a round chambered until absolutely necessary. Just to avoid catastrophic accidents.

"Yeah. No shit," she muttered.

"Okay, keep a good look, and sing out if you see something. You've got the only place they can get in in a hurry."

"Yeah. I thought about that. You think they're gonna try that?"

"Not really. They're probably hustling their asses out over the hills already. Wouldn't you?"

She smiled. "No doubt."

Not ten seconds later came the burst of fire that blew the nail fragment into Hester's face.

CHAPTER 23

MY CELL PHONE RANG. IT WAS LAMAR.

"Okay, Carl. The ambulances are startin' up towards the barn. Don't come out yet, but get ready to go after they leave."

"Okay."

"The two officers with 'em are TAC team members. Just so's you know."

"I feel better already," I said, lying.

"Yeah," said Lamar, "me, too."

I turned to Hester. "Better get ready, the ambulances are on the way."

She got to her feet slowly. "It hurts really bad when I stand," she said. "Give me a minute."

"Take your time," I said. I could see a flickering shadow on the far wall of the barn as the ambulance headlights shone through all the cracks. "They're just coming up the lane now."

I motioned Sally over. "You stay with her, too. We don't go out with her if she can do it herself."

"I'm just fine now," said Hester. "You guys be careful. Don't take chances."

"We'll be just fine. We get to split just as soon as the HRT gives us the word. They're here, probably gettin' set up. Don't worry about us."

She nodded. The three of us stood back a bit and watched the shadows move as the ambulances came closer. When I thought they might be nearly in place, I walked over to the east wall and peered out through the crack in the door.

"They're getting into the area under the yard light now," I said. "Let's get ready to move."

My cell phone rang. It was Marty, the TAC team leader.

"Okay, as soon as the ambulance closest to you stops, you can start Hester to the rig. The officer will go toward the other ambulance. The EMTs will come to meet her as soon as they have her in sight."

"Good," I said, and broke the connection. Marty was going to be busy.

I watched the ambulance roll to a stop, and the passenger door for the cab open. The floodlights came on, and the back doors began to swing open. The driver angled the rig toward the road, so that the back was facing us, and came to a stop.

An officer got out the passenger side and began to walk toward the second ambulance. The driver stuck his arm out of his window and motioned for Hester to come out. We opened the door, and I accompanied her for about ten steps, as the EMTs in the back got out and broke out the stretcher. We met about halfway between the barn and the back of the rig.

They had Hester on the stretcher and were strapping her in before I could really say goodbye to her.

"We'll get you where it's warm," said Diane, one of the EMTs from the Maitland ambulance. "Let's see that..." she inspected the wound. "I'll bet that hurts, yeah? It looks pretty good, though. The docs will..."

I stopped listening, and out of habit, grabbed one side of the stretcher and helped them over the rough ground. I knew I was breaking a rule, but I didn't think it could be too damned important. I'd just go back into the barn when we were done.

We got to the rig and had Hester inside and the stretcher secured in five seconds. "Take good care of her, Diane," I said.

"You bet," she said, and the back doors closed.

I turned and started toward the barn, watching the activity around the other ambulance. I could see the injured terrorist being set down by two of his buddies. As they got close to the floodlight area from the ambulance, I saw they had used an old door for a stretcher. The injured man was all wrapped up in a winter coat, with a huge, blood-soaked bandage on his left leg. It looked like they'd used anything they had to try to stop the bleeding, and I had the distinct impression of a large towel being the outer layer. It, too, was reddish brown with blood. He had to have a severed artery, I thought.

While one of the TAC officers stood with his eyes locked on the two terrorists who'd brought the wounded man down, the other TAC officer patted him down for weapons before any of the EMTs were allowed to approach. I noticed that one of the EMTs on the terrorist rig was Terri Biederman. I wondered if anybody had told her where her friend Linda was. It had gotten very quiet.

The officer motioned the EMTs over, and as they began to lift the wounded terrorist from the door to the real stretcher, the two officers spread apart a bit, providing better coverage.

One of the bad guys said something, but I have no idea what it was. It didn't sound like English. He slowly raised his hand and waved at the wounded man. Then he and the other man just turned around and walked briskly back into the shadows.

I saw the wounded terrorist being hoisted into the back of the ambulance, and the two officers moving slowly backwards, keeping their eyes on the shadowed area where the men had faded back into the darkness. I breathed a sigh of relief. Smooth as silk. Now we could get out ourselves.

I walked back to the barn and gave a thumbs up to the dark area where I knew Sally and George were.

"Perfect," I said as I slipped through the door. I looked back, and saw the taillights of Hester's ambulance begin to turn onto the roadway.

The second ambulance was turning in the yard, with both TAC officers trotting alongside.

"I wonder if I should leave my pack?" said George, half to himself.

"You can always come back for it," I said, turning back into the barn.

The force of the blast knocked me to my knees. I only remember seeing the floor come at me, and catching myself with an outstretched arm, Sally letting out a yell, and George running by me and out into the yard.

The pressure wave had felt like getting slapped with a good-sized couch. I got to my feet as fast as I could and turned toward the barnyard.

The second ambulance had blown up. The sides of the modular body had bulged out, the rear doors had blown open, and the rear corner of the top was peeled up. The access doors were blown across the yard. The whole rear body was off the chassis, about five feet away from it, and at an angle. There was an enormously bright flame, like the back of a jet engine, and a shrieking sound as the big onboard O_2 bottle vented and burned. The flame was so hot, I could literally see the opposite side of the ambulance begin to distort and melt.

It was raining tiny little pieces of plastic and Styrofoam and paper-wrapped medical supplies.

The driver's cab had come off, and there was nothing left of the front except the engine and the steering column that had been bent forward by the force of the explosion.

There was no fuel fire. Diesel fuel tends not to go up like gasoline would.

There was not only no sign of life, there wasn't even a sign of a body.

"Jesus Christ!" yelled Sally.

I could hardly hear her because of the blast effects, but I got the message.

George turned and motioned us back into the barn. He said "Hurry!" and I guess he must have shouted at the top of his lungs, because I heard that all right. It was just that the cobwebs wouldn't go away, and I was having a hard time turning thoughts into action.

He grabbed my shoulder, spun me around, and pushed me back toward the collapsed barn wall. It was then that I saw fragments flying all around. It took me a second to figure out that these weren't fragments from the ambulance, but dirt and wooden fragments being thrown up by gunfire.

They were shooting at us.

That finally got me going. We both grabbed Sally and pushed our way into the barn.

The old building had partially collapsed, so we were now in what amounted to a three-story lean-to with a big kink at the level of the first floor.

I pressed against the stone wall and moved toward my right, toward the silo. It was the last place I'd seen terrorists, so it seemed to me to be the logical place to look. I peered out. Nothing moving. Nothing. But I did notice puffs of dust popping up all over the silo. Somebody was returning fire, and I didn't think that anybody in that area had much of a chance. Good.

I felt something touch my back and I jumped six inches.

It was George. I only heard the phrase "suicide bomber."

It had never occurred to me. Not once, in all the time I saw the terrorist being loaded into the ambulance. Not once. Even after watching all the suicide bombers on CNN, taking out buses and restaurants. It was something every Israeli would have assumed. But this wasn't the Middle East. This was Iowa.

In about five minutes, George tapped me on the shoulder again.

"Yeah?"

"Your phone! Answer your phone!"

I pulled it out of my pocket, and sure enough, it was lit up. I opened it and handed it to him. "I can't hear well enough yet. You take it."

He did. I saw him nod twice, and then he shut the case and handed it back to me. "They're coming for us now," he said. "Don't shoot at anything. They're friends!"

"Okay."

He moved over to Sally, and I assumed he gave her the same message.

About a minute later, three black-clad members of the FBI HRT just sort of appeared in the barn. They had kneepads, which was the first thing I noticed. I would have given a lot for a set of those. They also had night-vision goggles, automatic weapons, and lots of gear I'd only seen in equipment catalogs.

"Hostage Rescue Team, FBI," said the first one in the barn. "We need to ID you," said one. "Which of you is Pollard?"

George raised his hand.

"Houseman?"

I raised mine.

"Wells?"

Sally's hand went up.

"All of you okay?"

We were.

"Glad you're in good shape here," said one of them, quite loudly and distinctly. They were trained to deal with hostages who had been close to gunfire and "flash-bang" grenades, and therefore had temporary hearing impairment. "We have lots of people outside, just stand fast for a second, then we're going to move you out. We're going to take out the yard light, and then we'll escort you to the roadway."

He said something into his mike, then there was a sudden darkening in the barn. The yard light was obviously now gone.

"Let's go," he said. "Move as quickly as you can."

Outside, the smell of hot plastic, lube oils, and medical supplies was very strong. We walked right past the ambulance, and in the dim light cast by all the vehicles down on the road, it looked like so much Kleenex scattered around the yard. Little fragments of aluminum and plastic were everywhere. I stepped on a twisted piece of stainless-steel grab rail and just about fell down. Then it was just hustle down the ever-lightening lane to the waiting vehicles.

Lamar, Volont, and a whole bunch of people were waiting for us. My hearing problem got me bundled into an ambulance and on the way to the Maitland Hospital before I really had a chance to say much of anything to anybody. I hate it when they do that. I had to stall them while I unloaded my rifle, and gave it to Lamar. I hate to be rushed.

On the way, I handed my cell phone to one of the EMTs and asked her to dial my home number and tell Sue I was all right. Then I began to feel very, very tired.

I must have dozed off, because I remember being shaken awake as the ambulance pulled up to the ER.

I was answering the questions of the admitting ER nurse when Henry walked in.

"Did they really blow up an ambulance?" he asked.

"Yeah, they sure did. Suicide bomber, for God's sake. Got three EMTs and the driver, and I believe two officers alongside."

The ER nurse stopped what she was doing. "What?" She hadn't had a chance to talk to the ambulance crew that had brought me in, at least not about the details.

I told her what had happened.

"Which ambulance?"

"I think it was the Battenberg unit," I said.

"Do you know who was on it?"

"Terri Biederman," I said. "She's the only one I know for sure. It was dark."

"Isn't she the paramedic who came back from Milwaukee?" she asked.

"That's the one."

"I met her..." She shook it off, and started with the admissions questions again.

I could hear most sounds now; it was just that they were buzzy sometimes, and I felt like I had a head cold.

"How close were you to the explosion?" asked Henry.

"How close?" I saw him nod. "Oh, about twenty-five, thirty feet."

"Which side was to it?" he said, loudly.

"My back, I think."

"Lucky," said Henry. "Probably no ruptured eardrums."

"Good."

"Okay, my man," he said cheerfully, his professional manner taking over.

"How many fingers do you see?" He held up two fingers about a foot from my face.

"Six," I said.

"Very funny."

"Okay, seven."

"Humor gets you a night in the hospital," he said, "and lots and lots of tests."

"Two."

"Much better…now let me have a look in your ears…"

After making certain that I wasn't dizzy, didn't have any hypersensitive reaction to light, and wasn't experiencing any nausea, Henry assured me that I could be released. He also said that my hearing would return to normal. Or, at least, almost normal.

"Henry, you know if Hester Gorse came up here, or did she go to the clinic in Battenberg?"

"She's here," he said. "We fixed her up pretty well, and she'll be going down to Dubuque tomorrow for a little oral surgery after the swelling has gone down."

"Can I see her?"

"Sure, come on with me."

We went through two sets of those bang-and-they-open doors designed for gurneys, and down a long, brightly lit corridor.

"She seemed to be in a lot of pain," I said.

"X rays showed two teeth sheared off, and one other cracked. Must have been very painful. She's lucky it missed the nerves in there. She could have had a permanent paralysis of the facial muscles on that side."

That had never occurred to me.

"I was worried that it broke her jaw," I said. Just making hospital conversation.

"If her teeth hadn't gotten in the way," said Henry, as cheerful as ever, "she could have had very severe bleeding in the oral cavity. She's pretty lucky."

It's all in your point of view, I guess.

To see Hester in the light-blue hospital gown was a surprise. She looked a lot smaller and more, well, delicate that I'd ever imagined her. She was very pale, and had an enormous dressing on her cheek.

They had an IV drip going, and her eyes were closed.

"Hester," said Henry, and her eyes snapped open, "you have a visitor."

She smiled with the half of her face that wasn't covered in gauze. "How'd it go, Houseman?"

"You knew about the ambulance?"

"Yeah, I heard it go up." Her speech had improved greatly.

"No survivors. Suicide bomber. Can you believe that? A Goddamned suicide bomber."

She shook her head. "I'm glad you made sure I got a separate ambulance," she said softly. "Thanks."

"Me, too," I said. "And you're welcome."

"Did we get everybody?"

"I don't have the slightest idea," I said. "HRT was doing its thing when I got out, so I don't expect too many of the bad guys made it. I think they were being dumb enough to try to shoot it out with our troops, so they probably got flattened. I don't know, though. I'll find out what's happening down there. I'll let you know. You better get some sleep. I'll talk to you in the morning."

I think she was asleep before I left the room. I glanced at my watch. It was only 21:51 hours, 9:51 P.M.

CHAPTER 24

SATURDAY, DECEMBER 22, 2001 **22:08**

MY CAR WAS DOWN AT THE HEINMAN BOYS' FARM, just the first of several complications that were to crop up in the next hour or so. I called the office on my cell phone and asked for a ride.

The Maitland officer was at a domestic call, and their other car was down at the old Dodd place, where all the action was. I asked Dispatch to make sure that somebody drove my car back, and decided to walk up to the office. It was about fifteen degrees by now, and the fresh air would wake me up. I also wanted time to think. Things had started happening too damned fast after the ambulances got into the yard, and I need some time to try to figure stuff out.

My biggest question had to do with what the hell all those terrorists had been doing there in the first place. It looked like they'd sure been there when we arrived, and just didn't see us until we were standing around in the farmyard. What the hell could they have been up to that they didn't even have a lookout posted?

My house was only a half-block out of my way to the sheriff's department. I figured the county could afford the extra overtime if I stopped and saw Sue.

She was really glad to see me. We talked for about five minutes, mostly about how I was safe now, and how frightened she'd been when she'd seen the explosion on TV. One of the reporters had kept saying that the barn had blown up.

I told her that I had to go to the office for a while, but that I'd be very safe.

"You said that last time."

"Well, now I'm a witness," I told her. "We always take better care of witnesses."

It was about three-quarters of a mile to the office, almost all residential, with the last third being up a rather steep hill with cracked and tumbled sidewalk. I took my time in the dark, not wanting to break my ankle at this late date.

I passed a house with a dog in the yard. I was just about under a streetlight, and the porch light was on, but he didn't notice me because he had his head in the bare branches of some bushes, hot on the scent of a rabbit. It was kind of cute, because from my angle he was mostly wagging tail. I even stopped for a second, but thought better of whistling. I didn't want him to start barking.

I knew what was distracting the dog. Not because I could smell the rabbit, too, but because I knew about dogs. What did I know about terrorists? Not much. But I knew a lot about criminals, and people of that mind-set. Most of the people we were dealing with down at the old Dodd place, I reminded myself, were not terrorists in the strictest sense. They seemed to be criminal types recruited to fill gaps. Second-stringers, but controlled by a terrorist "boss."

If I assumed the "boss" was not present, I was left with a bunch of second-rate criminals doing their thing. I remembered one bunch we had busted years back, after the only member of the little gang with a brain and a personality had been hurt in a car wreck. The original four had broken into a toy store in Dubuque and stolen a whole consignment of those remote-controlled toy cars. After their car wreck, the other three were a piece of cake, and we got 'em when they were actually racing several of the little cars up and down the only street in a little town. One of our marked cars had come through on routine patrol and damned near ran over some of them.

So what did I know about second-rate criminals? They were not only pretty stupid, but they tended to hang around the stuff involved in their crimes because it was fun. It made them feel good. It gave them a sense of importance.

The parking lot, and the street immediately adjacent to the office, looked strangely empty. Not one single media vehicle present. Not one. They must have all gone down around the old Dodd place. I shook my head. It had to be really crowded on that gravel road.

Once in the office, I called Lamar.

"How you doin'?" he asked.

"Just speak up a bit, and I'm fine," I said.

"How's Hester?"

"Pretty well sedated, I think, but they say she'll be fine after some surgery tomorrow."

"Good. Good."

"So, how's it going down there?" I asked.

"Well, there was a bunch of shooting, but that FBI team went through 'em like a knife through butter. Hasn't been a shot fired in quite a while. FBI's going through the area, seein' what they got. You want," he asked, in a rare moment of insight, "to talk to Volont about this? He's right here…"

Volont came on the line. "How are you?"

I told him, and also about Hester. He seemed pleased. "How'd we come out down there?"

"This isn't a secure line," he said. "If you're up to it, come on down. We have some questions, and George isn't sure about everything."

"No car," I said. "It's down there where you are."

"You don't have a spare vehicle in the lot?"

"We don't have a single vehicle in the lot, as a matter of fact. The media must have you surrounded."

"We got all of that stuff way back out at the highway, except for one rig. Let me get back to you. You don't have to come back down unless you feel up to it."

"I'm fine."

I sat down at Dispatch and sipped a cup of coffee.

"Did they really blow up the ambulance?" asked Pam.

"Yeah."

"Why would they do that?"

"Maybe no particular reason," I said. "I don't know." I took another sip of coffee as Big Ears wandered in, looked at me and wagged his tail, and disappeared behind the dispatch desk. It dawned on me that there should have been a reason for the bomb. There damned well had to be a reason, in fact. Even if you had access to somebody delusional enough to blow themselves up for the cause, you didn't spend those people too lightly. I mean, how many could you convince to do that in any given week?

My slowly focusing train of thought was broken by a phone call from Volont.

"Houseman," I said.

"Your chariot awaits," said Volont.

"What?"

"Just step outside. Your ride should be just about in the lot."

Just then a voice crackled on the radio: "918, Nation County Comm?"

Pam told them to go ahead. It was the Cedar Rapids police helicopter. Volont had sent it up for me.

It was an ex-military OH-58, and I just fit in the backseat, behind the pilot and the observer/crew chief.

"You Houseman?"

"You bet!"

"You were one of the guys in the barn?"

"Yep!"

I fastened the minimal military seatbelt, the crew chief handed me a headset with a long cord and a switch that he clipped into my belt. "Just press the switch to talk," he said.

I put the headset on, and the noise level dropped right off.

"On the way," said a voice in the earphones, and the machine very slowly lifted up, above the tops of the trees and the surrounding buildings. Then we began to move south.

"FBI," said voice in my ear, "wants us to fly you over the scene. If you lean forward, you can see the FLIR screen here..."

The back of the seat in front of me was pressed firmly against my knees, so to look at the screen, I had to unfasten my belt and lean to the side. Encumbered with my winter parka, I found I couldn't lean very far in any direction. Since I kept the mike button firmly in my hand, just so I wouldn't lose it, it took a minute to adjust my position.

"Got it," I said finally. I peered into the screen. "Holy shit, we're there already!"

"The joys of powered flight," said the voice in my headset. "Okay, now we'll start with the barn..."

We flew in, hovered, and then slowly moved west, covering the entire area in one short sweep.

I could see people moving through the area, with blinking lights on their shoulders. "Those are ours?"

"Yep. The HRT guys have little infrared strobes."

As we banked, I looked down and saw nothing but darkness. Not even the blinking lights. I glanced back at the screen, and there everybody was. Magic.

"No bad guys left on the ground?"

"That's what they're looking for now. Once the sweep is complete, they'll bring in floodlights and start processing the scene."

As we made another pass over the area of the barn, I saw a glow. George's Mr. Heater. Still working.

The glow from the shattered ambulance was still pretty intense. The oxygen from the storage bottle had long since expired, but the intense heat had really cooked that aluminum. It was an ugly sight.

"Let me show you the shed again," said the pilot, and we moved slowly over the farmyard to the furthest shed. "See the outline?"

Sure enough. They'd shut the engine off, but the faint outline of a car was still visible through the thin steel of the shed roof.

"I'm surprised you can see that well through a steel roof," I said.

"We are, too," said the pilot. "We think it might be a new roof, one of fiberglass, you know the kind that lets some light in?"

Ah. "Bet you're right."

"You see, though," he said. "You can tell it's a car."

I could. So where was the van Hector had told me about?

"Could we swing around on the perimeter for a little way?" I asked. "I got a tip that a van was bringing some of the assholes up this way, and I can't account for so many of 'em with just one vehicle."

"Could be two trips," said the pilot, "but our time is yours."

We banked again, and the pilot began to follow the gravel roads around the farm. There were at least fifty cars parked all along the two or three miles of roadway that could be used to access the farm. No figures moved in the wooded area, or in the fields. Just cars.

"All cop cars?" I asked.

"We think so," said the pilot. "They always leave their engines running, so they look hot from here."

That was true. Probably not a single cop car would be sitting in this cold weather with its engine off. Why freeze?

We were inbound on the southern leg when the crew chief said, "What's that?"

"Where?" asked the pilot.

"Go right, about a hundred yards off the road, at the very edge of the monitor...see that smudge?"

We banked and swung abruptly, and I found my unbelted self pressed against the flimsy little aluminum door. I hoped like hell the latch held.

In a moment, we were hovering over a dim shape.

"Looks like it could be a van," said the pilot.

The shape seemed covered by black cobwebs. Tree branches, very cold tree branches.

"Let's get somebody down there," I said.

"Nation County One," said the pilot. "We'd like some people about a mile west of your position, on the gravel road, we have what might be a van parked in a stand of trees, about a hundred yards off the road..."

I keyed my mike after Lamar acknowledged. From my time in marijuana-hunting helicopters, I knew I was able to hear all the pilot's frequencies, but was only able to be heard on the intercom. "Tell him we think it's red," I said.

"What?"

"Tell him it's green. Trust me. They're gonna think you guys are magic."

We landed near our year-old mobile command post, which had been set up on the road about a quarter mile from the old Dodd place. Well, it was actually a trailer with a sixteen-channel dispatch radio setup, a TV, walkie-talkie and flashlight rechargers, and a refrigerator. It had sheriff's department decals on it, and it was Lamar's pride and joy. We used it at the annual drownings in the Mississippi, and it gave us a place to use to coordinate the dragging teams. It was generally referred to within the department as "the Lemonade Stand."

Tonight, the FBI, the state, and Lamar were using it.

I left the helicopter and made my way over to the Lemonade Stand, and was instantly greeted by Volont and George. I glanced inside, and saw Sally sitting on a folding chair near the dispatch desk, trying to explain to Martha how to do something with the radios. We were nearly back to normal.

"We got just one little problem," said Volont, after saying how lucky we were to have survived the barn. "We've been viewing the tape made by the chopper."

The CRPD helicopter was equipped with a videotaping unit attached to the FLIR, and had made a complete video record of its passes over the old Dodd place.

"We picked up eight terrorists on the first pass," Volont said. "That's not counting the two dead ones that barely show up."

"Okay."

"One for sure went up with the ambulance. Three of them over by the silo shot at the HRT troops and died for their trouble. We took two prisoners. The area seems clean. The HRT just finished its sweep and didn't find any survivors."

"You're two short."

"Great math skills," he said. "At least two. We think they went to ground under something pretty thick, like a building or a fruit cellar, maybe. So there're at least two still at large. We're getting a dog or two. Brings me to the next point. What's with the van you were talking about?"

I explained about Hector's call, and the four people supposed to be in the van.

"I'll bet they walked in after you got stuck in the barn," said Volont. "That's why the originals hung in and shot it out. They were waiting for somebody who absolutely had to get in there."

Well, it was a better explanation than I'd been able to come up with.

"I'll bet it was Odeh himself," he said. "I hope it was. If so, we should have him."

"Why would Odeh come here?" I asked.

I don't know how long Gwen had been standing behind me, but she piped up with, "They didn't have the spray cans of ricin up north yet. We talked to one suspect earlier, and he said that for some reason, the delivery had been delayed."

"At the farm?" I found that difficult to believe.

"Sure," said Volont. "While you were stuck down here," and he nodded, "at our request, good old Dirty Harriet got us a subpoena for some UPS records. Your girl Linda got eleven packages in two days. The individual weights are about what four cans of that stuff would weigh. That's forty-four cans, Carl."

"Shit."

"You bet. We think Rudy and Hassan brought 'em out to the farm and stashed 'em someplace. We haven't found 'em yet, and we don't want the hazmat people in until we can be positive that every last one of those bastards is in our custody."

"Then," I said, "it could have been Hassan in the van?"

"Well," said Volont heartily, "it sure as hell could have. Let's go ask the little shit tomorrow. He's one of the two prisoners we grabbed."

"What? You're kidding?!" The size of the grin said he wasn't. "Hassan's the one who shot Rudy Cueva!"

"You bet," he said. "He's a little worse for wear, he shot at the HRT guys who approached him. Took six 9mm rounds in the legs. He's been Air Care'd out to La Crosse Lutheran."

"He'll make it?"

"Oh, sure. He's damned lucky we're better trained than he is."

Well, that made my whole day. Even if he wouldn't talk, we had him in custody. That would mean prints, photos, a lineup... I felt that I was back on track with the murder. Finally.

"We need to talk to you about what happened in the barn," said Volont. "We better do it now, while it's fresh."

I knew what he meant. I'd killed two men. It hadn't sunk in yet, and I wondered when it would. But we were going to have to get my information down. A lawsuit was just about automatic for these things, and I had the good fortune to be working in one of about three states where, even if exonerated in a criminal court, an officer could still be successfully sued in a civil case. It was for my own good. But, my Lord, I was getting tired.

"First, though, let's set up that van you found for us. You've been doin' a great job. Hell, you people here got better 'n half our evidence!" He actually reached out and punched me in the shoulder. I was astounded.

"We got six men from the HRT setting up around the van up the road," he said. "Two of 'em are snipers. They'll stay by it until Odeh comes for it, or we get him somewhere else. He won't get by them."

I was certain of that. Day or night.

CHAPTER 25

VOLONT AND GWEN THURGOOD, who were basically there for information purposes, attended my debriefing. An Iowa DCI agent named Phillips did the recorded interview itself. I didn't know him.

It was pretty simple. Volont was particularly interested in the fact that, immediately before I opened fire at the group of men, there had been some sort of grenade thrown at the barn.

"What a screw-up," he said.

"What?" I thought he was referring to us in the barn.

"What we have here is some recruits, trained by somebody who might have been trained in a terrorist camp. The routine is, throw the grenade, then run into the objective, and *then* fire your automatic weapons. You don't fire first and then throw the damned grenade, because you get caught reloading. Good thing you knew what you were doing." He was saying that for my benefit, and for the record. "You got 'em just in time."

He made me sound a little more "heads-up" than I'd been at the time. I hadn't really known what to do. I'd simply made a pretty good decision. I kept that to myself.

Volont excused himself right after that, leaving Gwen to keep their notes.

As I emerged from the DCI van where the debriefing had taken place, Lamar spotted me. He'd obviously forgotten I was still there. I could forgive that, he was pretty busy tonight.

"Carl? You're still here…look, you better get home. ATF is going to be here tomorrow, and you, you gotta be here with 'em. The bomb in the ambulance is our baby, too."

"Can't we get somebody else?"

"I want my best officer on this one."

That was that. "You got somebody who can give me a ride to my car?" It was still parked up at the Heinman farm, a good mile and a half from where we were, and it was starting to snow.

"Sure. Just a sec."

"And who's got my rifle?"

"That's on its way to the lab in Des Moines. It's evidence," he said.

Of course. They needed to make sure that the rounds that had struck the first two dead terrorists had actually come from my weapon. And while they were at it, they'd check it to make sure it was functioning properly. God forbid that the sights were off, and I had hit terrorist three instead of terrorist two.

I made my way toward the northern edge of the cordoned-off area, where I was sure I'd find at least two or three cops securing the road. One of them should be able to break away for long enough to provide a ride to my car.

There was a little knot of media people clustered around a van. On top were three cameramen with impressively long lenses, attempting to get the best view of the action at the barn. As I passed, I saw movement in the east side ditch. I almost drew my gun before I realized the dimly lit figure was waving at me.

I walked over. "Jesus Christ, Hector," I said, as I reached him, "how in the hell did you get over here?"

"My sister dropped me off," he answered, climbing up onto the roadway. "Way over there, on the good road."

He must have walked a quarter of a mile through a field.

"You weren't stopped?"

"By who?"

"Cops."

"No way, man," he said. "I just walked over here. There ain't no cops until you get here to the road."

So much for our secure perimeter. I held up my hand, indicating that he should wait, and pulled out my walkie-talkie. "Three to the command post..."

"Three?" Sally answered almost instantly. I wondered how long she'd remain on duty.

"You might want to check with somebody, just to see if there's any security on the paving. I'm talking with an individual who just walked across the field, and wasn't even noticed."

There was a pause, then an amused, "Ten-four, Three. I'll relay that."

"That'd be nice," I answered. "Then you might think about going home."

I shifted my attention back to Hector, as Sally acknowledged. "So, you just had to see the place?"

"No, I didn't, man. But I got to talk to you. It's real important."

"Look, I'm on my way to my car. Come on. We can talk now." The two of us headed north. "Your sister wait for you?"

"Yeah, over on the other road."

"Okay. I'll give you a ride. So," I said as soon as we were out of the hearing of the media crews, "what's up?"

"Listen, Miranda called my sister and said that somebody called her and asked for a ride from this area somewhere."

"Who's Miranda?"

"She's a friend of my sister; she used to hang around sometimes with Rudy Cueva and some of his friends."

"You never said anything about her before."

"Hell, man, she is just a slut who my sister is trying to…make her into a better woman. She don't *know* nothing."

"Hector," I said, "you got some learning to do about police work. Anyway…what is it she said?"

"I think some of the people who got Rudy want a ride from her. She calls my sister, she don't know what to do because she knows there is trouble up here. So she tells them her car is broken. But she is very scared."

"When did they call her?"

"I doan know, man. But she talked to my sister, who called me after I talked to you. I came up looking for you because your office says you're coming back here."

"Okay. So, just where did they want her to go?"

"This I do not know."

That's always the way, it seems. Never a complete item, just pieces and bits of data that have to be put together.

As we were still heading through the congestion of press, fire, ambulance, and police vehicles, I heard a familiar voice say "Houseman?"

The intrepid Judy Mercer, KNUG.

"Hi. I see you got here…"

"In plenty of time. We were first," she said with a smile. "It just didn't do us a lot of good, because the rest were close enough to get here before airtime. We were here, but we didn't beat anybody where it counts. You were in that barn?"

I sighed. "Yeah. That was us."

"Wow. You got a minute?"

I was her advantage. None of the other media had recognized me as one of the officers from the barn.

"You know, Judy, I'm really tired. Look, I'm gonna take this gentleman somewhere, and then maybe head to the office. Most likely, though, I'll be going home."

"Okay."

I noticed another reporter and cameraman approaching. They were one of the national bunch, and were smart enough to key on a local reporter talking to somebody.

"Maybe tomorrow," I said. I meant it. I was feeling really tired.

"Sure. Sure thing," said Judy.

"You might check at the Lemonade Stand back there, for a release. I think the feds might have one pretty soon."

"Okay. Thanks," she said, and turned away.

Hector and I continued to the north roadblock on the gravel road. Four squad cars, all state troopers, had been parked two abreast, leaving about eighteen inches of roadway open. There must have been a dozen spectator's cars lined up on the southbound side of the road.

"One of you guys able to give us a ride to my squad?" I asked the oldest of the troopers. "It's at the next farm to the north."

While the northernmost trooper got his car into a position where he could open the passenger doors without having us stand in the ditch, I used my cell phone to call Sally at the Lemonade Stand.

"There's a pretty good chance that we're looking for a couple of suspects who are trying to catch a ride. Tell the TAC team that, and make sure the roads are patrolled really well. And tell Volont, too."

"Got it," she said. "You're coming back here, then?"

"No. I've got an informant that I'm going to take home to Battenberg. Then I'm heading north."

"Hey, great. You want to stop and pick me up on the way? I've just got myself relieved."

As I thought about it later, I figured I'd reached sort of an information overload at that point, with both pertinent and extraneous information piling up. It wasn't like I was tearing my hair out, but I was just a little distracted by unusual events colliding with routine stuff.

We hitched a ride with a young state trooper who was glad to have something to do.

"You the one who shot two of 'em up at the barn?"

"That's what they tell me," I said as I settled into his car.

"Good job!"

"Thanks." I turned to look over my shoulder. "You okay back there?" As I did so, I saw a set of headlights behind us.

"Ya, you betcha," said Hector, in his best Norwegian voice. The young trooper looked a bit startled.

We drove very slowly past the spectators, and then picked up a little speed on the way north.

"We still got headlights behind us?" I asked.

"Sure do," said the trooper. "It got lit up as we passed through the roadblock...it's a media vehicle. This place is lousy with 'em."

"Okay." I glanced back and saw that Hector was trying to become inconspicuous in the backseat.

About halfway to my car, once we'd cleared the congested zone, the trooper said, "Can I ask you question?"

"Sure." Between the hiss and heat of the defroster and the slow squeaks of the windshield wipers, I was almost asleep.

"How do you prepare for a thing like that? In the barn, I mean."

"Well...well, you pack lots of good food," I said.

It got quiet again for a few seconds. I was just starting to think about getting back down tomorrow and having to help with the blown-up ambulance, when he spoke again.

"There were four of you, right?"

"Yeah."

"Two women officers?"

"Two of 'em," I replied. "That's right."

"Boy," he said as we reached the Heinman mailbox, "I would have been nervous with two women. I mean, that's half your force, in a fight like that."

I pointed toward the dimly lit house. "This is it. Just let us out at the mailbox, so you don't have to try to turn around in that barnyard."

"Sure."

"You check with me again, about the women," I said. "In about ten years. If you're as good as they are by then." We stopped next to my car. "But you're gonna have to work really hard," I said as I opened my door. "Thanks for the ride, and you might tell your sergeant that 1-388's car is here, too. They better pick it up. She's gonna be in the hospital for a while. She kept working for a long time after she was hit."

By then, I was out of his car, and bent down to speak before I closed the door. "You be careful." I nearly said "sonny," but I stopped myself. Not out of consideration for him, but to avoid appearing to be a hundred years old. "And you might want to stop that media vehicle that was behind us. It'd be awfully easy for one of these terrorists to snag one of those and just drive away from the scene."

I truly didn't think that was the case, but I did feel that it was something that needed to be done, just in case.

"Right." He didn't sound very happy about it, but I noticed that he turned north out of the drive and accelerated in the direction the media van had been heading.

As Hector and I approached my car, I noticed there were lights on in the Heinman boys house.

"That's my car, there," I said, unnecessarily. "I'll be there in a minute; I've gotta see these folks for a second."

I trudged up their porch stairs and knocked. I thought it would be nice to thank them for their help and to give them just a little information about what had happened. Sort of an inside account, to be taken to the coffee shop in the morning.

I could see lights in the kitchen and in the living room, and saw that the TV was on. I knocked again. No response. They were probably asleep in front of the TV. I turned and walked down the steps, and across the yard to my car. The amber sodium-vapor yard light gave the falling snow a gold tint. I thought we just might have our white Christmas after all.

"I guess they're asleep, Hector," I said. "We can go."

I fumbled around for a second for my car keys, and unlocked my car door. I didn't hear a sound as the lock worked, but just assumed it was still my temporary hearing loss. I reached across the car as I got in and unlocked the passenger door for Hector. Being a cop car, the switch that automatically turns on the interior lights when the door opens had been disconnected, so I was sitting in the dark as I tried to insert my key into the ignition. My hand encountered a sharp edge, and a bunch of what felt like exposed wiring. I looked down, and saw that the plastic cover of the steering column was beat to hell, and some of the wiring was hanging down.

Somebody had tried to bypass the steering wheel lock. Somebody had gotten into my car. Somebody had tired to steal it.

"Get out of the car!" I said to Hector.

I got out of that thing as fast as I've ever moved and ran for the shadow cast by the barn. "Over here, this way!"

Hector slipped once, and then was right with me.

I stopped there, drew my gun, and looked back toward the house, catching my breath. I took in the quiet scene. There was no movement, no sound, nothing. Our foot tracks in the quarter inch of snow were the only ones in the yard.

It had been snowing for a good half hour, I thought, as I slowly scanned the area around the house. It might take ten or fifteen minutes for enough to accumulate to show decent tracks. That meant that there hadn't been anybody but me around the two cars since the snow had covered the ground. At least. I pulled out my walkie-talkie, and tried to call the sheriff's department. No luck. Way too far down in the hollow, and I already knew my cell phone wouldn't do the job from here.

I changed channels. "One, Three?" I spoke in a low voice and hoped I was clear at the other end.

It took him a second, but then Lamar answered. "Three?"

"One, I'm here in the Heinman's yard, and it looks like somebody tried to steal my car. Could be our suspects. You want to send somebody up this way?" I tried very hard not to whisper, because whispers are very difficult to copy over a radio. But I was talking so low with my damaged hearing that I found it difficult to hear myself.

"Ten-four, Three. Are they there now?"

"Unable to advise, One. I'm gonna try to wake up the Heinman boys and see if they saw anything. I'll be at the house."

"Ten-four. We'll get somebody right up."

"Be advised I have a Hispanic subject with me, in a"—I looked at Hector—"a blue jacket and a blue baseball cap. Repeat, he's a Hispanic male, and he's with me."

"Ten-four."

"Thank you," said Hector.

"Stay here. Don't move, and put your hands up every time you see a cop," I said.

"You got that right, man."

I put my gun away and walked back up to the Heinmans' porch. This time, I knocked harder. Nothing. I sighed, opened the outer door, and walked onto the porch proper. I knocked at the kitchen door hard enough to rattle the glass pane. I tried to see into the living room area to my right, but the refrigerator stuck out too far from the wall for me to see through the interior door. There was a wall rack between the fridge and me, and there were two coats on it. They were definitely home. After a second, I thought I heard somebody moving around, but couldn't tell for sure.

"Jacob! Jacob, it's me, Deputy Houseman." I knocked again. Silence. "Hey, Jacob! Wake up!"

I tried the door. Unlocked, of course. I turned the knob and pushed, and I was in the kitchen. "It's Deputy Houseman! I gotta talk to you for a second!"

This time, there was a "yes, coming" from the direction of the living room. It didn't sound like either Jacob or Norris, but they'd been asleep... no. No. That was a rationalization. My gun came out again, and I held it down at my side.

"That you, Phil?" I asked.

"Yes," came the reply. It sounded closer.

Phil, my ass. Nobody named Phil lived in this house. My gun came up, and I pressed my back against the wall, with the refrigerator now between the doorway and me.

"Where are you," said the voice, sounding like it was just about in the kitchen.

If I'd been really, really lucky, the refrigerator door would have been hinged on the left, and I could have just reached out and thrown it open to startle whoever it was. I found myself, however, staring at the right-hand hinge just below my chin. Shit. I heard the floor creak, and thought somebody had crossed the threshold to the kitchen. I was absolutely convinced that if I stuck my head around to see, it would be the last thing I ever did.

I lowered my shoulder and pushed that refrigerator harder than I'd ever pushed anything in my life. It shot across the doorway so much faster than I thought it would, I lost my footing and went down on one knee. The big white box tipped away from me, and I heard a startled yell from the doorway, just as the refrigerator crashed over onto the floor. It shook the whole room.

I brought my gun up and pointed it in the face of a man on his knees who was trying to pull his AK-47 out from between the fallen refrigerator and the doorframe. We were eye to eye.

"Don't!"

He didn't.

"Put your hands over your head. Now!"

As he started to comply, a second man suddenly appeared in the doorway, pointing the business end of an old shotgun at me.

"Drop the gun."

"Well, shit," I said. I don't know about me, sometimes. But that's just exactly what I said. I did not, however, drop my gun.

"Drop the gun!"

"Can't do that." I didn't look at him, concentrating on the forehead of his partner. "You just better give up right now."

"Arrogant American Zionist pig!"

The one I'd got with the refrigerator kept glancing up at the one with the shotgun. It struck me that the man on his knees was the subordinate, and the man with the shotgun was the leader.

"You must be Mustafa Abdullah Odeh," I said. Odeh, or whoever the guy with the shotgun actually was, sucked in his breath, and I figured I had the right guy. "Just give up now. You're done." I was still concentrating on the forehead of the kneeling man, and saw his eyes widen. He wasn't making the decisions. The "up" man must be Odeh, all right. Good.

"I must kill you." Odeh said it very coldly.

"Why on earth do you think that?" I asked, stalling. Make 'em talk. Always get 'em to talk.

"You have seen me."

I was very much aware that it was going to take a second or two for the kneeling man to retrieve his AK-47 from where it was wedged beneath the refrigerator. Therefore, he really wasn't the immediate threat. Odeh, on the other hand, had just announced his intentions. I merely flicked my gun about six inches to my right, and pulled the trigger as I fell to my left.

There was a scream, and the shotgun went off, and the man in the doorway disappeared. The other man on his knees jumped back, and he, too, left my field of view. He had heaved on the stock of his AK-47 and it came free, causing him to sort of fly backwards into the living room and out of my line of sight.

As I tried to maintain my balance and get to my feet, it was pretty obvious I had a choice to make. Either go charging into the living room, where there were two pissed-off armed men I couldn't currently see, or get the hell out of that place and regroup outside.

I'm not that fast, but I was on my feet and out onto the porch in two seconds, onto the steps, and heading for the shelter of the barn.

Call it instinct, call it a reaction to recent events, but I changed course halfway to the barn and went thundering down into the tall, frozen weeds between the barn and the driveway. "Come on!" I yelled toward Hector. "This way!"

I continued toward cover, moving as fast as I could. Hector caught up, and I think the only reason he didn't pass me was that he wasn't sure where we were going. I wasn't all that sure myself, but I knew one thing: No more barns for this deputy. As soon as I got into shadow, I knelt down behind a skinny crab apple tree, shoved my keys into my pocket, and grabbed my walkie-talkie. Hector slid in the fresh snow and came to a stop about ten feet past me.

"Three to anybody! Ten-thirty-three, I repeat, ten-thirty-three!"

Sally, who was apparently still at the Lemonade Stand, answered in an instant.

"Three, go!"

"Up here… at the Heinmans'," I said, breathing hard. "They're here."

"Who's there?"

"Two suspects from the farm. The one's we're looking for." I needed to catch my breath. I slowed my speech as much as possible and tried to sound matter-of-fact and calm as hell. "Somebody broke into my car and tried to hot-wire it."

"Ten-four."

"It sure as hell wasn't the Heinman boys," I said.

"Ten-four. They're on the way."

"Hustle it up," I said, and released the mike button. It occurred to me that I had heard Sally very clearly. Given the present condition of my hearing, that meant that I must have the volume turned up way too high to be able to hide. I fumbled around, found the little dial, and turned the volume on my walkie-talkie way down. Since I'd never be able to hear somebody sneaking up, I sure didn't want them to be able to hear me.

"Hector?"

"Why we running, man?"

"The bad ones are in the house. Listen, get a little closer here, and if you hear this walkie-talkie, let me know. My ears are all screwed up from the bomb at the barn; I can't hear all that well."

"Sure." He shifted closer.

"I shot one of 'em. I don't know how many more there are. I hope just one."

I started scanning the area. From where I was, I couldn't see a single light in the house. They'd turned them off. Great.

I wondered where the Heinman boys parked their car. For the life of me, I couldn't remember. I dimly recollected being able to see into their garage, and that the little building was chock-full of tools and shop things. No room for a car there. Had I ever really seen their car? I had an image from years ago, of the Dodge Dart they'd been driving when it had been hit by the bus. It was the only car I'd ever associated with them. Well, whatever kind it was, there wasn't any car visible but the two cars we'd driven into the place. Regardless of the reason for its absence, that was why Odeh had tried to steal my car.

My eyes were becoming better adjusted to the dark. From my new perspective in the shadows, the front half of the house was between the yard light and me. In the golden glow, I could see through the thinly curtained front windows on the upper floor, and into what I guessed would be the kitchen on the ground floor. There was no movement there, and the back half of the building was pitch black.

We'd left some pretty clear tracks leading right to where we were. Great. Nothing to be done about it, but I was beginning to feel that a white Christmas was a little overrated.

It always becomes quieter when the snow starts to fall, but the deadening effect of the snow-filled air was emphasizing the shriek in my ears caused by the nearness of the shotgun blast. It was a little distracting.

The crab apple tree that had become our little bastion wasn't nearly as thick as I was. I seemed to remember reading somewhere that an AK-47 round could easily penetrate ten inches of wood. Not good, but it was definitely time to stop moving around. In the dark, movement is the tattletale.

A staccato clang behind me just about scared me to death.

"What...?" escaped from Hector.

I twisted around and caught a silvery shape in the darkness. The hog feeders. We were almost at the wooden fence that separated the hogs from the yard. There apparently was a hungry hog behind us. "Hog feeder," I said, with a long breath I hadn't realized I'd sucked in, and turned back toward the house. Just in time to catch a flicker of movement in the upper window. It was one of those things that happens in the dark, where you just aren't sure you've actually seen anything. I looked back at the hog feeder, and then brought my gaze back to the house. I did that three times, and never once caught a hint of movement. That pretty well satisfied me that I'd actually seen something.

But what had I seen? Whatever or whoever it was, it wasn't there now.

I was beginning to wonder where the cavalry had gotten to. I placed my ear as close to the mike-receiver as I could, and called Sally.

"Three to Mobile Comm?" I heard something like a response, but it was too faint. I pressed the little speaker right to my ear and adjusted the volume upward.

"Three to Mobile Comm?"

This time, I heard Sally say, "Three, go ahead!"

Hector punched me in the arm, apparently to let me know the walkie-talkie was receiving. Just like I'd asked him to do. "Okay, uh, where's everybody at?"

"Some of them are there already," she said. "Where have you been? We've been calling...give me your exact ten-twenty."

My exact location. I did the best I could. "We're kind of southeast of the residence. About a hundred feet."

"Stand by."

Like I had a choice.

"Three," said Sally, after about five seconds, "would you be near a small tree?"

That was a surprise. "Ten-four, I am."

"Stand by."

I did. The "some of them" she'd referred to must have night-vision equipment.

"Three?"

"Go."

"Three, a team member has you in sight. Remain where you are if at all possible. And who's this 'we'?"

"The Hispanic male subject is with me. We'll sit tight, ten-four on that." That'd be pretty easy. "Be sure they know there's two of us."

There was a pause, and then, "They know."

I looked around me. Nothing moved. No indication of where the team member might be. I was hoping I didn't have to "remain" all that long, as the cold was starting to seep through my clothes.

"Stand by one moment, Three..." and it got quiet again. Then she was back. "Uh, and, Three, be advised that there's an unidentified subject just entering the yard from the east side of the residence, apparently armed, and about twenty-five yards from you."

Holy shit. I stopped talking and just clicked the mike button in quiet acknowledgment.

I could tell Hector had heard the conversation, because he instantly looked in the right direction. I wasn't sure about Hector's younger eyes, but I looked as hard as I could into the deep shadow cast by the house and didn't see anybody. I tried looking to one side and then the other, hoping to catch a movement in my peripheral vision. No go. But if he was on my side of the house, my tracks ought to be pretty apparent in the yard light. I fervently wished it hadn't snowed.

A moment later, Sally's voice was back. She spoke very fast. "Three, he's spotted you, get down!"

Since I was kneeling already, I just dropped down on all fours and then kicked my feet back. I was as down as I could ever get. I was aware of Hector flopping to the ground, too. He had good ears.

I kept looking toward my right, at the house, and heard a loud voice from my far left say "Police! Put your weapon down! Police!"

I saw the man with the gun, then. He was crouched down and had just stepped about two feet out of the shadow of the house. I heard a crashing sound, and saw an orange muzzle blast leap out of his shape, first horizontally and then vertical so fast it described a bright orange arc, and then it was gone as he fell backward, back into shadow.

"Holy shit!" said Hector.

"The unidentified subject is down, Three," said Sally. He sure was. I could very faintly make out his lower legs and feet. There was no movement.

I risked a 10-4.

"They advise stay put, Three. They think there's another suspect in the residence."

"No problem," I said, and meant it.

Now that I was stretched full length on the ground I was getting colder. A lot colder. Snow was beginning to fall on the exposed back of my neck, and I was reluctant to reach back and turn up the collar. Lord, that was cold. I stayed put, though. I hadn't seen a flash or heard a report, but I was certain that somewhere there was a very good sniper who had taken out the "unknown subject" with one shot. I could stand by as long as they wanted. I was in absolutely no hurry to get up and move at this point.

"Three, there's movement again," said Sally, just as I saw shadows near the kitchen area. The shadows continued to the porch, and the door opened.

Exposed to the yard light, two men stood crowded together in the doorway. One was Jacob Heinman in a shirt and overalls. The other was dressed in a heavy parka, and had a ski mask pulled down over his face. He also had a weapon, which looked an awful lot like an old shotgun. He was holding Jacob in front of him.

"I have this hostage!" he yelled. I recognized the voice. It was Odeh. "I am armed." He held the shotgun out at arm's length, just to prove it. As he did, I heard a crack, and his gun just kept on going, out of his hand, off to his right and onto the ground. It looked for all the world as if he'd thrown it. That sniper was a really great shot.

He hollered something I didn't get, and pulled Jacob Heinman back into the house with him. Instantly, I could see HRT people going up the little cement steps and into the door right behind him. I saw lots of movement, a flash, and then two HRT members came hustling out with Jacob and Norris Heinman. They hurried them off to my left and disappeared behind the barn. Immediately, there was a loud noise that apparently was a combination of a shot being fired and the yard light blowing up, and the barnyard was plunged into darkness.

It got vewy, vewy quiet, as Elmer Fudd would have said. I could imagine the HRT members going from room to room in complete darkness, using their night-vision goggles. Spooky, but very effective.

After about five very long minutes, I heard a helicopter approach. It sounded like "mine," but since I couldn't see it, I couldn't tell. I heard it make three passes over us, and then fade as it began to circle quite a way out from the house.

A moment later, lights started coming on in the house, and two cars and an ambulance appeared in the driveway.

"It's all clear, Three," said Sally. "One suspect in custody, two hostages secured."

"Ten-four!" I said. "Can we get up now?"

"Yep," said a male voice, very near. "Name's Howell," said the black-clad figure that stood up on the other side of the fence that separated the hogs from the house. As he stood, a hog squealed in surprise.

I stood, too, but Hector stayed down. "Christ, man," I said. "How long you been there?"

"Too damned long. He came over the fence and scraped his boots in the fresh snow. "Glad it's not summer. Frozen hog shit is bad enough."

Hector got to his feet, and the three of us walked together over to the cars, which were rapidly being covered with snow.

The Heinman brothers were being escorted back out of the barn.

"You're still alive," said Jacob when he saw me.

"Glad you two are, too," I said, noticing a large swelling on his forehead.

"Too old to go easy," he said.

The ambulance crew hustled past us and into the house.

"Better have 'em check you out, too, Jacob," I said.

He indicated one of the HRT members. "He's already told me to do that."

"Shit, I cannot *believe* this, man. I saw you running, and I thought, 'what is going on with him,' and then you said to come on with you, and I thought it was a good thing to do, and I didn't know where we were going to…and they took that dude out, man. They snuffed his ass like *that*. And then when this dude comes up behind us from *nowhere*, man, and scares the living shit out of me…" Hector was talking very fast, coming down from an adrenaline high. He wore an enormous grin. "This was just so fucking cool!"

"Glad you liked it," I said.

Volont came over to us. "You do tend to get into deep shit, don't you?" he asked.

"I do what I can," I said.

"Just FYI," he said, coming a little closer, "our prisoner is Odeh. For sure."

"Excellent."

"Somebody shot him in the thigh," he said with a broad smile. "You?"

"Yeah, I think so."

"Too bad you missed his nuts," he said. "The dead one over by the house is the one they call Chato. Odeh's told us that already."

"That was just stupid, Odeh holding the gun out that way," I told him. "I thought you said he was a trained terrorist."

"Oh, he is. He is. But he's not one of those who's at the tip of the spear, not by a long shot." Volont glanced around. "It helps if you think of him as a middle manager. Sort of their version of Hawse," he said with relish.

EPILOGUE

IT TURNED OUT THAT THE HEINMAN BOYS HAD TOWED THEIR CAR INTO a garage in Battenberg about a week before. It had a broken timing chain, and they'd just raised the back end up and towed it behind their tractor. It was taking a long time to fix because it was a 1975 Dodge Dart, and the parts were getting a little scarce. Odeh and Chato had clobbered Jacob Heinman because they thought he was lying about the missing car. It seems they thought that Hester's car, which was a Plymouth, belonged to the Heinmans for two bad reasons. First, it had the same pentagonal logo as the key that hung on the nail in the brothers' kitchen. Despite what Jacob and Norris said, they didn't believe Hester's Plymouth was a cop car because Hester has one of the undercover radios that fit in the glove box. You can't see it from the outside, and it uses the same antenna as the commercial radio. My car, on the other hand, has a pedestal mount for the cop radio, in plain sight through the window.

Thanks to my having the young trooper check out the "media van" that had followed us toward the Heinman brothers' farm, Judy Mercer of KNUG was on the scene and she and her cameraman got almost all of the action at the farm on tape. She'd apparently thought my reference to being very tired was for the benefit of the other media team, and it had been her headlights I'd seen behind us. Inadvertent though it was, it was nonetheless her scoop. I was glad, because they'd caught me thundering out the door and heading toward the pigpen. I refer to that sequence every time somebody implies that I'm slow.

Odeh, I was told, talked pretty readily. I can't prove that, because I never got to talk to him again, myself. What George told me, though, was that Odeh and Chato had been in the van, the one that Hector told us about. They had four others with them. They'd parked it, and walked in after one of the people who'd surprised us in the barn had called them on a cell phone and warned them that we were there.

Volont had been right. The ricin cans were at the farm, and their distribution had been delayed when we began working the area because of Rudy's murder. They'd apparently tried to get in twice, and there were either lab agents or cops there both times, so they just kept on driving. The DCI lab team had been within fifteen yards of the little fruit cellar, but the entrance was nearly impossible to see. When we went on our little picnic to the old Dodd place, the people who started shooting at us were actually in the process of pulling the ricin cans out of the cellar and taking them to the shed where they'd parked the car. Odeh and company were supposed to meet them there, but elected to walk in when they were told that we were on the scene. It was a risk for Odeh, but it was either that, or have the whole operation with the ricin go down the tubes.

Odeh and Chato originally fled the scene when the ambulance was blown up. They were headed over the hill to the hidden van, but saw four or five cop cars parked just about on top of the hiding place. We didn't know the van was there, but Odeh and Chato couldn't know that. They'd circled around, trying to avoid cops, and eventually came out onto the roadway near the media vans. There, they sort of mingled, and then got to the east side of the road and began walking north, away from all the commotion. The helicopter hadn't keyed on them because they were on the cop side of the fence, so to speak.

The ambulance was blown up solely to create a diversion for Odeh and Chato. There was no other reason. They'd used a terrorist named Aba, who along with Odeh was the only really thoroughly trained terrorist present. He'd been hit in the leg, so his injury was legitimate, and the explosives had been inside the rolled rim of his stocking cap. In the dark, and in the hurry, it had just been missed. We reviewed the tapes. One of the victim HRT guys actually did something at the bomber's head just before they released him to the ambulance. George thought he'd probably felt the cap to see if there was anything under it, not part of it.

We found lots of remains of the people who'd been either in or just by the ambulance when it went up. The driver was virtually intact, for instance, but under a part of the cab. Those who were actually inside at the time of the detonation were reduced to parts. We never found the head of the bomber, but got his torso, eviscerated abdomen, and legs. Terri must have been leaning over him when he set himself off. We think that because most of her head and torso had just disappeared. If anything about the whole incident pissed me off the most, it was that. Here she was, knowing he had tried to kill some of us, and still putting herself at risk to help the man. So what does he do?

Chato, as it turned out, was supposed to be affiliated with FARC. He was trained, but not a fanatic like Mustafa.

Odeh pled guilty to assault, attempted kidnapping, and wrongfully pointing a gun at another. That was me. I didn't believe that was all, but the feds needed him elsewhere, and Iowa wanted to get rid of him. He went into federal custody immediately after our trial, and I have absolutely no idea where he is today. Volont didn't volunteer anything, and I didn't ask.

Speaking of Volont, Hester woke up after surgery in Dubuque to find a huge bouquet of flowers in her room with a big blue ribbon that said, in gold letters, "Lady Agent." It came from the FBI Field Office in Cedar Rapids, but it had to have been George and Volont who were behind it. She was charmed.

Juan Miguel Alvarez, also known as Hassan Ahmed Hassan, pled guilty to second-degree murder in the death of Rudy Cueva.

After his sentencing, he was transferred into federal custody, and tried in the Northern District of Iowa for Terrorism. He pled guilty there, too. Last I heard was on the news, and he was being transferred to a federal prison.

Linda Moynihan pled not guilty. Well, what's an innocent girl to do? I guess the plan was that, since everybody who could testify against her was either dead, in federal prison, or had been deported, she had a good chance of skating. Our federal attorney friend Dirty Harriet shot that one down when she announced in a news conference that any federally held witness who was needed to testify in Iowa would be made instantly available. True or not, it worked. Linda changed her plea and got five years. I expect her to serve eighteen months.

Skripkin turned state's evidence for every governmental agency he could find in the phone book. We got him a fifteen-year sentence as an accessory, and then he went to trial in the federal system for "terrorism." I don't think he's actually been adjudicated yet, but I'm sure he's happy as a clam.

When the news got out that the packing plant had been a victim of a terrorist act, their business actually improved. Ben was flabbergasted, but happy. Me, too.

Although my shooting of the two terrorists at the Dodd place was ruled by the District Court as "justifiable," I got sued. The suit was brought by two sets of attorneys who were supposedly representing "familial interests" of the deceased. Only the court knew the actual families, as they were afraid of "retribution." They must have been really interested, though because each suit demanded a hundred million dollars. Both dead men, as it turned out, were from Honduras, and had been known to associate with the drug trade. During depositions, it became clear that the plaintiff's attorneys were going to maintain that their clients, far from being caught by my return fire while they were reloading, were actually *unloading* their weapons while *preparing to surrender.*

Don't you just have to wonder sometimes?

Anyway, the feds let us have Juan Miguel Alvarez for a witness. He was deposed by the plaintiffs, with suitable restrictions, and claimed that the dead men had been reloading because they intended to advance to the barn door, throw in more grenades, step in with guns blazing, and kill all of us. He ought to have known, as he was standing right beside them.

Even so, the suit dragged on for three more months, as the attorneys for the plaintiffs ran up the bill. I hope the "families" of the dead men could afford it.

Oh, and just for the record, I've never regretted shooting them for an instant. I went through a short period of time wondering what was wrong with me because I felt no remorse at all. Then I decided that I'd just done what needed to be done. Works for me.

My shot into Odeh's lower leg was also ruled justified. There was no suit over that one.

The only upside to being involved in a police shooting, I discovered, was that I didn't have to do the damned investigation. That alone probably saved me six months' work.

All things considered, we came through this case pretty well. Hester has a permanent dimple in her cheek that the plastic surgeons couldn't quite erase. It really doesn't detract from her appearance at all. She still has Big Ears with her. She brings him along sometimes when she has a case in Nation County. Sally and the rest of the dispatchers go nuts when they see that dog.

Hector is still in Battenberg, pretty much in control of the world he inhabits. He still informs for me, when he thinks justice should be done and I seem to be lagging a bit behind. I'm pretty sure he's doing the same thing for the FBI. I hope they treat him right. He's a good man.

Our intrepid county attorney Carson Hilgenberg has already started to campaign for office. His bumper sticker reads PROVEN TOUGH ON TERRORISM.

Honest. He's unopposed, naturally.

Lamar says he's going to retire. I'll believe it when I see it. As for me, I think I'll stick around for a while.

ACKNOWLEDGEMENTS

I WOULD LIKE TO ACKNOWLEDGE THE invaluable assistance of the following people in the preparations for this novel:

Richard F. Fiester, MD, F.A.C.P., who conducted an exceptionally interesting autopsy; Ellen M. Gordon, Administrator, Iowa Homeland Security, who provided very helpful information regarding emergency responses; Kevin Techau, Iowa Commissioner of Public Safety, who provided invaluable contact assistance; Penny Westphal, the Director of the Iowa Law Enforcement Academy, who very kindly permitted me to interview some members of a basic class; and Officer Jo Amsden, Monona Police Department, who provided considerable insight into at least two characters in this book.

I would like to especially thank Jennifer Clarke, ATF-NRT, SACES, for her exceptionally valuable insights and encouragement.

Another special thanks to former KGAN Iowa City Anchor Anne Ewald Dill, and KGAN cameraman Pete MacNaugton, who were kind enough to allow me to ride along as they covered stories in and around Iowa City. It was an impressive experience for me.

A big thanks to Rebecca and J. David Hood, whose advice and information on selected procurements and specifications proved invaluable.

I want to thank Melissa Addington, RN for taking the time from her busy schedule to explain not only nursing and emergency room procedures and techniques, but her personal and emotional reactions as well. She, too, provided insights into more than one character in this novel.

Ann Bahls was also a great help in understanding several points of view that were new to this story.

Dianne Strudhoff deserves thanks for insightful information into the experience of multicultural existence in rural Iowa.

I must always thank the law enforcement personnel of Iowa, especially in the northeastern area of the State, for continuing their excellent work.